THE WYRD SEQUENCE BOOK 1

HOUSE

OF

FEAR

FREEDOM

KIMBERLEY J. WARD

ཀོ◆ཁ

ALSO BY KIMBERLEY J. WARD

The Wyrd Sequence
House of Fear and Freedom
House of Blood and Bone
House of Gore and Gold
House of Dreams and Dragons

The Otherside Chronicles
There is Only Darkness
As Darkness Gathers
When Darkness Devours

*To the doubters and the self-doubt.
I did it.
I defeated you (kind of).*

*To all the dreamers.
Follow those dreams.
They'll lead to wonderful places if you want them to.*

HOUSE OF FEAR FREEDOM

Kimberleyjward.co.uk

The right of Kimberley J. Ward to be identified as the Author of the Work has been asserted by her in accordance with the Copyright, Design and Patents Act 1988.

First published 2018.

UK English Edition.

All rights reserved.

No part of this book may be used or reproduced in any manner whatsoever without written permission from the author except in the use of brief quotations in articles or reviews.

All characters in this publication are fictitious and any resemblance to real persons, living or dead, is purely coincidental.

Cover Image Copyright © Kimberley J. Ward
Text copyright © 2018 Kimberley J. Ward
Re-covered 2022- cover by Getcovers
The moral right of the author has been asserted.

ISBN: 978-1-5272-2994-5
Also available as an ebook and hardback.

www.kimberleyjward.co.uk

Chapter I

Where it Ends and Starts

The darkness offered no comfort. It only shrouded the true nature of that place. It hid the mocking and gloating eyes of the unseen. The cold, dank air chilled everything in the room and had long since seeped into the very marrow of the girl's bones. It gave no relief and only aggravated the already sore skin around her wrists and ankles. The skin that had been rubbed raw by the manacles that bit into them. The manacles that kept her chained to the stone slab on which she was forced to lie.

The girl did not know how long she had been there, nor where 'there' was. All that she knew was that she had been forsaken, and that there were only two ways she would ever see the outside of that room again, and neither of them were desirable.

In the distance, the girl could hear the faint cries of other people's pain, fear and hopelessness. In a sick way, they were a comfort to her, the only one she had. They meant that she was not the only one there, that she was not the only one suffering at the hands of *him*, The Monster.

The girl knew that she had once known his name, but she had long since forgotten it, along with her own and those of the ones who haunted her dreams.

They were her friends, she believed. At least that's what the girl liked to tell herself. Those dreams, those memories, they reminded the girl of a place outside the room, a place with laughter and sunlight, and with a boy who had amber eyes and another who could make flames appear in his bare hands. They gave the girl the strength to resist *his* demands, to fight back against *him* in any small way she could. They kept her going when all she wanted to do was give up.

The memory of *her* is the most vivid and warming, the creature with the deep amethyst eyes. They made the pain and fear fade away sometimes, and made the girl smile in the dark, despite all things. *Hers* is the only name that the girl has not forgotten.

Aoife.

It was like a breath of fresh air that swept through the girl's mind, blowing away her grim thoughts for a brief moment.

She was the reason that the girl was there.

There was no blame in the girl's heart though, only the silent hope that the little creature was safe and far away from *him*, otherwise all that the girl had been through would be for nothing.

There was a noise from outside the girl's room, knocking her out of her thoughts. It was the screech of old hinges protesting as a door was opened. The other prisoners fell silent as a sharp clap of footsteps sounded down the hallway, and a sense of doom befell the girl when she realised they approached her cell with single-minded purpose.

He had come again.

The lock clicked and her door swung open with eerie grace, revealing a tall man standing haloed by the soft light of the hallway's sconces.

With dread the girl watched as he came to stand over her, his icy eyes shining with triumph and malevolence.

Oh, the girl wondered miserably, *how had it come to this?*

Chapter 2

Deep in the forest, hidden by trees and hills, was something strange.

In a large bowl-like indentation were the sprawling remains of a long abandoned town, ravaged by time and neglect. Thick stone walls had fallen away, roofs had collapsed, and the cobbled streets were covered in cracks and pitted with holes. Nature had slowly been reclaiming this forgotten place. Trees pushed their way through piles of rubble and climbing plants trailed leafy fingers over buildings. The air was thick with the scent of bluebells and the sound of bird song.

Nessa surveyed the town from her high vantage point, wondering, not for the first time, about the history of this place. A month had come and gone since she had first stumbled across it, and in that month she had explored a great deal, analysing the architecture, the broken bits of vessels she would occasionally find. Yet she hadn't discovered anything about this perplexing settlement. Nessa had taken her search to the Internet, local history books, even the creepy old lady who lived opposite her house, but no answers were to be found.

The deserted town was a mystery, Nessa's little secret, and her hideaway from the new life in which she suddenly found herself. Here, amongst the ruins and the trees, her worries and problems melted away, fading, for a few blissful hours, from her mind.

Nessa stirred and reached into her backpack, pulling out her notebook. She flicked through the pages until she found her crudely drawn map. Calling it crude was being polite. Nessa had been blessed with the gift of imagination, however, she was a piss poor artist. It was little more than a doodle of the ruins, complete with wonky lines and X's all over the areas that she had yet to investigate. She considered it for a moment and then set off, heading down the steep slope that led to the ruins, her goal of the day set.

Over the last month she had explored much of the outskirts of the town, finding them to be the best preserved areas. Here most of the buildings still had standing walls, only missing the roofs. Nessa had spent hours walking around rooms and streets, daydreaming and badly sketching the sights, wondering what it might have been like living there once upon a time.

The slope was, to start with, a somewhat hazardous descent, riddled with gnarled tree roots and entrances to rabbit warrens. However, partway down, a series of steps appeared, made from pale stones and half hidden beneath leaves and undergrowth. They were old, broken and partially crumbling, having been pushed out of the way by large oaks as they had grown. Many of them were covered, but still, Nessa could just about make out the faded shapes of runes that had been engraved onto each step.

Cautiously, she made her way down them, her eyes quickly tracing the runes' elegant lines, just as she had done many times before. They stirred a bizarre feeling in her, similar to that of déjà vu, but more powerful. Each time Nessa came upon them, she swore that she had seen them before, that they meant something important. But when she'd spent an entire weekend glued to the computer, desperately searching for anything about them, she had come up with nothing, not even finding anything closely resembling them. It was as if the town belonged to another world entirely, one to which Nessa felt inexplicably drawn.

Stepping around a large tree swathed in ivy, Nessa's descent came to an end as the town's ruins opened up before her.

Standing in the middle of the square, which had

several streets leading off in different directions, Nessa thought about which one to take. There was only one avenue that she had yet to try, and its entranceway loomed over her like a gaping mouth.

Nessa stared at it with a touch of trepidation. There was something about this particular entrance, something eerie and different. It made the hair on the back of her neck stand on end. She had so far avoided it, preferring to explore the less foreboding streets. But not today. Today she was going to find the town's centre, and she knew that this street would lead the way.

Why Nessa had the unignorable urge to find the heart of the town, she did not know, but it had been on her mind for the last week, plaguing her thoughts and dreams. Something awaited her there, calling to her. She was sure of it, and she wanted to find out what it was.

Holding her notebook to her chest, as if it was a piece of armour that would protect her against any beasties that might lurk around the corners, Nessa started forward. With surprising swiftness, she found herself in the threshold, standing just below the great archway that had always felt like an invisible barrier to her. More runes like the ones on the steps covered it, filling in the gaps between the intricate carvings of two battling dragons.

There was no barrier stopping her from passing beneath it, no magic sparks or ominous sounds. No monsters came jumping out at Nessa as she passed by a small window. She relaxed her death grip on her notebook and quietly chuckled at her own foolishness.

"Over imaginative dumb-ass," Nessa chided as the tension eased out of her shoulders. She slipped the pencil free from the notebook's cover and began filling in the gaps in her map.

The trees' young leaves bathed Nessa's path in pale green as the sunlight shone through them. Twigs and ivy crunched underfoot, and a curious blackbird darted to-and-fro between branches and broken walls, following her unhurried pace.

Nessa meandered about the ruins, jotting down where some of the smaller streets went for a short distance. Usually they would come to a sudden stop, ending either in an enclosed courtyard or a fallen section of wall, and Nessa would then make her way back to the main road. All the buildings were made from the same pale stone, tucked in close to one another. The doorways and windows stood empty of glass and wood, and homes lacked any sign of their once inhabitants. Nessa's hidden ghost-town had been untouched by man for many years; there wasn't even a hint of the modern world, no street lamps or cables, no telegraph poles. There were just these broken, empty buildings and all manner of wildlife.

The springtime sun had crept slowly away from its peak, starting its slow descent, hitting the tops of the buildings and creating far reaching shadows.

With only a few more hours of decent light left in the day, Nessa consulted her map once again, deciding on which direction to go. The route clear in her mind, Nessa carefully manoeuvred around a pile of stones, leaving behind the main street and venturing down a long winding alleyway. Young hawthorns, still without leaves, lined the sides, along with wild clematis. Fresh grass and a thick bed of moss were spongy underfoot.

The alley led to a crowded yard, surrounded on all sides by tall walls and filled with bushes and fallen rubble. While there were no other passageways or doors, there were a few windows dotted around.

Nessa crossed over to the nearest one, peered inside and found a clear doorway opposite. She went to clamber through when, in a flurry of claws, leaves and screeching, a black shape sprang at her.

Nessa fell back, falling hard to the ground.

With an ear splitting shriek, the creature shot past her and settled on a low branch on the other side of the yard. It then proceeded to watch her with baleful blue eyes.

Nessa picked herself up, glaring at the raven.

"Oh, not you again," she mumbled, dusting herself off, tucking a few flyaway strands of dark hair behind her ears.

The raven gave an unfriendly *caw* and ruffled its wings. This was not the first time that it had scared the living daylights out of Nessa. In fact, it happened on quite a frequent basis. The bird had an uncanny ability to appear when she least expected it.

"How many times have I told you not to do that?" Nessa snapped as she pulled a twig free from her ponytail of waist length locks. "Why do you even need to keep doing that, scaring me half to death? It's not like you have a nest nearby or anything. You do it in a different place every time."

The raven just cocked its head.

Nessa scowled at the bird. "Stupid thing," she grumbled, to which the raven gave another *caw*. "Squawk all you want, but come at me again and you'll receive a backpack to the face."

Her threat went unheeded when, with her knees on the ledge, just about to crawl across the window ledge, something sharp tangled in her hair. With a powerful beat of its wings, the raven yanked her back.

Once again, thanks to the raven, Nessa fell to the ground.

Swearing, she jumped up, calling the raven every name under the sun. The infuriating, aggressive animal just sat on the windowsill, barring the way.

Nessa tried to shoo it off, but it wouldn't budge. Contrary to her threat, she didn't actually want to hit the damn bird. Hurting an animal was strongly against her moral code. Besides, having an argument with a gothic parrot was beneath her.

"Fine, have it your way then," Nessa said,

crossing over to another window. This one, like the one she was abandoning, opened onto a large room with a doorway across from her.

Keeping an eye on the raven, Nessa clambered through the window, managing not to be attacked by the winged menace. She stepped further into the room, and a beat of wings told her that the raven had followed.

Nessa moved over to the door, saying, "I'm ignoring you."

The raven *cawed* and hopped along the ground behind her.

Going through the doorway, Nessa found herself in another street, identical to every other one in her ruined town, filled with debris, trees and wild flowers. She went to go left, but the winged fiend blocked her path, its blue eyes glinting.

"Seriously?" Nessa growled, turning her back to it. "I'm still ignoring you."

Nessa continued with her mission in this fashion, the unwelcome raven following closely, periodically *cawing* angrily at her and often blocking the way. She managed to rein in her temper for a good hour or so, which made her feel particularly proud. However, she snapped when, for the fifth time, the damn bird pecked her viciously on the ankle, drawing blood.

"Damn it all to hell, you dumb-ass," she hissed, examining the wound. Its sharp beak had ripped her jeans and made a small puncture at the base of her calf. The cut wasn't deep, but it stung like a bitch. "Goddamn stupid bloody bird. What the feck was that for? I was only going to have a look in there." Nessa waved a hand at the remains of a taller building, one which looked rather like a watchtower.

The raven wasn't having it, squawking and flapping its wings at her.

"I don't understand," she said, staring at it. "It's like you don't want me..." The raven tilted its head and a light bulb switched on for her, and she realised. "It's like you don't want me to go in that direction. You want me to go a different way."

The raven *cawed* triumphantly.

"You're herding me somewhere."

The raven took flight.

"Hey!" Nessa cried, chasing after it. "Wait! I can't run that fast."

Nessa didn't think about what she was doing. She was suddenly acting on instinct, following the raven as if there was a magnetic force pulling her after it. She stepped over fallen branches and around tree trunks, pushing aside dense undergrowth. Fingers of twigs would knot in her hair, forcing her to stop and untangle herself. Even so, she continued to follow the strange blue-eyed raven.

The deeper into the ruins Nessa went, the worse the condition of the streets and buildings became, making the trek tedious and time consuming.

Already they had to make several detours around sections of collapsing walls that perched at perilous angles, threatening to fall on anyone daring or foolish enough to walk beneath them. The damage seemed to radiate outward from the centre of the ruins, as if a strong blast had happened there.

Daffodils and primroses sprouted from cracks in the cobbles, and what remained of walls were covered in a thick coat of ivy and blossoms, concealing them. Bees and song birds darted about, too preoccupied to pay Nessa any attention. She turned a corner and found the raven in the branches of an old pine tree, waiting for her.

When it caught sight of her, it took off again, flying between the trunks of two ancient oaks that reached towards one another, their branches knitted together, forming a mighty archway.

This was it.

This was the place that had been calling to her, haunting her dreams and thoughts all along.

Nessa was sure of it.

With eagerness she strode forward, excited to see what was beyond the great arch.

A small orchard spread out before her, filled with blooming apple trees. Here there was no debris from broken buildings, no walls half buried by ivy. Here, unlike the rest of the town, everything was in perfect order. The paved path was without cracks, the trees in perfect lines, the enclosing walls tall and strong. It was surely as beautiful as the day it was established.

The raven called to her in its croaking voice, drawing her attention. Following the sound, Nessa made her way slowly down the path, finding that it led to the middle of the orchard, where it widened into a large patio.

What Nessa had first assumed was a dried out pond turned out to be much more curious. Circular and so deep that the sunlight didn't reach the bottom, and with a staircase curling down the side, Nessa thought that it might have been a well.

That didn't seem quite right, though.

Nessa cast around, searching for anything else that may be of interest, but only found apple trees. Her blue-eyed raven seemed to have vanished for the time being— no loss there in all honesty— and disappointment and doubt began to creep up on her. Nessa had felt so sure, so confident that something had awaited her. But all there was were trees and an overly large, well-like feature.

Feeling deflated, Nessa turned away, planning on heading back home. The hour had grown late and the sun had slipped down in the sky, hiding behind the trees, casting long shadows.

Behind her, in the growing darkness, green light flashed like lightning.

Slowly, hesitantly, Nessa turned back to the well, where strange lights flickered erratically from its depths, and peered over the edge.

Faint sunlight illuminated the first ten or so feet,

but the rest was shrouded in a darkness as deep as a night without a moon or stars. At least, it was until those eerie lights flashed again, showing the bottom of the stairs in disjointed bursts.

"What the...?" Nessa muttered.

Curious, she made her way over to the top of the stairs, giving them a cursory inspection, ensuring that there were no obvious cracks and such. Crossing her fingers and praying they would hold her weight, Nessa cautiously put a foot on the first step.

It held firm, and so, she stepped onto the next one, and the next, moving deeper and deeper into the gloom.

Her feet touched the ground and the lights' source stood across the room from her, emanating from a small section of the curved wall, flickering steadily and silently. Nessa stared at it, watching, waiting. Inquisitiveness saw to her feet moving, seemingly of their own accord, propelling her forwards.

Dead leaves crunched underfoot, a noisy carpet of decay. The sound echoed, strange and whispery, unnerving Nessa. She gave a quick scan of her surroundings, but saw nothing other than a dim and empty space. The only things down there were her and the lights, which sparked like tiny fingers of mystical green lightning.

Nessa stopped a couple of feet away, unable to bring herself to get any closer, for there, under the flashing lights, standing in front of her was...

A girl.

A teenage girl, no more than eighteen, with large eyes and elfin features, cheeks flushed a delicate pink from excitement, red lips parted in surprise, dishevelled chestnut coloured hair tied back in a loose ponytail.

Standing in front of Nessa was...

Herself.

Beneath the lights was a mirror, an old corroded one. Standing as tall as the average man and oval in shape, it was set flush into the wall. Rust ringed the edges and moisture had leaked down the back, causing areas to bubble and chip. Webs of a white film covered the silver surface in a hazy skin, making it hard to see a clear reflection, but even so, Nessa saw her own startled brown eyes staring back.

That was until a large hand pressed against the surface.

Nessa jumped, surprised, and glanced over her shoulder, searching for an explanation and finding none. She was all alone in the room. She looked back at the mirror, seeing that the hand was still there, noticing that the fine webbing of film had started to swirl slowly, like smoke pushed in a gentle breeze.

Brows drawn together, Nessa reached towards the mirror. Her hand passed through the green lights, finding them to be icy cold. A slight tingling sensation ran up her arm as her fingers brushed against the mirror's surface, as her hand pressed against the other's, palm to palm.

Large and masculine, it rested there for a moment before withdrawing. A second later it slammed against the mirror, a fist that made the glass rattle and Nessa flinch. It vanished from sight again and she stood stock still, waiting for it to reappear, but the mirror merely glowed with the steady flicker of the lights.

"Weird goddamn place," Nessa muttered. "Should just go home and forget about it."

Despite her words though, Nessa found herself edging closer to the mirror to see through it. Beyond, the image was blurred and distorted, but she could just about make out the shapes of four people, standing tall and appearing to be wearing flowing robes.

"How strange..."

Knowing that the lights wouldn't hurt her, Nessa leaned against the glass, the toes of her ankle boots and the tip of her nose gently touching the cool surface. She cupped her hands around her eyes, attempting to block out the lights, hoping that it would help her to see better.

The hand's owner stood near enough for her to observe his side, his arm moving, gesticulating angrily. Someone behind him pointed, appearing to be shouting, arguing. He spun around and Nessa abruptly found herself gazing into a pair of icy green eyes.

Nessa sprang back.

The lights crackled and blazed with sudden intensity.

Rippling and flowing like liquid mercury, the mirror parted and a hand shot through, latching onto Nessa's wrist before she could do anything more than yelp. She braced her feet against the floor, trying desperately to get free, to break his grip and to stop him from pulling her any nearer.

The hand tightened painfully, and no matter how much Nessa struggled and screamed, she found herself being tugged closer and closer to the ominous mirror.

The lights flared ferociously.

With one last forceful yank, Nessa was wrenched into the unknown.

Chapter 3

Time had become a series of moments, intersected by darkness. Sometimes there was light, voices, the sensation of being carried. Nessa was adrift, floating steadily away from reality. Previsions held her firmly in their clutches. She was a leaf in a river of images, being tossed about in a current of her own mind.

Dreams... memories... They whirled around her, a torrent of disorganised chaos, bombarding her from all sides. Nessa didn't know what was real anymore.

A broken and forgotten town, drowning in young trees... Her notebook, a crude map displayed on its open pages... A raven, its beak glistening red with blood and its blue eyes bright and cunning...

Faster and stronger these flashes of surrealism

came, pulling Nessa further from the surface of consciousness.

Twin oaks stood proudly, their branches knitted together, forming a mighty archway... A mirror of liquid mercury, rippling and shifting as a hand emerged...

Nessa was falling... Screaming...

She was sat in a sitting room, on a dusty armchair, facing an ancient woman whose face was a mask of wrinkles. Nessa sipped her tea, all politeness, even though it tasted like watered down mud.

"That's it, dearie," the old crone said. "Drink up while I tell you all about ravens."

Nessa frowned. She wanted to know about the ruins, not bloody birds. The old woman prattled on, oblivious.

"Many cultures believe ravens are the bringers of death, but many also believe that they will lead a person to their destiny." Her milky blue eyes stared into Nessa's, seemingly able to penetrate right into the core of Nessa's soul.

Nessa jolted awake.

Her eyes felt as if they had been sewn shut, and her thoughts ran as sluggishly as honey. Her throat felt burnt, and her head ached so badly that it forced her to come to her senses.

With a groan, Nessa rolled onto her side and blinked blearily. The room in which she found herself was dark and cold, and it took long minutes for her eyes to adjust to the gloom. She was in a single bed, a couple of thin blankets thrown over her. To her right was a small window, without curtains or glass, which allowed a small measure of weak light into a corner of the room, highlighting a battered table and chairs. The walls and floor were stark stone.

Nessa's surroundings were unfamiliar to her, alien and foreign.

She sat up in a hurry and wrapped a blanket around herself like a cape, her breaths appearing as tiny clouds in front of her face, growing increasingly faster as panic began to take root.

This isn't right, she thought. *This isn't right at all.*

A bitter chill blew in through the window, making Nessa shiver and goose bumps rise. On unsteady legs, Nessa rose and made her way over to the door opposite, telling herself that there had to have been some kind of misunderstanding, some kind of mistake.

The door was large, made from solid wood and very securely locked. Nessa jiggled the door knob, twisting and turning the thing, but all it did was make a horrible nails-on-chalkboard screech and shed a few flakes of rust.

Nessa stumbled back a step, evaluating it with wide eyes.

Robust but worn with use, the door was varnished with the dull sheen of age. In the top half, around eye level, was a smaller door the size of a book. Nessa pressed a hand against it, hoping it would swing open and offer a glimpse of what was outside.

It was unyielding, holding firm.

This is wrong. Very, very wrong.

Nessa muttered a curse and tears of fear came unbidden to her eyes. She hurriedly swiped them away and pounded on the door, praying that the sense of danger she felt was unwarranted.

"Hello?" she called. "Is anyone there?"

Silence.

"Where the bloody hell am I?"

Nothing.

"I demand to know why I've been locked in here." Nessa moved back when no response was forthcoming and cast a forlorn look around the room. Her prison, it seemed.

"Where is 'here?'" she asked herself.

The room was empty of answers, but the window seemed to summon her.

It was small and set high in the wall, with three iron bars sitting in the place of glass. Leading up to it from waist height were a series of small steps, narrow and steep, but steps nonetheless. On trembling arms, Nessa pulled herself up onto the first one, and quickly scaled the rest of them. At the top, she wrapped an arm around one of the bars to prevent herself from pitching backwards, flicked stray tangles of hair out of her eyes, and gazed out the window.

Shock.

Horror.

Uncertainty.

They swirled around inside Nessa for long moments, freezing her in place. She sucked in a shaky breath and stared disbelievingly at what she saw.

"I've a feeling we're not in Kansas anymore."

Her window stood a daunting fifty feet above the ground, with a sheer drop of a rugged cliff face leading down to a fog shrouded city below. Rays of watery light from the rising sun haloed it in gold and made the dirty blue river that ran down the middle gleam like lapis lazuli.

The river divided the city into two parts. On the left-hand side, streets zigzagged through densely packed wood framed buildings. People the size of ants rushed to-and-fro, filling neighbourhoods with the noisy hustle and bustle of everyday life. On the right-hand side, however, it was a different story. It was neat and orderly, with large identical buildings spaced evenly apart. Straight streets split them into blocks, and groups of people marched back and forth, like soldiers in a drill.

Nessa frowned, her grip on the bar tightening, and suddenly grew lightheaded as she stared at the unfamiliar city, as the memories came rushing back with overwhelming clarity. She remembered the ruined town, the raven with cunning blue eyes, and the mirror covered with those eerie green lights.

Nessa recalled the hand that had shot through it, somehow pulling her into its shifting surface.

Nessa tried to make sense of it all.

Obviously the mirror wasn't *just* a mirror. It also couldn't be a door. That wouldn't account for the view outside. What it could be, then, eluded her completely. Her mind shied away from such possibilities as magic and portals. It was the twenty first century, for God's sake. Things like that surely didn't exist. Right? However, when she searched for another explanation, she found herself coming up empty. All Nessa could see in her mind's eye was that mirror and those flickering lights that had danced over its rippling surface.

"Magic," Nessa whispered.

Surely it wasn't possible.

It couldn't be possible.

But it appeared it was.

With the notion that magic was in fact real slowly dawning on her, she found herself faced with a million more questions, and a lot of conflicted thoughts. Amazement at discovering that there was another world, one filled with enchantment and who knows what else, thrummed through her blood, exhilarating and thrilling. As intoxicating as finding oneself in another realm might be, though, it was short lived. The reality of her situation was swift to strike her, and as wonderful as the idea of magic was, Nessa couldn't help but see a darker, more sinister side to it.

Nessa sighed, trembling, realising just how scared she was.

She looked out of the window, noting the differences between home and there, at the sea of wood framed buildings and the orderly barracks, and briefly wondered at how many other things might differ, such as language and customs. She watched the city thriving with life, staring at the people in their bright clothes rushing around, cheerful and carefree.

Free.

Nessa frowned at the sight before her, feeling as if it was mocking her. She wished that she was out there. Perhaps then, Nessa thought, she might find some answers. Sorrowful and plagued by the uncertainly of how she got there, and more importantly, the meaning behind why she might be locked up, Nessa left her roost, unable to bare the barred view that was beyond her comprehension.

Nessa was trapped in the unknown.

She didn't know what to do.

In desperation, Nessa went to the door and rattled the doorknob over and over, praying that it would budge. When it remained stubbornly locked, Nessa's temper flared and her hand shot out, punching the door.

It was a stupid and pointless thing to do, Nessa knew that, and bloody painful besides. However, it did make her feel marginally calmer. Turning around, she crossed over to the bed, rubbing her hand as she went. Her knuckles were red and throbbed dully.

"Stupid thing to do," she chastised herself, flopping down on the thin mattress and staring blankly at the sunlight that streamed through the narrow window, streaking across the ceiling and growing brighter with the passing hour.

It was quiet in her cell. Silent. The noise from the city below didn't reach the window, didn't permeate through the thick stone walls. Nessa felt trapped and utterly alone.

Isolated.

Time passed, measured only by the slow trek of the sun across her room. When boredom started to creep in and as her mind began to settle into an uneasy doze, Nessa heard the quiet but sharp tap of hurried footsteps from outside her door, growing louder and closer. A gut feeling told Nessa that they were heading for her cell, so she swung her legs over the side of the bed and sat, waiting uneasily.

The footsteps grew closer.

Tension radiated through Nessa in powerful waves as they came to a stop outside, and with an ear-splitting screech, the door was thrown back on its hinges.

An overweight man held the door open, his beady eyes fastened on the floor as another man swept past him with inhuman grace.

A beautiful deep green robe fell to his ankles, made from raw silk, and around his trim waist was an intricate belt of delicate gold strands that were braided together, intersected with large gemstones. From it hung an ornate sword, which Nessa eyed with a touch of trepidation.

Her alarm grew when the door clanged shut, locking her in the room with this man, a man who oozed power and strength. She fought her growing panic and raised her eyes, forcing herself to meet his gaze.

Show no weakness, Nessa told herself. *Show no fear!*

Through steel coloured eyelashes, jade green eyes stared icily at her, filled with sly cruelty. Silver-white hair fell to his shoulders, framing cold, beautiful features that were twisted by the darkness in his eyes and the mocking sneer that curled the corners of his lips. Around his neck rested a stunning torc of highly polished strands of silver that ended in two large gemstones, either jade or emeralds.

He was a chilling sight to behold and Nessa's stomach clenched with dread when she realised that there, standing just a few short feet from her, was the man who had pulled her through the mirror of flickering lights. Lights, Nessa noticed, that matched the green of his eyes perfectly.

Nessa tried not to shake as he loomed over her, large and imposing, but when he reached down and grabbed her, she couldn't stop herself from flinching. His hands closed around her upper arms, and she saw that one of them was wrapped in a bandage of clean white cloth. The fingers were exposed, painfully red and with patches of skin peeling off. It was a ghastly sight, but it filled Nessa with a small amount of glee to know that the trick with the mirror had hurt him.

Her joy, however, was short lived.

Harshly, he pulled Nessa to her feet, forcing her to stand close to him. She cringed, desiring a greater distance between them. He smelled of shadows and ice, and of all things filled with malice. Contempt filled his eyes as he looked her over, taking in her dirty t-shirt and ripped jeans. Nessa became self-conscious, feeling incredibly small and inadequate against his height and otherworldly appearance.

He shifted, moving to arms-length away, and looked her up and down, analysing her strengths and weaknesses. His eyes were so bright, so piercing, they made Nessa feel naked under their gaze. She wanted to say something, quip a sarcastic remark, make demands, but she was frozen, the words stuck in her throat.

He raised his hands and gently cupped her face, a thumb slowly caressing her cheek. He was being too intimate, and he was invading her personal space far too much for her liking. Nessa didn't want him touching her.

Her fear was forgotten.

Nessa slapped his hands away.

His eyes sparked dangerously and rage radiated from him. Nessa instantly regretted her actions. She didn't have time to back away or to defend herself before he backhanded her.

Nessa's head snapped to the side, her cheek on fire.

Pain shot down the right side of her face and her eyes watered. Nessa clenched her hands into tight fists, refusing to let the tears fall as she stared him down. A new look crept into his eyes, one she couldn't quite decipher, but one that chilled her to the bone nonetheless.

He spoke, the words flowing like water through her ears, without any recognition or understanding. Nessa frowned. He grabbed her shoulders, shaking her, repeating himself, his words vibrating with anger. It didn't matter how enraged he got, or how much he shook her, Nessa didn't understand anything that came out of his mouth.

"I don't understand," Nessa said slowly.

He cocked his head to the side, his pale eyebrows pulling together.

"Me no-under-stand-oh."

His hands slid from her shoulders as he took a step back, his lips curling into a sneer. He murmured something, talking to himself, and then barked a loud command. The door instantly swung open, and turning on his heel, the man strode swiftly away, his robe twirling around his ankles. He was out of the room in a blink of an eye, abandoning Nessa without so much as a backwards glance.

The door banged shut behind him, and this time, Nessa could hear the click of the lock.

She stared at the door, shocked and more than a little fearful that he might return. Her cheek throbbed and she raised a hand to it, finding it hot to the touch. Only then did everything sink in and the tears began to fall. Her legs trembled with such force that she collapsed on the bed, sobbing. She curled into a ball and pulled the blankets over herself, burrowing under the them, feeling awfully sorry for herself. Never had she been hit like that before, she had never been smacked as a child or got into violent fights. It had shaken her, making her mind numb.

Eventually, under her cocoon of thin bedding, the tears stopped, the shaking subsided, and a sad thought crept into Nessa's mind. *What does everyone back home think has happened to me?* She'd been missing all night and most of the day now. Surely someone would have noticed her absence by now? School? Her mum? Yes, her mum would have. Nessa knew that her mum, no matter how strained their relationship had become in the last few months, would have known something wasn't right when Nessa hadn't returned home yesterday evening. Were search parties hiking through the forest, calling her name, hunting for any sign of her? Was her picture being shown on the news, in local papers, on a missing person poster?

Do they think I'm alive, lying injured somewhere in

the forest, or that I'm dead? Nessa bleakly wondered. *Worse yet, do they simply think that I've ran away, finally had enough of everything happening at home and escaped from it. Do people even search for runaways?*

Possibilities and scenarios flew around and around in Nessa's head, creating a vortex of maddening thoughts. She doubted that anyone would be able to find the ruins, or that they would discover the town's centre and the mirror hidden beneath. Even if they did, Nessa knew that it was impossible for anyone to come to the conclusion that she had been pulled through the mirror and was somewhere... *else.*

Elsewhere.

Chapter 4

Nessa was yanked from the bed, abruptly woken from her doze. She had slept through the door opening, blissfully unaware that two men had entered the room, approaching her with swift strides. Only when one of them had grabbed her did Nessa wake, finding herself being pulled over to the table. She fought like a wildcat, screaming, clawing and kicking. Her assailant was strong, though. He merely spun her around and wrapped his arms around her, pinning hers to her sides, and carried her forward.

The blond man had returned and stood waiting by the table, stone-faced and impatient. His eyes were cold, so very cold, as they keenly watched Nessa struggle. She snarled at him, and his lips twitched into a narrow smile as she was hoisted over the table and laid on her back. Nessa squirmed and bucked, trying to throw off the hands holding her down.

Blondie, as Nessa had dubbed the blond man, came to stand over her. Hating the sight of him, she looked away, only to find herself staring into a pair of deep blue eyes the colour of sapphires; eyes that were oddly familiar to her.

Before Nessa could figure out why, Blondie placed his hands on her forehead, the tips of his long fingers gently pressing in a line from temple to temple, forming a series of light pressure points. He closed his eyes, took a deep breath, and then Nessa was bombarded by pain.

Metal spikes were surely being driven through her head. Nessa screamed and thrashed, and was held down all the harder for her efforts. The pain grew in intensity and the world shrivelled to nothing, becoming dark and sinister. Nessa was floating in a sea of black flames, burning to ashes.

A strange sensation snapped through her mind, not unlike a *ping* of an elastic band ricocheting around. Then there was the impression of someone else there, in her head, taking over. Nessa tried to recoil from them, tried to push them out, but they had no intention of leaving.

Intangible words whispered in Nessa's mind, filling it with thoughts that weren't her own. Images began accompanying them, flashing here and there, and then vanishing before she could consciously identify what they were. Nessa sank deep within herself, almost entranced, the fight leaving her as her head was muddled by the will of another.

Finally, when all perception of time had long since vanished, it all stopped. The presence of the other withdrew, leaving Nessa completely and utterly exhausted, and the fingertips left her forehead, as did the hands holding her down. Not that they were necessary anymore. Nessa didn't even have the energy to open her eyes, let alone get up and fight. Dimly in the background, she could hear a murmured conversation, then the sound of retreating steps. The door opened and closed, and Nessa felt a small measure of relief when she thought that she had been left alone.

A quiet sigh came from somewhere near her elbow.

Not quite as alone as she had hoped.

Nessa froze, trying not to flinch or even breathe. She didn't want to draw anymore unwanted attention to herself. Particularly when she was that weak, not when she couldn't even defend herself in the slightest, for all the good it had done before.

Cool fingers brushed against her clammy brow, pushing back damp hair.

"You'll be fine," someone said.

Nessa flinched and the hand instantly withdrew, but only to slip under her shoulders a second later. She was lifted upright, legs dangling over the side of the table, and an arm wrapped around her back, holding her steady as she trembled. Something cold pressed against her lips, and not knowing what it was, she turned her head, knocking it away. Pooling what little energy remained, Nessa battled to open her aching eyes.

Everything was blurry to start with, but things slowly came back into focus, and Nessa discovered that it was a mug that hovered in front of her. She didn't think, just drank, guzzling down the crisp water, finding that she was parched. Quickly her shaking became little more than intermittent shudders, and the fog that clouded her mind began to fade.

With the world around her steadily becoming clearer, Nessa blinked heavily, her eyes taking in the old mug, now empty, and the hand holding it. The hand that wasn't hers. Her gaze travelled up an arm, taking in the muscles that lay under black leather, and over broad shoulders, lingering on the torc that sat elegantly around the base of his neck, similar to Blondie's but with blue gems instead of green. Her eyes flicked up.

Longish black hair gleamed like raven's feathers, a beautiful contrast to his pale skin, and framed strong and handsome features. Eyes such a dark blue that they were nearly black ran over her, taking in her features just as she was with him, and were edged by eyelashes that most girls would kill for.

He was tall, well over six foot, and cut a fine figure; muscled and strong, but not excessively so. If it weren't for the present unpleasant circumstances, Nessa might have fallen head over heels for him, but as it was, all Nessa felt towards him was fear and a fair amount of contempt. Beneath all of this was the sense of familiarity, of recognition. His eyes, they stirred something inside her. Such an unusual deep blue, Nessa swore that she had seen them before. But surely that was impossible?

Nessa tried to move, to get away from him. Her exhaustion betrayed her though, for she had little to no control over her muscles. The arm behind her back shifted and a hand clamped down on her shoulder, preventing her from pitching forward and falling.

"Don't move," he said, his voice a deep rumble. "You'll only wear yourself out," Nessa stilled as he continued, "and right now, you need all the strength you can get."

His words. Nessa could understand them.

"What?" Nessa whispered. "How?" With as much ease as she spoke English, the words she now uttered belonged to a language that decidedly wasn't it.

"It's complicated," he murmured.

Slowly, hesitantly, as if he was worried she might fall, his hand loosened from her shoulder. Nessa swayed, but managed to catch herself. Her strength was slowly returning, her headache nearly gone.

Wearily, Nessa watched him as he walked around the table, questions poised on the tip of her tongue. He grabbed a chair and dragged it over, setting it down in front of her. He sat with arms crossed and his long legs stretched out. His face was impassive, like he didn't want to be there. But as Nessa stared into his eyes, she could see something concealed behind their dark depths.

Whatever it was made her pause, made the questions and demands quieten.

He laughed softly, giving her a grin that almost breached the thin line between a smile and a smirk. "Go on," he said. "Ask your questions. I won't bite."

So Nessa said the first thing that sprang to mind.

"What's your name?" she found herself asking. It was far from what she had originally planned on saying, much of which had mostly consisted of shouting, profanities and a lot of demanding. No, now she wanted to put a name to the face.

He leaned forward, resting elbows on knees, and looked contemplative. "Name," he sighed. "You wish to know my name. You get right down to it, don't you?" Nessa frowned, but he continued on, unaware or simply ignoring her bewilderment. "These days most people call me Shadow, for that's all I am anymore, a shadow."

Shadow.

Shadows were dark, intangible things, the vague suggestion of something. *What a strange thing to call yourself,* Nessa thought.

"Where am I?"

"In a new world, filled with wonder and danger,

challenges and horror. Where beauty and foul things are one and the same, and not all things are as they appear." A terrible light shone in his eyes for a second, one full of pity and despair. Nessa felt dread settle over her shoulders like a fine cape. "You'll need to keep your eyes and ears open, Nessa," Shadow murmured, "and lock away your delicate *heart* where no one will ever find it. Otherwise you'll never survive here."

He was speaking in riddles, surely? Mad as a hatter. For some reason though, Nessa felt a chill creep up her spine. As much as she wished she could put his words down to shear madness, something in her gut told her that there was more to him than meets the eye.

Nessa opened her mouth, about to demand a straight answer, when Shadow's head whipped to the side. She paused, following his gaze over to the door, seeing and hearing nothing. However, her skin prickled in warning.

Without taking his eyes from the door, Shadow said, "Listen, and listen well. Things aren't the same here as they are where you're from. Everything is different, literally a world away from what you have ever known. More often than not, you will have to make choices and do things you don't want to. Things that will break you down if you let them. You need to be strong now, Nessa, stronger than you have ever been before. Do not break, Nessa. Ever."

The door screamed as it opened, making Nessa jump as Blondie re-entered the room. In his hands he held a dark wooden box, square and varnished to a high sheen. He shot Shadow a sharp glare as he approached.

"Having fun?" he snapped, his voice as hard and cold as glacial ice.

"Aren't I always," Shadow said dryly, grimly amused.

"Did it work? Can she understand us now?" asked Blondie, putting the question to Shadow, ignoring Nessa completely, as if she was beneath him, unworthy of his attention. Her hatred of him grew by the second.

Shadow shrugged, looking bored, and Blondie's jade green eyes settled on her.

Do not break, Nessa, Shadow's words whispered to her. *Do not break.* She held Blondie's stare, strong and unflinching. His eyes ran over her, evaluating.

"You can, can't you?" he said. "Good. That will make things easier." He set the box on the table, within arm's reach of Nessa, handling it like it contained something of weight and fragility. Blondie stepped away, although he remained too close for Nessa's liking. Her cheek throbbed in remembrance of his cruelty.

Nessa looked down at the box and a peculiar sensation ran over her, making her shiver and her skin tingle. Goose bumps broke out on her arms and her heart started racing. Her reaction didn't go unnoticed. Cold green eyes gazed at the box, an almost feral joy shining in them. Shadow stared at her, his shoulders tight with tension.

The odd sensation returned in a wave, sending a cold jolt down her spine. Eyes drawn to the box, she took in its details, taking in the high lustre and the intricate patterns of the wood's grain; whirlpools of deep colour and rounded shapes. Carved with exquisite detail on all four sides and the top were elaborate images.

Dragons snaked over the box, torrents of flame bursting from their roaring mouths. Each and every one of them had hundreds of tiny scales on their bodies and their splayed wings had the fine detailing of veins upon them. The dragons were in the dance of war; flying with and fighting one another with such lifelike prose that Nessa half expected them to come to life. The box was fastened by an unusual diamond shaped lock that was without a keyhole.

Shudders of unease ran through Nessa, the cause of which emanated from the box, from whatever was in it.

"What's inside that box will change the game that we are players in," Blondie said. "It's going to help me win it. Inside is, shall I say, a lock. A metaphorical lock which only opens to one particular key, one person alone. Until now, I didn't have the key." His eyes glinted and Nessa felt her stomach drop. "Now I do. My metaphorical lock needs to be opened for me to win my game, and I need my key to open it. So the question is, are you going to open it for me, my little key? Hmm, are you?"

Prowling near, Blondie came to a stop perilously close to Nessa, making her squirm at the proximity. He raised his arm and pointed at the box, and with a single whispered word, a spark of green light flashed between the tip of his finger and the box's lock. With a *pop* it sprung open a finger's breadth, and with a casual swipe of his hand, Blondie flung back the lid.

A deep purple glow shone from the depths of the box. Nessa saw it from the corner of her eye, too perturbed to have a closer look. Light flashing from Blondie's finger troubled her greatly, and she feared that whatever was in the box would be just as alarming. Nessa felt that she really couldn't handle any more surprises.

The light was soft and flowing, dimming and brightening, swirling around in hues of amethyst and violet, plum and wine. Eerie and chillingly beautiful. Blondie reached into the box, giving the light's source a caress.

Nessa gazed up at him, finding his face bathed in shifting illumination, his features distorted by madness. The silver of his torc glinted, the gems sparkling darkly, the vibrant green turning a murky black.

"There are two paths open to you," Blondie said,

eyes drilling into Nessa's, "but they both lead to the same destination. One path is an easy and pleasant journey. The other, however, is a grim road, filled with anguish and suffering. Which route you take is entirely down to you. Although I do recommend being a good, obedient little girl."

Ire kindled inside Nessa. She hated him, despised him for kidnapping, imprisoning and threatening her. She sure as hell wasn't going to be 'obedient' for him.

Blondie saw the defiance in her eyes and smirked. "I'll give you a couple of days to mull things over. I'll even gift you that," he said, tipping his head to the box before turning away. "Perhaps some time with it will help you to decide what to do." The door swung open, squealing only slightly that time, and with a neat twirl of his robes, Blondie left, no further explanation given.

Nessa watched as the door shut, not even bothering an attempt of escape. Suddenly everything seemed so very hopeless, pointless. Her shoulders sagged in defeat.

"Don't," Shadow said.

Slowly, Nessa looked up, finding him staring at her, frowning.

"Don't what?"

"Don't let him get to you. Not now. Not so quickly. He'll win otherwise."

"What do you care?" Nessa snapped. "You just sat there, scowling in silence as he said those horrible things, threatening me."

"I have my reasons."

"Oh goodie. You have reasons. I don't suppose you're going to tell me what they are?"

Shadow's eyes flashed and he sat a little straighter. "No. At present I am not. Not until I know whose side you are on."

"Side," Nessa sputtered, "I'm on no one's side. I just want to go home."

"But you can't," he barked, temper flaring dangerously. "Not now, and not for a long while yet. So you had best start accepting that and get on with deciding what you're going to do, and where you are going to stand." He stood, the purple light hitting his face with rosy hues and catching on the woven strands of his torc.

"You don't know it yet," Shadow said, walking over to the door, his voice suddenly softer, kinder, "but you are in a very powerful position. If you do the right thing, make the right choices, you can crush cities and topple empires if you wished to."

"But all I want is to go home," Nessa whispered as the door locked behind him.

Chapter 5

A cold, bitter emptiness filled her, consumed her. Nessa was devoid of feelings, bereft of anger, fear and hopelessness. There was nothing left in her just then, only energy sapping weariness. Too drained to move or to cry, she peered down at the box.

Nestled within deep folds of mauve coloured velvet was an orb of spectacular beauty. Its surface glimmered like a diamond, crystal clear and without blemishes; a perfect shell to encase the glowing mist that swirled slowly inside, as if caught in a gentle breeze. A soft, calm light emanated from deep within the sphere's core, oddly soothing. A sense of peace settled over Nessa like a warm blanket.

Strangely comforted by the orb's mesmerising light, she reached a curious hand towards it. The air inside the box felt different, heavier, as if the orb gave off a charge. The hair on Nessa's arm stood on end and her palm tingled as it pressed against the orb's surface. It was incredibly smooth and warm to the touch, and her hand glowed red as the light passed through it.

Nessa caressed it, savouring the warmth it offered. The room was dim, and with the budding darkness came a chill that went straight through her. She watched, entranced, as the orb illuminated the dimness around her, filling the area around the table with enchanted luminosity.

The orb shone brighter.

Nessa frowned, and looked at the window, noticing that the sky was now a deep azure blue. Night was coming, and swiftly, but it wasn't there just yet. No, she was sure that the orb had grown brighter. Much brighter.

Under her hand, deep in the swirling mist, a shadow stirred.

It moved against the flow of the mist, making it churn around like storm clouds in its wake.

With a yelp, Nessa sprang back, hopping off the table.

"What the hell?"

Nessa took a cautious step forward, leaning over the box and peering down. All appeared normal. The orb glowed softly, the mist moved slowly, and the shadow was absent. Nessa stared at it. Perhaps she had imagined it? Maybe it was just a trick of the light? But that wouldn't account for the tremors she had felt, like something scraping against the surface, tapping at it.

Deftly, she flipped the lid shut, hiding the orb from sight, and breathed a sigh of relief. It was spellbindingly beautiful, but in an unnatural way. Nessa was both instinctively drawn and repelled by it.

Needing to clear her mind, to have a breath of fresh air, Nessa moved over to the window. She scaled up the stairs and perched on the narrow ledge, shoulder pressed against an iron bar. The scent of rain was carried on the wind, and black clouds rolled across the darkening sky, rapidly enveloping the city and smothering the sunset in a blanket of grimness.

Night descended early as thick curtains of rain fell, falling heavily on the buildings below. The rumble of thunder sounded in the distance and the far horizon flashed with lightning. Drops of rain were blown through the window, hitting Nessa, slowly soaking into her jeans and shirt, making her shiver with cold. Still, she stayed there, watching as the rain fell harder, as the lightning grew ever closer.

"A whole day," Nessa murmured. "I've been gone for a whole day." It had now been twenty four hours since she had been pulled through the mirror, since so much had happened. All Nessa knew was that she was still trapped there, an unwilling pawn in a madman's game.

Her stomach clenched, emitting a loud growl which rivalled that of the thunder, and she wrapped her arms tightly around herself. *Will they bring me food?* Nessa wondered. *Or am I to be starved until I agree to help him?*

The thought was a bleak one, and filled Nessa with unease. However, she didn't let it trouble her too much. Her mind was made up. No matter how awful things got, no matter what he did, Nessa swore that she would never help him.

From her perch, Nessa gazed down at the table, at the box. She wondered what was so important about the orb, what it was and what it did for Blondie to desire it so badly. *What does it do?* Nessa pondered as she stared at it, eyeing the purple light that shone through the gap where the lid hadn't quite shut completely. *Was it a weapon of some kind?*

Nessa didn't know. She didn't have the faintest bloody idea.

A mighty boom of thunder made the wall tremble and lightning forked across the sky, shockingly bright, illuminating the world for a split second. The city was desolate, not a single soul daring enough to be out in such a storm. Rain fell in a deluge, flooding the narrow streets, turning them into streams that flowed into the river that was now a bloated monster that raged and churned through the middle of the city.

The hour grew late and the storm continued,

unrelenting. Nessa yawned and finally left her roost, cold, hungry and tired. The bed, though small and hard, was oddly inviting. Nessa settled down on the lumpy mattress and wrapped the blankets tightly around herself, curling into a ball to fight off the chill that had seeped into her bones. Her clothes were damp, sticking to her skin, but she refused to take them off, even if that would have warmed her. No, Nessa would rather be wet and cold than partially dressed.

Nessa closed her eyes, wishing for a deep, dreamless sleep. Her wish went unanswered though, for sleep of any kind eluded her. The thunder made her jump every time it clapped overhead, and the lightning would spark through the narrow window, showing her cell in eerie light and weird angles.

Worse yet was the scratching sound, which seemed to come from the other side of the room. Nessa thought that it belonged to either mice or rats, perhaps both, but every time she peered over in that direction, she could see nothing scurrying around in the gloom.

Nessa groaned and once again rolled over, wiggling and trying to get comfortable. Something gnawed at the edge of her mind, an unformed thought that she couldn't quite identify. Whatever it was made her toss and turn, unable to find any form of rest, even as the storm slowly rolled into the distance.

Nessa sat up, glaring accusingly at the box. A thin sliver of light shone through the join of the lid, gleaming like starlight. Something about it, some kind of calling, saw to Nessa jumping out of the bed and going over to it, to the treasure nestled within. Her mind and body begged for sleep, but she had been unable to find it for hours. Nessa was sure that the source of her insomnia was in front of her.

Perhaps it was her tired brain, or maybe something else, but Nessa found herself picking up the box and taking it over to the bed, where she then set it down on the floor next to it. She hastily laid back down on the mattress, tucking the blankets snugly around herself, hiding from the cold. She closed her eyes, hoping that sleep would now find her. Only it didn't.

Growling in frustration, eyes so heavy they would barely open, Nessa flipped back the box's lid, revealing the orb. A gentle burst of warm air brushed against her face and the deep purple glow gently illuminated the dark corner where she lay.

Nessa wiggled to the bed's edge, where she could gaze down into the box and watch the mist swirl around in its many shifting shades of purple. It was hypnotic and soothing, and instantly she felt better, calmer. A sense of warmth, of companionship, settled over her. She didn't feel quite so cold and alone. The distant rumble of thunder and the constant drumming of the rain suddenly didn't bother her anymore.

Nessa's eyes drifted shut and her breathing deepened, and with the orb's light warm on her face, she finally fell asleep.

☙ ✦ ❧

The morning was still and quiet, and grey light spilled through the window. Nessa woke slowly, her night of ill sleep making her sluggish. After a long doze, she sat up and rubbed her face, tired beyond belief, and spotted something on the table.

Food.

On a tray was a large bowl of stew, hot and steaming, accompanied by a couple of thick slices of bread, fresh and buttered. Nessa was enticed from the bed, from her small cocoon of warmth. She dashed to the table, to the food, paying no mind to the cold or to the other objects there.

Nessa was ravenous and the food was soon devoured. Only then, when her stomach was happily full, did she take notice of the other things on the table; a couple of jugs and a pile of clothing that had a pair of black boots perched on top.

One of the jugs was filled with clean, fresh water, and had a small tin cup sitting next to it. The other jug was larger, sat in a washbasin, and had a delicate whisper of steam rising out of it. Nessa took an inquisitive sniff and found that its contents were perfumed. The clothing was neatly folded, consisting of two tops, a pair of thick socks and some trousers.

Nessa placed the boots on the floor and closely inspected the clothing. One of the tops was long-sleeved and a creamy brown colour, with three little buttons on the front. The other was a deep brown, sleeveless and fairly loose fitting. The trousers were simple and not unlike leggings.

Nessa eyed the clothing thoughtfully. They weren't her usual style or much to her taste, however, they were clean and would be considerably warmer. She looked down at herself, at her ripped and dirtied jeans, at her t-shirt that hadn't fared much better, and made her decision. Being pulled into another world wasn't good for one's appearance.

She undressed swiftly, keeping a watchful eye on the door, and using her old top as a flannel, she dunked it into the scented water and washed the worst of the grime from her skin. Shivering, Nessa hastily donned the long-sleeved top, then pulled the other one over it. The leggings were snug and she tucked them into the socks, then quickly wormed her feet into the boots, which were nearly knee-high with laces running up the front.

Nessa looked at the widow, at the dreary morning light beyond, and at the sodden ledge. Without the barrier of glass, last night's rain had blown through the window, making its surroundings slippery and wet, and had created a puddle on the ground below. Deciding that she rather liked her new clothing to remain dry for the time being, Nessa milled around, doing laps around the room to keep warm.

It was then that something rather odd caught her eye.

There, on the floor, was a pile of sand.

"What's this?" Nessa mumbled, moving over to it.

She knelt down and inspected it. In front of her, tucked up against the wall, was an accumulation of grit measuring a few inches in height. It was grey in colour and a mixture of coarse agate and fine powder. Nessa rolled a pinch of it between her fingers, puzzled at what could have caused such a bizarre build-up.

Suspicious, Nessa gazed at the wall, her eyes running over it, searching. The grit matched the mortar. She quickly found, a couple of feet up the wall, that a small hole had been chiselled between two stones, unnoticeable unless specifically looked for.

"How peculiar."

It was a rough little hole, fitted snugly into the mortar. Nessa leaned forward, peering through it, curious to see what was on the other side. It was a peephole of sorts, a crude spy-hole, and offered very little in the way of a view, merely showing a tiny section of the dingy space beyond. It lacked any substantial light, making it hard for Nessa to see, but she was sure that it was a room like hers, just a bit smaller.

At first Nessa thought that it was empty, but then a dark shadow moved in front of the peephole, and a second later she found herself staring into a bright amber eye.

With a startled shriek Nessa fell back, the memory of icy green eyes flashing in her mind.

"Wait!" a muffled voice cried. "I only want to talk."

Nessa was half sprawled on the ground, heart racing from shock. She swore, picked herself up, and glared through the peephole.

"Who are you?" Nessa demanded, dusting herself off, alarm swiftly turning to relief and a small measure of curiosity.

"I'm a friend. I hope," the owner of the amber eye said, blinking slowly, sounding somewhat desperate. "Who are you?"

Nessa frowned. Whoever they were, they sounded youngish and faintly amused. 'They' were also a *he*. With mild annoyance, Nessa said, "I asked that first."

"So?"

"So, since you're the one who, I presume, chiselled a hole in the wall, which I must say is a rather odd thing to do, you can say who you are first."

Nessa heard a sigh.

"Fine," he said glumly. "Be unfun then. If you must know, I go by the name of Hunter, fine thief and traveller extraordinaire. Is that satisfactory?"

"For the time being."

Hunter snorted. "And what, pray tell, shall I call you?"

"Nessa."

"Nessa." Hunter rolled her name on his tongue, testing it out. "Nice to meet you, Nessa."

"Nice to meet you too, Hunter, fine thief and traveller extraordinaire." Nessa bit her cheek, a thought suddenly coming to her. Was this some kind of trick, a trap set by Blondie to get her to lower her guard? She didn't know. The conversation stalled, neither of them seeming to know what to say next.

"I… Umm…" Hunter said haltingly. "I'm sorry if I startled you."

Nessa gave a bark of laughter. "You scared the bloody daylights out of me."

"I didn't mean to," he argued. "I just... I don't know... just wanted to know if anyone else was around. I spent a day chipping away at the other wall hoping for some titillating conversation, but the chap in the next room wasn't particularly chatty, or very friendly, come to think of it. A shame really. I would have enjoyed a bit of male bonding. Anyway, I thought I would try again and found you, which I'm very happy about. Already I've found the banter between us very satisfactory."

"Fantastic," Nessa said dryly, and something then dawned on her. A suspicion arose. The scraping sound last night must have been him, but all had been quiet that morning. The peephole had been completed by the time she had got up.

"Did you watch me get dressed this morning?" Nessa asked.

Hunter was slow to answer.

"Of course not," he eventually murmured.

Nessa was less than impressed. "What do you want?"

"Ahh," Hunter sighed. "You do get right to the question at hand. And the answer to that question is freedom. I want freedom."

"You're planning a breakout?" Nessa exclaimed.

"Yes," Hunter said proudly. "Yes, I am. And I may need some assistance."

"You're mad."

"Perhaps, but not mad enough to stay here, rotting away in this dank place. I want a partner in my escape. Be my partner, Nessa, and I'll take you with me. Unless, of course, you wish to stay here?"

"No," she spat. "I'd rather die than stay here much longer. Take me with you. I'll help."

"Excellent," Hunter said, and Nessa could hear the smile in his voice, and she thrummed with excitement, with hope. She would be free from there, from Blondie, finally able to seek a way back home.

The thought made tears of joy spring to her eyes.

Home.

"What do I have to do?" Nessa asked.

A dark chuckle filled the room.

Nessa's blood turned to ice and terror washed over her, making her movements slow as she turned to face the source.

There, standing by the door, was Blondie, vibrating with anger and with his green eyes glinting with malice.

So absorbed with talking to Hunter, Nessa hadn't heard the door opening, hadn't noticed him entering.

Blondie swept towards her, his robe twirling around his ankles, his face filled with evil delight. He was upon Nessa before she could react, backhanding her once again.

Nessa's head snapped to the side and she slumped to the ground, vision blurred and jaw throbbing. Her scalp smarted as Blondie grabbed a handful of hair, yanking her up and forcing her to kneel awkwardly before him. Nessa yelped and clawed at his hand, digging her nails into his flesh. He snarled and shook her, pulling cruelly on her hair, almost ripping it from her scalp. She froze, still clutching at his fist, gouging deep bloody grooves into it.

Blondie sighed, his lips set in a sinister smile. "Oh, Hunter, my dear foolish boy," he purred. "Getting yourself into even more trouble, are we? It really is a shame that you keep bringing other people down with you. What was her name again, the pretty little raven haired girl?" His tone turned mocking. "Ah, I remember now. Kaya, wasn't it?

Poor little Kaya. Terrible business what happened to her. But, the law is the law, no matter how ugly it is."

Nessa heard a growl and the dull *thud* of a fist hitting stone. "Don't you dare say her name!" Hunter shouted, his voice strangled by the peephole. "I'll have blood for what was done to her. Do you hear me! I will have blood!"

"The only blood being spilt around here will be yours," Blondie snarled, his grip tightening on Nessa's hair. He forced her head back, making her meet his gaze, which was filled with cunning appraisal. "I expected many things from you, Nessa, my dear girl, but not this. I don't know whether to be disappointed or impressed." He cocked his head to the side, white-blond hair brushing over the silver torc that rested elegantly around the base of his neck. "Maybe a little of both," he mused. "I never thought you would have the guts to disobey me like this, to abet in an escape. Tell me, where would you have gone? There's nowhere for you to run to, no one who would be able to hide you from me. And I'll tell you this now: While I still draw breath, you will never go home. The mirror is sealed, closed to you forever. None other exists in this world."

His words were like shards of glass, slicing into Nessa with sharp, jagged edges.

"Lies," Nessa hissed, digging her nails harder into his flesh.

Blondie ignored her, instead staring at the wall as

if he could see through it. "You're very quiet, Hunter. Cat caught your tongue? No matter, we'll have our little chat later." His eyes shifted to Nessa and turned flinty. "Now what to do with you?" he crooned, making her heart clench with dread as his smile grew, as his hand twisted in her hair.

Nessa was abruptly shoved forward, her head striking the wall with terrible force. The world slowed and her body became heavy and numb. Her ears rang and her sight was filled with blinding light before motes of black began unfurling from around the edges, like the wings of a new butterfly emerging from its chrysalis, damp and velvety soft.

With her senses deadened, Nessa barely perceived the grip on her hair loosening, of a short fall before hitting the ground. The absolution of unconsciousness washed over her, drowning away the, "I'm sorry," that was whispered through the little hole in the wall.

Then oblivion swallowed her whole.

Chapter 6

Something was poking Nessa unkindly in the cheek. It was an unwelcoming wakeup call. However, it was somewhat more pleasant than the onslaught of pain that followed. From the top of her head to the tips of her toes, everything ached horribly.

Her temple hurt the worst, throbbing with each heartbeat, and her scalp felt as if someone had lit it on fire and left it to smoulder. A thick and unpleasantly sticky substance coated the side of her face, making it feel tight and itchy. Nessa tried to raise her hand to rub at it, but it wouldn't heed her command, remaining limp somewhere by her side.

Nessa forced her eyes open, something that made her headache a hundred times worse, and was greeted by darkness. A touch of panic crawled up her spine, fearing that she had gone blind. But ever so slowly, her eyes adjusted to the bleak dimness, and she thought that perhaps being blind might not have been so bad. At least then she would be ignorant to the unpleasantness around her.

Confused and sore, Nessa found herself lying in an unfamiliar room. High above, thick wooden beams held up a conical roof, watery light trickling through gaps in the tiles. She turned her head, following the line of a weak ray, seeing that it hit a rounded wall, weathered and otherwise swathed in thick shadows.

Nessa's dazed eyes widened, and her situation harshly slapped her into action.

She pushed herself up, eyes watering as stabbing pains shot though her skull. She groaned, hands rising to cup her head, gagging as her mouth filled with the overwhelming taste of bile and copper. Breathing deeply, the nausea faded, for the most part after a few minutes, and Nessa was eventually able to look around.

She grimaced, wondering if her eyes were playing cruel tricks on her.

Nessa found herself sat on a pile of rotting straw that acted as a thin mattress. She surveyed her surroundings, noticing that there were no comforts; no bed, no table or chairs. It was quite the opposite of her former room, which, while lacking in luxury, at least had some dingy light and something to sleep on. No, this room was dark and bitterly cold, with dampness covering every surface. The roof was riddled with holes and the floor littered with puddles of rainwater.

Set excessively high in the wall was a single window, narrow and far too small to allow any decent amount of sunlight through. Opposite her was an iron door, wide and red with rust.

Nessa went to stand, but fell back with a cry, pain blossoming all over her body. She sobbed, and with shaking hands, pulled up the hem of her tops, revealing her stomach. A mass of blue-black marks were just about visible in the room's dimness, large and slightly puffy to the touch. She inspected them, and judged from the shape and size, that they were the result of a very sound kicking. From the way the rest of her ached, Nessa felt that it was safe to presume that it had been an all over pounding.

"Son of a bitch," Nessa swore, tugging down her top. "It just wasn't enough that he smashed my head into a wall, he just had to kick me too?"

Hugging her middle, Nessa stood on weak legs and shuffled over to the door. She knew that it would be locked, knew that they would never give her an opportunity of escape. She just wanted to examine it, search for weaknesses, if there were any.

The door was large, rusted but still solid, and had no signs of a lock or handle on her side. A small flap was on the bottom, and Nessa nudged it with a toe. It didn't budge and she concluded that it must be locked from the other side.

Nessa turned around and leaned back against it, staring listlessly at her new room. At her new prison cell.

It was a harrowing scenario Nessa found herself in, beaten by a madman and locked away somewhere unknown to her. She realised that any chance of escaping with Hunter, no matter how small it had been to start with, was now lost entirely. Hunter was gone and she was utterly alone.

Nessa hobbled back over to the bed of straw and saw a couple of dark objects nestled in it. Slowly, so not to trigger anymore pain, she knelt down next to them, instantly recognising the intricately carved box. Beside it was a sad excuse of a blanket, rough and threadbare. She used a corner of it to wipe her face, rubbing off the congealed blood that streaked from temple to jaw.

Sighing, Nessa laid down on the straw, trying to ignore the smell of mold that wafted from it. Every part of her was sore, her legs, her chest, her head. She swore that even the tips of her hair hurt. She couldn't stop the self-pity that welled up inside her.

"What a Goddamn bloody mess."

The life of rural adventures, of woodland walks, had come to an awful end. One that Nessa could never have seen coming. It all felt like a half forgotten dream, the crumbling town and the mirror.

Not a dream, Nessa decided, *a nightmare.*

One she wished would end.

Nessa longed with all her heart to be free from that dreadful place and to just go home. That's all she wanted, to go home and forget about everything that had happened in the last few days. Nessa now knew that the only person she could rely on was herself. She had to get herself out of that situation, not wait for someone to rescue her.

The way Nessa saw things, at the moment, she had two options. Either do whatever Blondie wanted her to, hoping he would allow her some measure of freedom after, or escape and find a way home herself. The latter was her preferred choice. However, it came with an awful lot of challenges.

The fact that Nessa had no idea where she was wasn't helpful, nor was the reality that she didn't have the slightest idea of the layout to the prison...dungeon...*place* where she was locked.

Nessa came to the decision that she really needed a plan, and more importantly, to heal. Both of which would take time.

She shifted into a moderately more comfortable position and reached for the blanket, spreading it over herself. She closed her eyes and imagined what it would feel like to be free and in the world outside, finding answers.

The thought made Nessa smile.

☙ ◆ ☜

Time became a fickle thing, with minutes feeling

like hours and entire days rolling by unnoticed. The only thing that signalled the shift of time were the ever changing colours of Nessa's bruises, fading from angry blue-black to a sickly yellowish-green. There was nothing for her to do in her lonely cell other than sleep and pace. No one came to see her, and no one spoke when food was slipped through the flap in the bottom of the door.

Nessa had never felt so abandoned, so neglected. It played with her head. At times she worried that she was growing mad, but usually she didn't mind, welcoming the waking dreams that were her only company.

The first few days, after she had awoken in her new cell, all Nessa could do was doze, too sore to fall asleep entirely, yet too broken to move around. It was in this state that the visions came to her.

Once again she saw the forest and the town's ruins, saw herself being led towards the mirror by the cunning blue-eyed raven. She watched as she was pulled through its liquid mercury surface, as she was yanked into that nightmarish place. She saw a great many things besides, things too strange and outlandish to be real; coiled serpents and roaring dragons, flames of blues, greens and purples spewing from their mouths; Shadow, fingers toying with the golden torc around his neck, studded with blood opals instead of sapphires, his eyes black instead of blue and ever so menacing as he sat on a mighty throne with a crown perched upon his head.

There was much more, too many things for Nessa to recount; armies in silver and gold armour battling each other, the sky filled with a cloud of arrows, a river of blood flowing down the hillside, a waterfall of gore. Screams had filled her ears and whispers of lies and truths, of promises and prophecies, had hung in the air for a long time after she had awoken from each dream-like haze.

Once the bruises began to fade, Nessa started to feel human again. The muscles in her legs had screamed in protest at first, cramping and tightening, but after doing a few laps around the room, they had eased somewhat. Now, the main discomfort Nessa felt was hunger. Every now and again food would be shoved through the small flap in the bottom of the door: a thin, tasteless soup that did little to fill her stomach.

All the while, the orb sat in its box, softly glowing away.

୧୦ ♦ ଓଃ

The sun was at its peak and the room was at its brightest, although that wasn't saying much. The pale light shone through the holes in the tiled roof, hitting the floor with a mild touch of warmth. The window seemed to be a useless feature, never permitting in any sunlight. Nessa had, on occasion, wondered why someone had even bothered to construct it. The answer came to her in a moment of bleak clarity. It was there as a taunt, she realised, to mock whoever was locked away with a small glimpse of the outside world.

Walking around the edge of the room, where the light never reached, Nessa trailed her fingers over the stones, thinking of nothing and everything. Halfway around her circuit, she encountered a particularly rough patch, sharp stones catching on her fingertips. Nessa paused and peered at the wall.

There, beside the ghostly silhouette of her hand, was something scratched into the stone. It was too dark to see clearly, so Nessa relied more on touch than sight, and carefully traced the shapes, quickly figuring out what they were: letters. But not the ones she had learnt growing up. No, these were different, swirling and intricate, and she somehow knew what they spelled.

Kinlandi.

She frowned and backed away, feeling uneasy. The name rang like a bell in her head, though she didn't know why. The reality of her situation came rushing back to her, suddenly impossible to ignore. Troubling thoughts entered her head. *Where are they now? Are they alive? Did they escape or are they still trapped here, locked away somewhere?*

Nessa turned and gazed over at the far side of the room. The sun had shifted and the rays of light came in at angles, now mostly hitting the wall, highlighting sections of its pockmarked surface and making something jump out at her, something Nessa had overlooked a hundred times before.

A line of stones protruded slightly from the wall, forming a rough path leading up to the wooden rafters high above.

Elated, Nessa ran across the room, never taking her eyes from the pathway in case she lost sight of it. The stones poked out just a few inches, barely perceivable in the muted light that was already moving past them, rapidly making them harder to distinguish. Nessa dashed over to the straw, grabbed a handful, and used it to mark the base of the path.

Gawking, Nessa followed the line of stones with her eyes, committing each one to memory, trying to figure out the best way to go about it. It wouldn't be easy, that was for sure, getting up to the beams. Nessa wondered if she would actually be able to climb them. During her younger years she had tried and failed to clamber up trees, discovering that she wasn't a natural like the other children. She had stopped trying fairly quickly, before she broke something vital. However, desperate times called for desperate measures.

Scaling up the wall was one thing, but what would she do next?

Chapter 7

Fingers slick with sweat and arms trembling, Nessa hoisted herself up from handhold to handhold. *Only a few more to go*, she told herself, gasping for air. A bead of moisture cruised slowly down her forehead, ticklish and itchy, then fell to the floor thirty feet below. *Don't look down. Do not look down.* Her fingers latched onto the next stone, and upwards she went. *Nearly there...*

It had been three days since Nessa had discovered her means of escape, roughly two weeks since she had been confined to the tower room, covered in bruises. The marks had all but faded, and Nessa had felt that she had recovered enough for the climb. She might have been wrong.

Her ribs burned with each laboured breath, and every time she reached for a new handhold, she was rewarded with a sharp stab of pain in her side. Her shoulders were stiff and her arms shook, making Nessa think that she would lose her grip and plummet to the hard ground.

Despite the pain, she continued on, using the last of a small reserve of determination that would hopefully see her to the top. It was too late to turn back now. Nessa had to reach the beam. She just had to. She had gone past the point of no return. Nessa either reached the top or she would fall. Those were her only options, and she didn't think that she would survive a thirty foot drop.

Nessa wasn't willing to die just yet.

With the remainder of her strength, Nessa managed to pull herself up to the last handhold, the beam finally within grasp. She allowed herself a quick second to catch her breath, holding onto the wall like a large spider, then shakily, she reached for the rafter.

Her sweaty hands struggled to find purchase on the smooth wood, and for a heart stopping moment she was suspended in open air, legs kicking wildly. Sheer panic gave her the power to swing one leg over the beam, allowing her to straddle it.

Instantly, Nessa wrapped her legs around it, locking her ankles together, and rested her cheek against the cool surface. Shudders shook her body as her tired limbs clutched weakly at the beam, preventing her from pitching over the side. She closed her eyes, finding it somewhat easier to pretend that she wasn't up so high.

Nessa stayed like that for a long time, until she didn't feel quite so panicked, until her heart didn't feel like it was about to combust. Slowly, carefully, she sat up, hands holding the beam's edges and her legs tightly twined around its girth. The weight on her back shifted, threatening to throw Nessa off balance.

With one hand firmly on the beam, Nessa slowly reached behind her, grabbing at the makeshift backpack that she had fashioned from a blanket. Cautiously she brought it in front of her, setting it down on the beam, and with gentle tugs untied the knots that held it all together. The edge of the blanket slipped away and the treasure inside was revealed.

The orb glowed merrily away, lighting the conical roof with shifting purple luminosity. Nessa found it easier to see the damage to the tiles, and spotted a group that had begun to slip. She thought that it would be fairly easy to knock them loose and create a hole big enough for her to clamber through.

Nessa gazed down at the orb. She didn't really know why she had decided to bring it with her. She supposed that it wasn't exactly a decision. It just seemed to happen. On her way over to the wall, ready and determined to climb to her freedom, a nagging feeling had came over her, pulling her back over to the straw, over to the beautiful carved box.

Without much thought, she had opened the chest

and removed the orb, swiftly fashioning the ratty blanket into a makeshift backpack. Nessa had then slung it over her shoulder and continued with her plan. The only explanation she could find for bringing it was for comfort. Though it was only an inanimate object, beautiful as it was, it had been the only constant thing she had since arriving there. Perhaps spite had something to do with it as well. A part of her hoped that Blondie would be seriously pissed when he discovered that not only she was gone, but his precious 'lock' too.

The edges of the beam were digging painfully into the insides of Nessa's thighs, forcing her into action. She looked away from the orb and up at the roof. The sky, a pale bluish-grey from the setting sun, was visible through holes where tiles were missing, offering glimpses of pink clouds which drifted from one gap to the next. Fresh air drifted down and Nessa breathed in deeply, realising just how moldering the room had been.

A bell rang deep and loud, the tolling *dong...dong...dong...* making the beam tremble. Nessa froze, a bad feeling taking root, becoming uncertain. After weeks of silence from the outside world, she wasn't sure what the sudden commotion meant. Should she abandon her escape?

Nessa peered at the floor, fighting a wave of vertigo as she did so, her decision finalised. Onward and upwards, as they say.

A loud crash sounded below, making the room

rattle and a plume of dust swirl. Nessa jumped, losing her grip on the orb. It wobbled precariously for a millisecond, all too close to the beam's edge. Nessa caught it with clammy hands and she let out a shuddering breath, heart racing.

She looked down and stared.

The door swung silently on its hinges, crumpled and warped. A long streak of yellow light streamed out beyond it, a narrow strip on the floor which showed that something moved in the shadows on the far side of the room.

Damn it, Nessa cursed. *Out of all the possible times, Blondie just had to choose now to pay a visit?*

But why break down the door?

Nessa watched as whoever they were crept around the room, keeping to the sides. Although they stayed in the darkness, and she couldn't make out much detail, Nessa saw that it wasn't Blondie. Neither was it Shadow. Both of them moved with panther-like grace, practically gliding over the floor. The person moved with stealth, sure enough, quiet and certain of each step. However, there was something that differentiated them. Their movements were more *human* than Blondie's or Shadow's.

Her silent analysis eased her nerves somewhat, although her suspicions grew as they moved over to the bed of straw, all the while looking over their shoulder at the open door. Nessa frowned when she realised that they were probably looking for her.

"Nessa?" they hissed.

That was her confirmation.

Quickly, Nessa covered the orb, concealing its soft glow beneath the blanket, hiding the roof space, and her, in dimness once again.

The bell still rang, loud and deep, and Nessa's heart thundered away. She could feel an oncoming panic-attack dig its claws into her. She prayed for them to leave, for them to think that they had the wrong room and go search for her elsewhere.

They didn't.

In each lull of the bell, Nessa could hear their quiet call, growing evermore desperate, and sounding almost familiar.

Nessa felt a sliver of hope.

"Hunter," she called, "is that you?"

"Who else would it be?"

༄ ♦ ༄

Hunter moved to stand in the light, looking up at her with a quizzical frown. For the first time since their brief meeting, Nessa was able to put a face to the name. He had dark brown hair that curled carelessly around his temples, dishevelled and in need of a trim, and a strong jaw that was peppered with stubble. Nessa already knew that he had intense amber eyes. His lean frame was swallowed beneath stained clothing that had seen better days.

"What are you doing up there?" he asked conversationally, as if being perched on a rafter thirty foot up in the air was a perfectly normal thing to be doing.

"Escaping," Nessa said.

"Oh, right. Of course." He nodded. "Interesting method."

"The stones create a pathway," Nessa explained, pointing them out. "I climbed up them." She didn't even attempt to keep her pride from showing.

Hunter peered at the wall, a peculiar expression settling on his face, and he crossed over to the base of the pathway, committing the protruding stones to memory. Then, to Nessa's astonishment, he started to climb.

"What do you think you are doing?"

"Climbing, dear Nessa. I am climbing up a wall so that I may aid you in your rather eccentric escape attempt." He was being facetious, but his laboured breathing marred it a little. "Now, if you would be so kind as to keep the questions to a minimum, I would be most appreciative, as I would like to concentrate on not falling."

Knowing how difficult it was, Nessa kept quiet, watching and marvelling at how swiftly he scaled up the wall, already over half way. It had taken him a mere few minutes to achieve what Nessa felt had taken her so much longer to do.

His ripped sleeves slid down his arms, revealing muscles and fading bruises, and a strange feeling settled over Nessa as she observed him, one she couldn't identify, but which brought a blush to her cheeks and made her heart flutter just a little. He had found her, had come back for her. That meant an awful lot to Nessa. She looked away, and to settle her thoughts, began to retie her makeshift backpack.

By the time Nessa had tucked the orb away and had the backpack strapped in place, Hunter had almost reached the top, and she realised that there was no space for him on the beam. So, very slowly, she shimmied backwards, creating a small gap for him to swing on to.

His head of curly hair bobbed beside her as he reached the end of his assent, and then his hand reached out, grabbing at the weathered wood. With such ease that Nessa felt a touch of envy, Hunter pulled himself up, straddling the beam and facing her, a mischievous grin twitching his lips.

"There," he said. "That's better. Now I can finally put a face to the name."

"Indeed."

His smile grew and he gazed up at the broken tiles. A thin shaft of sunlight hit his upturned face, and while he was preoccupied, Nessa took the opportunity to look at him from beneath her lashes, noticing that he appeared to be only a few years older than her. She also realised that what she had first assumed was a large belt was, in fact, a length of rope coiled around his waist, in which two items were tucked. Nessa's eyes widened. Hunter was armed with a small dagger and a short sword.

"So, I presume that the next step of your escape

was to go through the roof?"

Nessa dragged her gaze up from the weapons and found Hunter looking at her questioningly. Words lodged in her throat, so she simply nodded.

"And then what?"

Nessa cleared her throat. "I haven't planned that far ahead yet."

"Huh. Improvisation." Hunter nodded happily. "I like it."

With catlike agility, he leapt up onto the beam, standing tall, the top of his head brushing against the sharp slope of the roof. He pulled his tattered sleeve over his hand and, before Nessa realised what he was about to do, curled his hand into a fist and punched hard at the edge of a hole.

Tiles cracked and shattered, raining down in a shower of broken slate as Hunter's fist slammed against them over and over again. Nessa winced at each blow, at the sheer determination on Hunter's face. The hole grew into a sizable opening, and with a few deft tugs, Hunter pulled free a few loose tiles.

"There," he said, looking down at her, his smile growing. "Part two of escaping can now commence."

Nessa stared at him, utterly gobsmacked. "Didn't that hurt?" she croaked, nodding to his hand. "Because it looked like it would hurt. You know, punching something like that."

He unwrapped his hand and held it out to her, showing Nessa that, other than a bit of redness across the knuckles, he was otherwise unhurt. "Tough as an ox, I am."

"Good to know," Nessa murmured.

Hunter offered her his hand and she took it, using it as a much needed aid as she slowly rose to her feet. The beam was fairly wide, nearly a foot thick, offering plenty of foot space. When she was standing however, it felt like it was a tight rope, narrow and unsteady. A wave of vertigo crashed over Nessa, making her dizzy and her knees weak. She gripped Hunter's hand with bone crushing force until the light-headedness passed.

When she tentatively opened her eyes, she found Hunter staring at her with a measure of concern. His hand tightened on hers for a moment, reassuringly, and Nessa felt a little bit of courage grow.

"You alright?" Hunter asked.

"Oh, I'm just great," Nessa said dryly.

"Not scared of heights then?"

"Not in the slightest," she lied.

"Good, because you really don't want to be scared of heights when you're standing thirty feet above the ground, now would you?"

Nessa glared. "If we weren't standing thirty feet above the ground, I would punch you."

Hunter chuckled. "It's a good thing we are then." He released Nessa's hand and nodded at the hole above their heads. "You first or me?"

Nessa looked up at the steep slant of the roof, and at the joists and battening that were covered with signs of woodworm. She wasn't particularly sure they would be able to support much more weight. Besides, if anyone were to fall off the roof it would be her. If Hunter went out first, Nessa reasoned, at least she would be able to see how the joists faired under his weight first, and he would be able to steady her once she got up there too.

She smiled, liking that idea.

"You," said Nessa. "Please."

Hunter smirked, as if he could read her thought process, then reached up, grabbing the edge of the hole. Without much effort he pulled himself out, and Nessa could hear him shifting around on the tiles above, getting into position.

She stood as still as a statue, fearing that if she was to move even the slightest bit, then she would plummet to the floor below.

Hunter popped his head through the hole, arms reaching down. "Give me your hands. I'll pull you up."

Careful not to lose her balance, Nessa did as she was ordered, hating how her hands shook, displaying her fear for him to see. With a strong grip around each other's wrists, Hunter hauled her up through the hole, her feet scrabbling for purchase as soon as she was clear of it. Her boots' leather soles gripped the tiles securely, and she swiftly settled herself down beside Hunter.

Up there, perched atop the spire, which in turn rested upon a high rocky outcrop, the world was spread out before Nessa, seen from a bird's eye view.

Fading light from the setting sun bathed the heavens in magnificent colours. Oranges and watery reds saturated the gathering clouds that blanketed the horizon, turning their undersides pink and yellow. The city was haloed in a soft glow as the sun sank behind the earth, showing the buildings in a mystical light. Nessa searched for the river, but it was out of sight. She presumed that she was on the other side of the prison.

Hunter shifted. "So, any ideas from here?"

"I hadn't thought of a way down," Nessa confessed. "In all honesty, I didn't actually think I would get this far."

"Well, considering the ground is a good sixty foot below us, I reckon we can rule out jumping."

"I think that's a wise decision."

"So we need to find a shorter distance between us and the ground, and then use my rope to climb down."

"That sounds like a reasonable course of action."

"Glad you agree."

Nessa quickly checked that her makeshift backpack was firmly in place, ensuring that the knots were tight, and then indicated that she was ready.

"Stay close," Hunter said, "and try to be as quiet as possible."

Nessa briefly wondered why they needed to be

quiet when the bell still rang clear and loud, a near continuous *dong* that made the earth rattle and shake, but kept her mouth shut. What the hell did she know about escaping from a fortified prison? Nothing. Hunter, on the other hand, seemed to be pretty damn sure of himself, like he had done this before.

Ever so slowly, they shuffled around the spire's roof, making sure that they wouldn't slip before moving an inch. Nessa was, not for the first time, grateful that she was wearing sensible clothing. If the tunic had been much longer or a dress, then she was sure that she wouldn't have got far.

On the other side of the roof, Hunter seemed to find what he had been searching for. Spread out before them was a castle. A keen, contemplative look settled on his face and he stilled, watching, planning. Nessa stared, disbelieving of what she was seeing.

A dominating square building stood in front of her, a hundred feet high and built from dark stone that glinted malevolently. Thin, slitted windows shone with yellow torch light, and shadows moved within. Perched on each corner, and crowning the top were tall turrets which reached towards the sky like desperate fingers. Surrounding the imposing fortress was a thick wall of protection, made from a mixture of adjoining buildings, towers and spires. It was there that Nessa and Hunter found themselves momentarily trapped.

Between them and the castle was a courtyard, filled with numerous figures running to-and-fro. Some carried blazing torches whilst others bore swords.

"It's a hive of activity down there," Nessa murmured, voicing her worry.

"It most certainly is," Hunter said with an alarming amount of excitement. "But that might work to our advantage."

"I don't like the sound of 'might.' I would prefer something a lot more definite."

Hunter thought about it for a second. "It will most probably work to our advantage?" He quirked an eyebrow. "Was that better?"

"Almost, but not quite."

"Pity." He tugged at the rope, untying it from his waist. "If we get out of here alive, I'll be sure to work on being more definite." Then, almost too quiet for Nessa to hear, he muttered, "I really hate this place."

Nessa frowned. "Have you been here before?"

His amber eyes went stark. "Unfortunately yes, I have."

"And where exactly," Nessa asked, "is here?"

"Welcome to Ironguard, home to the demented, the damned and the ignorant."

Chapter 8

The sun sank beneath the horizon, turning the sky midnight blue before true night settled upon Ironguard. With the arrival of darkness, Nessa found herself hanging perilously from a rope, abseiling slowly down the side of the spire's wall. The roof of the adjoining building was somewhere beneath her, but she couldn't see where. The feeling of nothing under her feet was the worst, unnerving and terrifying, and the rope she clambered down felt far too thin. Nessa wound her legs around it for extra grip, and continued to work her way down, all the while thinking that when she got home, she'd be a frequent visitor to a gym.

Hunter was stationed on the spire's roof, steadying the rope as much as he could. When Nessa perceived something large in the dimness just a short distance below her, the rope jerked alarmingly, swinging wildly as Hunter began following her down. Nessa barely stifled a shriek.

Blessed solidness came beneath her feet, and she swiftly untangled herself, springing away from the rope like a cat in water. The slope of the roof was considerably less than that of the spire's, and Nessa found it easy to stand without the threat of slipping. As she waited for Hunter, she shook out her aching arms and brought up her hands, blowing on the rope burns that streaked across her palms, soothing the sting a little.

Nessa looked up and saw that the sky was devoid of stars. The moon peeked around from behind the castle, its pale light catching the front of a mighty cloud that was swiftly devouring the night. A chilled breeze tugged at the hem of Nessa's top and at the loose strands of hair around her face.

A storm was blowing in. A big one.

Hunter jumped and landed beside Nessa with a *thump* and a muffled curse. She flinched at the noise and didn't have time to wonder what was happening before he grabbed her wrist, yanked her over to the other side of the roof, and pushed her against the base of the neighbouring tower. His body covered hers, trapping her between him and the tower's wall, and his hand clamped over her mouth, smothering her cry of outrage.

Nessa squirmed, alarmed, and Hunter's grip tightened in response.

"Shhh," he hissed.

With his free hand, Hunter pointed to above them, where Nessa could now hear the sound of studded boots stomping around. A ring of burning light shone down from the tower's battlements, narrowly missing them but brightening the rest of the roof.

"I'm telling you," a gruff voice growled. "I heard something down there."

They had been found.

Nessa froze, muscles tensing in panic.

"Wait," Hunter breathed into her ear.

"Nonsense," a second said. "How in the Nine Devils would you be able to hear anything over that bloody bell? Bollocks, I say. You're as deaf as a post most of the time. Besides, what would they be doing on the roofs? There's no way for them to get to the city, at least not without a fatal fall first. Anyway, the commander said that the door had been busted down. They're scurrying around the castle grounds somewhere, just like rats."

The light was withdrawn with a grumbled, "Don't like rats," and the sound of the footsteps faded away.

They remained undetected for the time being.

Nessa slapped Hunter's hand from her mouth. "That was far too close for comfort."

Hunter gave a low chuckle, taking a slow step back. "Perhaps, but now we know that they don't suspect what we're doing yet. Good escape plan.

Very good." Nessa sucked in a deep breath, trying to ignore her burning cheeks as he crossed over to the dangling rope, pulling at it. With a sharp flick of his arm, the rope cracked like a whip and fell to his feet, dislodged from where it had been looped over the spire's point.

"What now?" Nessa asked, coming up behind him.

"Now? Now I'm going to lower you to the ground and then jump down."

Nessa peered over the side of the roof, trying to judge how much of a drop it was. The darkness made it hard, but she guessed that they were about first floor height. "Won't you hurt yourself jumping that far?"

"Nonsense, it's all in the technique. I'll be fine. I've jumped further distances before and haven't been too badly hurt."

Nessa was not impressed. "Too badly?"

"Stop worrying," Hunter said, placing the end of the rope in her hands. "Hold on tight, and don't wander off when you get down there."

"I'm seventeen, not seven. I do know not to walk off into the midst of people armed with swords who are searching for me."

"If you say so."

With that, Nessa clutched the rope firmly and allowed Hunter to help her over the edge of the roof. He lowered the rope slowly, and all Nessa had to do was hold on and steady herself against the wall with a foot.

Once she was on the ground, she gave the rope a small tug to let Hunter know.

Feeling rather exposed, Nessa crouched down, back against the wall, trying to make herself as small as possible. Hunter timed his jump perfectly with a *dong* of the bell so that it drowned out the sound of his landing. One second she was alone, and the next Hunter was beside her, nearly scaring Nessa out of her skin. Silently he knelt down, and together they surveyed the courtyard.

Spread out before them, it looked even larger and more daunting than it had from above. The wide expanse of it was filled with burning torches and large groups of armed soldiers, their chainmail glinting in the firelight.

A ring of shadows clung to the outer wall of buildings, where Nessa and Hunter hid. To their right, the courtyard curled around the castle, and to their left, a long building stretched between it and the outer wall, connecting them and cutting the yard in two. In the centre of it was a large, open gateway, and beyond it a similar scene could be observed.

Hunter handed something to Nessa, and her fingers automatically closed around it. Whatever it was had some weight to it, and quizzical, she gazed down at her hand, discovering that she held the dagger that Hunter had so far been carrying.

"You might be needing that," he whispered.

"Might I?" Nessa hissed. "It's a dagger. I don't

know what to do with a dagger. I've never even held one before."

"Well," Hunter said slowly, "it's quite simple really. If anyone other than me comes near you," he flicked the tip of the blade, "then use the pointy end."

Nessa swallowed, nervous and a little sick at his words. He wasn't joking, not even in the slightest. The place was filled with enemies, and if it came to it, Nessa would have to fight her way out, would have to use the 'pointy end' if need be.

"Follow me," the softly spoken words floated in the air.

They set off, moving at a painfully slow pace, keeping tight to the wall, hiding in the shadows. They crawled on hands and knees, making themselves as small as possible to avoid detection. Twice they were forced to stop as small groups of soldiers marched frightfully close to them, and once when a troop of cavalry cantered past.

But at a snail's pace, they continued on, creeping ever closer to the gateway.

༄ ✦ ༄

They huddled in the corner, the gateway a stone's throw away. Light poured through it, chasing away the shadows that Nessa and Hunter had so far been using as a cover. The darkened corner was their last refuge.

"Stay here," Hunter whispered in Nessa's ear.

"I'll be back in a sec."

Nessa nodded as he stood, and pressed herself into the corner until the wall was firm against her back. In silence, she watched as Hunter slowly approached the threshold between the light and the shadows. In his hand was the short sword, tucked in close to his side. With sharp eyes he scanned the courtyard, and then darted from the gloom, disappearing around the corner of the gateway.

Nessa almost went to follow him, desperate not to be left alone, worried that they might become separated or that one of them would get caught. She stopped herself though, just. Long, tense minutes passed with no sign of Hunter. Nessa watched the gateway, the courtyard. Her heartbeat sped up and her hands grew clammy, making it hard for her to hold the dagger. She felt vulnerable there by herself, open and weak.

Hunter rounded the corner and Nessa had never felt such relief as she did just then. He rushed over to her, eyes trained on the courtyard and the soldiers, and grabbed her hand, pulling her up and tugging her after him as he raced back to the gateway. They turned the corner and Nessa was yanked sharply to the left. A door closed behind her, and she found herself in a long, narrow room filled to the brim with *things*.

Nessa turned questioningly to Hunter, and paused. His hands fumbled at the door's lock, his fingers lightly holding two metal skewers that he had inserted into the keyhole.

"What are you doing?" Nessa asked, bewildered.

"I'm locking the door behind us," Hunter said. "That way we won't have any unexpected visitors."

"You can pick locks," Nessa murmured, mildly impressed.

"That," he turned and gave her a wink, "and so much more."

Nessa left him to it and moved further into the room, eyes sweeping from left to right, taking in everything. The far wall was curved slightly inward, and between it and Nessa hung three large candlelit lamps, illuminating the space in muted light. Running down the sides and in the middle of the room was an assortment of low tables, shelves and hangers, all of which held a wide collection of shields, helms, chainmail shirts and tunics, and an impressive array of weapons.

"What do you think?" Hunter asked, coming to stand by Nessa's elbow.

"I think you've taken me to an armoury?"

Hunter nodded happily. "Indeed I have."

"Why?"

"Why? Why? Because this room holds the greatest things ever."

"Pointy things and unflattering clothing?"

"Camouflage," Hunter corrected.

"Right," Nessa muttered. "Of course."

Hunter, grinning, moved deeper into the room, searching for something with bright eyes. He approached a line of neatly hung midnight blue tunics and plucked out the smallest one, holding it out to Nessa. She took it and measured it against herself, finding that it appeared to be a reasonably good fit. Looking up, she found that Hunter was holding up a chainmail shirt. He passed it to her, and the weight of it nearly sent her to the ground.

"Put the chainmail over what you're wearing now," Hunter instructed, "and then the tunic over that. I'll go find something that will fit me." He went to move away, but paused, gazing over his shoulder at her warily. "You hanging in there alright?"

Nessa stared at him, surprised that he would ask something like that. The truth was, Nessa wasn't alright. She was drained beyond measure, exhausted to the core of her being. She was confused, unsure and frightened, weighed down by the knowledge that she was a world away from home and had no idea of how to get back.

Nonetheless, Nessa nodded, murmuring, "I'm fine."

Hunter looked as if he wanted to press the issue, but he simply dipped his head in acknowledgement, and slipped away between some shelves, off to procure himself some camouflage.

Nessa sighed and dumped her armful of clothing on a nearby table, and began untying the knots holding her backpack together. It slipped away from her shoulder and she set it down carefully, folding back a corner and giving the orb a quick check over, making sure that it wasn't damaged. It was fine, sitting quite happily in the ratty blanket, glowing softly away. Nessa gave it a stroke, and then covered it back up, lest Hunter should catch a glimpse, deciding that she would find it a proper bag once she had dressed.

Picking up the chainmail shirt, Nessa slipped it over her head and slid her arms through the sleeves, which only reached to her elbows. The weight of it dragged down on her shoulders, and it was an effort not to stoop over like an old woman. The tunic was made from a soft, high quality fabric, and sat lightly over the chainmail, neither too baggy nor too tight. It fell to her knees and had slits in the front and back for ease of movement. Laces tied up the front, and upon the left breast a black rose was finely embroidered, surrounded by tongues of flame. Nessa gently brushed her fingers over it, and as she did so, a faint shiver ran up her spine.

Nessa grabbed her dagger and scooped up the orb, cradling it in the crook of her elbow, the blanket loosely wrapped around it, and went in search of Hunter. Her boots clapped softly on the floor as she worked her way through the tables and shelves, and over to where she could hear him moving around. Nessa felt jittery, her mind repeating one thought over and over: They needed to get out of there. They needed to get far, far away and hide. The thought took over and Nessa's body filled with the sense that something dreadful was rapidly approaching.

She found Hunter tucked away in a corner, his fingers working at his tunic's laces. He heard her approach and looked up, a faint grin starting to appear, but which immediately drooped when he caught sight of Nessa's expression.

"What's wrong?" Hunter asked, going to her. "You're as pale as death."

"I don't know," she said. "I'm not sure. I just suddenly have this feeling that something is coming, that we need to leave." Nessa worried that she sounded crazy, but Hunter didn't appear to think so.

"We'd best be heading off then," he said.

Hunter turned and picked up something, passing it to her, and Nessa saw that it was a leather messenger bag, old and battered, but still in good condition. She placed the orb inside, blanket and all, and set the strap on her shoulder, eager to be going. As they made their way back over to the door, Nessa buckled the flap shut, ensuring that her precious treasure couldn't be knocked out.

Placing his ear against the door, Hunter listened to what was outside. He removed the lock picks from a hidden pocket and inserted them into the key hole, swiftly unlocking the door.

"Once we leave here, keep close to me," Hunter said. "We'll be going to the left, across the bailey, heading over to where the old kitchens used to be in the castle."

Nessa nodded, even though she didn't have the faintest idea of what a bailey was.

Hunter opened the door, poking his head out briefly, and grabbing her hand, he pulled her along as he dashed out. The door fell shut behind them, but Hunter made no move to re-lock it, instead turning to the left, and with Nessa close at his heels, walked through the gateway.

The courtyard they entered was larger than the previous one and contained a lot more activity. Brightness spilled from the windows of the towering castle, casting a monochromatic rainbow of long shadows and beams of light on the ground. Braziers had also been stationed throughout the yard, adding more illumination, and jutting out from the outer wall were more armouries, their wide doors flung open, showing men inside arming themselves to the teeth.

Nessa swallowed nervously, her movements stiff and jerky. She felt incredibly visible, and she worried that she stuck out like a sore thumb.

"Relax," Hunter whispered. "Act like you're meant to be here."

Too visible, her mind whispered to her. *Someone will notice us.*

Nessa frowned, mumbling under her breath, "Belong here. Act like you belong here." The problem was, Nessa certainly didn't belong there in any possible way. Nonetheless, she held her head high and tried desperately to move like the soldiers, confident and strong. Nessa wasn't entirely sure she pulled it off convincingly, but Hunter whispered encouragement anyway, spurring her on.

Hunter led Nessa through the courtyard, striding straight through the very centre, yet somehow avoiding most of the activity. He angled them towards a base of a tower, and as they grew closer, Nessa saw that hidden away in a nook was a small, unassuming door.

Their destination.

Once again, armed with his lock picks, Hunter began tinkering with the lock. As he did so, Nessa kept an eye on the courtyard, making sure that no one noticed what they were doing. Her eyes landed on the gateway, now a fair distance away, and she saw a figure move within its shadows.

Nessa's blood turned to ice.

Whoever they were, were too far away for Nessa to identify, but the feeling of dread arose as she watched them enter the armoury. She was about to voice her concern to Hunter when she heard the lock click open, sounding more beautiful than a chorus of singing angels, and a lot more welcome at present. On squeaking hinges, the door swung back.

A rush of warm air brushed softly against their faces in greeting, and an empty hallway stretched out before them, lit by glass lanterns hanging down from the ceiling at intervals. The air was warm but limp, giving the hallway a dead, timeless feel to it, as if people rarely ventured there.

Hunter pulled the door shut behind them, sealing them in, and with a touch to Nessa's elbow, urged her down the corridor. It was narrow and filled with many twists and turns, making it impossible to tell how far they journeyed into the belly of the castle. When they rounded yet another corner, the hallway came to an abrupt end, a large door blocking the way.

"Well," Hunter said, frowning. "That wasn't there before."

Nessa looked between him and the door.

Large and wooden, it sealed the end of the hallway, stopping them from going any further. Hunter grabbed his picks and aimed them at the key hole, only to find that there wasn't one. He paused, looking over his shoulder at Nessa, his bafflement clear.

"That makes this difficult."

"Is it actually locked?" Nessa wondered. "It makes sense that if it doesn't have a lock, then it can't actually be locked."

"That's a good point." Hunter pocketed the unrequired picks and raised a hand, intending to push the door open. His hand went clear through the wood, disappearing into it.

They both yelped and Nessa sprang forward, catching Hunter's wrist and pulling it back. The door gave no resistance, releasing his hand without a fight. Taken by surprise, they fell back and toppled to the floor, landing in a startled heap.

Hunter rubbed his wrist in contemplation, staring at the door, and then jumped to his feet, laughing.

"It's an illusion," Hunter said, giving Nessa a hand up.

"What?"

"The door, it's an illusion, an image. It's not real. That's why my hand passes right through it." Hunter reached out again, demonstrating. His hand disappeared up to his wrist, looking to be embedded in solid wood. "Someone must have put it here as a deterrent." He grinned. "A bloody brilliant idea, if I do say so myself."

Hunter took Nessa's hand and leaped forward, pulling her with him through the illusion. It rippled around their passing, not unlike water. Nessa tried to wrap her mind around the fact that the door was nothing more than an apparition, for every ridge of the wood's grain could be seen, and their shadows stood neatly against it, their forms blocking the dancing torch light.

On the other side of the illusion, the sight of an identical hallway greeted them, empty save for themselves and the lanterns. A scowl grew on Hunter's face as he stepped forward, searching for something.

Nessa trailed after him. "What are you looking for?"

"Somewhere around here should be a door. However, it seems to have vanished."

"Doors don't just up and move."

"No," Hunter agreed, "but they can be covered up and hidden."

"Another illusion?"

"Another illusion," confirmed Hunter.

"So, I suppose that if we run our hands over the wall, and the door is under an illusion, then our hands will sink into it."

Hunter looked at her appraisingly. "Oh, I do like you."

"Excellent. Now, go forth and find."

Hunter nodded and turned, striding down the hallway, hand against the wall. He paused just a few yards away and shot Nessa a feral grin over his shoulder.

"I think I have something," he sang.

Nessa joined him and saw that his hand had sunk into the wall slightly, the illusion covering his palm, as if he had placed it into a plate of dark water. Hunter slid his hand down and across, the illusion rippling in its wake for a second as he searched for the door handle. He found it, and with his trusty lock picks, soon had the door open.

As soon as the door swung back, the illusion shattered, breaking apart in a symphony of dancing lights, revealing the doorway and what lay beyond. Heavy shadows clung to the walls and stairs, concealing all but the first few feet in inky darkness.

Nessa shifted uneasily.

"Ready?" he asked.

Nessa looked at him, nodding, and saw that he had plucked one of the lanterns from its chain, holding it up ready to light the way. She smiled, waving him forward. "After you."

With eagerness in his step, Hunter started down the stairs. Nessa stuck close to his heels, pausing only to shut the door behind them, for all the good it would do since the illusion concealing it was gone.

The darkness was smothering, battling against the lantern's meagre light. The steps were steep and narrow, worn smooth by years of use from once upon a time. The air was dry and dusty, and Nessa was forced to muffle a sneeze on more than one occasion.

Deeper into the bowels of Ironguard they went, the stairs becoming more worn and broken, the air colder and more unpleasant. Finally, when Nessa was shivering, the stairs came to an end and she found herself standing in a long room that was caught in the ravages of time and disuse. Watery moonlight filtered in through a small, dirty window that was set high in the far wall, mixing with that from Hunter's stolen lantern.

A kitchen was revealed, trapped in the refuge of its last days in use.

Cooking pots and pans glinted dully, stacked atop each other on long, wooden counters. A large, ash filled fireplace sat to their right, a heavy cauldron hanging from a hook in the centre, and tall shelves dominated the wall beneath the window, covered in glass jars filled with unidentifiable contents.

"Where are we?" Nessa asked, her voice echoing.

"A few years ago, before Ironguard became a major military outpost, this was the castle's main kitchen," Hunter explained. "Then they built an entire wing of kitchens to meet the soldiers demands, and this room was put out of use, which so happens to make escaping a whole lot easier without it being filled with maids and cooks." Hunter looked over at Nessa, grinning like an excited child. "There's a secret tunnel behind the fireplace."

He ushered her over to the fireplace, which looked like a gaping mouth, the cauldron dangling down like the thing at the back of a person's throat. A mound of black ash, riddled with clumps of coal and semi-burned logs, covered the hearth. The light from the lantern shone dully on the flame licked tiles.

Hunter bent under the mantle and moved to the back of the fireplace, his boots kicking up little clouds of ash in his wake. He set the lantern down and inspected the tiles in front of him closely. Nessa took a step to the side, observing what he was doing from over his shoulder. Whilst his back was to her and his attention was elsewhere, Nessa's hand drifted down to her massager bag, feeling the smooth curve of the orb through the leather.

Hunter tinkered around at the back of the

fireplace for a few minutes, his fingers scrambling along an invisible seam. With a sound of frustration, he abruptly turned and stalked past Nessa, annoyance on his face.

Nessa stayed where she was, watching with bemusement as he moved around the kitchen, opening and closing several draws and cabinets before he found what he was searching for.

"A soup ladle?" exclaimed Nessa. "What do you want a ladle for?"

"What wouldn't I want a soup ladle for?"

"You're mad," she decided. "Utterly and completely mad."

Hunter grinned as he darted past her, ducking beneath the mantle and going to the back of the fireplace again, soup ladle in hand. He positioned the end of the handle in a grove that ran beside a line of tiles, sliding it up and down, trying to wedge it in.

Nessa watched his antics for a second, then said, "If you're trying to pry the damn thing open, then why not just use your sword? It's sharper and a lot more robust."

"Because," Hunter said, grunting, "if I were to do that, I would blunt the edge. Besides, my ladle is working spectacularly well." The sound of grinding stone punctuated his words, and Hunter stepped to the side, letting Nessa see what he had done.

At the back of the fireplace was a crack measuring an inch or so wide.

"Come have a look," said Hunter, waving her forward.

Nessa, fascinated, went over and peered through the slit, curious as to what might be on the other side. All she could see was darkness. However, judging by the light breeze that brushed against her face, Nessa could tell that the void was a deep one.

"It's a secret tunnel," Nessa murmured.

Hunter nodded. "It's a secret tunnel." He stepped closer, his shoulder brushing against hers, and grabbed the edge of the crack, pulling with all his might. It held steady for a moment, and then, with a grinding moan, slowly slid to the side, creating an opening just big enough for the two of them.

The tunnel awaited.

Nessa stared at the small, narrow entrance, and at the bottomless darkness that stretched out before them, so complete that the lantern did little to brighten any respectable distance.

"Where does it lead?" Nessa asked.

"It curves down into the rock outcrop that the castle is built atop," Hunter explained. "Then it joins onto a series of old mining tunnels that run under the castle and the city. Once we're in those, I reckon we can wait for the searches to calm down and then make our way over to somewhere safe."

He spoke with such confidence, such ease, that Nessa was sure that he knew what he was doing and that he had experience doing it. Nessa wondered, though, about how successful he had been. Whether or not he had escaped by this route before, he had still ended up back in Ironguard, only for the cycle to start again. She was tempted to ask Hunter if he had actually managed to escape before, but she wasn't entirely sure if she wanted to know the answer, in all honesty. Instead, Nessa enquired about the 'somewhere safe.'

"Still trying to figure that one out," Hunter confessed. "But don't worry, I'll find us a place out of harm's way. You can trust me on that. It's a promise. And I always keep my promises."

There was only one problem with that. Nessa didn't trust him, not completely, not yet. Perhaps not ever. From past experiences, Nessa had learnt the hard way that it was best to rely on no one but yourself. That way, you could only be disappointed in your own actions, and not those of others.

But while Nessa didn't fully trust Hunter, she did need him. From that came a sense of faith in him. After all, he had come back for her, hadn't he? He had come back and was helping her out of the castle, even though it would have been quicker and easier if he had done it alone, leaving her behind.

That meant something to Nessa. That meant everything to her. So few people had come back for her in the past. She only hoped that Hunter's loyalty wouldn't bring down the barriers that had taken her months of heartbreak to build.

Chapter 9

The lantern produced very little in the way of heat, and did nearly nothing to drive away the bitter chill of the tunnel. It did offer a small ring of semi-protection from the darkness, which one person was grateful for, and that person wasn't Nessa. Although it left her shivering from the cold, she lagged behind Hunter intentionally.

To start with, the tunnel had been wide enough for both of them to walk side by side, but quite quickly it had started to narrow, forcing them into a single file. Soon after that, the ceiling had gradually curved down, giving them no choice but to crawl on their hands and knees. The floor descended steeply, puncturing deep into the hard earth, and a cold slime covered it in a slippery blanket. It seeped into their clothing, clinging to their skin. They were freezing, damp, and their escape was made incredibly unpleasant.

With the appearance of the slime came the creepy crawlies. They clung to the tunnel's sides and ceiling, things with ghostly white bodies and lots of long legs. Creatures Nessa would rather not see. They fled from the lantern's light, scurrying away, and every now and again, much to Nessa's horror, falling on her, tangling in her hair or landing on her back. Each time, she would shake herself like a wet dog, dislodging the critter and sending it flying. Nessa felt a grim sort of pleasure each time she heard the *plop* as the creature landed somewhere in the slime.

However, after one of them, something small bodied but incredibly long legged, landed on her head and burrowed into her hair, Nessa lost her resolve of suffering in silence and promptly shrieked.

She swatted at it, slime splashing all over her face, her hair. Hunter, surprised by the commotion, turned around, or at least tried to.

Whacking his head on the tunnel's wall, he cursed and peered awkwardly over his shoulder at her, the narrow confines of the tunnel preventing him from going to her aid.

He had the nerve to ask, "How you doing back there?"

Nessa growled at him, and with one last slap, the thing loosened from her hair and tumbled to the ground. Without looking down, she started forward, crawling over to Hunter, who eyed her curiously, taking in the goo oozing down her face and neck. Wisely, he kept his mouth shut, and continued leading the way.

The tunnel curved to the side, and then, all of a sudden, opened up onto a large underground passage. It must have been the mine that Hunter had mentioned. He clambered out of the tunnel, slipping and sliding as he went, and then, finally free, placed the lantern on the ground. He offered Nessa a hand up, and she saw that it was covered up to the wrist in dark green slime, just as hers was. This, they quickly discovered, made it incredibly hard to grip one another's hand, and rendered Hunter's assistance of little use.

After a fair deal of yanking, pulling, grappling and quite a bit of muttered swearing, Nessa was finally out of the horrible little tunnel. Her back and legs, after crawling for so long hunched over, protested against her standing, and retaliated by cramping. Nessa sighed and leaned back against the wall, stretching out her aching muscles, slowly relaxing.

Hunter picked up the lantern and held it high. The ring of light showed ten or so feet of the mining shaft before melting into pitch black darkness that surrounded Nessa and Hunter on two sides. Walls of solid stone were smoothly cut, supported by thick wooden beams, as was the ceiling. The ground was even and the air was still and dead.

Nessa looked over at Hunter, finding him staring into the gloom, his eyes sharp and a crease between his brows.

"What do we do now?" Nessa asked him.

"Move on, I guess." Hunter's answer was quiet, subdued even. His eyes were glued onto the darkness, unblinking. A shiver ran down Nessa's spine. She cast a quick, nervous glance over to the spot that held his interest, but saw nothing there. Still, Hunter was beginning to make her uneasy.

"Is everything alright?" Nessa whispered, laying a hand on his arm.

Hunter stirred and looked down at her, the frown fading away.

"It's fine," he said reassuringly. "Everything is fine." It seemed like he said it more for his benefit than hers. He turned and began walking in the opposite direction, not once looking back. Nessa, more than a little perplexed, hurried after him, unable to resist a quick peek over her shoulder as she did so. She thought she spied movement, a flicker of something in the darkness, as indistinguishable as a shadow moving within a shadow, the blur of a bird's wing in a blackened sky.

Nessa paused, staring, but no further movement could be seen, and the darkness lay still and unwelcoming. She rushed after Hunter, who was further down the tunnel, not realising that she had stopped for a moment. Nessa was in a panic, wondering what that could have possibly been. Had it merely been a play of the light? The shadows dancing as Hunter had walked away with the lantern? Or was someone down there with them? Goose bumps rose on Nessa's arms as a thought entered her mind. *What kind of person would be down in an abandoned mine without a light?*

What if it wasn't a person... what if... what if it was a monster?

Nessa kept close to Hunter.

They walked in silence, both of them deep in their own thoughts. Tension radiated from Hunter in waves and his eyes were deep and reflective. Nessa knew that if she were to ask him a question, it probably wouldn't be heard or answered. She grew nervous and jittery, every slight noise making her flinch or jump.

At times, water dripped from above, sounding eerily like footsteps when the droplets hit the ground.

Eventually, Nessa and Hunter came across a crossroads, and standing in the middle, with the lantern held high between them, they peered at the other entrances. The light barely reached them, but after a slight pause, Hunter went over to the one on their left.

The tunnel was near identical to the one they had just left, with thick wooden beams holding up the walls and ceiling, and with no hint of wind or fresh air. The only sounds Nessa could hear were their footsteps and the drips of water, which were steadily increasing in tempo. The only difference was the tunnel's size, smaller and narrower, the sides pressing in on them, the ceiling almost brushing against the top of Hunter's head. There was a feel of claustrophobia about it.

Their surroundings were unchanging, and time was only measured by the steady *drip...drip...drip* of falling water droplets. With each step, Hunter grew tenser, his shoulder's tightening, his hand drifting closer to the short sword tucked into his belt. Nessa was sure that someone was following them, but each time she had mustered enough courage to look over her shoulder, she saw nothing, no moving shadows or a hint of a light in the distance.

Unable to endure the torture of silence any longer, Nessa turned to her ghost of a companion.

"We're being followed, aren't we?" she murmured.

Hunter nodded stiffly. "I've got a plan. Act natural. Don't let them suspect we know."

Act natural? Nessa thought. *What the hell is natural behaviour when you're being followed by a creature in the darkness, encased by walls of solid stone?*

Hunter having a plan was of some comfort to Nessa, but not much. His stride lengthened, and he led Nessa down the tunnel at a swift pace with no attempt at stealth. Then, suddenly, he grabbed her hand and yanked her to the side, pulling her sharply down a narrow passageway that branched off. The walls were rough, jagged, and there was barely enough space for them as they rushed down it.

A cavern opened up before them, small and rounded. The ceiling was low and smooth, the shape of an inverted bowl, giving the room a squat feel. Nessa quickly realised that there were no other exits.

It was a dead end.

Panicked, Nessa turned to Hunter, but he *shushed* her before she could voice her alarm. He pulled her over to the side and knelt, tugging her down with him. He let go of her hand and opened the lantern, quickly extinguishing the candle. The darkness swallowed them immediately, making them blind.

Nessa shook, the fear nearly overwhelming. In the dark, Hunter's hand found hers, holding it tightly. Unable to see, her other senses became heightened, and she could not help but be aware of his presence beside her.

They remained there, crouched down for what felt like an eternity. Nessa's breaths echoed in her ears and her body swam in adrenalin. She itched to run, to fight, to do something other than wait.

Everything seemed to grow abnormally quiet as time went by.

Just when Nessa began to think that they had been wrong, that no one was following them, she heard something that was out of place; the subtle crunch of stone, as if someone was treading light footed over the uneven floor.

Hunter shifted and Nessa heard the steely slither of the sword as he pulled it free. She gripped his hand tighter, shivering as their stalker entered the cavern, their steps seeming overly loud in her ears. They appeared to have abandoned any attempted at a furtive approach and moved with bold strides. Dimly, in her growing panic, Nessa wondered if she should draw her dagger, but she feared making a noise.

The footsteps came to a stop in the centre of the room. Hunter stiffened and slowly, carefully, rose from his crouch, tugging Nessa up with him. She tried not to make a sound, tried not to disturb the loose stones on the ground. She daren't even breathe.

It was all for nothing, though.

After a loaded pause, their stalker moved, heading straight for them.

Nessa wanted to run, to scream, but Hunter's grip on her hand tightened painfully, holding her still. Only when their stalker was close enough for them to feel the air stir, close enough for their breath to be heard, did Hunter move.

Hunter lashed out, striking as fast as a snake, and a mighty bellow filled the cavern, ricocheting off the rounded walls, amplified to a deafening degree. Together they sprinted through the darkness, Hunter leading the way.

Since they didn't immediately run into any walls,

Nessa guessed that Hunter somehow knew exactly where everything was. The tunnel closed in around them, and Nessa's hand clutched at his, her other closing around the bag that bounced against her side, holding it down. Behind them came an agonised shout and a sudden burst of blue light. The two of them pushed themselves harder, barrelling along the tunnel as fast as they could.

Nessa's legs burned and her lungs gasped for air. She refused to let that slow her down.

Unseen hands of jagged stone reached out to her, ripping at Nessa's clothing as she bumped against the tunnel's walls, cutting and bruising her arms. Hunter pulled her to the right, and her shoulder whacked a corner as they turned into the larger mining tunnel. How Hunter could tell where they were going, Nessa couldn't fathom, and she didn't have the time to figure it out either.

All too soon, Nessa heard the sounds of pursuit behind them.

Blood roared in her ears and her legs felt as if they were made of lead. Her breath got caught in her throat and she sobbed, nearly stumbling as their pursuer grew closer. Nessa and Hunter rocketed around another corner, and ahead, a dull light appeared.

The end of the tunnel was within sight.

Nessa ran with everything she had, the mine's exit getting delightfully closer with each step.

Before Nessa knew it, they were there, being

bombarded by howling wind and cold rain. They leapt through the threshold, the air stirring behind them as their pursuer drew frightfully near, and tumbled down an embankment, landing in a tangled heap in a puddle. Hunter didn't pause, jerking Nessa to her feet, pulling her over to the first row of houses and tucking them into the gloom of an alleyway.

Together they turned, looking up at the mine.

Hunter flinched and Nessa felt the hope of escape die.

Standing there, as still as a statue, looking like a god of death personified, was Shadow.

Chapter 10

Shadow gazed down at them, his handsome face pale and expressionless, giving no hint of what he was thinking. In one hand he held a long, sharp sword, the tip pointed towards the ground, whilst his other was pressed to his side, where blood shone a stark red against his black clothing, just visible in the gloom of night.

Hunter had injured him, clearly, and Nessa could tell by the amount of blood that it must have been a bad wound, a deep one. Despite this, though, Shadow showed no pain, no weakness. He stood tall and strong, radiating strength and power. Misgivings grew in Nessa's stomach.

Shadow stepped down the embankment, walking easily, not slipping or falling. It was unnerving to witness. He moved like a cat stalking its prey. Nessa braced herself, ready to run, but Hunter muttered a curse and moved in front of her, his sword raised and ready.

"What the hell do you think you are doing?" Nessa hissed in his ear.

"The only thing I can do," Hunter growled, watching as Shadow prowled closer. "I'm pretty sure he's not just going to let us walk away."

"And you reckon you can take him on in a fight? With swords?"

Hunter shrugged.

"I hate to point it out to you, but his sword is a lot bigger than yours."

"It's not about size, Nessa, but how it's wielded."

Before Nessa could talk him into reason or pull him back, Hunter lunged forward, stabbing at Shadow. The element of surprise may have helped Hunter back in the cavern, but Shadow was not to be tricked twice. He blocked Hunter's jab with an easy swing of his sword, batting Hunter's away as if it was a mere nuisance. A second later their blades met again, the metal ringing loud and as clear as a bell.

Nessa stumbled back, not wanting to be struck in the ensuing fray. She watched in horror as they fought. She had seen fights before, scuffles at school involving kicks and a few punches, but they were tame compared to this, almost pathetic. The battle between Hunter and Shadow was feral in its brutality, barbaric. They weren't fighting over an insult or a girlfriend, they were fighting for life and limb, and perhaps something that meant a lot more: freedom.

She watched, flinching at each blow. Hunter held his own to start with, blocking each strike of Shadow's sword, even counter attacking, but the toll of his imprisonment began to show. Weeks without proper food and rest made him weak, and the exertion during their escape wasn't helping. Not even Shadow's injury gave Hunter the upper hand in the end.

Hunter's movements slowed and became laboured, and at each of Shadow's hard hits, he struggled to keep his balance, forced to retreat.

And then he made a mistake, and Shadow pounced.

With a steely slither, Shadow's sword slid down Hunter's, locking them together at the crossguard. They struggled against one another, wrestling for control, then an evil glint shone in Shadow's eyes and his head whipped forward, bashing against Hunter's forehead.

Hunter recoiled, his sword falling from numb hands, landing on the ground with a clang. He stared at it with a dazed expression, making no move to retrieve it, making no move to defend himself as Shadow gave a mighty kick to his chest, sending him flying. Hunter hit the wall of a nearby house, smashing against it heavily, his head striking stone. Instantly he went limp, falling to the wet ground in a heap.

For a heartbeat Nessa was frozen, fearing the worst. But then, thankfully, his chest moved faintly with a breath, and she gave a cry, running over to him.

Nessa made it halfway across the alley before Shadow was upon her.

She screamed as his hand closed on her arm, as he swung her around and pushed her up against a wall. He moved in front of her, blocking her view of Hunter, and raised his sword, pressing its fine edge against her throat.

Nessa stilled, hardly daring to breathe.

Her head was level with his chest, and too afraid to look up into his eyes and see her death written in them, hers fixed onto the torc that sat around the base of his neck, seemingly shining with its own inner light. It was different to the one he had worn before, beautiful and intricate, with both fine and thick silver wire twisted together over and over, studded with small blue gems that were nestled between the strands, and capped with two large faceted sapphires that shimmered with every slight movement.

Shadow shifted, and the sword edge pressed harder against Nessa's skin, a thin line of fire burning with threat and intention. Nessa barely suppressed a gasp, and of their own volition, her eyes flicked up, instantly captured by Shadow's dark gaze.

Time became suspended.

It suddenly felt as if there was nothing else in the world but them.

With her eyes locked with his, her fear seemed to dim. She could not help but observe certain aspects about him, qualities that made him seem more human and a little less monstrous. She noticed trivial details, like how long his eyelashes were, and how his eyes were such an amazing blue; how his long hair had lost its wave and was slick with rainwater, reaching to just past his shoulders, and that he had a small, silvery scar that marred the skin just beneath his ear. Shadow swallowed, his throat working, and Nessa awakened from her daydream-ish daze.

Shadow's eyes gazed into Nessa's, and she saw that they were filled with a great many things that made fear rear its ugly head again. Those beautiful blue depths were filled with rage, sorrow, and what scared Nessa the most: regret.

What could he possibly be planning to bring such emotions to his eyes? Nessa didn't know. She didn't want to even start thinking about it. He had the looks of a fallen angel, and the temperament to match, wretched and cruel to the core.

Nessa shivered and bit her lip, trying to think of something to do, anything.

Praying that her thoughts were concealed from him, Nessa inched her hand towards her messenger bag, reaching for the dagger that was tucked inside.

The drum of the pouring rain muted the noise as she pulled it free, and her shivers hid the movement as she angled it, ready to thrust it into his side. Shadow frowned, and faster than Nessa could blink, his free hand was clenched around her wrist, slamming it up against the wall by her head. Nessa yelped as pain blossomed in her wrist. Her fingers spasmed, losing their grip on the dagger. It fell to the ground, lost to her.

Shadow bent down, bringing his head level with hers.

"Not such a meek little mouse now, are you?" he murmured, his voice deep and resonating.

Nessa struggled to free her arm, wriggling and twisting her wrist, uncaring about the sword at her throat. "I was never meek."

"No?" Shadow asked softly, his eyes sparking, his hand tightening against her efforts. "Then you put on a mighty fine show before. Had me thinking that all hope was gone. But there's a fire in you. I knew there would be. It just took you a while to find it."

Nessa growled.

Shadow chuckled and straightened, his grip on her arm loosening. It flopped to Nessa's side and remained there, limp, and she watched with weary eyes as he took a step back, still keeping his sword poised at her throat.

"Be careful, little mouse," he said, his words nearly washed away in the rain. "You're playing a very dangerous game, and I would hate for your flame to be extinguished too soon. Don't disappoint me now."

He turned and stalked away, disappearing into the darkness.

All strength left her and Nessa slid down the wall, huddling on the ground in a confused and shocked mess. Her breaths rattled in her chest, something between gasps and sobs, and great shudders wracked her body. Rain fell, washing over her face like tears, and soaked through her clothing, painfully cold. She stared ahead, her eyes unseeing until a low moan broke through the fog in her mind.

"Hunter!" she gasped.

He lay where he had fallen, face down on the ground, unmoving even as a puddle of dirtied water formed around him. Nessa clambered to her feet, her legs feeling like they were made of jelly, and stumbled over to him.

She fell to her knees, bruising them against the hard cobbles, and carefully rolled Hunter onto his back. A groan came from deep in his throat, but other than that, Hunter didn't react. The heavy rain pushed back his hair, and even in the darkness of a stormy night, Nessa could see the angry red mark on his forehead. She bit her lip, worried beyond belief as she placed a hand on his chest, gently shaking him.

"Hunter," she called softly. "Wake up. Hunter?"

Nessa shook him again, making his head loll.

"Please wake up," she pleaded. "Please."

Hunter didn't moan or groan, or even twitch a finger. Nessa's heart raced and she looked around, searching desperately for some kind of help. No one had come to investigate the noise of the fight, and no light shone from the closed shutters of the nearby buildings. The street was deserted save for her and Hunter.

Nessa deliberated about calling for help, wondering if anyone would come, or if it would just draw unwanted attention. An image of the soldiers from the castle flashed in her mind. They had been readying themselves, preparing to enter the city to expand their search. She grew anxious. How long until they were in the city, armed and looking for them? Were they there already, getting closer and closer to them?

Hunter groaned and his eyelids fluttered.

Nessa leaned over him, placing a gentle hand on his shoulder. "Hunter, it's time to wake up now."

And with excruciating slowness, Hunter regained consciousness.

With long blinks and confused eyes, he gazed at her without recognition at first, but then his mind cleared, and in a rush he scrambled up, trying to get to his feet. He didn't even get to sit before Nessa pushed him down.

"Slowly, damn it," she said. "You've been knocked out, probably concussed, and you need to take things easy."

"Fine," Hunter mumbled. "I'm fine." He raised a hand to his forehead, wincing as his fingers grazed the swelling there. "Where's Shadow? Where's he gone?"

"You're not fine," Nessa cried. "None of this is fine. Escaping from castles, brawling and fighting with swords... it's just not... fine." She slumped forward, cradling her head in her hands, hiding away the tears that were suddenly in her eyes. "And as for Shadow... I haven't got the faintest idea what happened. He had us, could have easily taken us back to the castle, but all of a sudden he just left. I don't know why."

"Perhaps I scared him away?"

"Or maybe he's gone to get reinforcements?" Nessa sobbed, the terrible image of them back in Blondie's clutches springing to mind.

A cold hand touched hers, startling Nessa, and she peered through her fingers, finding Hunter reaching out to her, his worry clear to see. She let him take her hand, entwining his fingers with hers.

"I'm not accustomed to things like this," she said. "Not at all."

"It's alright. Everything will be alright." Hunter sat up slowly. "It takes two or three wild escapes before you get used to all the excitement."

Nessa scowled at him, but it lacked heart.

"Come on," Hunter said, "help me up and I'll get us somewhere warm and dry. That will help raise your spirits." With some degree of effort, Nessa managed to get him to his feet.

Hunter was unsteady at first, wobbly and unbalanced, his coordination off-kilter. Nessa placed his arm over her shoulders, taking as much of his weight as she could, becoming his crutch. Her bag slid, settling uncomfortably on her hip, but with Hunter heavy against her, Nessa couldn't risk shifting it, not if she didn't want to drop him. Hunter wasn't doing much in the way of holding on.

"Which way?" Nessa asked, staring down the alley, which branched off in several directions.

Hunter nodded to the right. "If we head off in that direction, we'll end up by the river. Once we reach that, we can follow it down to a friend's place. They'll keep us safe for a little while." He kept saying 'we,' but Nessa had the feeling that she would be doing most of the hard work.

Heading off in the direction that Hunter had gestured to, Nessa set as swift a pace as she could. Hunter stumbled over his feet every other step, and he struggled to keep his eyes open, but she was determined to get out of the rain as quickly as possible, especially with him so badly injured. The cold wouldn't be doing him any good. The looming threat of being found by Blondie's search parties was another motivator for finding safety.

༄ ♦ ༄

It was a long walk to the river, one that was not

made any faster by Hunter or the weather. With each passing minute, with each of Hunter's fumbling steps, the worry in Nessa's heart grew. It had been some time since they had left the castle's courtyard where the soldiers had been gathering, and Nessa could practically feel their breaths on her neck as they surely grew ever closer. They would be in the city by now, Nessa was confident of that. A seed of purpose germinated. She would get them to safety, get them out of the rain and the cold, and hide them where they wouldn't be found until Hunter regained his strength.

Nessa's back straightened and she marched on, practically dragging Hunter.

While Nessa had never been there before, she kind of knew where she was from the time she had spent in the prison cell that had overlooked the river. She was in the residential part of the city, where the timber framed buildings had been built with no clear organisation. She supposed that this was a blessing. If the tunnel had exited on the other side, where the barracks were, Nessa guessed that she and Hunter wouldn't have made it far before being caught.

An occasional candle or lantern shone within a room, throwing weak light through gaps in the shutters, illuminating small parts of their trek, but other than that, Nessa wandered through the darkness of the stormy night without aid. No other souls, save for Nessa and Hunter, were around.

Nessa could tell that Hunter was trying his best not to rely on her completely, that he was trying not to put too much of his weight on her, but even so, he still weighed a bloody ton. In the distance, over the heavy drum of the rain, Nessa could hear the faint roar of a thundering river. At least, she hoped that it was the river. After the whole episode of the illusionist doorways, Nessa wasn't entirely sure what was real or not anymore.

Whether it was another illusion or not, Nessa forced herself to keep going.

The roar grew louder and closer, and the houses opened up onto a large lane, a main street that ran beside the river. The rain poured from roofs and down the alleys and streets, emptying into it, making it swollen and angry. Dark, dirty water sped past Nessa at a shocking speed, carrying debris and things that had been caught in its churning path.

With a murmured direction of "left" from Hunter, Nessa followed the river, keeping as far away from it as she could. The river was a raging monster, tossing and spraying water everywhere, threatening to burst its banks any minute. The street was uneven and slippery, and Nessa was careful where she placed each step, making sure she had firm footing.

A few short weeks ago, Nessa had been looking down at this very river, wishing that she could be down here. Now she was. Nessa could not resist the temptation to look behind her.

The ominous fortress rose high into the night's sky, haloed by the light of a thousand torches. Its spires and towers reached to the clouds, a crown of jagged shapes that loomed over the city below, keeping watchful eyes on the citizens. Nessa gazed at the castle, knowing that she had been locked away up there, wishing for answers and freedom. The latter she had now gained, although she was still searching for answers. Nessa found herself wondering at how many people were up there, sitting by their windows, watching the storm and wishing they were free to experience it, just as she was now. That thought sent a pang of sorrow through her.

Nessa turned her back on the castle. Over her dead body would she ever willingly step foot in that dreadful place again.

She continued down the street, half dragging Hunter with her, waiting for him to mumble the next direction. They rounded a bend and up ahead was a beacon, calling to her.

Streaming across the street was warm golden light, pouring out from the windows of a large dwelling. Hanging above the door was a sign: The Iron Horse.

Hunter's head lifted, and without being told, Nessa knew that this was their destination.

The promise of light, of warmth and shelter from the rain, drew them in like moths to a flame. They shuffled past the first of the windows, and a clatter sounded from within. As they neared the door, it flew open, letting out a burst of heated air. They paused.

Standing framed in the doorway, hands perched on ample hips, was a stout woman who stared at their sodden forms, scowling. Her eyes slid from Hunter to Nessa, missing no detail, and then flicked back.

"Hunter, you scoundrel!" she all but shouted. "Where the blooming heck have you been? Your mother has been worried sick. I've been worried sick. And look at the bloody state of you. What have you done this time, you good for nothing overgrown man-child?"

Hunter raised his head, smiling weakly. "Hello, Margret. You have no idea how happy I am to see you."

Margret snorted, but then her steely eyes slid once again to Nessa, who suspected that she looked like a drowned rat, and softened a touch. With a sigh, Margret stepped aside, opening the door a little wider, and ordered the two of them inside.

Chapter II

With Margret's help, Nessa manoeuvred Hunter into one of the chairs beside the fireplace. He settled into it with a sigh, instantly sliding into a slouch, a look of relief on his face.

"Business a little slow, Margret?" he asked, gazing around the empty room.

A growl sounded from Margret's throat as she stared at him, taking in the stolen uniform and the large multicoloured mark on his forehead. Hunter's lips twitched with a smile, and Margret looked like she wanted to throttle him.

Nessa shifted, feeling uncomfortable and unsure of what to do, or if this really was the best place to seek refuge. Perhaps Hunter, in his current state, had made a mistake, for Margret didn't seem particularly pleased to see him.

Eyes of steel moved from Hunter and settled on Nessa, running over her wet form and the puddle of rainwater that was pooling beneath her feet. Nessa looked down at herself, unable to bear Margret's hard gaze, and felt a stab of embarrassment. Her clothing was soaked through, sticking to her skin, and since she hadn't seen her reflection in around a month or so, she knew that she couldn't have looked good in the slightest. She was also shaking from the aftereffects of adrenaline and the cold.

What a pitiful sight Nessa must have been, because softness entered Margret's steely countenance, and she pulled up another chair, setting it beside the fire. Nessa was quickly ushered over to it, and she quite happily sat herself down, watching in bemusement as Margret abruptly headed over to the front door.

As she pulled it open, Margret glared over her shoulder at them, her eyes loaded with warning. "Stay here," she ordered. "If I discover that either of you have so much as moved a toe, then there will be dire consequences."

Nessa shot Hunter a look of alarm as soon as Margret was gone.

Hunter gave her a tired smile, and said, "She'll return in a bit." He leaned further back in his chair, stretching out his long legs. His head drooped, chin coming to rest on his chest, and his eyelids fluttered closed. In the light, Nessa could see the mark on his forehead in all its glory.

It was swollen and sore, a bright red lump the size of a fist above his left brow. The skin around the edge of it was pink and puffy, with the touches of the vivid blue of a freshly forming bruise. It would be a real beauty in the morning.

Hunter's skin was growing frightfully pale and clammy, and his state of exhaustion was a concern to Nessa. She rose from her chair and knelt beside him, placing a hand on his shoulder. His eyes opened, bleary, and he gave her hand an absentminded pat.

"You alright?" he asked, his words slightly slurred.

A grim laugh escaped her. "Shouldn't I be asking you that?"

Hunter's lips twitched. "I'm fine," he murmured. "It's all fine. My head just hurts, that's all. I'm tired. Quite tired too."

Nessa kept her hand on his shoulder, stopping him from sliding further off the chair. "You're also rather wet."

Hunter chuckled. "A torrential downpour will do that to a guy."

"Indeed." Nessa was about to say more, but the door thumped open, startling her. She spun around, half expecting a group of Blondie's soldiers to march in, but it was only Margret. She stomped her boots, knocking off mud, and stepped to the side, allowing an elderly man and another woman to enter.

The three of them wasted no time, descending upon Nessa and Hunter in an instant. For a second, Nessa felt the urge to run, to escape, and she had to remind herself that Hunter had said Margret was a friend, that they would be safe here. Besides, as Nessa looked at him, she saw that Hunter didn't seem overly concerned as Margret fussed over him, clucking like a mother hen.

Nessa stepped back, giving the others some room. The man swiftly approached, his long coat flapping around his ankles, shedding drops of water. In his hand he held a small wooden case, and propped in his mouth was a spindly pipe, a whisper of smoke puffing from it. Nessa briefly wondered how it had survived the deluge outside.

The man, whom Nessa presumed was a doctor of some kind, placed the case on a nearby table, clicked open the little lock and flipped back the lid, revealing rows of coloured bottles, a few pairs of different sized tweezers, and a sharp implement that Nessa hoped Hunter wouldn't have used on him.

The man peered at Nessa, his eyes quickly scanning her from head to foot in a practical manner. "No injuries, girl?" he asked. "No sickness of any kind?"

Nessa's response caught in her throat, trapping her words. She shook her head. The man ran his eyes over her again, not quite believing her. He pursed his lips around his pipe, looking doubtful.

Nessa swallowed her nerves and forced out, "I'm perfectly fine." Her teeth chattered and it was then that she noticed, despite her proximity to the roaring fire, she was freezing cold, the heat unable to warm her through her layers of wet clothing.

The man frowned, clearly displeased, but turned with a sigh to inspect Hunter, who was either asleep or unconscious. "Margret, my dear," he said as he knelt beside Hunter, poking at him, "you might want to get the young lady out of those clothes before she catches a chill."

Margret looked up from her fussing, eyes landing on Nessa, and nodded, more to herself than anyone else. With a kind hand on Nessa's arm, Margret guided her away from the fire and through the large front room, which was filled with groups of tables and chairs. They weaved their way over to the back of the room, where two doors stood behind a long counter. Arranged around the doors, leaning back against the wall and stacked atop each other were large barrels, their taps sticking out for ease of use.

They skirted around the counter, and as Margret held the door open for her, Nessa quickly peeked over her shoulder, allowing herself one quick look at Hunter before she was led away. He was still propped up in the chair, the doctor standing over him, prodding at the wound on his forehead. For some reason, Nessa's eyes flicked up, and she met the gaze of the woman, the doctor's companion.

She stood behind Hunter, hands on his shoulders, stopping him from sliding to the floor. The rain had slicked down her hair and dampened the long dress she wore. There was something about her that seemed odd to Nessa. She stood as still as a statue, staring at Nessa with deep-set eyes the colour of whisky. It unnerved Nessa, for her eyes seemed to have the ability to look straight into Nessa's soul, evaluating it, and appearing not to like what she saw there.

Nessa darted through the door, relieved when it swung shut, severing the strange woman's stare. Dying embers in a large open hearth produced faint light, revealing a large rustic kitchen. It was filled with long worktops that had tall stacks of cups and plates all along the backs of them. Hanging from the timber beams were pots and pans of every size and shape, and a length of string stretched across the room, bundles of dried herbs dangling from it.

Margret picked up a small lantern and twisted a cog on its side, making a small flame appear, and started up a narrow staircase. Nessa hurried after her.

The light bounced off the walls as they went up one story, turned a corner, and climbed up another. The stairs ended in a small hallway dotted with closed doors. Margret opened the first one to their right and ushered Nessa inside.

"This was my daughter's room before she married," Margret said, setting the lantern on top of the chest of drawers. "You're welcome to it tonight, until Hunter's mess has been sorted out. Again."

Nessa stood in the doorway, feeling awkward, and watched Margret rummage around in a draw. A moment later she pulled out a long, plain dress and laid it on the bed, and then busied herself at the small wood burner at the back of the room, chatting merrily away. Nessa didn't hear a word that came out of her mouth, too busy staring at the all too inviting bed. It was small and narrow, but looked ever so soft and comfortable and warm. The pillows were as plump as marshmallows and the duvet was a thick quilt that held the promise of a good night's sleep.

"There," Margret said, clapping her hands together, knocking Nessa out of her trance. "That will get the place toasty in no time." She stood and eyed Nessa. "Now, you get yourself out of those wet *clothes*, dry yourself off, and get that dress on," she ordered kindly, nodding to the one on the bed. "While you do so, I'll go and fix you something to eat. You look practically half starved."

Nessa smiled in gratitude and shuffled into the room, dripping water.

Margret left, shutting the door behind her, giving Nessa some privacy.

Nessa didn't waste any time following her orders. She kicked off her boots with relish and jumped over to the fire, pulling at the socks that clung to her feet. Once they were off, revealing pruned toes, she placed the messenger bag on the floor and began working at the ties of her tunic. Her fingers were numb, and she fumbled for a little while, but she finally managed to untie them, and then everything ended up on the floor in record time, a pile of crumpled clothing that slowly leached water.

The dress was several sizes too big, the hem pooling on the floor and the sleeves dangling past her fingertips. Nessa sat on the bed, rolling them up around her wrists, and then loosened her hair, letting it fall down her back in a damp and messy wave.

Free from her wet uniform, Nessa warmed up quickly, her skin turning pink and her fingers thawing. Gazing around the room, she wondered what she was to do now.

The room was small, quaint, with a single bed, a chest of draws, and the fireplace. A basket of logs sat next to it and there was a worn rug on the wooden floor. The curtains had little pink flowers on them and were drawn across the window. The back half of the ceiling had a slope to it, and Nessa guessed that she was up in the loft space.

Her eyes fell on the bag and she crouched beside it, opening it up and pulling out the orb. It was still bundled in the grubby blanket, and she set it down on the rug in front of her.

Nessa unwrapped the orb and felt a spike of alarm when she saw it.

The bag and blanket had protected it from the worst of the rain, but still, moisture had seeped in and clung to the orb's surface in little beads. Nessa ran her hands over it, wiping away the water droplets, and discovered that it was as cold as ice.

Nessa suddenly felt a bizarre amount of worry. She didn't know why, but she did. Something instinctive told her that the orb needed to be warm, else... Nessa bit her lip. *Why did it need to be warm?* she wondered. For a long minute Nessa stared at it, questioning why worry grew like a dark flower in her chest as the orb's light dimmed.

With a sound of frustration, of annoyance, Nessa reached over to the draws, opening the lowest one and pulling out the first thing her hand came in contact with, a shirt, soft and clean. She used it as a towel, rubbing it over the orb in gentle circles, drying it.

Soon it began to warm up, not a lot, but just enough to ease the tightness around Nessa's heart. Before she could do much else, she heard the creak of the stairs as someone climbed them. Margret, Nessa presumed, with a rather late dinner.

Hastily, Nessa wrapped the orb in the shirt and stowed it under the bed, not wanting Margret to see it. She moved to perch on the edge of the mattress, waiting, her stomach growling in anticipation. She made a silent prayer, begging for the food be piping hot and flavourful, and preferably a pizza. Nessa decided that she could really use a pizza right then.

Covered in cheese. Cheese and pepperoni.

Nessa nearly moaned at the thought.

Margret opened the door and stepped in, carrying a tray ladened with a steaming bowl and a small loaf of bread. She handed it over to Nessa with a smile.

"There you are," Margret said. "You tuck into that. It's a good old stew, my mother's recipe. Cures almost anything, that. It will have you full and warm, and ready to doze off in minutes." She turned to leave, then paused in the doorway. "Don't worry about Hunter. He's just banged his head up some. He'll be right as rain by tomorrow morning."

"Thank you," Nessa murmured, relieved at the news.

"I think it's me who owes you the thank you, child, for bringing our Hunter back to us." With that, Margret left the room, quietly closing the door behind her. Nessa sighed and sat up against the headboard, eating her dinner quickly, not unlike a starved dog. While it wasn't a pizza, her prayer had been answered in part, for the stew was hot and delicious, and true to Margret's word, had Nessa ready to doze off in minutes.

Kicking back the duvet, Nessa settled down on the soft, soft bed. The mattress was a cloud, and the pillows were as comfortable as they looked. After weeks of sleeping on a pile of rotting straw with nothing but mouldering blankets, this room, this bed, was a paradise. Nessa rolled onto her side and curled up into a ball, pulling the duvet up over her shoulders. It was thick and heavy, settling around her like a warm embrace, one that faintly smelled of lavender.

Nessa smiled, and with the knowledge that Hunter was being taken care of, closed her eyes.

The storm continued to rage outside, with raindrops pelting the windowpane and the wind howling down the chimney. Nessa didn't care, though, for she was warm and her stomach was full. For the first time since she had arrived at Ironguard, Nessa felt a measure of peace.

Sleep soon found her, pulling her into blessed darkness.

Only the darkness didn't last for long.

℘✦ℭ

Light slowly bloomed, like the petals of a flower unfurling for the first time, and Nessa found herself in a long, barren hallway. At the very end was a door, slightly ajar, with the sound of arguing voices spilling from it. Nessa frowned, looking around, wondering with a sleepy mind what the hell was going on.

It was a dream, surely? A vivid, detailed one.

But something wasn't quite right, it didn't *feel* right. Nessa couldn't even be sure she was asleep. In dreams you are in a bubble, one that blurs the edges of reality and makes the normal slightly odd and the odd seem normal. In the bubble you have no sense of time, of confusion or strangeness. In your little dream bubble, you are somewhat detached from what's happening. You can't feel things like cold or pain. That's what confused Nessa, because she could feel the cold flagstones beneath her bare feet, and the heat from the flaming sconces that lined the hallway's walls.

Nessa stood, trying to figure out if it was real, if she had lost her mind completely in the last month, or if it was just a bizarre dream. She felt like she was there, and that she wasn't, all at the same time. Nessa raised her hand, pinching her arm. Hard.

It hurt.

You can't feel things in dreams, the rational part of Nessa's mind told her, *certainly not pain.*

She looked down at herself and barely bit back a scream.

Nessa was a ghost.

There, but not fully.

Nessa raised a hand before her eyes. Well, the vague shape of it, at least. She stared at it in horror, able to see the hallway through it. There was no skin or bone, just a pale translucent shape, nothing but a mere suggestion of a hand. Gazing down, Nessa discovered that the rest of her was equally affected.

Nessa swore and looked around, desperately seeking answers, a clue to her whereabouts, her predicament, anything. *Keep clam, keep calm*, she kept telling herself, repeating it like a mantra.

Behind her was solid darkness, an intimidating

wall of nothing. The doorway in front of her, though, was bright and inviting. It beckoned to her.

Feeling like it was her only option, Nessa started forward, half expecting to fall through the floor, vanishing into it like a phantom, like she didn't exist anymore.

The door was only a short distance away, but it seemed to take forever to get there. It felt like for every two steps she took, she only moved forward one. The argument fell silent for a heartbeat, and then continued in hushed tones. Frustration grew and Nessa wished that she was at the door.

A wave of dizziness came over her and Nessa closed her eyes. She felt sick and disorientated, as if the world was sliding under her feet. After a few deep breaths it lessened, and when she opened her eyes, she found herself standing in front of the door. Bright light poured through the gap, dazzling her. She squinted and looked back over her shoulder, confused as to what had just happened.

Footsteps from within the room drew Nessa's attention. She sidled closer and peered through the gap, spying a narrow section of a lavish study. A plush rug covered the floor and towering bookshelves dominated the far wall, filled from top to bottom with every size and colour book imaginable. Over to the left was an open fireplace, green tinged flames reaching high, and sat in front of it, lounging in a large armchair with a glass of wine in his hand, was Blondie.

Nessa's heart skipped a beat, and she wanted to turn away and run, to hide. Then there was movement, making her pause, and Shadow came into view.

"This could be a problem," he was saying, beginning to pace.

Blondie raised pale eyebrows. "I fail to see the problem. No one of consequence will help her. She knows no one here."

"Oh, really? That boy, Hunter, seemed pretty damn determined to help her."

Nessa's lips parted in shock. They were talking about her! Hunter, too. She inched closer, listening intently.

Anger seethed in Shadow's voice. "The little bastard even managed to stab me."

"Indeed he did," Blondie murmured, eyes thoughtful as he watched Shadow's pacing. "Has someone got a hurt pride?"

"Now is not the time for you to be playing games," Shadow snapped. "This is serious. She has escaped with someone who is a potential risk to us. Don't forget that Hunter was in your prison for a reason. He's already demonstrated where his loyalties lie. Now we have no idea where he has taken her or what they might do next."

"She's taken the egg, though. That's something, at least."

"The egg," Shadow muttered. "Yes, she has taken the bloody egg with her. If it hatches before we find her, if the king discovers that the egg is no longer in our care, then he will have our heads."

"The king," Blondie snarled, taking a sip of wine. "The king doesn't have the slightest inkling of what is going on. All will be well, just you wait and see. As I've said, no one of great importance will hide her from us. She's a child, Shadow, a mere wisp of a girl. She has no idea where she is, or more importantly, *what* she is. Sooner or later she'll get scared and realise that the only place where she's safe is here. When that happens, she'll return of her own choice. Until then, all we need to do is keep her presence hidden from the king."

"She's not a dog, Margan. She might not come running back to us with her tail between her legs. What then?" Shadow spun, facing Blondie. No, Nessa corrected herself, facing *Margan*. "You and your bloody plots and plans and scheming. If you had just listened to me in the first instance then this wouldn't have happened! She would have been on our side from the start!"

"You had your chance to retrieve her. You failed. What can I say? She's a feisty little thing." Margan scowled. "And speaking of your failure, how did that come about? In all the years that I've known you, you've never let a simple thing like a flesh wound stop you from achieving your goals."

Shadow's eyes darkened. "As I said. The cut was deep. It bled a lot. I must have passed out."

Nessa's eyes widened. He lied. He was lying. He

could have easily brought her back to Margan. Only he hadn't.

"So you must have," Margan agreed, his tone as dry as dead leaves.

Shadow growled and muttered something that Nessa couldn't quite hear. She edged closer, hoping to catch what he was saying, and her knee banged against the door. Shadow and Margan fell silent, then the latter sprang from his chair, rushing to the door, rage on his face.

Before Nessa could jump back, he was there, yanking the door open, staring at her with those icy green eyes of his.

His gaze cut through Nessa, not seeing her at all. With a snarl, he slammed the door, smashing it into Nessa, knocking her back, throwing her to the ground. The floor whooshed up and darkness engulfed her, swallowing her whole.

Nessa jerked awake.

The dimness of the inn's room was a welcome sight. The once burning fire had dwindled down to embers, showing the cosy space in a rosy glow, and although the wind still howled down the chimney and rain pattered against the window, it felt warm and safe.

Nessa pushed herself up, sitting against the headboard, trying to calm herself down. Whatever had just happened wasn't your Average Joe kind of dream. Nessa felt clammy and jittery. Needing a dose of normality, she got out of bed and on shaky legs, she went over to the fire.

Nessa stoked it, placing a couple of small logs onto the embers, nursing it back to life. Once the flames were lively dancing again, she settled down next to it and wrapped her arms around her legs, resting her chin on her knees. God, how she wished she could confide in someone. She had just been in the castle, had overheard a private conversation between Shadow and Margan, had witnessed Shadow's lie.

Yet there Nessa sat, utterly alone and confused, wishing for, at the very least, a hug. Her mind jumped to Hunter for a second. He would listen. Then she remembered that he was injured and needed time to rest and heal.

Nessa sighed unhappily and gazed blankly at the fire, trying to think about what she should do.

Margan's words came back to her, whispering through her mind, restless and cruel.

She has no idea where she is, or more importantly, what she is...

Nessa wondered what he meant by that.

What she is...

A small ball of misgivings grew in her stomach.

Nessa might not know exactly what Margan was up to, but she did know that he was playing a game of some kind.

Just as Shadow was.

႘◆ఇ

Warm sunlight touched Nessa's face with gentle fingers, turning the insides of her eyelids red. She groaned and rolled over, searching for a few more minutes of sleep before she had to face the realities of the day. She dozed for a little while. Then, slowly, the events of last night began to filter in, and sleep became impossible to find.

Nessa sat up, burdened with the decision she had come to after hours of deliberation.

Today she would tell Hunter the truth.

Well, some of it.

Feeling jittery, Nessa got out of bed and reached for the orb, pulling it out from under the bed and tucking it into its bag. She crossed over to the door and cracked it open, peering out. The hallway was empty, all the doors except one were closed. A candle sat on a small table off to the side.

Nessa inched into the hallway, not wanting to disturb anyone, and crossed over to the open door, hoping that Hunter was inside.

He was.

In a room similar to hers, lying reclined on the bed, a mound of pillows around his shoulders, was Hunter. A large bruise marred the skin above his brow, an ugly mess of blue and green. Colour had returned to his face, and the swelling around the mark had gone down significantly. His eyes were closed, despite the curtains being open and cheery sunlight flooding the room.

Nessa's shoulders sagged and she decided to let

him rest. As she turned around, about to head back to her room, there was a sleepy groan from the bed, making her pause. Hunter blinked heavily and pushed himself up a little higher on his pillows, grinning when he caught sight of her standing by the doorway.

With a murmured greeting, Nessa took a hesitant step towards him, suddenly feeling shy and a little bit afraid. She held her bag tight, as if it might shield her from what was to come.

"How are you feeling?" she asked, shutting the door behind her.

Hunter's smile was bright as he said, "Oh, I'm fine. Just as I said I would be." He moved to the side, making space for her on the bed.

"That's good," Nessa said, sitting next to him, "because I really need to tell you something, and I need your help to understand all of it."

Hunter's smile drooped, replaced by a look of uncertainty. "Alright then, I'll do my best, if you so wish it."

Nessa made herself comfortable, for her story wasn't the shortest, and placed the orb on her lap. She opened her mouth, but the words instantly caught in her throat. Her cheeks burned and she fiddled with the bag's strap, growing unsure of herself.

Nessa's didn't have the faintest idea of how to start.

After several failed starts, Nessa was about to call

it quits when Hunter gave a quiet sigh and said, "Sometimes, I find that it's easier just to blurt it out. No restraints, no thinking about what to say. Just spit out the first thing that comes to mind."

So Nessa closed her eyes, leaned back against the pillows and the headboard, and with Hunter's gaze on the side of her face, the words loosened and her story spilled from her tongue.

Chapter 12

"I'm not from here," was the first thing Nessa said. It left her lips slowly, hesitantly. She had paused for a second after those four words, then the rest of her story had soon followed, a flood rival to that of the raging river from last night, fast and without mercy.

She told Hunter of her discovery of the town's ruins, and her subsequent explorations of it, although the reasons why she spent so much time there she kept to herself. Nessa explained how she had been drawn to the underground room, and how the mirror had been flickering with icy light. With a knot in her stomach, she revealed how she had been pulled through the mirror, and how she had later woken up, locked in the castle of Ironguard.

"Then," Nessa said, looking anywhere but at

Hunter, "last night, I had a dream. Only it wasn't a dream. At least, I think it was real. I was there, but not fully. I could see through myself. I could see the stone floor through my foot. In front of me was a room, and I could hear two people arguing. Naturally I went over to it, only to find Shadow and Margan inside. They were talking about us, bickering really, and then they mentioned this." Nessa handed over the orb, bag and all, to Hunter.

Nessa watched from the corner of her eye as Hunter handled the bag with caution, slowly opening it and unwrapping the orb. Purple light shone softly, and Nessa turned away a little, frightened of witnessing his reaction. Hunter was silent for a long time, making Nessa uneasy, and then he made a strangled noise. Nessa looked at him, worried, and the expression on Hunter's face was what she had been expecting and fearing. It was one of utter wonder and horror. The orb was in his hands, and with its light, Nessa could see the blood leave his face.

"Hunter, what is it?" Nessa asked urgently. "Is it an egg? They mentioned something about it being an egg." Hunter continued to stare at it, his eyes alarmingly wide. "Jesus, Hunter, breathe." She elbowed him hard in the ribs.

"I'm fine. It's all fine." He frowned. "Who's Jesus?"

"No one you know, clearly," she mumbled, taking a deep breath, trying to collect herself. She nodded at the orb. "So, do you know what it is?"

Hunter swallowed and tucked it back into the bag, thoughts whirling behind his eyes. "I might have a vague idea, but I'm not completely sure. It could be several things. No point in getting worried over something that might be nothing."

"Should I be worried?"

"No. No." Hunter gave her a forced smile. "I'm sure it's perfectly fine. It just reminded me of something when I first saw it, that's all. Honestly, I don't know all that much about things like this." He swiped a hand over his face. "I have a friend who could say for sure. He might even be able to help you understand that whole mirror thing. Although it seems to me, the easiest and safest thing to do is take the orb down to the river and throw it in."

Nessa stared at him, surprised that he would say such a thing.

"Look," he continued. "It was given to you by two of the most depraved men in the Twelve Kingdoms. I can assure you that they don't give out mystical gifts to just anyone, particularly to someone they've just kidnapped, without strings attached. Like, I don't know, enslavement and mass slaughter."

Nessa blinked. "Wow."

"I'm sorry to tell you this, Nessa, but the brutal truth is that no matter what that is," he nodded at the orb, "they want something from you, and that's not a good thing."

Nessa had no words, and tears were quick to spring to her eyes. Never in a million years did she think that she would be in a situation like this. Yes, she had dreamed of adventure, only more along the lines of backpacking around Europe or maybe even North America. She felt so overwhelmingly alone and afraid.

Hunter wrapped his arm around Nessa's shoulders, tucking her against him. "The truth is brutal," he murmured, resting his cheek on the top of her head, "but it will make soldiers of us all."

Nessa didn't respond, but after a little while she managed to pull herself together. No sense in wallowing in self pity. She sat up, wiping away the tears that clung to her eyelashes.

"Sorry," she mumbled, "this is a lot to deal with."

"No worries," Hunter said breezily. "I can't even imagine what you must be feeling right now."

"I'm not even sure what I'm feeling right now."

"Come on," Hunter said, nudging her with his elbow, "I know what will cheer you up a wee bit."

He shooed her from the bed like she was a cat and jumped up. Grabbing her hand, Hunter pulled her across the room and into the hallway. Nessa wondered if it was wise to leave the orb just lying around, but Hunter seemed inclined to leave it be. Besides, she reasoned with herself, the orb was wrapped up and tucked away in the bag. It wasn't like anyone would easily stumble across it.

Hunter quickly led Nessa downstairs and into the kitchen which, unlike last night, was now teeming with activity. Several cooks were busy preparing plates, filling them with fried eggs, bacon, and other such things. A few women darted between the kitchen and the adjoining door, taking out filled plates and bringing empty ones back. Each time the door opened, the sounds of conversation and laughter filtered through.

Ignoring it all, Hunter headed over to the back of the kitchen, where an open door led out to an enclosed courtyard. Realising that's where Hunter aimed for and spying the thick mud outside, fresh and wet, Nessa jerked to a stop.

Hunter turned to her, surprised. "What's wrong?"

"There's like a foot of mud out there, and I'm not wearing any shoes."

"What's wrong with going barefoot through some mud?"

Nessa shrugged. "It's gross." She turned, eyeing up one of the plates, pilled high with egg, sausage and bacon. Her stomach grumbled and she stepped forward, fully intending to beg a cook for it. However, Hunter had other ideas.

He swooped up behind her, catching her and slinging her over his shoulder like a sack of potatoes. Nessa yelped, but before she could worm out of his grip, Hunter leapt through the door.

Mud squelched beneath Hunter's feet as he

strode across the yard. Nessa clutched the back of his shirt, praying that he wouldn't lose his footing and send them both into the muck. A couple of pigs wallowed in the corner, content in the wet slush around them, snorting as Hunter moved past, and a few chickens milled around their coup, pecking at a scattering of corn and straw on the ground.

"This is very unnecessary," Nessa said.

"On that I must disagree."

Hunter took her over to an outbuilding at the far end of the courtyard, stone walled and low roofed, and set Nessa down on a rug that covered the entranceway. A closed door stood on either side of her, and Nessa watched as Hunter went over to the one on the right, struggling with the stiff handle for a second before it opened with a rush of warm air that smelled of soap.

Intrigued, Nessa peered over his shoulder.

It was a small room, square and dimly lit, with an old battered tub sat in the middle, filled almost to the brim with steaming water and glistening bubbles. A round table was at the head of the tub, holding a candle and an assortment of dainty glass bottles and bars of soap.

With a hand between her shoulder blades, Hunter gently pushed Nessa forward. "Margret and I thought you could use a nice surprise, a thank you of sorts. This was the best we could whip up on short notice."

"Oh, Hunter," Nessa murmured, oddly touched

by the gesture. "Thank you." She went over to the little table, picked up one of the little bottles and looked at it with curiosity.

"I have no idea what all of that stuff is for," Hunter said, nodding to the table, "so good luck finding out." He began backing out of the room. "I'll leave some clean clothes out here for you."

"Thanks," Nessa called as the door clicked shut.

With the door closed, the room became hot and humid. Nessa grinned and pulled off her dress, dumping it on the floor in a pile, and practically jumped into the tub, not caring that the water was nearly scalding. She hissed and held herself ridged for a moment, slowly adjusting to the temperature, bubbles fizzing around her shoulders. Her skin pinkened and her muscles relaxed, and she sank back against the tub, allowing the grime to soak away.

After a while, Nessa began investigating the contents of the little bottles, finding that some contained oils, sandalwood and lavender, and others held liquid soaps, one of which she used on her hair, making it smell of flowers.

Nessa scrubbed herself several times, feeling like the prison of Ironguard had left a dark stain on her skin. Only when the water had cooled did she stop. A towel had been folded and placed by the table, and as she stepped from the tub, she wrapped it around her body.

She crossed over to the door, pulling it open an

inch, and found that Hunter had been true to his word, for there, on the floor, was a stack of clean clothing, her boots sitting next to it. A new set of muddy footprints led to and from it.

Nessa picked them up and closed the door, retreating to dress.

The clothing wasn't too dissimilar from what Nessa had been given in Ironguard's prison; black legging-ish trousers, a long sleeved tunic, cream this time, and a white over shirt that was something between a dress and a blouse, falling halfway to her knees. Nessa laced up her boots and left the bathroom, going in search of Hunter, and hopefully some breakfast.

Nessa trekked through the ankle deep mud and headed over to the kitchen door, where she hesitated, not wanting to track mud everywhere. She spied Hunter over in the far corner, seemingly harassing one of the cooks. As if sensing her gaze, he turned, saw her, and ambled over, much to the delight of the cook, who shook his head behind Hunter's back and mumbled under his breath.

"There you are," Hunter said, grinning. "I was beginning to think that you had either turned into a mermaid or had dissolved."

Nessa rolled her eyes. "Ha-ha. Should I take my boots off?" she wondered, not wanting to be a nuisance and make a mess.

Hunter shrugged. "It's fine. I expect Margret will be making me clean the floors later anyway." He waved a hand, indicating to the trails of semi-dried footprints all over the kitchen floor. "Come on, I have procured us breakfast."

Hunter turned, and Nessa, feeling slightly guilty about the mud that was left in her wake, followed after him. He went over to the cook he had been harassing a moment ago, who, without looking at him, handed Hunter two full plates.

Together they entered the front room and found a vacant table. Unlike last night, the inn wasn't deserted. Many of the tables were occupied by families, or small gatherings, who had come for a social breakfast out. A few solitary figures kept to themselves, drinking a morning pint of ale before they continued on their way; travellers who had stayed the night lodging in the inn's guest rooms, which were on the first floor. The air was loud with conversation and the scrape of cutlery on dishes. Nessa and Hunter settled themselves into a quiet corner by the window.

They dug into their food and Nessa savoured every mouthful, particularly enjoying the sausage and egg, and gazed out the window. The street's wet cobblestones glistened in the pale sunlight, and a few sad grey clouds drifted high in the sky, casting dreary shadows if they dared to get too close to the sun. The river still ran bloated and dirtied, but at a slower pace, no longer threatening to burst its banks. A small number of people walked past, some carrying baskets laden with fresh bread and fruit.

"So, umm," Hunter said, swallowing either a mouthful of breakfast or nerves. "What do you want to do now?"

Nessa looked at him, surprised and slightly confused. "Do about what?"

"Well, I suppose you want to go home and such. If so, you'll need to find someone who knows about the type of magic that was used to bring you here."

Nessa stared at her plate, now empty, as a hand of despair wrapped around her heart. "Home," she whispered. "Of course I want to go home. I just don't know how or where to even start."

"Well, I know someone who might have an inkling of what Margan did, and how to undo it. Maybe." Hunter fiddled with his fork. "He seems like the best place to start. Pretty sure Margan's not going to be particularly helpful if we go back to him and start asking questions."

"Probably not," Nessa murmured in agreement as she remembered his words from her waking dream. "Margan seemed pretty sure that no one would be willing or able to help me."

"Margan is an arrogant arse and has no idea what goes on under his nose."

Nessa raised her brows at his dark tone, but didn't comment. "So you think that your acquaintance might be able to help me?"

"I think he's the best person to start with. If he can't help, then he'll know someone who can."

"There doesn't seem to be very many options

open to me."

"No," Hunter said honestly. "But at least there's one that doesn't involve going back to Margan."

"I suppose," Nessa sighed. "So where is your friend then, the one that might be able to help?"

"Orm? Well, truth be told, he could be anywhere. You see, Orm has a talent for getting himself neck deep in trouble, more so than me, and that's saying something. But," he scratched his head, "there's someone nearby who might know."

"That's something, I suppose. So we'll find Orm and hope that he can help me?"

Hunter nodded. "Sounds like a mighty fine plan. We'll go to the market and see if we can find his trail. If he's not local then we'll get some supplies and head out later. How does that sound?"

"Perfect. When do you want to go?"

Hunter stood. "No time like the present. Unlike you, I'm an early riser and have been ready for action for ages."

Nessa ran her eyes over him, noticing that he had indeed changed clothing and was considerably cleaner. His linen shirt was loose and a size too big, but it was free from stains and rips, as were his trousers. At some point during Nessa's bath he had also put on some boots.

Nessa rose, eager to get the ball rolling, as the saying goes. The sooner she found this Orm person, the sooner she could go home. Hopefully.

Together they wormed around tables and people

and entered onto the street. Nessa paused for a second, breathing in the fresh air. It was different there, cool and crisp, without the lingering smell of exhaust fumes or the rumble of engines. There was a sense of calmness around her.

The river ran beside them, and they followed it for some time through the city. Hunter was quiet beside her, wrapped up in his own musings. 'Away with the fairies,' as Nessa's mother would say. Nessa didn't mind and left him to his thoughts, for it allowed her time with her own.

Nessa looked at her surroundings with wide eyes, taking in the small details, like how the glass windowpanes were handmade, thick and slightly irregular, and how the buildings didn't have a straight line to them. *How medieval*, Nessa thought. There were no signs of cars or electric, nothing to hint of their existence. It was all rather refreshing.

The river curved to the side in a lazy bend, leading them into a more densely populated part of the city, and further away from the castle that loomed over them like a dark cloud. Even in daylight it was still a menacing sight, a black crown on a rocky outcrop, sharp and foreboding. No matter where you were, you could not escape from its glare for long.

The riverside lane widened, and after rounding a corner of a large building, they came upon a sprawling square that was filled with stalls, people and noise. Though it was fairly early in the morning, and the air had a chill to it, the market thrummed with life. Wooden waggons and carts overflowed with all manner of goods, and sellers stood behind makeshift tables covered with trinkets, calling out their wares to passersby.

Nessa stared, feeling something between awe and shock. Looking at the people, Nessa felt as if she had travelled back in time. Many women wore long dresses that fell to the ground, beautiful and elegant, made from silk and velvet. In groups they prowled around the booths that sold fabrics and jewellery, oozing wealth and elegance. The men wore similarly foreign clothing; smocks, tunics and doublets.

Nessa eyed a beautiful, raven haired woman, and felt quite lacking and out of place. The woman's dress was a rich red, the bodice covered in a fine pattern of metallic embroidery, the skirt full and shifted like water with the slightest movement. For a split second, Nessa felt a touch of jealousy, wanting to wear something so gorgeous, but then she noticed that the men and women behind the stalls were dressed like her and Hunter, and Nessa realised that she wore the clothing of the working class.

Hunter stood on his tiptoes, trying to see over the crowd. He nodded to Nessa and then started off again. She trailed behind him as he wove through the market, unable to stop herself from looking at the stalls as she passed.

At first glance, Nessa was disappointed, seeing nothing but the usual things you would find in a large marketplace; clothing, fabrics, jewellery and knick-knacks. But on closer inspection, she started to notice things that subtly stood out. In a stall that sold a multitude of fruit and vegetables was a basket of apples of such a deep red that they were nearly purple, and over in a booth that sold clothing was a cape that fluttered in a light breeze, shifting from black, to blue, to an iridescent beetle green. Nessa gazed around with growing wonder and curiosity as she spied an increasing number of beautifully abnormal things.

Hunter cut through the market square with single minded purpose, not bothering to stop and look at anything or talk to anyone. He headed over to a wide street that played host to shops, cafes and bakeries, and then turned down a narrow, shadowed alley that ended in a small yard. Over to the side was a shop, a sign hanging above the door announcing that it was 'The Bell, Book and Candle.'

The windows were dark and covered in a layer of grime that made it impossible to see what was on display.

"You may find things a little strange in there," Hunter said, pausing by the door.

"How so?"

Hunter smiled impishly. "The fun is in the surprise." He opened the door and disappeared inside.

Nessa stood in the yard for a second, bemused. "Fun for him or me?" she wondered.

With some degree of apprehension, Nessa followed Hunter into the less than welcoming shop.

Chapter 13

A bell chimed above Nessa's head as the door closed, ringing out across the cramped space. The air was thick with the smell of herbs and incense, making her sneeze and her eyes water. Nessa blinked heavily. Her eyes, though burning, slowly adjusted to the gloom, and she found herself standing at the entrance to a labyrinth of shelves.

"Hmm, Hunter's right," Nessa murmured, looking around and hurrying after him. "It is strange in here."

Free standing bookshelves held all manner of things, from bundles of dried herbs and flowers, books and crystals, to ornamental daggers. It wasn't so much *what* the shop sold that made it strange, though that didn't help matters, but the *feeling* that

Nessa got when she walked past certain things; as if some part of her knew they weren't used for good.

A noise came from the back, a creak of a floorboard, and Hunter moved towards it, Nessa sticking close to him. The narrow walkway led them around a corner, and took them up behind a woman who was knelt down on the floor, facing away from them, bent over a collection of jars, busy filling them with shimmering powders.

Hunter leaned a shoulder against a bookshelf and the woman's shoulders tensed. She paused in her task and turned, rising to her feet, her eyes instantly landing on Nessa, who immediately recognised her. She was the woman who had accompanied the doctor.

Nessa shifted, growing uncomfortable under the woman's heavy gaze, swearing that she wasn't even blinking. It felt as it had last night, as if the woman's whiskey coloured eyes saw through flesh and bone and could see into Nessa's soul.

Hunter frowned, looking between the two of them, and then stepped in front of Nessa, severing the woman's stare, much to Nessa's relief.

"That's enough, Helen," he said quietly, but with an undertone of warning. "We need to talk."

The woman, Helen, scoffed. "I'm busy. Go away."

"Helen, *please.*"

"No," Helen barked. "Leave and take *that* with you." She flung out her arm, pointing a finger at

Nessa, who flinched at the venom in her voice.

Hunter moved forward, grabbing Helen and shoving her over to the storeroom door a short distance way. "Don't leave the shop," he said over his shoulder, yanking it open and pushing Helen through, following after her. "I'll be back shortly."

Nessa stared, opened mouthed, as the door slammed shut. *What had she ever done to make Helen hate her so?* she asked herself. Surely nothing, Nessa reasoned, because she hadn't even had a chance to speak to Helen yet, not a single word. Maybe she blamed Nessa for Hunter's injury last night?

Nessa didn't let herself dwell on the matter for long, once she remembered that she was finding out how to get back home. Then this place would be nothing more than a bad memory, easy to put behind her and forget.

Hunter was gone for some time, no doubt enjoying more of Helen's delightfulness, and Nessa's curiosity got the better of her. Slowly, she perused the shelves, running her fingers over the intriguing things housed there. A diminutive silver box caught her eye, and when Nessa opened it, she found a collection of children's teeth inside. She grimaced and moved on, feeling a little sick, and meandered further into the heart of the shop. Figurines were dotted around, some small, some not so, but each and every one of them was stunning. Many of them were metal and depicted men in battle, either man fighting against man, or man fighting against beast. A few however, gave Nessa a chill as her fingers brushed over them, creatures so frightful that Nessa hoped they didn't exist and were just the fanciful ideas of an artist.

She turned a corner and the next row of shelves were occupied by knives and ornate daggers. They were either resting on velvet pillows or presented on small stands, the blades glinting with a malevolent sheen. Nessa had no doubt that the edges were razor sharp. Another corner and she came upon rows and rows of books, some thick, some thin, some small and some tall, but each and every one of them had gold or silver inlay on the spine. They were of every imagined colour, a rainbow of light in the otherwise bleak shop, and Nessa's fingers skimmed over them, as gentle as a butterfly's wing, feeling the textures of leather and suede and cloth.

They spoke to her, whispering sweet things in her ears, promises of being filled with knowledge and stories, and one of them was louder than the others.

Nessa's fingers hit a sudden dip and grazed against a small book. It sang to her, calling for her attention. She paused and looked at it, finding it tucked between two larger tomes, small and nondescript compared to them. She slipped it free and discovered that its red cover was without a title or mark, and that its pages were free from ink and words.

Nessa flicked through it, expecting to find something, but each creamy page was empty. "I wonder what's special about you," she murmured to it. It was a diary, she thought, an old and forgotten one. It was odd, though, for the pages were oddly thick and rough around the edges. She caressed one, wondering why the little book had called out to her.

It was then that the most peculiar thing happened.

Slowly appearing on the page, as if bleeding through from the one behind, was a line of elegant scripture in deep purple ink.

I am the book of all things known, it read.

Nessa stared as the ink faded.

She thought that it must have been a figment of her imagination, that she was going mad, but then it happened again.

I am the book of all things known, it said, the ink slowly bleeding back onto the page.

Nessa frowned and turned over to the next page, finding it empty.

I am the book of all things known, once again appeared on the page. *What are you?*

Nessa dipped a toe into the insanity that was unfolding in front of her. "I'm a human," she said quietly, answering the book's question.

Perhaps you are, said the book, *but perhaps not. What are you?*

"I'm a girl, a person," Nessa murmured.

Yes, the books said, *but also no. You are something not encountered before. What are you?*

The front door's bell chimed, gently knocking Nessa out of the book's thrall. Automatically she looked over her shoulder, but the rows of shelves hid the door from sight, preventing her from seeing who had entered.

When Nessa looked down at the book, she found that the ink was gone, and she hastily shoved it back between the other books. Apprehension grew in her stomach, and for the second time in just a few short hours, Nessa was questioning herself.

Nessa continued with her exploration, listening out for Hunter or the person who had just come in, but the shop was quiet. She thought that maybe the latter had opened the door, smelt the incense, and had been repelled. Hunter, she presumed, hadn't made much headway with Helen yet.

Somehow, Nessa found herself at the front of the shop, in a corner next to the window. On the floor, pushed up against the wall, was a large glass tank, filled with murky green water. The top was covered in a thick layer of mottled algae, and fine wire mesh fitted over the tank like a lid. Curious as to what might be lurking in there, Nessa crouched down, looking for any signs of life.

A moment later the water rippled with movement, the blanket of algae bobbing and then splitting, parting like curtains down the middle by a pair of tiny webbed hands. A head emerged and overly large green eyes gazed balefully up at Nessa.

She stared at the creature in awe, taking in its alien features of light green skin, pointed ears and long greenish-black hair. It was the size of a child's doll, and was as beautiful as it was strange.

Neither of them seemed to know what to make of the other, then the rustle of cloth whispered behind Nessa.

Without looking away, she asked, "What is it?"

"It's a water sprite," rumbled a deep voice that didn't belong to Hunter.

Nessa jerked, about to twist around, when something painfully cold and sharp pressed against the side of her neck.

"What do you want?" Nessa demanded, hating how her voice trembled just a little bit. Her hands clenched into fists and her body tensed. Every possible thought leapt around in her head. Should she try to fight, to run? Or should she do as she was bid?

"You, sweetheart." The blade pressed harder under her jawbone, threatening to puncture the delicate skin. "Now stand up."

With shaking knees, Nessa complied, and for a split second the blade left her neck. Instantly, Nessa drove back her elbow, striking the man in the gut. His breath left him with a muffled 'Oomph,' and she made to run.

Nessa barely made it a step before her assailant's hand tangled in her hair, and she was yanked off her feet. She landed on the floor painfully, stunned, and the man grabbed her arms, pulling them behind her back. Nessa yelped and the man gave her an angry shake, strong enough to rattle her teeth.

"Be quiet," he growled, beginning to bind her wrists together with a length of rope.

There was a low *thump* and the man's hands went limp. He groaned and fell to the side, and Nessa scurried away from him, the unfinished bindings slipping free. Bewildered, she looked up.

Hunter was standing over the man, his arm raised, a heavy statue in his hand. "Can't leave you alone for ten minutes without you getting into some kind of trouble, can I?" he said, putting the statue back on the shelf.

"This wasn't my fault," Nessa argued, picking herself up. "I stayed in the shop, just as ordered."

Humming in consternation, Hunter crouched down by the unconscious man, who lay sprawled on his back. He was stocky with thinning hair and a square jaw, average looking except for the tattoo that marked his left cheek. Once black, it had faded to a dull grey, making it look more like a birthmark, although it was too strangely shaped for that. Nessa peered at it, thinking that it looked like a snake, loose and uncoiled.

Hunter whistled and nodded at the mark. "He's a bounty hunter."

Quickly patting down the man's pockets, Hunter pulled out a crumpled piece of paper and placed it on the floor, smoothing it out. Printed in black and white were images of her and Hunter, complete with a brief description and their bounty price. Not knowing what the value of a hundred gold caps was, Nessa had to ask.

"A lot," Hunter answered grimly. "Enough to have every lowlife out there looking for us." He stood, crumpling the paper in his hand. "Come on, we should get moving before anyone else finds us." Nessa nodded, more than happy to leave the shop and to get as far away as possible from the unconscious bounty hunter.

Just as she got to the door, Nessa gazed over her shoulder at the tank. The little water sprite was watching their departure with wide eyes, and when it noticed Nessa looking back, it raised one tiny hand in farewell.

༺ ♦ ༻

Hunter took a different route back to the inn, avoiding the market and other busy areas. They went via the back alleys. It took longer, but the less people around, the lower the chances of them being noticed. Nessa was lost in her thoughts for most of the journey. That seemed to suit Hunter just fine, since he set a fast pace with a frown on his face.

Why had Margan gone to all the effort of bringing me here? Nessa kept wondering. *Why me above all others?*

"Hunter, why did Helen refer to me as a '*that?*'"

Hunter looked at her, surprised. "Don't read too

much into it. She doesn't know what she's talking about."

"What is she talking about then?"

"I'm not really sure," Hunter said elusively. "Just a bunch of mumbo-jumbo."

Nessa scowled at his back, annoyed that was all he was going to say. "That makes me feel so much better," she muttered as they turned down an alley that ended in a wooden gate.

It opened onto the courtyard behind the inn, and they crossed over to the kitchen, which was just as busy as it had been when they'd left. Leaving a trail of muddy footprints, Hunter went over to the stairs, starting up them. Having nowhere else to go, Nessa followed, beginning to feel like a lost puppy.

Her bag was where it had been left, untouched, with the orb still inside. Nessa perched on the edge of the bed and pulled it onto her lap, wrapping her arms around it. Hunter closed the door and leaned against it, his eyes darting between her face and the bag. Nessa pretended not to notice.

"So, what now?" she asked. Hunter swiped a hand over his face, as if he could wipe away the weariness there. "Well, it's up to you really."

Nessa's brows rose. "How so?"

"My dear friend Orm seems to be quite elusive these days, apparently gone into hiding after angering a lord or something," Hunter explained, moving away from the door to sit beside her. "Helen says that he's most likely gone to The Hidden City until things blow over."

"The Hidden City?"

Hunter nodded. "All things considered, if he is actually there, it's the best case scenario. It's one of the closer hiding places Orm keeps."

"Okay," Nessa said, feeling slightly more upbeat. "That sounds good."

"It's better than some of the other places he could have gone," Hunter agreed, leaning forward and propping his elbows on his knees. "But I had hoped that he would be a little closer."

Nessa fiddled with a buckle on the bag, growing worried. "So where is this Hidden City then, is it that far away?"

"It's a bit of a trek, but it won't take too long, a week or so on foot, faster if we had horses. But that's not what concerns me. I just don't want to drag you along on a long journey only for him not to be there."

"It is a long way to go," Nessa admitted. "But if he's not there, he'll be somewhere else, right? We'll just keep our fingers crossed and hope that we find him sooner rather than later."

Hunter nodded, a slow grin forming. "Optimistic thinking. I like it. So you want to go?"

Nessa considered her options, or rather, her lack of options. She had the choice to either stay or to go, and the thought of leaving Ironguard far behind was a very pleasant one. The idea of Margan getting his hands on her again was chilling. Nessa remembered his threat when he had presented the orb to her, the dark promises in his eyes. She didn't think that escaping the prison, running away with Hunter, and taking the orb with her was a particularly great way of getting into his good graces.

Yes, it was probably best to put as much distance between Margan and her as possible.

"We go," Nessa decided. "I think finding your friend is my best chance of getting back home. Plus, he might be able to answer a few other questions, like what this orb is and how my waking dream...*thing* works."

"Quite likely."

"So, we're going to The Hidden City?"

"We're going to The Hidden City." Hunter clapped his hands, excited, and bounced off the bed. "Best start packing. We'll leave the city come sundown."

Nessa was surprised. "So soon?"

"The sooner the better," Hunter replied, a mischievous glint entering his eyes. "Why? Is there something keeping you here?"

"No, and you know that. I just thought that you might want to, you know, make plans and get supplies. Stuff like that."

"Now, why would I need to get supplies when there is a very well stocked kitchen downstairs?" Hunter moved over to the chest of drawers and rifled through it, finding three bags. He tossed one to Nessa, who just about caught it before it slapped her in the face.

"One bag for you, one for me, and the other for provisions," Hunter sang.

"Hate to rain on your excitement," Nessa said, "but I have nothing to pack. You know, since I'm not from here."

"Just take things from your room. Margret won't mind."

Nessa wasn't quite so sure that Margret would appreciate some strange girl stealing some of her clothing; but since that was what Hunter said to do, Nessa did it, seeing that she couldn't be bothered to argue. She picked up the orb, and as Hunter began to stuff clothing unceremoniously into his bag, Nessa left to pack her own.

Not bothering to shut the door behind her, Nessa placed the orb on the bed and opened the empty bag. She went over to the chest of drawers and began looking for some suitable clothing. The bottom drawer held spare bedding, but the other three held an abundance of options for her to choose from.

Nessa picked out a few changes of clothing; a pair of dress-tops like the one she was wearing and a couple of spare leggings. She also selected a cardigan, in case things got chilly. Remembering the long dresses that some of the woman wore, Nessa rummaged around until she found a simple dress that consisted of a long, plain gown and a surcoat that was edged with ornamental trim. It wasn't nearly as spectacular as the red dress from the market, but it was quite pretty, and it would have to do.

Nessa neatly packed her bag, folding each item, and then left it on the bed next to her messenger bag.

She crossed the hall and found Hunter half under his bed.

"You alright there?" she asked, amused.

"I'm fine," came his muffled reply. "It's really dusty under here."

"Good to know."

With a bit more wriggling, shuffling and a few muttered swearwords, Hunter managed to extract himself from the narrow gap, pulling with him two large bundles. Standing, he set them next to his packed bag.

"And there," he announced, "are our luxurious sleeping accommodations."

Nessa eyed the bundles doubtfully, realising that they were, in fact, sleeping bags. "Aren't there, I don't know, other inns on the way that we could spend the nights in?"

"Of course there are. But with those warrants out on us, bounty hunters are going to be searching them in case we're there."

"I hadn't thought of that." The pleasant idea of a leisurely week-long stroll, sleeping in warm inns and waking up to a hearty breakfast vanished, replaced by the memory of how cold the nights could get. "I hate camping."

"That's just because you haven't done it with me before."

"On the subject of those warrants, how do we go about leaving the city without being recognised? Surely we don't want anyone knowing where we're going."

"Indeed we don't," Hunter agreed. "But I know a secret way out of Ironguard, one which allows us to avoid using the main gates. Once it starts getting dark, there'll be less people out on the streets too."

"So we're leaving at sunset?"

"Just before. We don't want the streets to be too empty. That would arouse suspicion. We'll merge in with the crowd of late leavers before the gates lock this evening, then take a detour, leaving via the secret way. No one will be any the wiser."

Nessa's eyes went to the window, tracking the ark of the sun. They would be leaving soon, and she would be taking the first step to finding out how to get back home.

Chapter 14

Late-afternoon rapidly approached, and Nessa was bursting with excitement. She and Hunter moved their packed bags downstairs, tucking them out of the way in a quiet corner of the kitchen. Nessa stood beside them, watching as Hunter moved around, filling the third bag with an assortment of cutlery, wooden bowls, and bundles of wrapped food that wouldn't perish over the next few days.

Once the bag was full, he placed it with the others, and motioned for Nessa to follow him as he walked over to the front room's door.

Margret stood behind the counter, serving several already intoxicated men another round. At the sight of them coming through the door, she abandoned her post and shooed them back into the kitchen.

The door closed behind Margret and she instantly rounded on Hunter, eyes ablaze. "One day," she hissed. "Just one damn day without someone unseemly coming into my inn and demanding to know where you are. Just one damn day!" Several wiry hairs fell loose from her bun as she continued. "What have you done now, boy? I've had every sort of lowlife in here searching for you this morning. Care to explain yourself?"

Hunter hung his head, not looking Margret in the eye. "You're a right piece of work. You know that, don't you?"

Hunter nodded.

"Good." Margret turned her steely eyes on Nessa, who braced herself for a similar tirade. "Hello dear, did you have a nice night?"

Nessa, somewhat stunned by Margret's turnaround, could only nod.

"Good, I'm glad. You looked like you needed a good night's sleep, and it seems to have done you a world of good." She turned back to Hunter. "Now, you little scoundrel, what do you want?"

Hunter thought very carefully about what he was going to say. "Nessa and I would be most grateful if you would lend us one of your horses."

Margret was most unimpressed. "Why do you want one of my horses?"

"I would like one to carry some of our bags, although if you want to provide us with two horses to carry us, that would be splendid."

"Where are you going that would require one or two of my horses?"

Hunter looked over at Nessa, seeking some assistance. She shook her head, deciding that she wasn't going to get in-between him and Margret. Hunter sighed and said, "We're going to find Orm."

"Orm," Margret mused, thoughtful.

"Yep," Hunter confirmed. "I haven't seen him in a while and I thought that Nessa could come with me until things here have blown over." He gave Margret a winning smile. "We'll be out of your hair for quite some time."

"Well, when you put it like that," Margret said, turning back to the door, "you can take the beige one."

Nessa stared after Margret, wondering what her and Hunter's relationship was.

"She's very abrupt," Nessa said.

"It's how Margret shows she cares." Hunter looked at her. "We should go and find the horse before she changes her mind."

Nessa nodded and collected her stuff, slipping the messenger bag's strap over her shoulder. Hunter gathered his baggage and led the way out the kitchen and across the yard, heading over to a long building that was to the side of the bath house. Hunter opened the door and the smell of old straw and horse wafted out, assaulting Nessa's nose.

It was dim inside, and rows of stalls ran along

both sides, ending at the far wall which was covered in an assortment of equine equipment. There were only a handful of occupied stalls, and they quickly found the horse that Margret was loaning to them.

Nessa's lips twitched into a reluctant smile as she looked between the horse and Hunter.

"Margret's doing this to punish me, isn't she?" Hunter asked

Nessa grinned, unable to help herself, and stepped closer to the stall, holding out a hand to the small, fluffy horse. It was a soft brown colour, with a long mane and thick, almost curly fur. It only stood as tall as Nessa's shoulder, and it nuzzled her hand with a warm nose. Tacked onto the stall's door was a plaque engraved with the name 'Betty.' Nessa thought the name suited the horse perfectly.

"She's so cute," Nessa said, petting Betty.

"And looks like she couldn't even carry your weight," Hunter finished, running doubtful eyes over the horse.

"Then it's a good thing that the bags aren't heavy then, isn't it."

Hunter shot her a withering look as he moved over to the back wall. "I asked for a horse," he muttered, "not a pony. I hope there's a saddle small enough for it."

"Don't mind him," Nessa told Betty, giving her head a gentle pat.

Hunter was back in no time, carrying a saddle, a blanket, a small bag and some reins. He set the saddle on the stall's door and the rest on the ground. From the bag he pulled out two hand brushes, one of which he handed to Nessa, and opened the door, moving to stand by Betty. Nessa followed suit, not quite knowing what Hunter was doing. She stood on Betty's other side, watching Hunter from over the horse's back.

Following Hunter's lead, Nessa ran the brush down Betty's back and over her side, removing dust and shedding hairs. "Why are we brushing her down?" Nessa asked, curious.

"Just so that there's nothing that could cause her any discomfort when the saddle is on." The task finished, Hunter put the brushes back in the bag, and then picked up the reins and the blanket, quickly fitting them on Betty. "Have you never saddled a horse before?" he asked, faintly astonished. Nessa shrugged. "You've never ridden a horse." Less of a question and more of a statement. It oddly made Nessa feel as if she had an inadequacy about her.

"I've never really had the opportunity to be around horses." Nessa felt like she needed to explain. "I've mostly just admired them from afar. Especially after one bit me."

"A horse bit you?"

"And stole my sandwich."

Hunter snorted.

"It's nothing to laugh about. Bloody thing chased me around a tree."

Hunter's shoulders shook as he picked up their bags and began arranging them on Betty's saddle, tying them securely in place. Thanks to Betty, the only thing Nessa had to carry was her messenger bag, and that was purely by choice.

Still chuckling, Hunter led Betty over to the stable's main door, Nessa trailing behind him. The door opened onto one of the main streets, presumably the one that ran behind Margret's inn. Small groups of men and workers slowly made their way home after the day's work. The sun was starting to dip behind the surrounding buildings, turning the sky a deep blue and casting long shadows.

Betty plodded between the two of them as they walked through the city, keeping to the winding back alleys. Nessa wondered how they wouldn't be recognised, since they made no effort to conceal themselves, but Hunter didn't seem at all concerned.

They traversed further than they had that morning, walking until the city's outer wall rose up before them. Made from the same dark stone as the castle, it was a foreboding and unwelcome sight, with battlements lining the top and armed soldiers stationed on watch. At the sight of them, decked out in their dark tunics and chainmail shirts, swords belted at their waists, Nessa's heart sputtered and she longed to be back at The Iron Horse, far away from watchful eyes.

The street turned onto the main road, and the base of the wall came into sight. The river ran through a wide square before escaping Ironguard via an archway on the far side. Next to the archway was the entrance to the city, the huge wooden doors spread wide, bluntly framing the outside countryside. A few people were still coming and going, carefully scrutinised by the guards stationed on either side of the gateway.

Hunter, upon seeing the number of guards, casually directed them away, heading down a road that ran next to the city's wall. The sight and sound of the river faded behind them. When Nessa didn't hear the sound of pursuit, she relaxed a touch. The road had a gentle bend to it, and that, combined with the row of buildings that were on their other side, soon hid the river and gateway from sight.

Hunter drew them closer to the wall and looked up. Nessa realised that from this angle, any soldiers up there wouldn't be able to see them.

"Here we are," Hunter said, pulling them to a stop.

Nessa gazed around, seeing that the only things of relative interest nearby was a ginger cat watching them from an upstairs window, and a small storm drain set low in the wall.

"Our secret way out?" Nessa hedged a guess.

"Indeedie." He handed Betty's reins to Nessa, who, never having handled a horse before, held them somewhat tentatively as Hunter knelt down and peered into the storm drain.

Nessa looked at Betty. "You wouldn't bite me, would you?" she murmured.

Betty blinked big brown eyes at her.

"Didn't think so," Nessa muttered, turning back to Hunter, who was rapping his knuckles against the drain. Curiously, he then gave a tuneful little whistle, which echoed behind the metal grate. He paused, then whistled again. This time, accompanying the following echo, came the sound of running.

Although Nessa was half expecting it, it still came as a surprise when someone's head popped up behind the storm drain.

"What ya want?" they demanded.

"Hello to you too, Ritta," Hunter said, grinning up at Nessa.

"Hunter!" Ritta, the man in the drain, exclaimed. "I did think I would be see's you around soon."

Amused, Hunter said, "Did you now?"

Ritter nodded. "I knew, I knew. You always be gett'en in trouble, you is."

"Well, in that case, you'll also know that I'll be requiring passage for two, plus a horse."

"Of course, of course." The head disappeared and Nessa wondered what the hell was going on. She cast around, thinking that Ritta was about to come out of a secret door or something. The street was quiet and Hunter began humming, bouncing on his toes while they waited.

Then, after long minutes, the ground beneath their feet rumbled and shook, and there was a grinding sound, not unlike the noise of shifting gears. Next to them the earth moved, a large rectangle of the cobbled street sinking inch by slow inch downward, forming a slope that angled under the city's wall.

Nessa stared, astonished, and Hunter stepped past her. He took Betty's reins and descended, smiling like an imp as he went. Roused from her shock, Nessa hurried after him, the dingy darkness swallowing her. As soon as her feet touched the damp ground, the grinding of gears sounded again, and the section of street rose, fitting back into place above their heads as if it had never moved.

The only light source was the storm drain, and that offered barely any illumination. From the still, moist air, Nessa presumed that they were in a small room.

A door opened and Ritta came scurrying out, carrying a small lamp, stopping in front of Hunter.

The lamp's flame was limp and unhappy, but gave off enough light for Nessa to see this mysterious Ritta. He was short and painfully thin, even smaller than Nessa, with hair that was shorn in uneven clumps. His hand had a nervous twitch and he watched her and Hunter with beady eyes that reminded Nessa of a rat.

Ritta held out a hand, fingers wriggling like worms, and Hunter sighed. He rummaged around in his pocket and fished out a couple of coins, depositing them in Ritta's waiting palm.

"Now, now," Ritta said. "Which tunnel you be wantin'?"

"East one please, Ritta."

Ritta nodded and moved over to the far wall and pulled a lever. With a creak the wall fell backwards, lowered to the ground on rusted chains, revealing a long dark tunnel. Nessa looked at it, nonplussed.

"Not more tunnels," she groaned, too low for Hunter to hear.

Hunter peered at the darkness and turned to Ritta. "Don't suppose we could trouble you for the light?"

Ritta clicked his tongue and handed over the lantern, then scurried back into the shadows. Hunter turned to Nessa.

"You ready?"

Nessa nodded, less than thrilled at the prospect of going into another tunnel. At least this time, she tried to tell herself, it would be a lot harder for someone to follow them, what with the hidden entrance and Ritta acting as a guard of sorts.

With her boots scuffing against the dirt, Nessa reluctantly entered the tunnel with Hunter. It was like every other tunnel that Nessa had the misfortune to find herself in recently; horribly dark, damp and dreadfully claustrophobic. After several yards, Ritta closed the door behind them, sealing them in. Nessa felt uneasy and Betty seemed to be of the same mind, nickering softly. Nessa laid a comforting hand on Betty's side.

The lantern offered little light, barely enough to prevent them from tripping on the uneven floor. Nessa searched for any sign of the exit, but couldn't see anything other than solid darkness outside the lantern's pale glow.

"So, where does this tunnel go?" Nessa asked.

"It takes us east out of Ironguard. There's one that goes south and another that goes northwest, but this one is the quickest route for us. Once we get out of here, we'll angle northeast to get to The Hidden City."

"Sounds good."

"Indeed. We'll be out of the tunnel in about an hour. We'll make camp for the night, have dinner, then set off tomorrow morning."

"Sounds like a plan."

"A beautiful plan," Hunter agreed.

They chatted for a while, filling the hour with lively conversation. Soon, before they knew it, they were at the end of the tunnel.

A round iron door stood before them, old and rusted, with a turn wheel in the centre. Hunter, after placing the lantern on the ground and handing Betty's reins to Nessa, gripped the wheel. With hard tugs, he began tuning it. It was stiff and reluctant to budge at first, squeaking and shedding flakes of rust. Eventually though, Hunter got his way and it loosened, spinning and unlocking the door.

It swung open, nearly knocking Hunter off his feet. A fresh burst of evening air rushed in, replacing the stagnant smell of the tunnel with the scent of grass and early spring. It was dark outside, the sun having sank beneath the curve of the earth when they had been below ground. A few lingering rays shone on the horizon, turning a scattering of clouds a pale pink and showing rolling hills and clusters of trees as black silhouettes.

Nessa hurried out of the tunnel with Betty in tow, grateful to be free from its stifling darkness. Hunter picked up the lantern and swung the door closed, turning the wheel so that it was locked once again. Nessa surveyed her surroundings, taking in the thick tangle of brambles that obscured much of the doorway, and the silvery sheen of Ironguard's river in the distance. Her eyes followed the river, tracing it back until she saw the dark shape of Ironguard.

There was, to Nessa's guess, a good four or five miles between her and the city. The castle was lit up for the night, the windows glowing with light, making the stone appear even darker against the deep navy of the sky. With such distance between her and Margan, Shadow too, Nessa felt a smidgen more relaxed.

Hunter moved up beside her, mouth open in a wide yawn. "Don't know about you, but it's a bloody nice feeling to be outside the city."

"It does feel pretty damn good," Nessa agreed.

Chapter 15

They set up camp for the night nearby, deeming it too late and dark to go any further. The clearing was small, with just enough space for two people and a horse, and was sheltered by a ring of trees, helping to keep them safe from any eyes and from the breeze that rolled in over the hills.

Betty was tethered to a low branch, preventing her from wandering off at the first opportunity, and Hunter was busy unsaddling her. Nessa made herself useful by getting a fire ready, gathering small twigs and some dried leaves for kindling. She piled them up in the centre of the clearing and then stood, dusting off her hands.

Hunter walked past her, carrying the sleeping bags, setting them down on what looked like the most level area of the campsite.

"I'm going to find some logs," Nessa said, heading into the woods.

"Good, good," Hunter said. "Don't go too far. Wouldn't want to lose you so soon."

The woods were young, composed mostly of juvenile trees that offered little in the way of fire wood, and Nessa found herself having to go deeper into the trees. The storm from the previous night had blown free spindly twigs mostly, but scattered amongst them were a few decent sized branches, and Nessa swiftly collected any she came across.

Bending down to pick one up, Nessa heard the quiet rustle of leaves behind her.

She froze.

The sound came again, slightly to the left this time. Slowly, Nessa released all the branches except for one, letting them roll almost silently to the ground. She rose, heart jumping wildly, and raised the branch like a bat.

She spun around.

No one was there.

Leaves whispered a short distance away, the perpetrator concealed by darkness and a shrub. Bit by bit, Nessa crept around the side of the bush, branch held at the ready. The rustling came again, close this time, and Nessa leaped forward, ready for confrontation.

Was it a peeping-tom of sorts? Had Margan found her? Had Shadow?

No.

It was a squirrel.

It shifted through the leaves, little hands working away, bushy tail quivering. Nessa lowered her branch, breathing a sigh of relief. "Bloody place," she muttered. "Got my nerves in tatters. Stupid squirrel."

Nessa quickly collected up her branches and made her way back to the campsite.

Hunter was in the middle of their camp, arranging the kindling. The sleeping bags were unrolled and Betty was unsaddled, dozing off to the side. Nessa deposited her armful of branches beside Hunter and sat cross-legged next to him. He eyed her haulage and began selecting firewood, arranging it over the kindling. "Good job," he said as he pulled a fire pouch from his pocket. "Although I was beginning to wonder where you had got to."

"I had a run in with a squirrel," Nessa explained, watching as Hunter took a pinch of tinder out of the pouch and nestled it into the leaves. "It delayed me."

"A squirrel, ehh?" Hunter grinned, placing his firesteel near the tinder, striking it. "I hear they can be bloodthirsty little bastards."

Nessa snorted. "Gave me a shock until I realised what it was."

Hunter laughed.

The firesteel shed sparks, then an ember grew on the tinder, making it smoke and blacken. Hunter nursed it, carefully placing dry leaves on top, allowing a flame to take root. It grew, devouring the leaves and twigs that Hunter fed to it, and he piled large branches around the fledgling fire, allowing it to establish itself.

The flames brightened, flooding their campsite with dancing light, and soon warmed the air around them.

"That's better," Hunter said, settling down and packing away his fire pouch.

Nessa nodded and watched the flames for a moment, then pulled the messenger bag's strap from her shoulders, placing the bag on her lap. She checked that the orb was safe and wrapped up tightly against the cold, and then set it over to the side as she positioned her sleeping bag a little closer to the fire, to benefit from its warmth later in the night.

"You hungry?" Hunter asked, reaching for the supply bag.

"Only a little." The hearty breakfast from The Iron Horse was still working its magic.

Hunter snapped off a corner of cheese and tossed it to her, before breaking off a chunk for himself. Nessa nibbled at it, not particularly hungry but eating just for the sake of it.

"So," Hunter said, "are you ready for your adventure?"

Nessa shrugged. "I suppose, though I do hope it's uneventful. I've had my fill of mad men since

I've come here."

"Haven't we all," Hunter sounded a little wry. "But you have a week to experience new sights, see things you never have before."

And be reminded of how far away from home I really am, Nessa finished silently.

"If you want," Hunter continued, "we could take a detour and visit a few of the Twelve Kingdom's wonders, like the Fire Falls or the Crystal Lake."

Nessa finished her bit of cheese and tugged off her boots, feeling rather melancholy all of a sudden. "If you don't mind," she said quietly, "I would just like to find Orm and see if there's a way home."

"Oh. Of course," Hunter sounded a touch surprised. "Of course you would want to see if you can get home first."

"Yes," Nessa said, slipping into her sleeping bag. "The sooner the better too."

"You in a rush or something?"

Nessa could tell that he was trying to be upbeat, trying to be nice, but she discovered that this was becoming a sensitive subject for her. "My mum's having a baby soon," she murmured, snuggling down into the sleeping bag. "I should be there with her, to support her, to tell her I'm sorry for how things have become lately, that things will now change."

Hunter was painfully quiet for a time, then Nessa heard him shift around for a moment, sliding into his sleeping bag as well.

"Then we had best get some rest," Hunter said quietly. "Otherwise we'll be too tired to cover much ground tomorrow." Even though he didn't say it, Nessa knew he was disappointed that she wanted to leave so urgently, and a part of her felt guilty about that.

Nessa rolled onto her side and closed her eyes, dreaming of all the things she would say to her mother when she got back. The thought of home, of righting the rift that had formed between them over the last few months was a slight consolation to Nessa, and eased the ache in her heart a little.

But as the old ache dulled, another one formed, making sleep elusive.

Nessa twisted in her sleeping bag, which was lined with dense fur for warmth, and peered over at Hunter. He was asleep already, his eyes closed and his chest rising and falling with deep, steady breaths.

Yes, a large part of her wanted to go home. However, a small part wondered what it would be like to stay a little longer.

৩০ ♦ ঙ

The morning was brisk, and the sun was just beginning to peek over the horizon, not quite ready to chase away the chill of night, allowing a thin layer of frost to cling to blades of grass. A bird sang in a nearby tree, its tune swiftly turning from a pleasant alarm clock to a persistent annoyance.

Nessa blinked tired eyes, only half awake, and propped herself up on an elbow, intending to scare the little menace away and get a few more minutes of shuteye.

"Good morning sleepyhead," Hunter said. "You're up just in time for breakfast."

Nessa turned, finding Hunter crouched by the fire, stirring a cooking pot. She sniffed, instantly awake, her stomach grumbling. Something smelt good.

Hunter chuckled. "I see someone's hungry."

"I suppose I am," Nessa said with as much dignity as one could whilst their stomach growled like an angry bear. "I confess, this is a better start to the morning than I was expecting."

"Oh, really?"

"Yes, a clear sky, a fairly decent night sleep, breakfast in bed, of sorts. What more could a girl ask for while on the run?" Nessa sat up, the sleeping bag pooling around her hips, keeping her legs covered and warm.

"Well," Hunter said, arranging two bowls on the ground, "I did say camping is a lot better with me as company."

Nessa grinned and rubbed the sleep from her eyes. She hadn't lied when she said that sleep had been fairly good, for she had slept solidly for much of the night. However, her troubled mind had kept her awake to start with, and while the sleeping bag was soft and warm, she had still been on the hard ground, and it took some time to find a comfortable position. As Nessa watched Hunter dish up breakfast, the fog in her mind started to clear little by little, and she told herself to be grateful that she hadn't had any more waking dreams.

Hunter handed her a bowl and a wooden spoon, and Nessa discovered that breakfast was a stew, thick with chunks of meat and vegetables. Herbs had been added too, and Nessa wolfed it down.

"That was lovely," Nessa said, scraping the bowl clean.

Hunter grinned. "I aim to please. Can't have your first adventure starting off with nothing less than the best breakfast I could provide."

"Your efforts are greatly appreciated."

"Glad to hear it," Hunter said as he gathered up the dirty cutlery and rinsed them clean using a water pouch. He then packed them away.

Nessa ran her eyes over him, noticing that he had changed into fresh clothing, his hair was brushed and his demeanour said that he was ready to go. He had clearly been awake for awhile. Nessa stretched and reached behind her, pulling her hair over her shoulder and giving it a cursory brush through with her fingers, working out the worst of the knots, and then quickly braided it.

After worming out of her sleeping bag, Nessa slipped on her boots and helped to pack up their camp. She rolled up her sleeping bag, placing it and her other bag next to Betty, who Hunter was currently saddling, and then collected Hunter's belongings, adding them to the pile to be loaded up.

Hunter swiftly had Betty saddled and all their bits and pieces tied in place. All except Nessa's messenger bag, which she had decided, for some inexplicable reason, to carry again.

Nessa sat by the fire as Hunter finished up, and when he came back to join her, he was carrying a roll of paper. A scroll, Nessa realised, when he unrolled it on the ground. Hunter used a few nearby stones to weigh down the corners, which were determined to curl back up, and Nessa saw that it was a map.

On creamy parchment, harsh black ink depicted the world that Nessa was in: The Twelve Kingdoms.

A large ocean dominated much of the left hand side of the map, empty save for a small cluster of islands near the centre. The land curved around it, filled with swathes of mountain ranges and forests, and a river ran down the middle, splitting the land but connecting two large lakes together. Scattered throughout were dots and small stars showing the locations of villages, towns, and a handful of cities, their names written in elegant swirls beside them.

Nessa stared at the alien layout of the map, so unfamiliar that it made her feel completely out of her depths.

Hunter tapped the parchment, finger poised over a small mountain range in the lower half of the map that had a river running through it. "The Hidden

City is here," he said, then his finger slid a little lower and to the left, "and we are here." The mountains had no marker for any towns or cities, but where Hunter's finger now pointed, Nessa could see the elegant scripture spelling out Ironguard.

"The quickest route, which we'll be taking, is to go through the Burning Forest," Hunter's finger came to a rest by the side of the mountains, "and then go through one of the mountain passes that leads into the city."

"Sounds good to me," Nessa said.

"There are a few villages on the way," Hunter continued. "But we'll skirt around them, avoiding them completely unless we need supplies. Although food shouldn't be a problem, since I can always set traps to catch some small game."

"Excellent," Nessa murmured.

Hunter rolled up the map, stowing it back in the bag.

Nessa stood as Hunter untied Betty's reins from the tree, and picked up her messenger bag. She frowned, feeling its weight. It seemed heavier than it had last night, considerably heavier. Nessa flipped it open, expecting to find several rocks or something equally heavy inside, but there was only the orb. She wondered if it had somehow gained weight. The idea seemed absurd, though, and Nessa discarded it.

She shouldered her bag, grimacing at the weight,

and moved over to Hunter, who stood waiting with a nickering Betty by his side.

"You ready to go?" he asked, eyeing her bag warily, which was already becoming uncomfortable. Nessa simply nodded, deciding to ignore his loaded look and get going. "Then we shall head off. But before we do, I have one request."

Nessa was surprised. "A request?"

"Now, I know that your introduction to this place wasn't the best, and that things are different to what you're used to." He frowned. "Or, at least, I think they are. Anyway, I would just like to ask you to keep an open mind and not let the events with Margan and Shadow taint your time here."

It was, perhaps, a bit of a weird request, but Nessa saw no harm to it and said, "I'll try." There was no sense in keeping Margan or Shadow in her mind any longer. Hopefully, in a week or so, she'll be on her way home and never have to think of those two again.

For some inexplicable reason, as she gazed at Hunter, with his growing smile and his merry eyes, that thought didn't give her quite as much joy as it should have done.

Chapter 16

Nessa left the safety of the trees with a level of buzzing excitement. She took Hunter's request in her stride, and cast away her worries and doubts. A week, that was all. Just seven days and everything would be put to right. Nessa was determined to enjoy each and every one of those days as best as she could. She might as well, because she would never be returning once she got home, that was for sure.

The sun had risen a little more, establishing itself low in the sky. It held the promise of some warmth later in the day, and already the delicate layer of frost had vanished from the tips of the grass. They set off and soon the shadow of Ironguard disappeared behind the rolling hills that spread out for miles in either direction. Without its watchful eye on her, Nessa felt as if a weight had been lifted. She felt lighter, happier than she had been in months, eager for her cross country adventure.

It would be the furthest she had ever travelled, going between worlds excluded. Previously that record had been held by the last house move she'd had to endure. Compared to that, which at the time had seemed monumental, moving from a big city to the middle of nowhere, this was on a whole new level.

This time round, though, instead of feeling angry and hurt like before, Nessa was beginning to burn with enthusiasm.

They trekked across a strip of grassland dotted with small clusters of young trees, then they climbed a particularly high hill. Atop the summit, Nessa could see for miles. Vast fields spread out before her, covering the earth in a multi-hued carpet of greens and the gold of ripening wheat. After descending the hill, they kept to the grass verges that divided the fields into blocks.

As the day continued on, and as the sun rose ever higher in the sky, butterflies emerged from their hideouts, flitting through the air, and colourful birds darted to-and-fro around them, calling out their curiosity.

Midday came and Nessa and Betty began flagging under the unexpected heat. Hunter pulled them to a stop by an irrigation stream, giving them time to rest. Tall reeds lined the sides, offering some dappled shade on the grassy bank where they sat. Hunter allowed Betty the freedom to roam, but the horse remained close, munching on the grass and drinking from the stream.

Hunter laid back in the long grass, throwing an arm over his eyes against the glare of the sun, and Nessa slipped off her boots, dipping her feet into the stream. The water was cool and soothed the patches of sore skin on her heels. Her boots were good quality, sturdy black leather with a robust sole, but they were new, and they had yet to mould to her feet.

For a time, Nessa basked in the sun, feeling it kiss her face, watching the light breeze stir the tops of the rushes, as Betty wandered over to a patch of lush grass.

This isn't so bad, Nessa thought. In fact, it was a rather pleasant way to spend the start of the afternoon.

Something tickled her toes and Nessa peered into the stream. There, darting around her feet, were several small fish. She leaned in closer, and they swam away as her shadow fell over them. They were quickly back, though, investigating the curious sight of her wiggling toes.

At first, Nessa thought that they were just minnows, due to their size. But then she noticed that their bodies had an iridescent shimmer to them, and they had large splayed fins and tails. Perhaps they were fighting fish? But the water was too cold for that species, Nessa knew, and their colouring and shape wasn't quite the same.

"They're baby Mangers," Hunter said, looking over Nessa's shoulder, blinking heavily. "They're common in the irrigation systems in the south. When they mature, they turn a beautiful green-blue." He rubbed his face. "I think I fell asleep for a spell."

"I think you did."

"Little good it did me. I'm even more tired than I was earlier." Hunter looked around, eyes suddenly growing wide. "The horse," he gasped. "Where has the horse gone? Margret will kill me if I lose her bloody horse."

Unworried, Nessa pointed.

Betty had crossed the stream a while ago and stood a short distance away, happily munching on a weed that had little pink flowers.

Hunter followed the line of her finger, and upon seeing Betty, relaxed. "Thank the Devils," he muttered. "I don't think I'll be able to talk myself out of anymore trouble with Margret."

"You and Margret," Nessa mused. "The two of you do make a rather curious pair. How did that come about?"

"Margret knows my mother," Hunter explained. "And a few years ago, when I got myself in a wee bit of trouble with the local authorities, she was kind enough to help me out. On mother's behalf, she keeps reminding me. But I like to drop in every now and again." He grinned. "Keeps her sweet, you see, for situations such as the one we got ourselves in the other night."

Nessa recalled Margret's worry when she and Hunter had stumbled into The Iron Horse. "She cares about you a great deal."

"I know." A little bit of sorrow entered Hunter's eyes, there and gone before Nessa could read too much into it. "She's kind of like a second mother to me these days. A home away from home, if you wish. Which is why I daren't lose her horse." Hunter looked at her, only half joking, "She'd slap me stupid."

Nessa raised her brows.

"I would rather be kicked in the face by a horse than slapped by Margret ever again. That woman has an unnatural amount of strength. I've been punched by grown men before that have hurt less than the slap I received when I..." Hunter paused, his cheeks turning bright pink. "Anyway," he coughed. "You don't need to know what I did. But let's just say that Margret was less than impressed and my cheek stung for a week."

Nessa grinned, imagining all kinds of trouble that Hunter could have got himself into.

Hunter rose, still red faced, and offered Nessa a hand. She took it, allowing him to help her to her feet. She pulled on her socks and boots as Hunter retrieved Betty, who was reluctant to leave her pink flowered weed, and together they set off once again, keeping to the sides of the fields, just as they had earlier. The long grass rose up to their knees and whispered softly with each step they took. While the fields looked like they were tended, Nessa didn't see another soul around. Which was probably why Hunter was taking them that way, she reflected. With less people to see them, the smaller the chances of bounty hunters being able to track them down.

Usually when Nessa walked, she would think about things, and naturally, her mind wandered back to those jolly little fish. That thought soon led her mind back to The Bell, Book and Candle and to the creature trapped in the algae filled tank.

"Hunter, you remember Helen's shop, right?"

He looked over his shoulder at her. "Yeah. Why?"

"In a tank she had something, a water sprite? I was just wondering why she would have one of those in her shop."

"To sell, I would presume."

"As a pet?"

"Perhaps. There are some people who think that if they own one, then it will bring them good luck."

"And the others?"

Hunter hesitated before answering. "The others use them in spells and potions."

Nessa didn't like that thought, and it must have shown on her face, for Hunter continued. "Some people buy them just to release them back into the wild, you know, that kind of thing. Either way, no matter what the buyer does with the water sprite after purchase, Helen makes a lot of money out of it. Money stealing witch is expanding her business."

"Do they actually bring you good luck?" Nessa asked out of morbid curiosity.

"I doubt it, in all honesty."

"How sad."

Hunter made a sound of agreement.

They conversed throughout the day, sticking to more pleasant subjects. Hunter delighted her for a time by telling stories of the trouble he would get himself into with the aid of his friend, Orm. Nessa hadn't known Hunter for long, but she knew that he was a natural born trouble maker; she could see the mischievous glint often in his amber eyes. Apparently, Orm was a kindred spirit.

As the sun began its descent, the terrain they crossed slowly changed from rolling farmland to natural meadows intersected with clusters of young trees. The streams dwindled in number until, just before nightfall, they stopped coming across them all together.

The light faded and Hunter deemed it safe enough for them to camp out in the open, so they settled down for the night on the brow of a low hill. They fell into the same routine as the one from the previous night. Nessa busied herself collecting firewood while Hunter saw to Betty. Dinner was a quick and simple affair, and they were soon tucked away in their sleeping bags, worn out by the day's march.

Hunter was instantly asleep, but Nessa found herself unable to keep her eyes closed for long. Although tired, sleep eluded her for a time, her mind buzzing with noisy questions. Nessa supposed that it wasn't too bad, though, because otherwise she would have missed the night's sky coming alive.

At first there was just the moon and a scattering of stars, beautiful without the pollution of urban light marring their gentle radiance, but not an otherworldly sight. But then bursts of colours began to unfold, reds and purples, blues and greens. It was as if a god had spilt watercolour paints across the blackened sky. It was breathtaking; the slow swirl of gently shifting colours calmed down her turbulent thoughts and eased some of her worries.

So Nessa watched the nebulae until her eyelids grew heavy.

ೞ✦ಅ

It was happening again.

This time, at least, Nessa knew what was going on. Her vision filled with foggy light that faded away to muted darkness. She knew that if she looked at her hand or down at her body, it would be translucent, barely there, as if she were a wisp of smoke.

Nessa's eyes slowly adjusted, and she found

herself standing in the middle of a circular room, a room she was familiar with. It was there that Margan had abandoned her to solitary confinement until she had escaped through the roof with Hunter. Nessa peered up and frowned, finding no sign of the hole they had made. In fact, there didn't seem to be any holes up there at all. The roof looked new, as if it had just been constructed.

Nessa looked over her shoulder, finding that the iron door had been fixed too, or perhaps, since it was now free from rust, replaced. Nessa had an odd feeling. How had they done all of that so quickly?

She began pacing around the room, just as she had done a hundred times before, wondering why her waking dream had brought her back there, and more importantly, how the hell she could wake up from it?

Nessa was just about to finish her first lap around the edge of the room when she narrowly missed tripping over someone. So still and silent and hidden by the darkness, Nessa didn't notice the figure until she nearly stood on them.

Barely perceivable, huddled against the wall, was a lone man. His hair was long and shaggy, hanging around his face in a knotted mess, and he sat with his back to her, one shoulder propped against the wall. In his hand he held a broken spoon, the handle of which was snapped in half. He was using it to scratch something into the stone wall.

Nessa watched him with pity, and her heart went

out to him, whoever he was. She knew what it was like to be locked away in that horrible room with nothing to occupy your mind. Nessa remembered the gut-churning loneliness.

After a fevered moment of scraping, he flung the spoon away and turned around, pressing his back against the wall and wrapping his arms around his legs. He buried his face in his knees, shoulders shaking with sobs or from the cold. Nessa moved closer, feeling the need to try and comfort him somehow.

She knelt in front of him, reassured by the knowledge that he wouldn't be able to see her, and placed a hand on his shoulder. The fabric of his tunic was torn, and through the rips, she could see the dark marks of bruises and cuts from harsh beatings. Nessa hoped that in someway he would be able to sense her and not feel quite so alone.

Nessa's eyes were drawn up, and she felt a spike of apprehension at what she saw.

Freshly etched on the wall was the word *Kinlandi*.

"Impossible," she whispered.

It was the name that she had ran her fingers over just a short time ago, the name that had been etched into the wall long before she had been locked there...

But it *was* the one that she had ran her fingers over.

But that would mean...

"I'm in the past."

The man stilled, shoulder tensing beneath her hand. He raised his head and stared at Nessa as if he could actually see her.

Nessa reared back, shocked.

Shadow looked at her with mournful eyes, eyes that weren't quite the colour they should have been. Threads of purple were woven into the midnight blue. They hadn't been like that the other night, when his sword had been at her throat, and when the rain had been falling around them in a spellbinding moment.

"You shouldn't be here," Shadow said, his voice rasping and broken.

Nessa's vision wavered and turned black.

ఠ♦ఠ

Nessa's eyes snapped open. Sweat covered her forehead and her heart thundered away as loud and as fast as a galloping horse. She sat up, shaking and wrapped her arms around herself, as if she might hug away the fear and uncertainty that grew as a painful knot in her stomach.

"What the hell was that?" she whispered.

Nessa wished that it had been a dream, a nightmare, but no amount of arguing would make the voice that told her it was real go away. The way the room had felt, cold and damp, the air smelling of mildew, had been all too familiar. And Shadow... his words... his eyes... His eyes looked like they had once been a deep purple, but were slowly transitioning into the sapphire blue she recognised.

A part of her, deep down, felt that her waking dream was a warning. Of what, Nessa didn't have the faintest idea, but that was the impression it gave her.

Hunter groaned and rolled over, opening drowsy eyes. He spied Nessa awake and did a double take.

"What's wrong?" he asked, pushing himself up on his elbows. "Has something happened?"

Nessa opened her mouth, ready to tell him what she had seen, then snapped it shut, teeth chinking together. A voice whispered to her that it was a secret, something between her and Shadow, and it wasn't her secret to tell, not yet. "Nothing," she lied. "Just had a bad dream."

"You sure?"

"Yeah, just a dream. Nothing more." Nessa forced herself to lie back down. "You should go back to sleep, get some rest."

Hunter didn't argue, curling back up on his side. Nessa listened as his breaths slowed, and when he was back asleep, she rose from her sleeping bag, too riled up to even contemplate trying to lay still. It would be time to get up in an hour or so anyway, she thought, judging by the lightening sky.

The fire had burned out during the night, reduced to a few ruddy embers. Nessa knelt beside it, adding a handful of twigs and a few branches, nursing it. It was slow to catch, but eventually the flames sparked and began to slowly climb over the firewood, and Nessa took the opportunity to change into some clean clothes.

Once she was dressed and the fire was burning nicely away, Nessa decided that she would be the one to cook breakfast today. Rummaging through the supply bag, she found a pan, which she placed on the fire to heat, and selected some sausages and a couple of thick slices of smoked bacon.

While Nessa waited for the sausages to finish, she pulled over her messenger bag and opened it, taking out the orb and setting it on her lap. It glowed, just as it always did, and she smoothed a hand over its surface, enjoying the gentle warmth it emitted. Hunter groaned and rolled over, making Nessa pause, ready to shove the orb back into the bag. For some undisclosed reason, Hunter didn't like it, periodically eyeing her bag throughout the day like it contained a severed head.

Something tapped against the orb's surface, and from within the purple haze, a shadow moved, shifting against the flow of mist and light. For a second, Nessa thought that she had imagined it, but then it came again, gently rubbing against the inside of the orb, making the surface vibrate beneath her hand.

Very quickly, without dwelling on the matter, Nessa stowed the orb back in the bag, deciding that she wasn't in the right frame of mind to be dealing with any more weirdness. Waking dreams were one thing, an oddly glowing orb that seemed to be changing was something else entirely. Separately, Nessa would almost be able to convince herself that everything was relatively normal. However, having both of them happen at once was too much to deal with before breakfast. Which, as it happened, was pretty much ready.

Nessa turned the sausages one last time as the bacon sizzled to perfection. It would be a modest meat feast.

Hunter awoke, nose twitching.

"Breakfast?" he enquired hopefully.

"Breakfast," Nessa confirmed, scooping up some bacon and sausages and wedging them between two rustic slices of bread. She handed it to Hunter, who marvelled at such a magnificent invention, and Nessa quickly made her own, devouring it.

"What a beautiful way to start the day," Hunter said around his mouthful. "I'm glad I helped you escape from Ironguard."

"Me too, Hunter," Nessa absently murmured, staring at her bag. Was it just her imagination or did it look fuller, as if the orb was growing? "Me too."

Chapter 17

The second day of their journey passed much like the first, with lots of walking and a few periodic breaks to rest their feet, have a drink and eat a snack. On the third day, clouds began to form overhead, offering a reprieve from the balmy weather, something that Nessa was extremely grateful for.

On the morning of the fourth day, Nessa woke to the sight of a dreary grey sky. It started drizzling soon after, the fine kind of rain that misted the air and soaked into your clothing without you noticing until you were wet through. Nessa didn't mind it overmuch, although it did make her top stick uncomfortably to her back. She found it rejuvenating, fresh. Hunter, on the other hand, whined about the weather near constantly, much to

Nessa's amusement. He had a way with words that few possessed. While no stranger to swearwords, Nessa still learnt a few new ones that would blister the ears of any hardened, foul-mouthed sailor.

They took turns cooking their meals, which gradually grew simpler as their supplies dwindled, and Nessa and Hunter fell into a kind of rhythm with one another, splitting the chores evenly between them. During that time, the homesickness that Nessa had felt for a month steadily faded away, and she slowly began to realise that she and Hunter were something akin to kindred spirits. They had known each other for a mere four days and yet, to Nessa, it felt as if their friendship had spanned years, such was how relaxed they were around one another.

Each night, Nessa snuggled into her sleeping bag, fearful that she would have another grim waking dream. So far, though, she hadn't had another one since. That made it easier for her to ignore the issue, to pretend that nothing abnormal had happened.

What was hard for her to ignore though, was the orb.

The few times that Nessa had taken it out of the bag, the eerie shadow had moved within, and while it was hard to prove without the help of a tape measure and scales, she swore that it was growing, getting larger and heavier with each day that passed. Not enough to be completely definite, but enough for it to continuously plague her thoughts. Nessa was tempted to talk to Hunter about it, to tell him what she thought was happening. Each time she went to open her mouth, though, she got tongue-tied, the words, the worries, refusing to leave her tongue. They were her secrets to keep, it seemed, and keep them she would, adding them to the pile with all the others.

On the fifth day, they came upon a small village.

Sat far in the distance, all they could see were the vague shapes of buildings and the smoke that rose from a few chimneys.

"Do you think that we should go in for some more supplies?" Nessa asked, squinting against the glare of the sun, which was slowly setting behind the houses.

Hunter looked up from his map. "I think we can risk it. It's small and remote, so I doubt that any bounty hunters will come this way, and no one would bother sending out a wanted poster either. It's unlikely anyone there would be able to read it." He rolled up the map and stowed it away. "At least, I hope so."

They started off again, walking across the sprawling grassland, just as they had been all day, and the day before, and the day before that...

The village was tiny, scarcely more than a few houses clustered around a dirt road that barely extended outside the settlement. The buildings were small and roughly made, a step above being a wooden shack. Their shutters were tightly closed, which Nessa found strange since it was still light out, and the village was quiet, too quiet. Whilst tiny, she thought there would be someone around at least. Nessa knew it wasn't completely deserted, for a handful of chimneys spewed dark smoke. It seemed that the inhabitants were reluctant to venture outside their dwellings.

In the middle of the village was a square. A post stood in the centre with a small number of aged posters tacked onto it. Hunter hurried over, his eyes running over them, instantly relaxing. There was nothing related to them on there.

Nessa eyed the village square with a critical eye. Though small, it had an alehouse, which was strangely boarded up. A few benches and tables were set up out front, sheltered from the sun by a tarpaulin, and a small group of rough looking men dozed in the shade. Opposite them were a few stalls made from planks placed on top of wooden crates.

They were crude, but Hunter made his way over to them, saying, "These look like our best bet."

Nessa trailed after him, keeping a watchful eye on the sleeping men, making sure that Betty kept close to her. She didn't like the look of them at all. They made her uneasy.

Hunter perused the stalls with a keen eye, picking up an item or two before putting them back down. It was a random assortment, Nessa thought, bits and pieces that mainly consisted of dented pots and pans. A few trinkets were dotted around in the mess too, little jewellery boxes and some hair clips. Hunter pocketed a couple of small items, and after a rummage around in a pile of fabrics, found a knotted length of fishing wire.

"Excellent," Hunter said, grinning from ear to ear. "This was just what I was hoping to find."

"If you say so."

"I did want to get more bread and cheese, maybe some veg too," his eyes darted to the sleeping men, "but I've since changed my mind. This will fix us up with a decent dinner. Nothing's better than a freshly caught fish smoking over a hearty fire at the end of the day."

"I'll take your word for it."

"Just you wait and see." He looked around, frowning slightly. "Who am I meant to pay, I wonder?"

"Not exactly lively here, is it?"

"No," Hunter agreed. He fished out a pair of copper coins from his money pouch and placed them on the tabletop. "I'm not liking the vibes this place is giving off."

"Good to know that I'm not the only one."

Hunter stowed away his fishing line and together they hastily left the village, Betty trotting beside them. They kept a fast pace, eager to put some distance between them and the settlement. They didn't slow until it was nothing more than a brown smudge on the horizon.

Bringing them to a stop, Hunter spread his map out on the ground and studied it, seeking their location. "Now, if I'm correct," he said, "we should be right about here." He pointed to a bare patch between a dot that marked the village and a thin squiggling line that traced its way through much of the map. "We're just a mile or two from the river Nyland."

༄ ✦ ༅

Less than an hour later, the river Nyland stretched out before them like a gigantic blue snake. At a quarter of a mile wide, the water ran slowly and smoothly, and was crystal clear. Both banks held a thin covering of trees, and weeping willows trailed leafy fingers in the cool water while silver birches reached spindly arms into the sky.

They made camp in the trees, where trunks and branches would help shelter them from the wind that blew in off the river. The patch they had chosen was nestled between two mighty oaks, their roots creating an indentation that was filled with a thick layer of moss. Nessa was looking forward to sleeping on something softer than hard earth.

Hunter swiftly unsaddled Betty and had their bags in a pile on the ground. He then sat on his sleeping bag and pulled out the tangled fishing line, working at the knots, slowly, arduously. While he did that, Nessa went about her task of gathering wood for the fire, a task that was made considerably easier since they were in an established wood. By the time she returned back with her second armload of firewood, Hunter had succeeded in untangling the fishing line, and was busy making some crude hooks from some needles he had found amongst the junk. Nessa dumped her load on the ground and started to arrange it, just as she had seen Hunter do each night.

Just as Nessa finished, Hunter went over and handed her his fire pouch. She took it with bemusement, setting it down on the ground like it was the most bizarre thing in the world.

"You get the fire going," Hunter said. "I need to start fishing before we lose the light. Otherwise no dinner for us."

Nessa found herself saying, "Okay," and Hunter bounded away, heading for the river. She sat, staring after him, wondering what the hell she was supposed to do. Lighting the bloody fire was his job, damn it. She had never used a firesteel before, had never needed to. She picked up the fire pouch and pulled out a pinch of tinder, deciding to mimic what Hunter usually did, and set it in a small mound of dry leaves. Then, holding the firesteel, she wished desperately for some matches.

Working from memory, she copied Hunter's actions, running the blade sharply against the steel. Nothing, not even one goddamn spark. The tinder sat unsmoldering, mocking her lack of success.

Nessa tried again and again, and it became a

matter of pride. Over her dead body would she be defeated by a fire, or lack thereof. Frustration finally won out, and she struck the firesteel angrily. Sparks flew, igniting the tinder in a glorious display. Hurriedly, she scooped up the burning bundle, blowing gently on it until small flames took hold. Then, before it burnt her hands, she placed it by the firewood, feeding it twigs until it grew big enough to handle the larger branches.

Nessa tended to it, making sure that it had plenty of wood to last for a spell, then went off in search of Hunter, giving Betty a quick pat as she passed. She found Hunter on the river's bank a short distance away, fishing line already deployed, and sat down next to him. He looked over at her, frowning a little.

"Are you okay?" he asked. "You're looking a little flustered."

Nessa waved a hand. "I'm fine. The fire's all sorted."

"That's good," Hunter said slowly. "Didn't have any problems then?"

"None whatsoever."

"I'm glad to hear it. It must have been the wind and the trees swearing with great gusto a few minutes ago, then."

"It must have been."

"Hmm." Hunter turned back to fishing, lips twitching with a poorly suppressed grin.

Nessa grumbled under her breath, adding a few more select words to those of the wind and trees.

They relaxed into a comfortable silence, and Nessa watched as the sun slowly set, turning the sky pink and orange. It dipped behind the trees and the warmth gradually left the air. Nessa shivered from the cold breeze that blew in from across the river, and she pulled her knees to her chest, wrapped her arms around her legs, and rested her chin on her knees.

Hunter reeled in the fishing line, winding it around a small piece of wood, and checked that the worm was still on the hook. Satisfied, he cast it out again, sending the hook and the unfortunate worm flying. A gust of wind caught it, sending it further downstream than originally intended, and loosened Nessa's hair, blowing it across her face. She gathered it back and tied it into a loose ponytail, but strands still came free, going in her eyes and mouth. She had lost her hair bobble upon arrival and had since been tying it back with a strip of cloth, which just wasn't up to scratch.

"Here," Hunter said, seeing Nessa struggling and handing something to her.

Nessa held it in her hand, finding that he had given her a hair clip. It was old and tarnished, but she was fairly sure that it was solid silver. He must have picked it up from the village without her noticing.

"My sister had hair as long as yours, although it was darker in colour," he said. "She had always said that hair ribbons were a waste of time and that you had to have a decent hair clip. Otherwise, you'd spend all day worrying about what your hair was doing and fussing with it."

Nessa was taken back, somewhat surprised that he had been so thoughtful. Then his words sunk in. Sister? Hunter has a sister? A second later she realised that he was using the past tense, and Nessa had to correct herself. Hunter *had* a sister, one who was no more.

There were so many things that Nessa could say, words of condolences, questions. But the sad, tender expression on his face as he gazed ahead, reminiscing about days gone by, made her settle with a simple and quiet, "Thank you."

Hunter nodded, reeling in his fishing line and then casting it out again.

For a time, the fish were reluctant to bite, but when the sun sank beneath the horizon, dinner was quickly procured. Hunter caught several fish, a pale trout of some kind, their iridescent scales glinting in the dying light. Hunter informed her that they were called Moonies, named such due to their colouring and because they were mostly active once the sun went down.

"They'll taste fantastic when I'm finished with them," Hunter reassured her, seeing her inspecting them with a critical eye.

"I'll be holding you to your word."

"That sounds like a challenge," Hunter said, grinning. He stood, offering Nessa a hand up, and gathered his catch, taking it back to their campsite, where the trees and the fire beckoned to them with the promise of warmth and some shelter.

As soon as they entered their camp, they instantly realised that something was wrong.

The fire burned with more enthusiasm than it should after an hour of neglect, highlighting the fact that Betty was nowhere in sight, and that their bags had been ransacked, their belongings scattered all over the place.

Nessa's eyes landed on her messenger bag, finding it empty, deflated without the orb filling it. She felt a peculiar level of horror at discovering it gone, which only grew when she could see no sign of it amongst the mess.

"My orb's gone," Nessa whispered.

"Margret's horse is gone," Hunter said, face growing pale.

"Indeed it is," a gruff voice remarked, "and it will fetch me a pretty penny at market too."

A man stepped out from behind one of the oaks, big and rough looking, with a bald head that shone in the flickering light and a large nose that cast a long shadow across his face.

Held carelessly in his hand was Nessa's orb, glowing with soft purple light.

Without thinking, Nessa started forward, intending to snatch it back. Hunter stopped her with a firm hand on her arm, pulling her back. He shook his head, eyes never leaving the man in front of them.

"Bandit," he muttered in warning to her.

Nessa forgot her frustration when three other men stepped out from the darkness, moving to flank their leader, each of them holding a weapon, either a club or a knife. Grouped together as they were, Nessa recognised them.

"They're the men from the village square," Nessa murmured. "The ones asleep outside the alehouse."

Hunter nodded, his hand tightening on her arm, eyes darting from man to man, taking their measure.

The leader shifted, leaning back against the tree, and played with the orb, bouncing it from hand to hand. Nessa grew angry at his arrogance, and her hands clenched into fists, wanting to drive them into his gut as hard as she could.

How dare he follow them, rob them, handle her orb in such a callous way. How dare he!

"What a pretty thing," the man said, holding it up, making Nessa's blood boil. "Odd that two people such as yourselves would have such a fine thing with them. Has a whiff of magic about it, doesn't it? Steal it, did we?" The man smirked.

"You'd know all about stealing, wouldn't you?" Hunter growled.

"That I would," the man agreed. "Now tell me, where'd you came by it and my men won't break your legs. It is a rare thing, pretty and unique. I want to know all about it to get a good price, you see? Now spill."

Hunter stepped in front of Nessa. "We know nothing about the orb," he said. "Now give me back my horse and leave us be."

"Leave us be, he says" the man laughed, an ugly sound. "How very rude." The men behind him grumbled in agreement. "What's your name, boy? Mine's Grover. I wish to know yours."

"No one of consequence," Hunter answered, much to Grover's displeasure.

"I think you've pissed him off," Nessa whispered to Hunter, watching Grover's face flush a ruddy red.

"I do believe I have." Hunter shifted his stance and dropped all the fish to the ground but one, holding it tightly by its tail. "Stay behind me," he ordered, "and let me deal with this."

"Yes master," she grumbled at his back.

"Enough of your whispers!" Grover bellowed. "Lads, teach the boy some manners."

One of the men stepped around Grover, twirling a large metal bar, grinning eagerly. "With pleasure."

Without warning, Hunter leapt forward, meeting the man in the centre of the campsite. Nessa's silent question of why he was armed with a dead trout was answered a second later when it hit the man right in the face at high speed. The slap was loud, and judging by the man's expression, painful. Stunned, he didn't notice Hunter move, not until Hunter's kick landed solidly in the fork of his legs.

The man's eyes bugged out of his head and his metal bar fell to the ground from limp fingers. Everyone watched with morbid fascination as the man's face turned an alarming shade of pink, then a bloodless white. He collapsed, curling into a ball, gasping for breath.

There was a moment of shocked silence, then, with loud shouts, the other two men rushed forward, weapons raised. Hunter flung the trout, forcing one of them to duck, and lashed out at the second with a kick that hit them in the gut. The first recovered, only to have one of Hunter's fists smash against his nose. Blood sprayed and the man went down. He stayed down.

Nessa flinched, unnerved by the violence, and across from her, she saw Grover scowl. With a mocking wave at her, he retreated back into the trees, taking her orb with him.

"Oh no you don't," Nessa snarled, starting after him, pausing only long enough to grab a heavy branch.

She chased after him, ignoring the voice that told her it might be a bad idea, instead following the faint purple glow that was just ahead of her, calling to her. Grover made it out of the woods before Nessa caught up with him, striding out onto the grasslands. Nessa paused at the edge of the tree line, wondering what she should do now. She'd never fought a man or attacked someone before, and found herself in new and uncertain territory.

Without the hindrance of roots and trunks, the distance between them quickly grew. Nessa was forced to act, else she faced losing her orb forever. She rushed after him, the grass whispering beneath her feet. Grover stilled, looking over his shoulder, the orb haloing him in subdued light.

"Stick? Ray?" he called. "Is that you?"

"No," Nessa said, stepping into the ring of purple-hued illumination. "I'm afraid Hunter's keeping them busy at the moment. It's just me."

Grover snickered, not seeing her as a threat. "Aww, love, did the scuffle scare you? Come for a hug, did we?"

She ignored his comment, eyeing the orb in his hand. *Her* orb. "That's mine," she said, pointing her branch at it, "and I want it back."

"It don't work like that, love." He hefted it up to eye level, taunting her. "It's mine now. And pretty though you are, I don't give things away for free."

"It's mine," Nessa argued, "and you will be giving it back."

"That sounds awfully like a threat, love."

"No, it's a fact." Or maybe a promise. Grover didn't see it, but Nessa did. The shadow was back, moving within the orb, scratching at the surface. There was no warning. Nothing save a bright pulse of light. Then Grover started screaming... and screaming... and screaming. It was a sound of utter agony, and it echoed on the grassland's hills for miles around. He fell to the ground, convulsing, his hands shaking, trying to dislodge the orb that seemed glued to his skin.

It was burning him, Nessa saw, turning his hands red and blistered and bloody. The orb blazed with blinding light, showing Grover's tortured face. His screams grew in ferocity. It was a horrible thing to see, a terrible thing, to witness someone in such pain. Nessa couldn't bare it. Before she knew what she was doing, the branch was cracking across Grover's head, making the screaming abruptly stop as he went limp.

The orb slid from his grasp, rolling in the grass before coming to a stop by Nessa's feet. She stared, alarmed, both by the fact that she had hit someone, and by what the orb was capable of doing.

Then she saw Grover's crumpled body laying on the ground, and the gravity of what just happened snapped her back into action.

"Shit," Nessa muttered, flinging aside the branch and kneeling beside Grover. "Don't be dead. Don't be dead." Cautiously, she pressed her fingers to the side of his neck, feeling for a pulse. She found a steady beat.

With a relieved sigh, she stood, dusting off her hands like she had touched something dirty. "You're a horrible man," she informed Grover's unconscious body, "but I'm glad I didn't kill you. Although, judging by the lump on your head and the bloody mess of your hands, I'm willing to bet that you'll wish I had when you wake up."

Beside her, the orb flared brightly, as if displeased.

Nessa stared at it, seeing it for the first time as something other than just an inanimate object. Perhaps it was alive after all. She considered it for a second, wondering if it would harm her as it had Grover. It never had before. But as her gaze went to Grover's hands, she suddenly had doubts. It had reacted to Grover. It still was, in all honesty, glowing brighter than usual, showing the damage it had caused; the shadow still moving within.

She prodded it with a toe, and when nothing happened, she bent over and gingerly picked it up. The orb was warm to the touch, but not abnormally so, not any more than usual. After a moment, the shadow disappeared from sight and the light dimmed, going back to its normal soft glow, as if content. She carried it back to the campsite, holding it at arm's length until she was sure that it wasn't going to flare up again.

Nessa found Hunter standing between three crumpled figures. He swung around when he heard her approach, still on alert, then instantly relaxed when he saw that it was her. He rushed over, taking her by surprise, and engulfed her in a tight embrace. "I told you to stay behind me," he growled in her ear. "Where the hell did you go, and more importantly, why?"

"He took my orb," Nessa explained, voice muffled against his chest. "I went to retrieve it."

Hunter stiffened, drawing back a little. "I see," he said tightly. "You were obviously successful."

"Yes." She shifted her grip on it, holding it protectively.

"And what happened to our dear friend Grover?"

"He is somewhat incapacitated over yonder way." She pointed roughly in the general direction.

A touch of humour entered his eyes, warming them. "Good," he said, lips twitching. He stepped back and crossed over to the sleeping bags, quickly packing them up. Nessa stared, then shook herself, tucking the orb back into its messenger bag, and helped to collect their stuff, pretending that she hadn't liked having his arms around her nearly as much as she had.

"We need to hurry," Hunter said, knocking her out of her thoughts, making her blush, "and put as much distance as possible between us and them before they wake up."

Nessa nodded in agreement and began stuffing her clothing into her bag. Something then occurred to her. "There were five of them in the village."

"One of them must have taken Betty away. He'll be back soon, wondering what's taking the others so long."

It was then, mentioning Betty, they realised that without the horse to carry their bags, they'd have to do it themselves, which would only slow them down. They abandoned everything other than their sleeping bags, a change or two of clothing, a cooking pot and what was left of their food.

Nessa picked up her messenger bag, heavy with the weight of the orb, and secured it in place before shouldering her other bag. She waited patiently as Hunter put out the fire, then together, they fled into the darkness of the night with nothing but the moon to show the way.

"Betty's been stolen," murmured Hunter, the fact just hitting home.

"She has."

"I've lost Margret's horse."

"Well, I think it was a joint effort."

"Margret's going to kill me."

"Probably."

Chapter 18

Nessa groaned, sleep still clouding her thoughts. She briefly wondered why her body ached so much, then the events of last night came rushing back. They had walked for hours, determined to put as much distance between them and the bandits as possible. They had collapsed at dawn, just as the eastern sky had began to lighten, with barely enough energy or inclination to slip into their sleeping bags.

The ground was hard and rough, but that wasn't what had so unkindly woken her. It was Hunter, crouched by a small fire, cooking a filleted fish over it. Dark bags marked the skin under his eyes and a bruise had formed on his cheek, a sibling to the fading one on his forehead. He looked worn out and cheerless.

Nessa sat up, tired beyond belief, and murmured a greeting. He gave her a small smile and handed her half of the cooked fish. Nessa ate it without tasting, and when she had finished, collapsed back down, snuggling deep into her sleeping bag. The sun was high in the sky, shinning bright, but it did nothing to stop her eyelids from sliding closed. Across from her, Nessa heard Hunter retreating to his own sleeping bag.

৩০✦ঙ

It was past midday when Nessa awoke once again, although this time it was of her own volition. She peered over at Hunter, finding him still fast asleep, an arm flung over his eyes. Nessa smiled to herself. In sleep he looked younger, more relaxed, the weight on his shoulders momentarily lifted. Nessa didn't know what the burden he carried was, but she knew that it was a heavy one. Perhaps it had something to do with his sister, or how he ended up in Ironguard in the first place? Maybe they were connected? Still, Nessa could only presume since she didn't have the heart to ask him.

Nessa got up, finally coming to a decision about something. Looking around, she saw that they had left the woods far behind and were now camped out in the open, the river only a stone's throw away. She left Hunter as he was and picked up her messenger bag, slinging it over her shoulder.

She didn't go far, just a short distance

downstream, giving herself the illusion of privacy. The river widened into a bend, and far in the distance, she could see the grey outlines of the mountains that were her destination. Her eyes traced their shapes. Somewhere over there was The Hidden City.

Lying between them was a river and a wide expanse of forest, on which a haze of smog resided over. It blurred the proud forms of the tall pines and the old oaks. Nessa wondered what that was all about. Forest fire, maybe? She would have to ask Hunter when he woke up later.

With a sigh, Nessa bent over, pulled off her boots, and waded into the river, her leggings soaking up the frigid water. She stopped when it came to just above her knees and took the orb out of her bag. She held it in her hands, feeling its warmth, its growing weight, seeing the shadow move inside.

Nessa steadied her emotions, or at least, she tried to. *You have to do this*, she reasoned with herself. *You have to. It brings nothing but trouble. It ties you to them, to Margan.* But still, she couldn't bring herself to drop it, unable to open her hands and let it fall. She was drawn to it, bound to it somehow. It was hers to protect and guard.

Nessa shook herself, resolved. *I can't take it back home with me, it has no place in that world.* She raised it over her head, preparing to throw it out into the river.

And then...

Crunch.

The sound of breaking glass sounded above her.

Nessa looked up.

The orb had cracked, dozens of fine lines spreading all over its surface, covering it in a spider web of delicate fractures. Nessa flinched in shock and stared, slowly lowering her arms, watching as the cracks grew and grew to the point where the orb looked like it would shatter in her hands.

It flared blindingly bright, and Nessa backed out of the river, slipping and falling on the bank in her haste. The sound of crunching stopped and there was a moment of loaded silence, as if the world had come to a sudden stop.

Then the orb exploded.

Nessa was thrown back, hitting the ground hard, her head smashing against a rock. Instantly everything went fuzzy, soft, then threatened to turn black. Something small and heavy landed on her stomach, and she tried to push it off, only to find that she couldn't command her arms to move.

She felt strange, detached.

Ahh shit, she thought faintly, *this isn't good...*

Nessa could hear someone screaming.

The world faded away.

༅ ♦ ༄

Everything came back to her in a rush. One moment, oblivion. The next, bright sunlight and someone calling her name over and over. She groaned, wishing for a few more minutes of peace, but whoever they were, they were bloody persistent. Nessa opened her eyes, wincing at the brightness, and shifted, about to turn to the source.

Something dug its claws into her stomach.

Nessa froze.

Then she remembered. The orb. It had broken.

What had been released?

She went to lift her head, only to discover that she didn't quite have the strength to do so.

"Oh, thank the Creator!" someone exclaimed. "You're awake."

It took her a moment, but she was eventually able to put a name to the voice. "Hunter?"

"It's okay, everything is fine. I'm right here."

With an inordinate amount of effort, Nessa was able to turn her head to the side, and saw Hunter sitting on the grass ten or so feet away. His face was pale and his eyes held an alarming amount of concern and fear in them. That didn't bode well.

"What's wrong?" Nessa croaked.

Hunter's eyes darted to the weight on her stomach, the weight that was incredibly warm and did, in fact, have claws.

"What is it?" Nessa demanded, panic beginning to rear its ugly head. "What's on me?" *Please be a cat*, she prayed silently. *Please be a nice, friendly, sleeping, domesticated animal of the feline persuasion.*

"I... um... well," his eyes widened as the weight on her stomach moved. "It's... uh... hard to explain."

"What's so bloody hard to explain?" Irritation gave Nessa the strength to raise her head. Her vision blurred and the world spun, but luckily, she didn't faint. Though, when she spied the creature curled up on her stomach, she wished she had.

Small and scaled, it was most definitely not a cat. A long neck and tail were nestled close to its body, partially concealed beneath a pair of leathery wings. Petite pearlescent white spikes ran down the length of the creature's spine, from the base of its head to the tip of its tail. A cloud parted ways with the sun, and a ray of light caught the creature at just the right angle, making its scales blaze the deepest amethyst, and turning its wings nearly black as they appeared to absorb the light.

The creature twitched in its sleep, digging in its claws. Nessa gasped at their sharpness and Hunter shifted, as if he was about to spring up and come to her aid. To her bitter disappointment, though, he didn't, and just settled back on his hunches with a pained expression.

"What the hell, Hunter? Get this thing off me!"

"I've tried to," he held up his hands, "but it seems to have issues with me going anywhere near it."

Nessa stared at Hunter's hands, which were covered in bloody scratches and bite marks, trying not to cry. "It's going to kill me, isn't it?"

"No," Hunter said soothingly. "It's only being

territorial. Just the standard thing when it comes to dragons." He winced, instantly regretting his choice of words.

"Dragon! Dragon?" Nessa peered at the creature. Yep, it was certainly a dragon if she ever did see one. "Why the hell do I have a dragon sleeping on me?"

"One presumes that the orb was, in fact, a dragon egg."

"No shit, Sherlock."

Hunter tilted his head. "I have no idea who this Sherlock fellow is, but I'm pretty sure you're insulting me."

"Hunter," Nessa hissed. "How do I get this dragon off me without it slicing my guts to ribbons?"

"Well," he said, pondering and analysing the situation, "I would go with a scoop and slide method."

"What?"

"Scoop up the dragon, then slide out from under it."

"What an excellent idea," Nessa said dryly.

"Best I've come up with so far."

"Evidently." Nonetheless, Nessa went with the plan, intending to slip her hands under the little dragon and carefully move it off her.

The dragon was still asleep, curled up like a cat on her. Slowly, painfully, she inched her fingers under it without it stirring, and discovered that its scales were as hard as the amethyst they were coloured after. Thin, delicate rib bones flexed under her hands with each breath the dragon took, and its heart pattered away, its beat fast and strong.

Nessa's hands tightened around its torso, ready to shimmy out from under it, when it shifted. She paused, hardly daring to breathe as the dragon pulled back its wing and its head snaked up.

Eyes the colour of violets stared at her, pupils slowly retracting into thin slits. It yawned, revealing rows of sharp teeth and two pointed fangs. Nessa gulped, fearing that it would go for her throat, when, to her astonishment, it picked itself up, stretched, and clambered off her on unsteady legs.

It sat on the ground, tail curled around its legs, looking at her like it sought approval.

Nessa slowly came to the understanding that the dragon hatchling wasn't about to attack her, and relaxed a little. If anything, it looked incredibly small and vulnerable, harmless.

"Explain," Nessa demanded.

Hunter looked perplexed. "Explain what?"

"That! Explain the bloody baby dragon that's looking at me like I'm its mummy."

Hunter frowned. "You don't know about the dragons?"

"Of course I don't know about the dragons. We don't have dragons where I'm from."

"How intriguing," Hunter murmured. "A place without dragons equals a place without Dragon

Riders."

"What are you mumbling about?"

"I'll explain it all to you," Hunter sighed, "but I'd rather do so on the move. Story telling is always more fun at a brisk walk."

"You look a little bit worried," Nessa remarked. He kept looking around, as if he expected trouble to jump out at them at any second. "A little twitchy."

"Oh, I'm fine. It's not like a dragon hatched for me or anything. But I'd be a lot more happy if we got going. The sooner, the better. We don't want anyone stumbling across us with a dragon hatchling on our hands. Else bandits and Margan will be the least of our problems."

"Who could be worse than Margan?"

Hunter was grim. "The king." He stood, and with some degree of caution, helped Nessa to her feet, keeping a watchful eye on the dragon hatchling. "And trust me, he is a thousand times worse than Margan."

"Then I suppose we should get going," Nessa murmured, staring at the little dragon, wondering if it would be at all possible to get it to sit in her bag so that she could carry it easily.

"Just pick the little bugger up," Hunter called over his shoulder as he made his way back to their camp. "I promise it won't hurt you."

Nessa eyed the dragon's needle-like claws dubiously.

Chapter 19

They went upriver, where the grass banks levelled out and the river transformed into an area of boggy marsh. Hunter led the way, testing the soft earth with a long stick before taking each step. Nessa shadowed him, the mud and water squelching underfoot.

Her bag jumped and bumped against her hip as the dragon moved around inside, and Nessa placed a steadying hand on it. Through the leather, she felt the dragon settle down. She had discovered that with a simple thought, a simple gesture, the creature would, to a certain extent, do as it was bid. While incredibly strange, Nessa didn't dwell on the matter, deciding that an 'ignorance is bliss' approach was best when it came to mystical creatures.

"So," Nessa started, finding herself steadily heading into deeper water, "when do I get my explanation?" Hunter looked over his shoulder at her and she stifled a sigh. "Yes, yes," she said. "I know. Later."

They had been walking for over two hours now, and other than a few words when they had hastily packed up camp, Hunter had remained quiet, only ever saying the word 'later' when Nessa made her enquiries.

Which was fine, Nessa kept telling herself. A lot had happened that both of them needed to process. Having time to think things through was good for them. Possibly. She just hoped that Hunter wouldn't come to the conclusion that she was too much trouble, hatching dragons and whatnot, and abandon her, seeking a quieter, dragon free life.

The dragon in question moved again, and curious as to what it was doing, Nessa opened the bag and peered inside. She found the dragon curled up into a ball, or at least it had tried to. While the dragon was no larger than a small cat, the bag wasn't exactly spacious. Without moving a muscle, apparently finding a comfortable position, the dragon slowly opened one eye, looked up at her for a second, then tucked its head under a wing, seemingly falling asleep.

Nessa closed the bag gently, letting the dragon have its nap in relative peace, and fished around in her pocket, pulling out a couple of sharp objects. In her open hand, twinkling in the sunlight, were a few pieces of the dragon's eggshell. Surprisingly thick and a deep purple, they matched the dragon's scales. She had only been able to save a couple of larger pieces before Hunter had collected up the rest, throwing what remained of the egg in the river, claiming that they couldn't leave any evidence behind.

But still, Nessa had managed to save a bit of it, a souvenir of sorts. She might not be able to take a dragon home with her, but she'll be able to take the pieces of shell with her, to remind her that this wasn't all just a dream, that she hadn't gone insane.

Nessa turned them over in her hand, marvelling at the play of light that danced over their smooth surfaces. They were only the size of coins, sharp edged and rough, but she thought that, with a little bit of work, they would make a couple of nice pendants, or maybe a bracelet.

From the corner of her eye, she spied Hunter looking at her, at the pieces of eggshell in her hand, and she quickly stowed them back in her pocket. He knew that she had them. He had seen her pick them up, but he hadn't commented. He had been deep in thought, and Nessa knew that he was thinking about her and the dragon. What he might be thinking about, she didn't know, but she saw the way that he looked at her bag, at what it was holding, and she saw the worry in his eyes. Worry, and an emotion that she couldn't fathom.

Whatever it was, though, made Nessa anxious and uneasy. She rested a hand on the bag, feeling the warmth that soaked through the leather, and felt protective towards the little creature that was inside it. Not from Hunter. Nessa knew that he would never harm an animal unprovoked, but from something else. She had a feeling, a sense that something dark and sinister loomed before her, a threat. One that was linked to the little dragon.

I'll find a way back home, Nessa decided, coming to a decision, *and before I leave, I'll find somewhere to hide the dragon away, somewhere it will be safe from those who would do it harm. From people like Margan and the king Hunter had mentioned.* The thought of hiding the dragon safely away gave Nessa a measure of comfort. She trailed after Hunter, feeling moderately more content then she had a few minutes ago.

"Long ago," Hunter began suddenly, "when cities and castles were a new invention, an explorer travelled to the far east and discovered the Forgotten Lands, a wondrous place filled with astonishing sights and spectacular creatures of the likes we had never seen.

"For a time, the explorer traversed all across the land, seeing and experiencing all that it had to offer. Then, when he had enough, he left the Forgotten Lands and returned home. But not alone. With him he brought a clutch of dragon eggs, the first in this land. When these eggs hatched, dragons were introduced to the Twelve Kingdoms."

Nessa listened silently, eager to hear the rest. Hunter paused, but only for a moment, collecting his thoughts. "For a thousand years," he continued, "these dragons grew and bred, and were the pets of the rich, the nobility. Times were peaceful, filled with growth and discovery. Cities were built and flourished, and the people prospered. But alas, it did not last.

"A boat came from the west, landing on our shores, carrying warriors, merchants and settlers. While the boat carried our human ancestors, our ancestors carried a disease, one that all but wiped out the dragons completely."

Nessa found herself placing a hand on the bag, as if she could protect it from the long passed threat. She could feel the shape of the dragon's back, flexing with each sleeping breath. A thought popped into her head, and as Hunter paused to jab his stick into the marshy water in front of him, Nessa voiced it. "If they were the first humans to come here, then what was the explorer?"

"He belonged to an ancient race called the Old Bloods. Not much is remembered of them now, nothing but fairy tales and fables, for they no longer inhabit this land anymore."

Nessa was surprised. "You mean they left, moved somewhere else?"

"No, I mean they died out," Hunter said. "Were killed off. Anyway, that story is for another time. Now take my hand, the current is starting to get stronger."

The river ran through the middle of the marshland. Slowly, Hunter and Nessa, hand in hand, waded through it, the water pushing against their hips, trying to wash them away.

"What happened to the dragons then?" Nessa asked, wanting something to take her mind off the freezing water that rose up to her navel. With her free arm, she pulled up her messenger bag, hugging it against her chest so that it, and the dragon, wouldn't get wet.

"Oh, well, for a number of years the disease ravaged the dragon population until there were only twelve left. For reasons unbeknown to us, the Old Bloods intervened. They wove a spell, one that was both a blessing and a curse. It bound the remaining dragons to the twelve ruling families, the Twelve Houses, who were the descendants of those who had first arrived. One dragon per House. That's how it was. They were meant to be our protectors, our guardians, our noble and mighty Dragon Riders.

"The bond between man and dragon saved the latter from the disease, immunising them against it. It also meant that each new generation of dragon would only hatch for someone of the Twelve Houses."

Nessa frowned. "How can that be when this one hatched for me?"

"Dragons only hatch for someone with the blood

from one of the Twelve Houses," Hunter said grimly. "As they have done for thousands of years."

"I know what you're insinuating," Nessa said, putting the pieces together. "You think I'm a member of one of the Twelve Houses."

"I'm not insinuating anything. I'm saying that you must be in order for a dragon to hatch for you."

"Well, you have it all wrong," Nessa said with confidence. "I know for a fact that I can't possibly be related to anyone here, let alone to someone from the ruling houses. My mum is a secretary and my father is a lawyer. They run a firm together." *At least they used to*, she amended silently, *before everything went to shit and she moved in with another man*. "I love them both, but there's nothing 'royal' about them."

"A bastard line, perhaps?"

"Impossible. I'm not from this place, and neither are my parents."

"And what about their parents?"

That brought Nessa up short and Hunter, damn him, noticed. "I know my father's ancestry," she argued. "I managed to trace his family tree back some two hundred years." *Thank you Internet and school history project.*

Hunter wouldn't drop the subject. "And your mother?"

"Mum's parents died when I was born. I never knew them, and mum never talked about them either. Said it hurt too much."

"Hmm," Hunter mumbled. Nessa could tell that

he was thinking about that, drawing on threads that weren't there, creating a tapestry of conclusions that couldn't possibly be true.

"Perhaps this dragon hatching is a fluke," Nessa said. "A mistake?"

Hunter shook his head. "That's never happened before."

"Perhaps it's a first."

"Not possible. I would know if it's happened before. I would have heard something."

Nessa cocked a brow. "You ever heard of someone being pulled through a magic mirror by a deranged psychopath before?"

"Can't say I have. Point taken." He didn't sound very convinced, but Nessa let it slide, not wanting to argue anymore. She knew who she was and who her family were, and that's what counted. Nessa was confident that neither of them had even heard of the Twelve Kingdoms, let alone had come from there. Hunter was grasping at straws that didn't exist.

"What is the point of the Dragon Riders?" Nessa asked, curious.

Hunter sighed. "They were meant to protect us, defend us against any threat. Help us when there was a flood or an earthquake or some other kind of disaster."

Were, as in past tense? Nessa thought. "And now?"

"Now we just hope that the last few Dragon Riders don't kill us all."

Alarmed, Nessa asked, "What do you mean by that?"

"Dragons give their Riders incredible power. But with power comes corruption and greed. The Dragon Riders we have today are the twisted image of what they once were."

Nessa didn't know what to say, so she let the subject drop.

※

As quickly as the grassland had turned to marshland, it reverted back to solid ground and rolling hills. A few lone trees dotted the landscape between them and the smoking forest that sat a couple of miles away. Even from this distance, the air smelt faintly of burning wood.

Nessa scrambled up the bank, finally leaving the cold, murky water. She was drenched, her clothing heavy and sticking to her body, making the task difficult and hindering her movements. The cool air hit her and Nessa found herself shivering.

At the top of the embankment, she stood beside Hunter, who had wrapped his arms around himself, shaking from the cold. "Come," he said, nodding to a nearby tree; an old, solitary oak. "We'll change out of our wet clothes and hang them on the branches to dry."

Nessa nodded, finding that her teeth were chattering too much to speak.

They dumped all their belongings on the ground

amongst the oak's fallen twigs and roots, everything save Nessa's messenger bag, which she gently placed on top of a rolled up sleeping bag, not wanting to disturb the resting dragon hatchling.

Nessa quickly discovered that while her messenger bag and dragon were safe and dry, the bag containing her clothing hadn't faired so well. The bottom was soaked through, as were much of the sides. Groaning, praying that something had been spared, Nessa poured the contents onto the ground. All hope of dry clothing faded as she looked at the half wet mess.

Muttering a low curse, Nessa dropped to her knees and dug through the sodden pile, ascertaining that not a single item had been spared. Every top, tunic and pair of leggings had a sizable damp patch somewhere on it. She sorted through her clothing, deciding to wear the least damp thing. While it wasn't ideal, it would be better than what she currently had on. With limited options, thanks to the bandits and the river crossing, Nessa was forced to go with the dress, which had been in the middle of her bag, protected from the worst of the soaking, only being wet around the hem.

Nessa looked over at Hunter, finding him digging around in his bag, which, infuriatingly enough, was bone dry. *Must be nice to be so tall*, she thought. *Comes with all kinds of perks.* Clothing in hand, Hunter stood and looked between her and her dress.

"I'll... um... go around the tree and change," he said.

"Right," murmured Nessa, realising that there was a lack of substantial cover around them.

As soon as Hunter disappeared from sight, Nessa stripped off her wet clothing as quickly as possible. The tops came off easily, but the leggings clung to her calves, making the task difficult. She managed to kick them off and, in a matter of seconds, was slipping into the dress.

It was deep blue in colour and consisted of a long, plain gown and a matching surcoat that was edged in an ornamental trim. It was a little large around the middle so Nessa fiddled with the laces that ran down either side, pulling them tighter for a more flattering fit. With surprising swiftness the chill left Nessa's bones, and while she waited for Hunter to return, she occupied herself by hanging her damp clothing on some low branches to dry.

Finished, Nessa frowned, wondering what was taking Hunter so long. How much time does one man need to change, damn it. She looked around. The marshland stood before her and the hills and forest were behind. There was no sign of Hunter anywhere.

"Hunter?" she called softly, stepping around the tree, hearing a quiet noise.

She found him scrabbling at the earth between the tree's roots, digging up a bundle of long green shoots with bulbous muddy roots. Brows raised, she asked, "What are you doing?"

Hunter looked up, surprised to see Nessa standing over him, hands on hips, staring down in bemusement.

"Wild onion," Hunter said, as if that explained everything. "It'll add a bit of flavour to our next stew."

"I'm not entirely sure how to respond to finding a grown man digging in the mud with his hands for some sad looking plants," Nessa mused.

"Mother is of the same opinion as you, oddly enough," responded Hunter as he shook the wild onions, making granules of mud fall off.

"Hmm. Do you do this often then, for people to form such opinions of you?"

"Strangely enough, yes."

At Nessa's quizzical expression, Hunter elaborated. "I'm a nineteen year old man. It would be weird if I didn't get mud under my fingernails on occasion."

"Nineteen year old man-child," Nessa corrected.

Hunter snorted, dismissing her words.

"You do realise that we don't have any meat left for a stew, don't you? Unless fish counts."

Hunter scoffed, "Fish isn't meat." He stood, stuffing the wild onions into his pocket, limp green shoots hanging out of the top, and moved around the tree to their bags. "And anyway, I plan on changing that."

"How so?"

"I'm going to set up some traps and hope that some nice, tasty animal will stumble across them."

Nessa surveyed the land around them, seeing nothing other than a few songbirds fluttering through the sky in the near distance. "And what poor creature do you plan on catching out here?"

"I'm sure there are a few pheasants lurking around in the long grass." His eyes brightened. "Or maybe we'll get lucky and catch a squirrel or two."

"A squirrel?" Nessa had never heard of eating such a thing.

"Sure, they're small, but I've heard on good authority that they taste something divine."

"I don't care how divine they taste, I'm not eating a squirrel."

Hunter laughed, and strode off to set some traps.

༄ ♦ ༄

A few hours later, a pheasant and two quails were roasting on a spit over the fire. No squirrels though, thank God. Nessa idly watched as they browned, her hand resting on the dragon that was curled beside her in the grass, fingers gently brushing over the ridges of its scales. They gleamed with hypnotic beauty, and Nessa's eyes were constantly drawn to them.

Slowly, she trailed her fingers down its back and over its wing, which was loosely tucked against its side. The little dragon watched her with lazy, half open eyes, unworried as Nessa traced the tapestry of tiny veins that sat just beneath the membrane's surface, which was as thin and delicate as a butterfly's wing.

A cold breeze blew in from the marshland, rousing Nessa. She rose and crossed over to the tree, hoping that her cardigan had now dried. Hunter was reclined against the trunk, long legs stretched out in front of him, absently twirling a lock of his longish hair around a finger. His brow was creased and his eyes were distant as he pondered silent thoughts.

Nessa stepped past him and moved over to the branch that her clothing was hung on to dry. The sun had set an hour ago and the night was dark. The fire gave off a ring of light, but it didn't quite reach where she stood. Nessa managed to find what she was looking for, and was searching for any sign of dampness when the air behind her stirred.

One moment, she was standing. The next, flat on her back.

Stunned, Nessa stared up at the stars, visible through the tree's branches that had yet to open their leaves. Hunter leaned over, his head blotting them out. "Hmm," he muttered, brows drawing together in a frown. "This might be harder than I first thought."

"What the hell was that for?" Nessa growled, pushing herself up onto her elbows.

"I'm teaching you how to fight."

"And what does throwing me to the ground

teach?"

"You, nothing. However, it tells me that you have absolutely no experience in self-defence."

"Couldn't you have just asked me that?"

Hunter shrugged. "I suppose I could have. That didn't occur to me."

"Of course not," muttered Nessa, picking herself up from the ground. "And besides, despite the lack of self-defence tutelage, I'll have you know that I handled myself pretty damn well when it came to the bandits. I even knocked Grover out when he stole the dragon egg."

"You got lucky when it came to Grover. He didn't expect an attack. If he had, then a fight would have ensued. A fight that he would have won."

Nessa was irked. "You can't know that."

"Fine then. If you can hit me, I'll leave the subject alone."

"Fine then," Nessa murmured, raising her fists. Hunter smirked and followed suit, looking a lot more sure of himself than Nessa felt. She circled him, trying to buy herself some time. Hunter mirrored her movements with keen eyes, shifting his weight ever so slightly.

Deciding that speed was her best bet, Nessa sprang forward, fist aimed at his face. It was caught before it hit his nose, never really being a threat. Nessa scowled as Hunter looked at her fist, suspended in the air by his hand, with an amused expression.

"A reasonable effort," Hunter said, releasing her hand, "but poorly executed." Nessa's mouth fell open. "I could see your punch coming from a mile away."

"You could not."

"I could. You projected your intention before the very idea had even finished forming in your head."

"Bollocks."

"Try again then."

She did, aiming her punch at his stomach this time. It never hit, once again being caught mid strike.

"How do you do that?" Nessa exclaimed.

"You have tells. Very obvious ones, I might add."

"Obvious tells?"

"Your eyes flick to where you're aiming at."

"Oh."

"And you have terrible form."

Nessa glared, irritated that it wasn't going how she had hoped.

"First off," Hunter said, "you need to maintain eye contact, or look at their upper body. It will help you to predict what they'll do. It's also a good intimidation tactic. It unnerves them, puts them on edge. It makes them realise that you mean business."

Nessa thought that was an awful lot of effort just to land a punch. "Can't I just whack people on the head if they come near me?"

Hunter blinked slowly. "No. No, you cannot."

"Why not?"

"Because it's impractical to carry a damn branch around with you wherever you go. Not to mention that it would raise a few eyebrows."

"I didn't mean that I would carry a branch around with me. I just meant that, if needed, I would grab the nearest available whacking thing, and... Whack."

"Whack?"

"Whack," Nessa confirmed.

Hunter shook his head. "As entertaining as that sounds, you need to know how to handle yourself if a situation arises."

"And is that likely to happen in the near future?"

Hunter hesitated.

"Because I'm not going to be around here for much longer," Nessa reasoned. "Am I?"

Hunter's eyes darted to the sleeping dragon.

Nessa decided to ignore the weight behind his gaze, continuing on. "Because we'll be at The Hidden City soon, and your friend Orm will be there, and he'll know of a way to get me back home."

"Humour me for a few minutes."

Nessa sighed, knowing that his heart was in a good place, and nodded. "Five minutes."

Hunter grinned brightly. "Excellent."

Nessa felt that she had just made a great mistake.

Chapter 20

Dinner was a simple affair. One that allowed Nessa plenty of time to brood over the self-defence class she had somehow found herself having. Five minutes had magically turned into an hour, and in those sixty minutes, Nessa hadn't been able to land a single blow. Not that she was bitter over that at all.

She followed all of his instructions, took on board all of his advice, and yet the end result had been her flipped over his shoulder. Yes, she might have lost her temper a bit at the end. But who doesn't resort to trying to hit someone over the head with a rather large branch if provoked? It might have been a little out of line. However, she hadn't planned on whacking him hard, and in no way deserved to be made airborne. Anyway, he was being as annoying as hell, looking smug every time he managed to dodge a kick or catch a punch.

Nessa nibbled at her piece of cooked pheasant, watching him devour a quail. Kicking my ass must have made him work up quite an appetite, she mused.

"How do you do it?" Nessa demanded. "Move so quickly and such."

Hunter peered at her from across the fire, one brow quirked. "Experience."

"And how come I couldn't even hit you once, even when I did exactly what you said to do?"

"Lack of experience."

"You are very infuriating."

"Mother is of the same opinion too, weirdly enough."

"Yes, how very weird."

Hunter snickered and Nessa turned her attention to the dragon, who sat beside her, staring with large cat-like eyes. She pulled off a sliver of pheasant meat and held it out between pinched fingers. The dragon stretched out its long neck and took a delicate sniff, then rejected it, turning away and tucking its head under a wing.

Growing frustrated, and more than a little bit worried, she set the piece of meat by it. The hatchling ignored it, folding its wing tighter against its body. It had hatched hours ago and still had no interest in eating.

"Don't worry yourself over it," Hunter said,

sensing her distress. "If it were hungry then it would eat the meat." Nessa was uncertain, nudging the meat closer to the dragon. "If you keep doing that, you'll just piss it off and it'll be making a meal out of your fingers." Nessa stopped with her attempts.

Hunter abruptly said, "You should name it."

"Why would I do that?"

"To call it off when it's attacking someone." Forever the practical one.

Nessa was unimpressed. "That's not helpful."

"Is it not? I would have thought the poor bugger it's chomping on would disagree."

"Hunter," she warned.

"Mankiller springs to mind," Hunter carried on, regardless. "Or maybe just Killer? The range of names open to us is simply overwhelming. I mean, just from those two ideas we can delve into names such as Destroyer or Exterminator. Oh, how about Slayer?"

Nessa shook her head.

"I'd put my money on either Destroyer or Slayer. They're my favourites."

Nessa was silent, trying to figure out if he was serious or merely joking. "You've given this some thought."

"I have."

"Too bad those names are terrible."

"Terrible?"

"Terrible," confirmed Nessa. "Whilst somewhat

amusing, they are not appropriate names for a dragon."

"I think you'll find they're far more appropriate than you give them credit for."

"I'm leaning towards a nicer name. You know, something that's not all doom and gloom."

Hunter's eyes lit up. "I understand now. You want a nice girly name. Fine, fine. If that's what you want, then that's what you'll get. Daisy? Poppy?"

Nessa groaned.

Hunter mock gasped. "Buttercup."

"I refuse to acknowledge your existence until you're helpful." Nessa stood and collected her sleeping bag, unrolling it.

"When am I not helpful?" Hunter laughed.

"Right now you're not," Nessa muttered.

Still chuckling, Hunter unrolled his sleeping bag near the fire. "Are you still mad because I flung you to the ground?"

Nessa gave him a stony glare.

"Alright, you are." Hunter laid down. "In all fairness, I didn't mean to do it that hard. You caught me by surprise, branch and all, and I just reacted."

"And laughing at me afterwards?"

Hunter looked at her with merry eyes. "That might have been a little out of taste," he admitted. "But the face you pulled was priceless."

"Well," Nessa said as she pulled off her boots, "I'm glad you find me so entertaining."

"Mmm, life right now would be a lot more

boring without you." His eyes slid closed. "I'll try to think up some of the names the dragons in times gone by had. Maybe you'd like them a little more than my ideas."

Nessa snuggled into her sleeping bag and smiled into the night. "Thank you, Hunter," she whispered, grateful for more than him just thinking up some names. She was thankful for his companionship, for his help, and for him getting her far away from Ironguard. He said that his life would be boring without her in it, but without him in hers, who's to say that her life would be worth living if Margan had got his way.

Hunter's snores rose into the air, oblivious to the gratitude both spoken and silent. With a smile on her lips, and with her hand resting on the dragon hatchling curled up beside her, Nessa dreamed of stars and friendship.

ಐ♦ಔ

Morning came all too soon. Nessa groaned and rolled onto her back, the sunlight turning her eyelids red. The hour was still fairly early, but the sky was a bright blue with tinges of violet. Nessa sat up and rubbed the sleep from her eyes, and found herself completely alone. Hunter was nowhere in sight and neither was the dragon.

Hunter's sleeping bag was neatly rolled up and his boots were gone, so he must have wandered off somewhere a little while ago, but the dragon…

Nessa stood and spun around, searching for a sparkle of purple in the long grass. "Dragon?" she called. "Where are you?" She circled the tree, hoping that it was hiding on the other side. It wasn't. She looked up at the branches over head, wondering if it had perhaps flown up there, but all she could see was a pair of dozing pigeons.

Nessa cupped her hands around her mouth. "DRAGON?" she shouted, as if she actually expected to receive an answer. Her voice carried over the hills, but no little purple dragon appeared.

"DRAGON?"

Nothing.

"Bollocks," Nessa muttered, turning in a circle. *Where could it have wondered off to? I really should have given it a name.*

She paused, her mind coming up with all kinds of scenarios that the little creature could have got itself into. She didn't like a single one of them. "Slayer?" she called hesitantly, trying out Hunter's name suggestions on a hopeful whim, "Destroyer?"

Nessa shook her head. "No, no. This is insanity. A stupid idea. It's more likely to respond to 'Dragon' than those." In any event, Nessa gave up calling for the dragon and instead tried to find Hunter, thinking that maybe it had followed him wherever he had gone.

On the second call of his name, Hunter appeared out from behind a tangle of bushes and brambles, hopping on one foot whilst trying to put on a boot.

"What's wrong?"

Nessa grinned at the sight and moved closer. "I can't find the dragon. Is it with you?"

Hunter shook his head. "It was still asleep when I left to freshen up and get changed. That was not too long ago. It couldn't have got—"

A shrill shriek pierced the air not too far from them, the sound of an animal in distress. Nessa's heart jumped and without thinking, she ran towards the source, only for it to stop suddenly. Nessa found herself running blind for a brief moment, then she came upon a scene that made her stop dead.

"Ha," Hunter said, coming up behind her. "I've come up with another name for it. Bunnybiter."

Nessa found herself speechless.

"At least you don't have to worry about it going hungry anymore."

In a circle of freshly flattened grass, was the dragon and a body of an unfortunate rabbit. Blood and bits of fur covered the dragon's snout, and Nessa turned away as it bit into the rabbit's soft belly.

"I really could have gone without seeing that this early in the morning. Or, come to think of it, ever."

Hunter clapped her on the back. "You're a delicate soul, Nessa. And I'll leave you to it. I'm going to check the snares again, although I bet the dragon's scared off the wildlife with its little display of its hunting abilities."

Nessa made a sound of acknowledgement, and

Hunter moved away, whistling a cheery tune as he disappeared over the hill with only one boot on, the other slung over his shoulder. She looked at the dragon, wondering if it had finished, and gagged.

Okay, rabbits have a lot more innards than I had thought.

There was a crunch of bone. Nessa grimaced and walked to a safe distance away where she didn't have to hear what was happening. Long minutes passed, then the grass parted and the little dragon sauntered over to her, rubbing its side against her ankle in greeting.

"All done?" she asked.

Another rub against her ankle.

"I'll take that as a yes." She gathered the dragon hatchling up in her arms and headed back to the campsite.

Nessa set the dragon down on her sleeping bag, where it proceeded to clean itself, tongue rasping over scales, and went over to the tree. Her clothing hung dry on one of the branches, and when she pulled them off, they retained their draped shape, stiff from the marsh's waters. They didn't smell all that fresh either. Nessa folded them up and packed them away, as they would be unwearable until they had been washed, and decided that she would have to wear the dress during today's march.

She had just finished rolling up her sleeping bag when Hunter returned with his catch of two small rabbits.

"Behold," he cried, dumping them on the ground, "the mighty hunter returns with his prize."

Nessa looked down at the poor creatures, and noticed that the dragon had paused in cleaning itself, staring intently at the rabbits. Hunter, too, saw this and quickly swiped them up, holding them out of the dragon's reach. For a second the dragon looked half tempted to try and retrieve them, eyes locked and tail twitching. It quickly lost interest, though, and went back to cleaning its gleaming scales.

"If it eats these rabbits, I'll kill it," Hunter informed her.

"No, you won't," Nessa said. "But I'll be sure to pass on your threat since it has such a clear understanding of the human language."

"Very funny, you little short-ass."

"I thought so. And I'll have you know that I'm not short. I'm of a perfectly average height."

Hunter quirked a brow and ran his eyes over her. It didn't take him long. "You're short."

"Maybe you're just abnormally tall. Ever think of that?"

"No, I haven't. Thank you for opening my eyes to my height. I will be more careful when it comes to low door frames from now on."

"You're welcome."

Hunter's lips twitched as he gazed over at the smoking forest. "Are you eager to have something for breakfast or can we make a move?"

Nessa gave it some thought. She wouldn't mind having something to nibble, but she could go a few hours before she got too hungry. And anyway, Hunter seemed filled with nervous energy, eager to head off. "I suppose I'm alright for the time being," she said. "Although a nice lunch will be greatly appreciated."

"Excellent." Hunter rubbed his hands together. "I want to find some decent shelter before the storm rolls in. It feels like a big one."

Nessa paused in her task of packing up camp, taking a moment to look up at the sky in amusement. Other than a few wispy clouds, which looked more like sad pieces of cotton wool than a mighty storm cloud, there was nothing but bright blue sky and the distant haze of the forest's smoke.

"Okay then," Nessa muttered.

A few minutes later their camp was cleared, the fire was extinguished, and the two of them, plus a very sleepy dragon hatchling, were making their way through the grassland, heading towards the forest.

The line of pine trees loomed before them, each as straight as a pin and packed closely together. As Nessa stepped into the forest, the ground beneath her feet changed, becoming soft and sticky. She looked down, finding that the earth was black and that heavy clumps were sticking to her boots, weighing them down. Nessa's lips curled in disgust. For a while, she plodded behind Hunter, trying, with some degree of success, to kick off the tacky mud. This, thankfully, became less of a problem the further they travelled into the forest, as the black earth became covered in a thick carpet of stodgy moss and brown needles.

A breeze gradually grew throughout the hour, making the trees around them whisper and sigh, but still, the sky remained blue. Much to her regret, Nessa found herself getting hungry faster than she had first thought. To take her mind off her growling stomach, she began thinking about the story Hunter had told her yesterday, and a few things piqued her curiosity.

"Hunter," Nessa enquired, "when you were telling me about the Dragon Riders, you mentioned something about them now being a twisted image of what they were..."

Hunter made a communicative noise.

"...what happened?"

Hunter frowned. "Well," he said slowly, "what I was told— and am starting to wish I had paid more attention to when I was being told it— was that what happened to the Riders was connected to one key event." He looked at her, then at her bag, which rested full against her hip.

"Dragons are creatures of magic," Hunter began, "and through the bond, their Riders become something else. They change, becoming stronger, immensely stronger, and able to access magic, something only an Old Blood or a small number of their lingering descendants can do.

"They have every advantage. And back in the day, very few creatures would be able to best a dragon, and nothing could take on a group of Dragon Riders and survive, not even an army. Or so they thought for a time."

Hunter looked at her over his shoulder. "As I mentioned yesterday, they took it upon themselves to govern the land, which at the time was only one kingdom. This proved problematic, though, and things unseen and terrible slipped through their grasp. So they split the kingdom, dividing it into twelve smaller ones."

"The Twelve Kingdoms," Nessa murmured absently.

"The Twelve Kingdoms," Hunter agreed. "One kingdom for each of the Twelve Houses to rule over. Twelve Kingdoms for the twelve Dragon Riders to protect.

"But as it is, all good times must come to an end.

"An army came from the west, shrouded in an eerie mist, invading our lands, lining our coastline with their black ships and filling the fields and rivers with blood."

"You seem to have a problem with people coming from the west," Nessa mused.

Hunter snorted, and then continued. "Battle by battle, the Dragon Riders began losing the war. Our army was nearly decimated, famine was rife, and things looked bloody bleak. But then, without reason, the invaders and their strange mist left. Just like that. When they were so close to winning the war, they just packed up and went, never to be seen again."

Nessa frowned. "One would have to question their motives for coming in the first place, then."

Hunter ignored her. "After the war, the Twelve Houses and the Dragon Riders were mere shadows of themselves, and the land was plunged into a crippling darkness. Out of that darkness emerged something far worse than anything they had ever faced before. A new Rider came forth, taking the lands for himself, ruling over them with an iron fist and his black heart for near five hundred years. Any Dragon Rider who refused to join him, or showed any weakness, was crushed, as was anyone who tried to stand against him.

"There are fields up in the north, where the first uprising tried to take root, that overflow with the bones of a town that King Kaenar had slaughtered in retribution. The Bone Fields are what they are known by these days, the name of the town long forgotten."

Nessa felt sick to her stomach at the thought. "Can't someone at least bury them? Give those poor people some dignity and honour instead of leaving them like that, just lying around?"

Hunter shook his head. "People have tried in the past, but the Bone Fields... They're a cursed place. None who dare venture there ever return. I've heard whispers that tell of ghostly creatures that skulk in the ruins." Hunter sighed. "Anyway, that was hundreds of years ago. Those poor souls are long past caring."

"It's a sad thought, though, to think of those people there, nothing but bone, abandoned by the world, their names forgotten."

"It's a terrible thought," Hunter agreed. "But it's the reality we have to face. The Dragon Riders we have today are made in his image, the king's: powerful, cruel, and without a heart. There was no one who could help those who call the Bone Fields their forever home, just as there's no one to stop something like that from ever happening again."

"That's bleak." It really was. Any questions Nessa might have had faded to the back of her mind, where they would stay. God, she would be glad when she got back home, far away from mad murderous kings and Dragon Riders. Where there was running hot water and comfy beds, and the worst hazard she had to face was boredom. Well, she'd be glad for the most part. Nessa's hand rested on her bag, on the dragon hatchling inside, and her eyes lingered on Hunter with a touch of wistfulness.

"Anyway," Hunter said, "I've made some progress with dragon names."

Relieved at the change of subject, Nessa smiled. "Oh yeah?"

"Yeah, and they're way better than the ones I came up with yesterday."

"I'm glad."

Hunter's eyes were merry.

When no names were forthcoming, Nessa was forced to ask, "Are you going to tell me them, then?"

"Maybe later," Hunter said after a second of thought. "I reckon they'll be best told around a fire this evening."

"Oh dear."

"The anticipation can build during the day."

"Oh God."

Hunter laughed. "You'll love these ones, I promise."

"Promise me that you'll actually give me a couple of serious names, at least?"

"Sure," he said, "if that's what you want. Although, saying that, we don't even know if it's male or female. If we knew that, it would make it easier to name."

Nessa thought back to the small yet razor sharp claws, and the needle-like fangs that she had seen in action that morning. "Well, since you have more knowledge of dragons than I do, I'll leave that job to you."

Hunter held up his hands, displaying scabbed over scratches. "Dragon doesn't seem to like me very much."

"I suppose it will remain a mystery for the time being then."

"Or until we find some claw-proof gloves."

Nessa opened her mouth, about to comment,

when a cold wind blew through the trees, carrying a chill and the smell of smoke. She wrapped her arms around herself as it strengthened, making the treetops bend and sway.

"Is that smoke?" Nessa asked. "Why does the forest smell of smoke? If we're heading towards a forest fire, I will be most unimpressed."

"We're not going towards any forest fire," Hunter chuckled. "This is the Burning Forest. Smelling smoke is the usual state of things here."

"And why is that?"

"Well, the Fire Lizard, a common species in this region, has the ability to breathe fire."

"There are lizards that can breathe fire?"

"Well, it's more like a spark. But it's enough to set fire to shrubbery and the peat reserves underground, which have a tendency to smoulder for a while. Hence the smoke."

"Huh," Nessa murmured. "Fascinating." *Fire breathing lizards. Who would have thought it?* Her eyes ran over the ground, hoping to catch a glimpse of these intriguing creatures, but they were playing coy. While she could hear things moving around in the undergrowth, she didn't see anything other than a few pigeons desperately trying to out-fly an ominous cloud.

Nessa stopped and stared at the approaching storm, wondering how a beast like that had managed to sneak up on them so quickly. It stretched from horizon to horizon, a black mass of churning chaos that was barrelling towards them with shocking speed.

"That doesn't look good," Nessa said.

Hunter paused and gawked. "No, no it is not."

An hour later, thunder rumbled overhead as the storm cloud overtook them with a rush of wind that made the trees groan. The sun disappeared behind a blanket of rolling darkness, plunging the land into premature night. Frigid rain poured down, soaking Nessa in a matter of seconds, making the dress stick to her skin, the skirts cling to her legs, tangling around them.

"Come on!" Hunter shouted over the howl of the wind, grabbing her hand. "There's a cave in the mountain's foothills just under a mile away. We need to get to it, and soon, before we catch our deaths!"

Nessa nodded, desperate to be out of the rain, and let Hunter pull her along at a breakneck speed.

The ground swiftly became riddled with rapidly growing puddles, and the trees seemed determined to knock into them or to trip them up. Hunter, though, seemed to have cat-like senses, and managed to avoid running into them, for the most part.

Thunder bellowed above them, making the ground shake and their bones rattle. Nessa clutched at Hunter's hand as he sped up, going full speed through the darkening forest. An instant later, lightning flashed. It showed, for a brief disconcerting moment, the world in blinding white light. The trees cast haunting shadows, their branches seemingly reaching out to grab at Nessa, and the ground appeared to be alive with snake-like streams.

As quickly as the lightning appeared, did it vanish, leaving them running blind and dazed.

A peculiar sensation came over Nessa, one that was unrecognisable yet somehow familiar to her. Everything faded until there was nothing but a silence so deep and profound, it was like the deepest reaches of space had wrapped themselves around her.

Then the world tipped sideways and Nessa fell.

Chapter 21

The ground was wet. Not with rain, but with blood. With a yelp, Nessa pushed herself up on translucent arms, trembling from her fall, and stared at the crimson liquid that covered her, fresh and running down her front in think rivulets.

"Not real," Nessa muttered, trying to convince herself of that fact. "Not bloody real. You've whacked your head. Or gone insane. Maybe both?"

If that was the case, then it was one hell of a hallucination Nessa was having. The term hell was surely an apt description of the scene she had fallen, quite literally, into.

All signs of the forest and the storm had gone, replaced by Armageddon.

The moon hung low in the sky, watching over with a slitted eye, and the air was filled with the sound of metal clashing against metal and unearthly screams. The ground rumbled with what felt like footsteps of a gigantic beast moving unseen. Nessa jumped to her feet, fearful that the creature might be upon her.

Standing, Nessa found herself engulfed in a thick cloud of smoke. Her eyes watered and she coughed, stumbling away before it choked her. She rounded a wall, which was mostly in pieces, and reeled back a step.

She stood by what had once been a stone building, one that now lay in burning mounds of wood and stone. Before her was a valley that opened up onto wide fields that were framed by the tall ridges of steep hills.

A town had once stood there. It had now met the same fate as the building beside her. Angry flames reached high into the sky from ransacked dwellings, belching great torrents of black smoke. The inhabitants lay where they had been cut down, bloodied and dead. No one had been spared in the slaughter, not man, woman or child. Their bodies covered the streets, their blood flowing over the ground. Some lay in piles, where they had tried to save one another, only to have that luxury denied, while others had been butchered as they had tried to run.

Bile rose in Nessa's throat, and she forced her eyes away from the harrowing sight.

A war was being fought out in the fields, twin

armies battling against each other, one clad in black armour and the other in gold. Shouts, screams and groans came from those fields as the men warred, the sounds cutting through Nessa's ears and making her want to cry in distress.

Nessa turned, no longer able to bear witness to the atrocities that were unfolding before her, knowing that there was nothing she could do to help those poor souls in the ravaged town or in those war torn fields.

The earth rumbled again, nearly knocking Nessa to her knees. The wall beside her crumbled and fell, narrowly missing her as she leapt away. Flames reached high into the air as they caught and spread, bright and fearsome, and a shadow moved behind them, a giant shape that slowly slithered down the side of what had once been a mighty tower.

The creature was monstrous in size and seemed to suck in all light. Its scales shone dully with splatters of blood, and its venomous red eyes gleamed with a terrible glee. Huge bat-like wings buffeted the air, stirring up flames and embers in a torrent of wind.

It took Nessa a moment for her mind to accept what she was seeing, but when it opened its jaws and released a thunderous roar into the sky, she couldn't deny it.

The nightmarish creature was a dragon, one a hundred times bigger than her hatchling. It skulked around the burning ruins, snout sniffing at the air. It twisted and stared upwards, nostrils flaring. It stood with its side to her, its wings tucked in close to its body, offering Nessa a profile view.

Perched in an unusual saddle was a man.

Though dwarfed by the monster he rode, the man was somehow an intimidating sight unto himself. Dressed in black armour with red inlay, he was a likeness of his dragon, whose scales shimmered with flecks of deep crimson. On his head was a helmet that concealed much of his face, leaving only his eyes and mouth visible.

Even from the distance of fifty or so feet between them, Nessa could see that his eyes glinted like black diamonds, filled with evil delight as he beheld the sight of destruction before him.

This, Nessa absently knew, *must be one of the Dragon Riders Hunter was talking about.*

The dragon growled, making the very air tremble, and the Rider followed its stare, gazing up at the sky over the battlefield. Nessa too, looked, and saw a sight that made her stomach drop.

There, flying over the fields of fighting men, was another dragon.

Silhouetted against the squinting moon, the dragon rapidly approached.

Large membranous wings flapped leisurely as the dragon dipped over the battlefield, dropping in close to a battalion of black armoured men. It seemed to happen in slow motion. Even from such a distance, Nessa saw the dragon open its jaws, saw the flames licking its tongue for a suspended moment before a torrent of purple tinged flames burst forth, released over the men in black. They screamed. They screamed until they fell abruptly silent.

In response, the man and dragon beside Nessa gave a thunderous roar.

The distant dragon, with mighty beats of its wings, swiftly descended upon them, leaving the battlefield far behind.

It landed with an almighty *thump* that made everything in the vicinity rattle.

While the black dragon was darkness personified, this dragon was all regal beauty and elegance. It was lighter in build, graceful limbs and a more angled face. A deep royal purple, it was only a few shades darker than Nessa's amethyst hatchling, and she found it easy to envision what it would look like grown.

The image took her breath away.

Saddled on the purple dragon's back was a man clad in golden armour. Nessa stared, realising that they were the leaders of the battling armies, finally coming together.

"Well met, brother!" the man in black shouted. "I must say, I am impressed. Never would I have ever thought that you and your band of vagabonds would achieve so much. You have caused me much grief these past few months."

"And here it will all come to an end," called out

the man in gold. "We will soon be free."

"Indeed, you will be free," the man in black promised, dark amusement dancing in his eyes, "but not in the way you think."

Growling at one another, the dragons began circling, trapping Nessa in the middle of their ring. She cast around, desperately searching for a way of escape. The dragons proved to be a very secure wall of scaled muscle, and Nessa couldn't see a safe way out.

The golden man scowled, the tightening of his eyes just visible through the eye holes of his helm. "Enough of this!" he barked. "Long enough have you got away with the tortures you have caused, the pain you relish in making. It must stop."

"Then let's have at it, brother dearest," the man in black cried. "Let us battle one another, sword against sword, and let fate decide who wins."

"So be it. If anyone should have to stop you, it should be me, as punishment for ignoring what you have done for so long, for being ignorant of your ways and of your cruelty." He had sounded so sure of himself, so confident to start with, but now the golden man's words were tinged with anguish.

Nessa paused at her attempted retreat. His voice, rasping and deep, was oddly familiar. She frowned, a touch unnerved, and peered at him, trying to see the man beneath the golden armour. It was an impossible task, one made harder by the moving dragon.

They seemed to have come to some kind of agreement, and both men dismounted, hitting the ground in union, landing with panther-like grace, their armour clinking sharply. Nessa swallowed nervously. Whatever was happening couldn't be good.

I need to get out of here, Nessa thought frantically. But how? The last two times she had a waking dream, she had been forced out of them, pushed out in one way or another. Nessa closed her eyes, picturing Hunter's face, the forest of trees and smoke, and wished to be back there.

She didn't need to open them to know that her wishful thinking hadn't worked.

Nessa swore under her breath. She was still there, trapped between a pair of aggressive circling dragons, and with two armed men coming towards her. Evidently they couldn't see her, which was a comfort. An incredibly small one, but one nonetheless. Otherwise, Nessa was sure, she would have been on the business end of the black armoured man's sword as he strode past her, twirling the weapon in question.

Nessa scurried back, only getting so far before nearly running into a dragon. The creature obviously couldn't sense her presence, as its focus didn't shift from the black dragon opposite. Nessa gulped, eyes wide as it paced past her, so close, she could see every detail; its pearlescent white claws, undoubtedly sharper than the finest blade; how scales the size of dinner plates met neatly together without a gap between them. In the firelight, those scales of the deepest of purples shone with inner light, shimmering with a golden hue as the creature moved. For a split second, Nessa thought she saw a glimpse of her future.

The dragon prowled past, making the ground rattle a little with each step. Nessa only came up to the creature's knee, barely. Her attention sidled away from it as the men met in the middle, swords drawn, muscles tense, ready to spring into action.

"Give up this lunacy," the golden man begged, "and let us begin again, as brothers should."

"No, *brother*," the man in black spat. "Too long have I stood behind you, too long have I been ignored. I will complete what I have started, and I will never be invisible again."

"You have never been invisible to me. You are my brother, my shadow. I would have been lost without you by my side all these years."

"Your shadow." He shook his head sharply, anger coming off him in waves. "Your faithful servant. Well, no more! Fate has always chosen you. You, who was born a mere minute before me. Yet that minute decided *everything*. You get *everything*, and I? I get *nothing*."

"Is that what this is about?" the man in gold cried. "You're upset about inheritance. You've done this over money and titles."

"It's about so much more than that."

"Mother adores you. I do too. Is that not enough?"

"No," the man in black hissed, "it was never enough." He grasped his black sword in both hands and swung it at his brother, who lifted his with lightning speed. Their blades collided with a burst of silver sparks. The man in gold shoved back, pushing his dark brother away, and started a complex series of hard blows, dancing light on his feet. He stabbed and parried, but his brother managed to hold his ground. They were both equally skilled and neither could gain the upper hand.

Then, watching them battle each other, Nessa realised something. Neither of them were fighting at full capacity. They were holding back, each for different reasons. The golden man, she could tell, didn't want to hurt his brother. Not badly, at least, despite his words. But the man in black was just biding his time, stalling and creating a diversion whilst his monster of a dragon got into position.

It was all a trick, a trap, into which the golden man had so easily fallen.

The black dragon pounced.

It struck the smaller purple dragon with bone crushing force, wings flared and claws bared. Together they hit a wall, sending it crumbling down in a cloud of dust and flying stones, concealing them from sight.

Then, suddenly, a loud *crunch* sounded out from

the mêlée... and everything fell painfully still and silent.

The golden man reeled back, clutching at his chest, his heart. His sword fell to the ground with a resounding clap, and he collapsed to his knees. A scream tore out of his throat, raw and filled with unfathomable anguish and loss.

It was a tortured, broken sound, and it made the hairs on the back of Nessa's neck and arms stand on end.

The debris settled, revealing the aftermath.

The black dragon stood over the lifeless body of the other, blood covering its gaping mouth, covering its jagged teeth. Nessa turned away before she saw any more, not wanting it to haunt her more than it would already.

The golden man was knelt on the ground, groaning and sobbing as if a part of his soul had been torn away. Maybe it had.

With slow, hesitant steps, Nessa found herself moving closer.

The man in black armour stood over him, staring down with dark, glittering eyes. A slow grin stretched his lips, a twisted version of happiness. "Poor big brother," he cooed. "What, oh what, am I meant to do with you now? Hmm. I do wonder." Contempt and pure, unadulterated joy oozed from him. "I thought this would be the end, dearest brother. However, I'm suddenly seeing a future with us in it together. Isn't that what you wanted just a few minutes ago? You and me together as brothers should be? I like that idea. I like it very much."

Nessa's hands clenched into fists. God, she had never wanted to punch someone so much. Well, maybe one person, but that was for another time... A punch seemed too good, too kind, for such an evil man. She looked around, searching for a suitable weapon, wondering if she could actually hurt someone in a waking dream.

Now seemed as good a time as any to find out, she decided.

The golden man's sword lay near at hand, and Nessa felt that it would be perfect. Such divine retribution it would be for him to be killed by the sword of the man he had just destroyed. His own brother's sword.

Nessa bent down, reaching for the sword, and paused when she heard a whisper escape the fallen man's lips.

"Aoife... Aoife..." he murmured. "Aoife..."

"You said that I was your shadow," the black brother intoned from above them, "but now you shall be mine."

❦

Nessa woke with a body jolting sense of awareness. She stared at the rocks above her with uncomprehending eyes, not quite sure what was real or not anymore. She frowned, blinking sharply, and pushed herself up onto her elbows, finding herself tucked snugly in her sleeping bag.

She was in a cave, naturally formed with rough edges and a domed ceiling. Layers of dark compacted stone sat upon one another, seeming to move in the light cast from the small fire in the middle of the room. The entrance to the cave was some distance off, not shown by the fire's light, but Nessa could hear the sound of the storm raging on outside. Over to the side, just visible in a ring of shadows, was Hunter, fast asleep and snoring. Curled up on his chest was her little dragon, its head hidden neatly beneath a wing.

Nessa stood, and as quietly as a mouse, crossed over to them. Neither woke as she crouched beside them and carefully picked up the dragon. She held it in her arms, feeling oddly tender towards it, especially after what she had witnessed in her waking dream. Nessa carried it back over to her sleeping bag and sat down cross-legged on it, cradling the hatchling as one might a baby, albeit a scaled one. It rested there, taking deep and steady breaths, then its tail twitched and coiled around her wrist like a jewelled bangle.

Nessa smiled, and without thought whispered, "Aoife."

The dragon stirred at the sound of the name. *Its* name.

Its wing drew back and its long neck snaked up, tilting its angular head at Nessa. It blinked those great, big eyes slowly, as if with a meaning that needed to be conveyed. Nessa felt a flutter in her chest, an odd sensation that she couldn't quite put her finger on.

Was that the beginning of the mysterious 'bonding' Hunter had mentioned? A part of her scoffed at the idea, finding it ludicrous. But then, in her waking dream... The smell of smoke still clung to her nostrils and the screams still rang in her ears. The image of the broken man, sobbing for his dragon, Aoife's namesake, sprang to mind, all too fresh. It was clear to Nessa that something had been between dragon and Rider, something a lot more complex than simple affection or love. There had been a tie between them, a bond as such. What that really meant, Nessa didn't understand, not yet, and she wasn't entirely sure that she ever wanted to find out.

"Do you like that name?" Nessa murmured to the dragon hatchling. "Hmm, my little Aoife?"

The dragon blinked slowly again, and then settled back down, curling up into a tight ball on her lap. For a time, Nessa just sat there, stroking the dragon, feeling every ridge and bump of its scales, of Aoife's scales, she corrected herself. Her waking dream haunted her, staying in the forefront of her mind.

"I wonder what happened to the man in gold?" Nessa wondered aloud.

Hunter snorted and absently patted his stomach.

Realising that the dragon wasn't there, his eyes flashed open and he sat up in a hurry. Instantly, he spotted Nessa and relaxed.

"Oh good," he said. "You're awake. You had me worried for awhile there."

"Really?" Nessa smiled. "You were so incredibly worried that you fell asleep?"

"Worry is a very taxing thing. And anyway, I had to drag your unconscious ass through a storm, with the wind howling and hailstones the size of walnuts hitting me. My poor, battered body needed a nap."

"Well, poor Hunter, my lad. When you put it like that, I suppose you do deserve a break."

"I'm glad you agree." He looked her over with bright eyes, missing no detail, not her pale face or the dragon on her lap. "And with that case closed, how do you feel?"

"Tired," Nessa said truthfully, "and a little sad."

"Oh?"

Nessa was too damn weary to have another secret. "I had another waking dream," she explained. "This one was the worst, filled with death and misery."

"Is that so?" Hunter said slowly. "What happened in this one?"

"It was a battle. An army of gold fought against an army of black. Each side was led by a man that rode upon a dragon." Nessa's hand stilled on her own dragon hatchling, on Aoife. "The man in black armour tricked his brother into a dual. But it was a distraction, a deception. His dragon attacked the other, killing it. The golden man fell to the ground, screaming." Even then, Nessa could still hear the blood curdling sound of loss and anguish. "I..." She couldn't find the words and sighed, staring off at nothing, trying to vanquish the memory, the cruelty that she had seen in the dark brother's eyes.

"What else is troubling you?"

"Was that experience not enough to trouble me?"

Hunter came and sat beside her. "That's more than enough," he murmured. "But that's not all of it, is it?"

"I've never seen someone die," Nessa confessed. "I've never seen a dead body. But there, the streets were filled with them, the bodies of innocents. There were piles of them, bleeding and burning. I've never seen something so horrific."

"Well, it may be of some comfort to you to know that whatever you saw isn't happening right now. Nor is it likely to in the near future."

"The future," Nessa mumbled. "It wasn't the future. It happened in the past. I'm sure of it."

"The past?" Hunter looked contemplative. "I've never heard of such a thing happening. Not like how you've described."

"Maybe it happened so long ago that it's been forgotten?"

"Perhaps." Hunter didn't look very convinced.

Nessa sighed. "There's something else."

Hunter raised his brows.

"The thing is..." She hesitated before continuing. "This might sound a little odd."

"Because everything else is completely normal?"

Nessa ignored that remark. "I'm pretty sure that the leader of the golden army was Shadow."

Hunter looked incredulous. "Shadow!" he snorted. "I might not know exactly what you saw, but I can guarantee that whoever it was, wasn't Shadow. I doubt he's ever done anything good or honourable in his entire life."

"It sounded an awful lot like him," Nessa reasoned.

"Sounded? So you didn't actually see him then?"

"No," Nessa admitted after a slight pause. "His helmet covered his face."

Hunter nodded. "And I bet that it muffled his voice a little as well, making you think that he sounded like Shadow."

"You're probably right." Nessa let the subject go, giving him a small smile of reassurance.

Hunter nudged his shoulder against hers. "Don't dwell on it too much. You'll give yourself a headache worrying about things that you can't do anything about."

"Again, words of wisdom from you. I don't know how you do it."

"You mock me," Hunter said with false hurt. "I'm wounded, truly."

Nessa found herself chuckling, albeit somewhat weakly. The more she thought about Hunter's reasoning, the more it made sense to her. To tell the truth, beneath all the sneering, the man in black armour had sounded rather like Shadow too.

"Anyway," Hunter was saying. "If it's still troubling you, you can always ask Orm about it when we find him. He'll be more likely to know. He always did pay more attention to our tutors than I ever did."

"Is that so?"

"Oh yes," Hunter said with a reminiscent smile. "He did love his studies, which everyone at the time found rather strange."

"And you?"

"I'm just not academically inclined."

"What a pity."

"Mmm, my tutors didn't think so." He laughed. "At least not by the end."

"What did you do?"

"Let's just say that they didn't have an appreciation for a bored mind and an endless array of pranks aimed in their general direction."

"I bet they didn't," Nessa murmured, easily envisioning all the mischief Hunter could have got up to.

"They weren't very fond of me," Hunter added.

Nessa laughed. "I can't imagine why."

"I'm sure Orm will love to regale you with the stories. He does like to do that."

"Orm seems to be a font of knowledge," Nessa said, her mood lightening.

Hunter nodded. "That he is. Although, you should be aware that some of the things he knows about are completely useless."

"I'll keep that in mind."

"We'll be there soon, once this storm lets up, and you'll be able to see for yourself."

"You really think he'll know of a way back home?"

"Possibly," Hunter said. "But a greater question is, would you still want to return if he did?"

Nessa looked down at the dragon hatchling, so warm and small on her lap, and refused to meet Hunter's gaze.

"I'm not so sure anymore."

Chapter 22

The storm continued without pause. Rain and hail fell in sheets and day turned to night without much difference between the two. Neither Nessa nor Hunter ventured outside, not willing to brave the weather. Not even Aoife showed the slightest inkling of moving away from the small fire.

Nessa yawned, eyelids heavy, finding that she was absolutely exhausted and that the cave was lulling and warm, even though the fire was beginning to burn low. They were starting to run out of dry firewood, but with the downpour outside, neither of them went to retrieve more. Not that there would be any wood dry enough to burn. With the warmth and the low ceiling, the cave had a den-like feel to it. Nessa found it to be rather cosy, and it had been an effort to keep her eyes open during their quick dinner.

As she nestled into her sleeping bag, she couldn't help grinning as she spied Hunter doing the same, wincing a little as he did so. Before dinner he had insisted they have another self-defence class. It went slightly better than Nessa's first one, and while she hadn't been able to land a single punch, much to her frustration, she had at least been able to sneak in a surprise kick to his leg, to her delight and Hunter's silent approval.

Nessa traced the red marks on her arm with a finger, oddly proud of the forming bruises on her fair skin. They were her evidence of her new found skill in blocking Hunter's hits, in her ability of almost being able to predict where he was aiming. She turned on her side and used her arm as a pillow.

Hunter, it turned out, was one of those people who could fall asleep in a blink of an eye. Nessa, however, wasn't, and she spent a good long while thinking and worrying about her waking dreams. Were those strange things trying to show her something? If so, what? In any event, no answers were forthcoming, and her sleep, when it eventually came, was dark and deep and without dreams of any kind, which was a blessing in disguise.

However, it wasn't for long.

A few hours later, Nessa awoke with an ominous feeling. Keeping her eyes closed, she feigned sleep, listening. All she could hear was Hunter's steady breathing and the wild noise of the storm outside. Slowly, she opened her eyes and peered into the darkness. The fire had burned down to embers, which produced a small amount of ruddy light that did little to illuminate the cave.

Nessa sat up and gazed around at the shadows, which clung to the sides of the cave in an impenetrable cloak of sinister blackness. Cold air found its way to her without the sanctuary of her sleeping bag, making her shiver. Seeing as nothing stirred in the gloom, she rose, going over to the fire, intending to stoke it.

Drowsy, Nessa spent a few minutes coaxing it back to life. She crouched back on her heels and watched as the small flames slowly climbed over the handful of twigs she had just added, leisurely devouring them.

A whisper sounded behind her, muffled steps over the cave's hard floor. Nessa stood, wiping the dirt from her hands, and turned, expecting it to be Hunter.

It wasn't.

Hooded and cloaked, and swathed in shadows that seemed to fight against the fire's light, the man stood between her and Hunter. Nessa froze as they stared at one another, weighing each other up. He was tall and had a threatening air about him, but other than that, Nessa couldn't tell much more. He was a shadow in the shadows, and as she watched, they moved around him as if they were alive, curling over his shoulders.

Nessa's eyes darted to Hunter, finding him solidly asleep. No help from him. Aoife was nowhere to be found.

The stranger flexed his hands.

Nessa reacted on instinct.

She made to run, aiming for the cave's entrance, wanting to get far, far away.

Nessa only made it a few steps before he was upon her.

As swift as a striking snake, his arm reached out, hand grabbing at her, swinging her back. She stumbled and fell, landing hard on the ground. Stones dug painfully into her palms as she tried to push herself up, more than a little stunned.

There was no time to scream before footsteps came up behind her. Hunter's words from just a few hours ago sounded loud and clear in her head: *Should you ever find yourself down, fight tooth and nail to get back on your feet before they're on you, otherwise it's game over.*

Nessa lashed out, kicking behind her, hoping to knock them off their feet. It didn't work. They moved with inhuman speed, and her foot met with nothing but open air. Hands reached down, seizing her with bruising strength, and jerked her onto her back.

In a blink of an eye he was on her, straddling her hips, forcing down her legs, preventing her from kicking at him again. A hand ensnared her wrists, locking them together, and pinned her arms above her head.

Nessa squirmed and wriggled, feeling like a lamb laid out for slaughter.

Nessa's assailant leaned over her, and the weak firelight caught the side of his face, giving her a small glimpse of the person hidden beneath the heavy hood.

Familiar sapphire-blue eyes stared down at her.

Shadow.

A scream finally broke free.

A gloved hand clamped over her mouth, smothering the noise. Nessa struggled against him, but his grip was unyielding and his weight held her firmly down. She wasn't given an inch of wriggle room.

"Hush," he murmured, his voice low, rasping. "I can't abide the sound of screaming girls. And it won't do you any good. I'm the only soul around for miles. And your friend over there, he won't be of any use to you either. He's dead to the world." Nessa, alarmed, struggled against Shadow, making muffled sounds of protest. His grip on her wrists became painful. "Stop it, girl," he said calmly. "You'll only tire yourself out. And in any event, you'd never be able to best me. It's a pointless waste of energy."

Nessa glared at him in the dimness, knowing that his words had a measure of truth to them, and stilled.

"Now," Shadow said. "I'm going to let you up, and you're not going to scream, try to run, or attack me. Understand?"

Nessa deliberated and then nodded, seeing that she didn't really have a choice.

Shadow was slow in letting her go, almost reluctant. His blue eyes, which were the only things she could see clearly from under his hood, ran over her face. His hand loosened on her mouth, and only when Nessa kept her silence, did it withdraw completely.

"Remember, no running."

Nessa gave a grudging nod. Shadow seemed to take that as confirmation of compliance and stood in one smooth movement. He stepped away and began pacing around the cave, not so much as glancing Nessa's way as she picked herself up from the ground.

She dusted herself off, watching him with wary eyes.

Shadow prowled over to the sad little fire, his floor length overcoat slapping around his ankles with each long stride, shedding rain drops in his wake. He looked down at the pitiful flames, shaking his head, and reached out a hand, muttering a word. The fire hissed and spat, then blazed high with a mighty roar.

Instantly the cave was filled with light and warmth, more so than it naturally should be. Nessa stared at the flames wide eyed, noticing that they were tinged blue. Shadow stood over them, warming himself for a moment, and then tugged at the hooded scarf that was wrapped around his shoulders and pulled tight over the lower half of his face, loosening it.

Nessa sidled closer to Hunter and prodded him with a toe. He didn't so much as snort. She frowned, glancing between him and the man by the fire, who was busy taking off his coat and hooded scarf to dry.

"What have you done to Hunter?" she demanded, voice trembling just a little bit.

Shadow looked at her with dark, assessing eyes. "Nothing permanent, I assure you. I'm merely keeping him from waking. That way he won't interfere or cause me any more trouble."

"And how are you doing that?"

"With the same means as I got the fire going." *With a few muttered words...*

Nessa shifted, uncomfortable with the concept. "Magic?"

"Magic," Shadow confirmed.

Nessa scowled, her mind screaming, *What do I do...? What do I do...?*

"How quickly fear turns to outrage," Shadow said with a small, grim curl of his lips. "Margan once called you a wildcat. I find myself inclined to agree with him."

Nessa bristled at the mention of Margan. "I guess that's why you're here," she murmured, "to take me back to him."

Shadow ran those sapphire blue eyes of his over her, taking in her uneasy countenance and balled up fists.

"I'm to bring you back to him, yes," Shadow said after a loaded pause, making Nessa's stomach drop with dread. "But not today, I think. I've yet to make up my mind about you. I'm not one to make hasty decisions, especially now, when so much weighs on them. But I do think, perhaps, that it is best to let you have your little run around for the time being, away from Margan. It does not suit me to have you under his thumb right now."

Hope flared in Nessa's chest. "So you're letting me go?"

"For now."

"Thank you," she said tartly.

Shadow appeared faintly amused. "Don't think I'm doing it for your benefit. I'm doing it because it suits me."

"Oh, I'm not making that mistake. I distinctly recall that the last time we were face to face, you held a sword to my throat."

"The last time?" he murmured. "Hmm, I suppose I did."

Nessa didn't see an ounce of regret or apology in his eyes. "Did you follow us all this way just to tell me that you weren't taking me back to Ironguard," she demanded, "or do you have another reason?"

"I have many reasons to follow the two of you.

You mainly, I admit, although your Hunter has piqued my interest on several occasions."

Nessa felt her temper flare at the knowledge that they had been so easily followed without them realising it, thinking themselves free from Ironguard and its master. "Is that why you haven't killed him, just turned him into the male version of Sleeping Beauty?"

Shadow blinked, taken slightly aback. "You have your uses, and Hunter, I'm sure, will have his."

"And Margan has his games, as do you," Nessa boldly retorted.

Shadow inclined his head.

"So why are you here now? You can't honestly think that I'll help you."

"Margan was foolish in thinking that he could simply manipulate and control you. I won't be making the same mistakes as him. And anyway, I'm here to help you."

Nessa was incredulous. "Help me?"

"Indeed, although I can see that you do not believe me. And since you are ignorant of our world, it is unlikely that you will feel like I did for some time. However, there will be a day where you will be thankful for what I'm about to do."

His words sent a spike of fear through Nessa, and she took a step back, instincts telling her to run.

Shadow stalked forward slowly. "Remember," he said, "no running. You promised." His hand went to his waist, where a dagger was sheathed. He pulled it free, holding it with intention.

Nessa swallowed nervously and took another step back, eyeing the dagger. It was small, the blade only three or so inches in length, but the edges were wickedly sharp. The handle was ornate, aged gold encrusted with rubies. That dagger had a purpose, she knew as a tingle of warning went up her spine, a specific use.

Her eyes locked with Shadow's. "To hell with that," she snarled, having absolutely no intention of being knifed. "You really think I'm going to stand here and let you stab me?"

He stepped to the side, blocking her exit. Nessa tensed.

Shadow inched closer. "I mean you no lasting harm."

"The sacrificial dagger suggests otherwise."

Shadow looked down at it, distracted. Nessa took her chance, dashing for the cave's entrance. In a blink of an eye, he was in front of her, barring the way. Nessa skidded to a stop, realising that she was well and truly screwed.

"Can't blame a girl for trying, can you?" Nessa said, vying for time.

Shadow smiled. "It was a predictable move." He prowled closer. "I understand that this might seem frightening, but we must do this. It's a part of who and what we are."

"That still doesn't sound particularly reassuring."

"A dragon hatched for you, and that means the

bonding must be completed before it's too late."

"Bonding?"

"The egg hatching was only the start," Shadow murmured, backing her up against the cave's wall. "Now the bond must be written in flesh."

"Written in flesh? So stabbing me is off the table in favour of a simple maiming. Excellent."

"A crude way of putting it, but we'll go with that."

"Is there a better way of putting it?"

"Now is not the time for me to teach you about the bonding ritual between Rider and their dragon." Shadow came closer, boxing her into a nook, trapping her.

Nessa feigned to the right. Shadow mirrored the move. "So you're just going to *cut* me?"

"Pretty much," Shadow said bluntly.

"Look, I know things are different here," Nessa told him. "But where I'm from, it's considered rude to attack someone. Illegal actually."

"Oh, attacking someone is widely considered against the law here too."

Nessa was bewildered. "And you're still going to do this?"

"Yes."

"Huh."

Shadow edged a step closer. "If you don't resist, this will go a lot faster."

"And if I resist?"

Another step closer. "It will have the same

outcome."

"Hmm."

Shadow grinned. "Come now. The bonding must be completed, for everyone's sake."

"Bollocks to them," Nessa snarled. "And bollocks to you as well."

Shadow shifted his grip on the dagger, and Nessa abandoned all sense of self preservation. She ran, or at least tried to. Shadow, damn him and his cat-like reflexes, caught the back of her top, pulling her up short. He wasn't gentle as he flung her to the ground, and the air was forced out of her lungs on impact.

Nessa lay on the ground, breathless and stunned, vision swimming. Shadow climbed on top of her, pinning her down just like before, using his weight to hold her immobile. He fumbled with her right sleeve, yanking it to her elbow, exposing the soft skin of her inner forearm. She blinked away tears and coughed, finally able to get a small amount of air into her burning lungs, and felt the cold kiss of steel against the inside of her arm. Clarity came to her in a terrible rush.

"Don't you bloody dare," she growled.

The pressure of the blade lightened for a second. "It must be done. If not by me, then by one of the others. And believe me, I am the lesser evil."

"You know what? I don't believe you. Not one bit."

"It's like you want to do everything in the most

difficult way possible," Shadow pondered aloud. "I mean, this is the second time you've been on your back with me on top of you. Is this a regular occurrence, or am I just lucky?"

Nessa sputtered, "Bastard."

Outrage wasn't a strong enough word to describe the feeling that burned through her. How dare he find this amusing. Nessa managed to pull an arm free and brought her nails down on his face, raking four beautifully bloody gouges across his cheek.

He reared back, the amusement fading from his eyes, and caught her wrist in a punishing grip. "Wildcat indeed," he growled, forcing her arm back down, pinning it to her side with a bruising knee. "A rabid one." His hand tightened on her outstretched arm, holding it still. "Now," the pressure of the dagger increased, "let me make you into what you were born to be."

The blade cut deep, slicing her skin as easily as butter. The pain was slow to hit, and in that delayed moment, Shadow drew the dagger around her forearm, curving down in a spiral that circled her wrist, ran over her palm, and ended on the back of her hand.

Nessa stared, absolutely horrified, as blood quickly welled to the surface of the wound. Warm and heavy, it ran in thick streams down her arm, pooling at her inner elbow before dripping to the ground. She made a sound of distress, biting back a scream, refusing to do so in his presence, refusing to let him see how much her arm burned with pain. Tears clung to her eyelashes, threatening to spill, making the world blur.

"Shh," Shadow murmured, sounding oh-so-far-away. "It's nearly over." He shifted, and Nessa heard the dagger sliding back into its sheath. She sighed, thinking that her ordeal was at an end.

Shadow released her arm and it flopped to the ground, limp and hurting. Nessa didn't have the strength to move it, and so it lay where it fell, weeping blood.

Aoife took that moment to return from wherever she had been, coming to stand by Nessa's head, watching Shadow with large eyes. Nessa felt a brief flare of hope, thinking, praying, that the little dragon would go for Shadow's throat. The hatchling was small, but its claws and teeth were razor sharp. It was also fierce, as Hunter had discovered.

Nessa's hope was for nothing, as it turned out.

Eyes locked with Aoife's, Shadow slowly pulled off one of his leather gloves, presenting his hand to the hatchling, who cautiously snaked out her long neck and sniffed the offered palm. Nessa blinked heavily, trying to clear away the tears that misted her sight, and stared.

There, wrapped around Shadow's hand, was a terrible mark. Warped and twisted, the edges stretched, the scar was a dreadful thing, thick and a strange blue-ish purple. It disappeared up under his sleeve, where Nessa had no doubt that it continued up his arm.

A low hum sounded from Aoife, coming from deep within the dragon's chest, more felt than heard. Nessa labouringly turned her head, finding that even a simple task such as that suddenly took an inordinate amount of energy. Was it shock? Blood loss? Everything swam and she felt incredibly lightheaded as the humming grew in intensity.

Nessa looked at Aoife and frowned, perplexed. Had she gone mad? Was she hallucinating?

Soft light glowed from the dragon's chest, directly over its heart. It was a gentle light, dimming and brightening in a steady beat, and reminded Nessa eerily of the orb's—its egg's— shifting luminosity.

"There," Shadow murmured as Aoife turned from him and went to stand by Nessa's bleeding arm. "Just as I knew it would be. She has accepted you as her Rider."

A puff of breath tickled Nessa's hand, cool and almost soothing on the wound. Then Aoife's nose came down and touched her palm, scales rubbing against tender flesh. Nessa hissed and tears rolled down her temples. It took a great deal of effort not to beg for it to stop, for her to bite back the whimpers. She didn't want Shadow to know how scared she was, or how much it hurt. It felt like he would win if she did.

The puff turned into a long stream, and the light in Aoife's chest shifted and swelled, rising in the dragon's throat, into its mouth. It spilt out in a glittering cloud, dancing in the air like a will-o'-the-wisp before seeping into the cut on Nessa's arm. The pain was excruciating and a strangled scream tore out of her throat.

Then, after a second, the pain vanished, as did the glow in Aoife's chest. Nessa was frozen, face covered in a mixture of sweat and tears, her lungs gasping for air. God, it felt like something had burrowed deep inside her, to a place that she hadn't known existed. Her arm throbbed in time with her thundering heart.

With a smooth movement, Shadow stood and offered a hand to Nessa. She gave him a glare that conveyed her immense dislike of him quite successfully, and his hand was swiftly retracted. Shadow moved away, giving her some much needed space.

Nessa slowly pushed herself up, sitting hunched over as the world spun, feeling incredibly worn out and abused. Her hair fell in a long curtain, hiding her face from Shadow's gaze as she pulled her bloodied arm onto her lap, intending to see what he had done.

Her breath left her.

She was unharmed. Under all the tacky blood, was smooth, uninjured skin. Bewildered, Nessa ran fingers over her hand, where she knew for a fact that she had been cut, where drying blood had pooled on her palm as evidence.

"What the..?"

The skin was tender to the touch and she looked closer, spying something beneath all the blood, a discolouration of some kind. Nessa peered at it, finding it hard to see in the muted firelight, but yes, she was sure of it, there was something there. Instead of a long winding wound, she had a tattooish-like mark, not too dissimilar to the one Shadow had. Whereas his was thick and stretched, the outline blurred, hers was neat and fresh, the edges cleanly knitted together.

Nessa couldn't be quite sure in the dimness of the cave, but while the cut had been a simple curved line, her mark seemed to have more shape to it. She looked through her hair, hoping to catch a glimpse of Shadow's, but he had put his glove back on, hiding it away from her. Suspicions whirled in her mind as to what it might mean.

Nessa found the strength to stand. "What the hell have you done to me?"

Shadow watched her from his place by the fire. "I did what needed to be done. You'll come to understand in time."

"I want to understand now."

Shadow appeared to stifle a sigh, barely. "The Bonding between dragon and Rider must be written in flesh, the mark of an unbreakable vow." He nodded to her arm. "I have given you your mark, tying you to your dragon. You are now the Twelve Kingdoms' newest Dragon Rider. Congratulations."

"But I don't want to be," Nessa said, moving to stand opposite him, the fire sitting between them. "I want to go home. I want to be far away from you and Margan and goddamn dragons."

"What you want is irrelevant," Shadow informed her, dark eyes alight. "Destiny is a hard thing to fight against, especially one that was written long before you were born."

"I don't believe in destiny," Nessa argued. "I'm going to find a way back home and then forget about this place."

"Your words lack a certain amount of conviction." His amused grin returned. "And anyway, you had best forget about your home. The Twelve Kingdoms are where your future lie. The sooner you accept this, the easier things will be for you. There is no way back."

His words stuck a painful cord, one that ran close to her heart.

"I might surprise you," Nessa said stubbornly.

Shadow picked up his overcoat, slipping back into it, and began wrapping his hooded scarf around his head and shoulders. "There is very little that you can do or say that will surprise me." He turned, heading for the cave's entrance.

Perhaps Nessa should have kept her mouth shut. Perhaps she should have just let him disappear into the night. But the words came out of their own accord.

"I saw you in my dreams," Nessa blurted. "You and Margan both. You on a couple of occasions."

Shadow stilled, shoulders tensing.

Nessa knew that she had made a fundamental mistake.

With swift strides, Shadow rushed back to her, stopping frightfully close. Before she could take a step back or put a hand out to stop him, for all the good that would do, he reached out and forced her chin up, fingers digging into her jaw. His eyes locked with hers, searching.

"Already?" he whispered, startled.

That was not what she had expected him to say.

Nessa's lips parted, although she could find no words, and her eyebrows drew together.

Shadow gazed at her, understanding dawning in his deep blue eyes. He released her and stepped back, almost stumbling. He looked as if he saw her anew, as if his perception of her had changed with such a simple and bizarre statement.

Nessa could see the thoughts whirling in his head as he backed away from her, thoughts she couldn't even begin to identify and unravel.

"How swiftly things come to change," Shadow muttered, shaking himself. He spun on his heel, suddenly leaving with great haste, abandoning the circle of firelight and disappearing into the darkness of the cave's mouth.

"You have your freedom for now," he cast over

his shoulder, "but I will be coming back to fetch you when the time is right. Which may be a lot sooner than you think. Enjoy it while it lasts, however fleeting it may be, for there is no place on this earth where you can hide from me. You, Nessa, are of great importance to a great number of people. People who I'd rather not get their hands on you."

"Why?" Nessa croaked.

"You are unique, a rarity, and will play a vital part in what is to come."

Then, in a flutter of movement, Shadow disappeared into the black storm outside, leaving Nessa to stare after him.

"But what is to come?" she whispered.

Only the crackle of the fire answered her in the sudden silence.

Her arm throbbed and her knees felt weak, and then all strength left her; sobbing, she fell to the ground. Fear, it was a terrible thing. It had the ability to keep you strong, but it also had the ability to crush you if you let it. In that moment, Nessa's fear, which had kept her *fearless* a minute ago, was suddenly threatening to devour her.

Nessa didn't react as Aoife rubbed up against her side, or when Hunter's arm slipped around her shoulders, pulling her close. He murmured words to her, soothing, meaningless words, and rocked her slowly.

Nessa held herself ridged, refusing to give in, refusing to appear any weaker than she already was. But his kindness and gentleness quickly broke her down, and the tears began to fall.

For a long while, Hunter held her and comforted her without knowing why she was so distraught, and he became her anchor, preventing her from splintering into a thousand pieces.

Chapter 23

The sound of birdsong flitted into the cave, quiet but obnoxious, and incredibly unwelcome at that particular time. Nessa groaned, disorientated and uncomfortable, the cheery chirps ringing in her ears and making a headache quickly grow. She tried to ignore it, tried to fall back asleep, but once she was awake, that was it. Sleep was nowhere to be found and Nessa became all too aware of how achy she was. Dozing became impossible.

She was resting at an angle, tucked up against something warm. The hard ground was digging painfully into her hip, and Nessa blinked open tired eyes, wondering why she wasn't snuggled in her sleeping bag.

Watery light filtered in through the cave's

mouth, faintly illuminating the cosy cavern. Nessa saw that the fire had burned out and that her sleeping bag lay off to the side, empty, as was Hunter's. It then dawned on her that she was, in fact, nestled against his side, her head on his chest and his arm draped loosely around her waist. He was slouched back against the wall, eyelids twitching in sleep. Confused as to how they had ended up like that, Nessa started to slowly sit up, careful not to disturb Hunter, and her eyes landed on her hand.

Realisation came crashing over her and she remembered with frightful clarity what had happened last night. She bolted upright, spine ramrod straight. Hunter mumbled and his arm slid from her.

Nessa stared at the mark that curled around her wrist, over her palm, and ended on the back of her hand. It was strange and she turned her hand so that the light caught it at a different angle, thinking that it was her imagination playing tricks on her. But no, the mark was more than a simple winding line. It had a distinct shape to it.

"Not possible," Nessa whispered, yanking her sleeve up to her elbow.

With the mark on full display, it became abundantly clear that it was more than just a simple scar. Nessa moved her arm around, watching as the light revealed what it was.

A long thin tail wrapped around much of her

forearm, with a lean body circling around her wrist, wings drawn in close to its sides, as if the creature was diving while in flight. An elongated neck stretched across her palm, ending with a tapered head on the back of her hand. Nessa had the basic silhouette of a dragon marked onto her.

It was fine, delicate even, and might escape notice in the first instance if it were a normal scar. But whatever it was, it had a faint iridescence, a purplish sheen telling all who saw it that it wasn't right.

Nessa scowled, feeling distressed, and pushed down her sleeve, hiding as much of the scar as possible. She stood and found that a large portion of her felt bruised, probably from when Shadow had thrown her to the ground. She then caught sight of Aoife, curled up on the other side of Hunter.

Nessa felt a shift in her feelings towards the dragon, finding that it unnerved her greatly. The way it had acted towards Shadow, as if there was an understanding between man and dragon. It was as if they had spoken to one another. Also, the look in the dragon's eyes as it had laid its snout on her bleeding palm had been a most unnatural gaze, one filled with ageless knowledge and an intelligence that no animal should have, let alone one that had just hatched. Everything Nessa had thought she had known about the dragon hatchling had been thrown into doubt. Although, thanks to Shadow, she did at least know that the dragon was female. That was something, right?

Aoife stirred, her head rising out from under a wing, and looked up at Nessa with wide eyes, the pupils contracting into thin slits. Nessa scowled at the little creature, rubbing a hand against her sternum, at the tight feeling that was suddenly there. She turned and went over to her bag, rifling through it until she found something clean to wear. Well, clean-ish. Nessa had yet to wash any of her clothing that had got soaked during the crossing of the river Nyland, and because of this, most of them smelled quite strongly of marsh water.

Nessa took the opportunity, whilst Hunter was asleep, to quickly change into a pair of relatively marsh-free leggings and a red half dress. Despite the sunlight, there was a slight chill to the air and Nessa rummaged for a cardigan, finding a large one that was a rich brown, and shrugged into it, wrinkling her nose at the odour that came from the right sleeve. It was several sizes too big, and hung from her frame like a large blanket, warm and soft. Nessa rather liked it despite the slight smell, which she hoped would air out soon.

Hunter startled awake, hand absently patting the ground where Nessa had been. Aoife let out a small hiss as she was disturbed from her nap, scowling up at Hunter as much as a dragon was able to.

"I'm here," Nessa called, sensing that she was the cause of his sudden panic.

His eyes jumped to her and he relaxed with a

sigh, slumping back against the wall. "Thank the Devils." He swiped a hand over his face. "For a second there, I thought you had been kidnapped by another madman."

"No kidnapping yet," Nessa said with a forced smile. "Although the day is still young."

Hunter snorted. "Oooh, dark humour, and so early in the morning."

"Well, it was one hell of an eventful night."

"It most certainly was."

They fell into a silence, unsure how to continue. Nessa crouched down and began rolling up her sleeping bag, doing anything she could to keep herself busy, to take her mind off what had happened.

Hunter stood, yawing, and stretched his arms above his head. He wandered over to his stuff and began packing it away, his eyes every now and again darting in her direction. Nessa ignored it to start with, but it got on her nerves after a while, especially when he kept going to say something and hesitating, coming up short.

"What's on your mind?" Nessa asked.

Hunter looked at her. "Who says I have anything on my mind?"

Nessa raised an eyebrow, disbelieving.

"Okay okay," he relented. "I just want to know if you're alright?"

"I'm fine. Why wouldn't I be?"

Hunter's eyes went to her hand, to the mark that

was hidden by her sleeve that fell nearly to her fingertips.

Nessa tensed, knowing that he was asking about more than just that. "It's fine," she insisted, embarrassed that she had let herself fall apart in front of him. "I'm fine. I'd rather not talk about it right now."

"Of course," Hunter murmured. "But if you need to talk, to vent, then I'm here for you."

"I'm fine," Nessa said quietly.

Hunter, thankfully, let the subject drop. "Do you want something to eat or shall we head off?"

"I'd like to head off, if that's alright." Nessa folded her arms, hugging her middle. "It's hard... It's hard to be here after..." Her words dwindled off as she found it impossible to convey what she felt.

Despite her difficulties, Hunter understood. "Then we should get a move on. The storm has passed and the weather looks to be quite fair today."

"Excellent."

Nessa shouldered her backpack and her sleeping bag, and then picked up the messenger bag. She went, somewhat reluctantly, over to Aoife. The little dragon looked at her with reproach. Nessa felt it more than she saw it, and that unsettled her a bit. In any event, she scooped up the hatchling, ignoring the tightness in her chest and the tingle that ran through the mark. Aoife curled up in the bag without a fight, seeming to fall back into a doze.

Hunter stood waiting in the cave's mouth, and

Nessa hastened to join him, eager to leave.

Stepping outside, Nessa discovered that the cave was nestled high in a craggy outcrop of rocks. She paused, breathing in the freshness that always came after rain, as if the very air had been cleansed. Closing her eyes, Nessa tilted her head back, welcoming the feel of the sun on her face. It was like a warm caress, a pleasant thing that brought a measure of quietness to her otherwise chaotic thoughts.

Opening her eyes, Nessa took in the view.

A sea of green stretched far into the distance; The Burning Forest, with its plumes of smoke rising into the sky. The day was young and the sun hung just above the tree canopy, not yet driving away the chill of the night or chasing away the puddles. Nessa sighed, weariness creeping up on her. It was so beautiful there, so peaceful without the sound of cars and lorries, without the sight of ugly pylons and telegraph poles. It was a shame that such despicable people like Shadow and Margan inhabited such a place. Otherwise, Nessa thought, she could stay there quite happily for a little while longer. But as it was, they were there, and they were the ones in power. Nessa felt that left her with no choice, no option but to get back home, otherwise she risked falling back into their hands.

Shadow's promise sounded in Nessa's mind, finalising her decision.

You have your freedom for now...

"For now and forever, jackass," Nessa muttered as she started after Hunter, who, not realising that she had stopped, had continued ahead.

Nessa quickly caught up to him, and together they slowly descended down the rocky outcrop. The ground was uneven, the slope fairly steep in places and littered with loose stones that would shift quite suddenly underfoot. Nessa feared, on several instances, that she would lose her footing and slip to her death, rolling in an undignified manner down the rocks until she broke her neck. Thankfully, though, that didn't happen, and they reached the forest floor safely. Barren ground swiftly turned into soft pine-needle covered earth, and it evened out, becoming easier to traverse.

"Where are we?" Nessa asked, marvelling at the trees. They were at least a hundred feet tall, soaring up to the sky, determined to reach it, it seemed.

"We're in the southern foothills of the mountains which The Hidden City lies under," Hunter said. "The storm has cost us some time and we still have quite a trek ahead of us, but I imagine we'll be there in a day or so."

"A day or so?"

"Yep, then we'll start hunting for Orm. See if he can answer any of your questions."

"And see if he knows how to send me back home."

Hunter stumbled a little, tripping over himself. Odd, considering he usually moved with cat-like surety. "You still want to find a way home?"

"Of course," Nessa said, mildly confused. "Why wouldn't I?"

"Well...um..." his eyes darted to her hand, to her messenger bag. "No particular reason."

"Uh huh."

"Well..." Hunter uncharacteristically floundered, struggling to find words. Nessa raised a brow as he continued. "It's... um... Just that I thought you were kind of enjoying the mini adventure we're having. You know, seeing some of the sights, sleeping under the stars."

Nessa sighed. "I have enjoyed travelling with you, Hunter. But what happened last night made things very clear to me. I don't belong here. This isn't my world."

"I think you belong here a lot more than you realise," he mumbled under his breath.

Nessa grunted, feeling incredibly torn between following her head or her heart.

Hunter was taciturn for the next hour, brooding over something. Nessa let him have his silence, content to just listen to the multitude of bird song that filled the surrounding forest. Without the interference of humans, the woodland was as it should be, free and untamed, a sprawling city that played home to an uncountable number of animals, many of which were unafraid of their presence. Through the tree trunks, Nessa spied a small group of deer. They watched her with curious brown eyes, so close, yet showing no alarm.

Her mind a thousand miles away, she didn't realise that Hunter had come to a sudden stop. She ploughed into his back, knocking him forward a step or two with an, "Oomph."

The deer, startled, ran away, swiftly disappearing from sight.

"Let me see what he did to your arm," Hunter demanded. "I haven't had a good look at it yet."

Taken by surprise, Nessa didn't move. Hunter rolled his eyes and reached out, grabbing her hand and shoving her sleeve up. The scar was shown in all its glory, shimmering in the sunlight with its subtle iridescence. Nessa cringed, trying to tug her arm free. Hunter wouldn't let her, his hand tightening on hers. He stood there, staring, his eyes wide as if he didn't quite believe what he was seeing.

That was all the confirmation Nessa needed. The mark wasn't normal, even in that world. Unbidden, tears came to her eyes and she hastily blinked them away, not wanting to embarrass herself any more in front of Hunter. She managed to jerk her hand out of his and shove down her sleeve, hiding the mark. She wondered if it was permanent. Would it be there when she got back home, serving as a constant reminder? Or would it wash away like a bad stain when she went through another portal?

"I suppose you know what it is?" Nessa forced out.

Hunter seemed at a loss for words, and struggled to answer her. "I've only heard stories. I've never seen one up close. Not like this."

Nessa supposed she could have asked what he had heard, but she didn't. In all honesty, while she felt a small degree of curiosity, she didn't want to know anything more than what she already did thanks to Shadow's vague explanation.

Shadow.

Without wanting it to, Nessa's mind turned back to him.

Hunter, frowning, abandoned the subject and turned around, once again leading the way to their final destination. Nessa trailed behind him silently, deep in thought.

Shadow, with those hypnotic blue eyes, eyes that were strangely revealing given his otherwise impassive demeanour. They had shown her something last night, something that made Nessa question a number of things.

In that moment of brief insanity, when she had called after him, telling him of her waking dreams, he had been shocked.

Shocked, but not surprised.

Nessa found that to be rather puzzling. It was as if he had expected it, as if he had known it would happen sooner or later.

༮◆༒

The sun climbed ever higher into the sky, and then

midday was upon them. Hunter called for a break, citing hunger. Nessa dumped her backpack and sleeping bag on the ground with a sigh, rolling her shoulders. They weren't particularly heavy, but after several hours of trudging through woodland, they began to feel like lead weights, making the straps dig in painfully. She gently lowered her messenger bag and let Aoife out. The little dragon blinked sleepily and arched her back, having a nice long stretch.

Hunter quickly had a small fire going, heating a pan of last night's dinner. While she waited, Nessa paced, growing increasingly uncomfortable for some bizarre reason. Something had changed in her, something she couldn't quite put her finger on. It was a niggle at the back of her mind, an itch beneath her skin, and it wouldn't go away. Aoife was sniffing a moss covered tree trunk nearby, and Nessa eyed her with suspicion.

Nessa turned away and peered up through the tree canopy, spying the mountain range that was slowly getting closer and closer.

The first mountain loomed over them, the peak half hidden behind thin, vaporous clouds. The forest covered the base in a lush green carpet that gave way to jagged grey rock. The tip was swathed in crisp white snow. Nessa, having never seen a mountain other than in pictures, drank in the sight, marvelling at it.

Lunch was soon served, and when they had

finished, they set off once again. This time, Aoife was reluctant to go back into the messenger bag, and there was nothing that would persuade the dragon hatchling to stay in it for long. The few times Nessa had managed to get her into the bag, she would only lie still for a few minutes before she'd start squirming, claws scratching at the leather, threatening to tear it. So, the little purple dragon walked beside them, and in front of them, and quite often behind them.

Nessa didn't worry, not after a while. She had learnt that if she just relaxed her mind, then she could, somehow, sense where the dragon was, even when Aoife wandered off, going out of sight.

While Hunter had been rather reserved earlier, he was now the opposite, open and carefree, talking practically nonstop. He'd point out various bits of wildlife, telling her all about it. Like Macklock, a small shrub that had bundles of tiny flowers that would snap closed if touched. Or a climbing plant called Babblebush, which looked like a decorative version of ivy, but had the properties to make people, as Hunter put it, babble inanely. At first Nessa thought that he was joking, but it turned out that he was actually serious. She learnt that in most cases, people would touch it, unaware, and fall victim to a light bout of babbling. Hunter had then gone on to tell her, with a twinkle in his eye, that if a leaf was ingested, the babbling would be severe and last for hours.

The conversation between them was casual and easy, and Nessa found herself enjoying their march. The day sped past and before she knew it, the sun was sinking behind the trees, casting long shadows. They found a small clearing to set up camp for the night, just big enough for the two of them, an adventurous dragon hatchling, and a fire.

Nessa set her bags down against the base of a gnarled oak tree, claiming it as her spot for the night, then busied herself collecting logs for the fire, such as the routine they had naturally fallen into. Soon a fire was burning cheerfully with a decent pile of logs next to it.

While dinner cooked, Nessa settled by the tree, sitting up against it. She wished for a book to read, something to relax her mind. Reading had always had that effect on her. The ability to be sucked into a story was magical, and coincidently the only magic Nessa wanted in her life. She found herself longing for her notebook that was filled with her scribblings. It would have been nice to spend the evening sketching away, drawing the sights, jotting down some thoughts. She guessed that it was now in Margan's possession, and that made her a little bit sad, and on further reflection, slightly embarrassed.

Nessa frowned, feeling uncomfortable at the idea of him flicking through it, seeing what she had drawn, what she had written in those pages. It was a diary of sorts, stuffed full with her inner thoughts and ideas, not just her sketches of the abandoned town, although they did dominate a large part of it. There were her secrets in that notebook, things she had shared with no one.

Like her failed attempts at writing poetry.

Having Margan, of all people, look through it, seeing such things, was a massive violation.

Nessa folded her arms, cheeks glowing, and tried to turn her mind away from such mortifying thoughts. Her eyes landed on Hunter and she watched him as he moved around the side of the clearing, kicking away twigs and branches.

"What are you doing?" Nessa asked, amused.

"I'm clearing a space."

"I can see that. But whatever for?"

"For our training session," Hunter said as if it should be obvious. "I'd hate to accidentally impale you on a branch or something."

"Impale me..." Nessa's eyebrows shot up in understanding. "You want us to spar."

"Of course."

"Of course," Nessa muttered. "Hate to break it to you, but I'm not in the mood to be hit and thrown to the ground. Not today."

"Nonsense," Hunter grinned. "There's no better way to end the day than with a wee bit of violence."

"I've had my fair share of violence in the last twenty four hours," Nessa argued. "I'd like to have a day or two without getting another bruise, or two, or ten."

"Come on, people think bruises are sexy."

Nessa frowned. "I'm pretty sure that's scars." Hunter looked a little too meditative for Nessa's liking. "And no," she added, "I don't want any more scars."

"If you did, it could easily be done."

"I don't."

"Alright then."

"I'm glad we have that sorted."

"I still expect you to train, whether you want bruises or not."

Nessa was feeling stubborn. "I don't and I won't," she said, as if that was final.

Hunter's eyes tightened. "Oh, yes you will."

"Because it proved to be so helpful last night?"

Hunter glared. "Practice makes perfect."

Nessa wasn't swayed.

"Come on," Hunter murmured. "Remember how proud you were when you managed to sneak in that kick. Imagine how good you'd feel if you actually took me down."

Nessa did remember, and it had felt pretty damn good. Still did, in all honesty. "You really know how to sweet talk a girl, don't you?"

Hunter winked. "I have a way with words."

"And motivational speeches." She joined him in the cleared circle, readying herself for whatever he had planned.

His arm whipped out, shoving her back with tremendous force.

Nessa lay on the ground, stunned and more than

a bit pissed off. "I wasn't prepared for that!"

Hunter stood over her, looking down with his hands on his hips. "Rule number one: Always be prepared for anything in a fight."

"My fondness of you lessens by the hour."

"You love me really."

"I wouldn't be so sure of that."

Hunter just grinned and ordered her up.

༓✦༓

Dinner put an end to what Nessa likened as half-an-hour of torture, and before Hunter could demand they do anymore sparring, Nessa hastened over to her sleeping bag, unrolling it. She sat on it and pulled off her boots, getting ready for the night. As she did so, her hand brushed against a newly acquired bruise, making her hiss.

Aoife sauntered over, rubbing up against her, looking, for a lack of a better description, amused. Nessa rubbed way the sting, muttering under her breath. Aoife snorted, giving Nessa the distinct impression that she was being laughed at by a baby dragon. She scowled and slid into her sleeping bag, snuggling into the warmth and stared up at the stars overhead, just peeking through the tree's branches and budding leaves.

Nessa felt uneasy at being so out in the open, vulnerable even. Hunter, it seemed, didn't have her reservations, and appeared perfectly happy to spend the night under the open sky, so she kept her worries to herself. Aoife settled on Nessa's stomach, curling up into a ball, a happy hum coming from deep within her chest.

At first Nessa didn't move, but then, when sleep began tugging down her eyelids, her hand crept up and rested on the dragon.

Aoife's hum grew a touch stronger.

Chapter 24

Gloomy shadows reached long and far, swathing the rocky foothills in a cloak of dimness. Nessa and Hunter had left the sea of trees behind and now crossed through tundra that was intercepted by large slabs of grey granite. The earth rose in a steep incline and, slowly but surely, Nessa found herself hiking up the base of a mountain for the very first time. The experience wasn't lost on her, even if her legs burned with each step. The mountain stood to her right with the sun trapped behind it, silhouetting it, bright rays beaming out from either side.

Hunter was slightly ahead of her, whistling a merry tune, and Aoife was somewhere in-between them, hidden by the heather. Occasionally, there was a glimpse of purple as the little dragon slipped from bush to shrub. Seeing Aoife play, being happy and free, brought a smile to Nessa's face. The dragon picked that moment to shoot up a pile of rocks, eyes locked onto something below, the tip of her tail twitching. Nessa paused, watching her, wondering what the little dragon was up to.

Aoife pounced, leaping into a large bush, disappearing from sight. Branches quivered and shook, and with a chattering cry, a bird darted out, wings flapping furiously as it took to the air. Aoife's head popped up out of the shrub, watching the bird fly away with large, disappointed eyes.

Hunter laughed, "And the dragon should keep to catching rabbits."

Aoife's lips twitched at Hunter's words, a half-hearted growl.

"Out flown by a sand warbler too." Hunter shook his head. "Oh, the shame."

Aoife was eyeing Hunter's ankles a little too intently for Nessa's comfort.

"I don't think mocking a dragon is a particularly wise idea," Nessa said.

Hunter grinned. "I don't think it can understand the human language."

"Really? Because it's glaring at you with a murderous glint in its eyes."

Hunter looked at the angry little creature, eyebrows raised. "Maybe you're right."

"And anyway," Nessa continued, "the dragon now has a name."

"Oh?"

"Aoife."

"Ee-fa?"

"It was the name of the dragon in my waking dream," Nessa explained. "I thought it just fit. You know?"

"Sure," Hunter said. "It's a good a name as any, I suppose. It means 'beauty' or 'radiance' in the old tongue. Did you know that?"

"I did not," Nessa murmured. She looked at the little creature, at Aoife, and thought that the name was pretty damn apt. Even in the mountain's shadow, her scales seemed to glow with an inner light, shimmering with every movement no matter how small.

The incline rapidly steepened and before Nessa knew it, turned into a rugged cliff face. They found a section where the slant was less severe and scaled up it, legs burning in protest and hands becoming scratched as they grabbed at rocks and bushes to prevent themselves from pitching backwards.

Hunter reached the summit first, bounding up the last few yards with ease. Nessa scowled at him, wondering where he got all his energy from. Lacking his speed, she joined him a few minutes later, finding him standing beneath a crippled tree. It leaned hazardly to the side, having been pushed over by the prevailing wind for years. From its gnarled branches hung some withered fruits, dried brown husks that Hunter was eagerly gathering, making the tree shudder.

Nessa moved up beside him, curious to see what he was picking so enthusiastically, and got sidetracked by the view that stretched out before her.

"Wow," Nessa said, staring, her breath catching in her throat.

It hadn't been an easy trip, reaching the top of the cliff, but the sight was more than worth the effort.

"It's beautiful, isn't it?" Hunter said.

Nessa could only nod.

Mountains, too many to count, stood on either side of a wide valley. Steep-sided, they soared high into the sky, their snow-covered peaks jutting above the wispy clouds that clung around them. Distance had only given a mere hint of their size, but now, being trapped in their shadows, looking up at them, Nessa found them to be immense.

The valley floor was lush green, mostly covered by a thick blanket of moss and small red and purple succulent plants. A few pine trees and majestic oaks lined the sides, some valiantly trying to grow on the rocky bases of the mountains. A river, slow and wide, snaked down the centre, crystal clear.

The River Nyland, Nessa presumed.

She followed it with her eyes, watching it gently bubble along, flowing against the clusters of stones that flanked its sides, until it disappeared out of sight, heading towards the Burning Forest.

"Jesus," she whispered, awed.

"You say that a lot," Hunter said, standing next to her with his hands filled with fruit husks.

"I do?"

Hunter nodded. "You mutter it under your breath quite often."

"Huh. I hadn't realised."

"You do it all the time."

"I'm sorry."

"I assume it's a swearword. Admittedly, I've never heard anyone else use it. But when you do, it's usually accompanied by a few other words that I am well acquainted with. Especially when we're sparring."

"Oh." A blush came to Nessa's cheeks when she thought of what those select words could be.

"I'm impressed really," Hunter continued. "It's a rare thing to find a girl who can cuss better than a hardened, seafaring man. Can I put these in your bag?" Without waiting for an answer, Hunter reached out and deposited the fruit husks in her empty messenger bag.

"I suppose so," Nessa murmured, rolling her eyes. "I swear during sparring?"

"Quietly, if it's any consolation."

"Mmm."

Nessa, feeling mildly mortified, turned away from Hunter, her eyes sweeping over the breathtaking view once again.

"It's called the Valley of the Haunted Kings. Few

people come here, in fear of the ghosts."

"Ghosts?"

Hunter nodded. "Legends tell of a battle that was fought here long ago. A king started a pointless war that killed thousands of innocents needlessly, and once sent his men here to fight against his enemy. They were slaughtered, and as punishment for his warmongering and selfish desires, the Gods cursed the king, making him walk for all eternally in this valley, never sleeping, never resting, forever haunting the place where he killed so many for his own gain."

"How lovely," Nessa said dryly. It didn't detract from the valley's beauty, though, maybe even enhanced it in a desolate way.

"Come on," Hunter said, giving her a gentle nudge with his elbow.

They started off again, slowly leaving the rise and heading downhill, venturing into the valley.

"Are there really ghosts here?" Nessa asked.

Hunter shrugged. "Who knows? Maybe there are, maybe there aren't. I've been here a few times and have never seen anything."

"That's a comfort then."

He looked at her, brows raised, faintly surprised. "Scared of ghosts then?"

"Maybe."

"Mmm." Hunter turned thoughtful.

"Mmm, what?" asked Nessa, curious as to what was going on in his head.

"Nothing," Hunter said. "Just putting another piece of the puzzle into place, that's all."

"A puzzle," Nessa laughed. "You think I'm a puzzle."

"You're an enigma to me," Hunter argued. "I know hardly anything about you. And most of what I do, I've had to piece together myself. You're not exactly forthcoming, you know."

Nessa was quiet for a moment, wondering if he was right. "I've told you how I came to be here."

"You said that while exploring the ruins of an old town, you came across a glowing mirror that Margan pulled you through, thus ending up here. You haven't told me where you've come from, what family you have. I presume it's all a world away from this."

"Quite literally," Nessa murmured, taken aback by what Hunter had said.

"I mean," he continued, "there can't be things like dragons or magic users, then?"

"Magic doesn't exist," Nessa said, biting the inside of her cheek. "It's just in children's stories."

"So this must be quite a surreal experience for you?"

"It's unbelievable. Sometimes I think I must have whacked my head and this is all just a dream."

"You don't have to keep everything bottled in," Hunter said. "You can tell me. I'll keep your secrets."

"I've known you for a week," Nessa reminded

the both of them. "Of course you're not going to know everything about me. And to be honest, I'm not sure why you'd want to. I'm very boring. Very average."

Hunter smiled. "Oh, I'm sure that's not true."

"I don't open up to people a lot," Nessa explained. "I haven't for months. I find that people think they want to hear your thoughts, your opinions. Then when you voice them and they're not what that person wants to hear, they get angry or upset."

"You can't let that silence you on all things."

"Not all things," Nessa argued. "Just most."

"I'm not like that," Hunter murmured. "If you want to speak your mind, I'll listen."

"I don't want to speak my mind," Nessa sighed. "I want to forget."

"Forget?"

"Well…" Nessa struggled to find the right words. "It's like… I feel that… if I were to talk about everything that's happened, then it would make it even more real. If that makes any sense? And since we've nearly reached Orm's, and he might be able to send me back home, then perhaps it's best just to forget everything, push it aside and focus on the future. Forget that magic exists and that dragons are real. Forget about people like Margan and Shadow…"

"And forget about me?" Hunter mumbled.

"No!" Nessa turned to him. "Never! I would

never forget you and your kindness. You're the only thing that I will look back on with fondness."

"Fondness, you say." His eyes brightened. "I'll take that. For now."

"For now?" Nessa grinned. "You think your charm will convince me to stay?"

Hunter winked. "That, and once you see The Hidden City, you'll wonder why you ever wanted to go home."

"Will I now?"

"It will knock your socks off," Hunter promised.

"Well, lead the way then, my charming friend," Nessa laughed. "I'm burning with anticipation."

With a spring in his step, he did, whistling happily away. Nessa eagerly trailed behind him, pushing away grim thoughts.

"You don't think I'm normal?" Nessa said after a little while.

Hunter looked over his shoulder at her. "I mean that in a good way."

"I'm sure you do." Nessa stepped around a low shrub with unusually pointed branches. "It's just that no one's ever paid me much attention before."

"I don't believe that."

"Not that anyone was particularly mean or neglectful or anything like that," Nessa mused. "I suppose people just left me to my own devices."

"That's not a bad thing."

"No, I suppose not. It can get a bit lonely, though."

"There's no better company than one's own mind sometimes."

"Wow, Hunter. You just spouted words of wisdom again."

"Hey, I can say something profound every now and again. Don't look so shocked."

Nessa smiled and made a non-committal sound.

They crossed the valley, heading away from the river. The terrain steepened and became rockier, barren of bushes and shrubs. Huge slabs of grey granite loomed before them, steep blocks that barred their path. A few lone trees grew around the bases of the sheer cliff faces, with a couple clinging on a little higher up.

Nessa waited for Hunter to divert from his course, thinking that he was perhaps planning on hugging the bottom of the mountain until there was a clearer path. He didn't, and aimed straight for those granite blocks. Nessa eyed them with trepidation, hoping, praying that Hunter wasn't expecting her to climb up them. A rock climber Nessa was not.

Jesus, Nessa thought, *it's hard enough walking through the bloody tundra without tripping over, let alone having to scale up damn mountains.*

Nessa's prayers, it seemed, were answered, and instead of being forced to climb up a vertical wall of stone, Hunter found a small crevice between two slabs that was slightly less steep.

It turned out to be a fissure, narrow and long,

and went on for quite some distance. The sides crowded in on them, and the ground angled up, driving them higher into the mountain. Nessa pulled herself up, grasping at any handhold she could find, wishing for some form of railing. Over countless years, rain had worn the granite slippery smooth. If not for the gripping leather soles of her boots, Nessa was sure she would have slid down the fissure like it was a slide; a very hard, very painful, and very long slide.

Slowly, the crack widened and evened out, giving Nessa's tired legs a much needed reprieve. It led onto a small space, a gully were two mighty mountains joined together. The air was cold, never warming due to being perpetually trapped in the mountain's shadows. A mist clung to the ground, slow moving with curling tendrils that snaked and coiled around boulders and protruding fingers of rock.

Hunter stepped forward, making the mist churn in his wake. Nessa trailed behind him, tugging her cardigan tight around her, shivering from the chill that seemed to seep into her bones.

Something brushed against her ankle. Nessa yelped and jumped back.

Looking down she found that it was only Aoife, who had merely rubbed up against her.

Hunter sent her a quizzical glance.

Nessa bent and picked up the little dragon, who was nearly completely hidden by the mist, only her head visible above it. Hunter rolled his eyes and continued on. Nessa held Aoife to her chest, wrapping her cardigan around the both of them. The smooth granite gave way to an uneven and rocky ground. Stones crunched underfoot, the noise echoing in a ghostly fashion.

Together they wormed their way deeper into the mountains. The towering rock faces pressing in on both sides and the mist growing ever denser, cool, damp and concealing. Nessa craned her head back, looking up at the sky. Twin peaks framed a thin sliver of blue, the sun nowhere to be seen, tucked far away from sight. Despite climbing up a mountainside, Nessa had the bizarre feeling of being underground, swallowed by the earth.

Further they went, climbing ever higher.

Nessa's breath puffed out in front of her in a thin white cloud, and she hugged Aoife all the tighter, savouring the warmth. The dragon, she found, had put on weight, growing a few inches. It wasn't much, but just enough to make carrying the hatchling a chore after a while. She shifted her hold on the dragon and turned the corner that Hunter had just disappeared around.

She stopped dead in her tracks.

A void opened up before her, one filled with impenetrable darkness.

Nessa swore and took a stumbling step back.

"Bloody terrible time to discover you're afraid of heights," Hunter called. He was to Nessa's right, standing on a perilously narrow ledge that ran along the side of the abyss.

Nessa scowled at him, heart thundering away. "What the buggery bollocks is this?"

"It's the quickest way."

"Only if you don't fall to your death first."

Hunter laughed. "I'm sure that won't happen."

"That ledge is barely two foot wide."

"You're thin. That's plenty of room."

Nessa stared, aghast at his reasoning, and inched closer to the edge, peering over. The darkness was deep, the bottom of the chasm well beyond sight. Nessa eyed the ledge which clung to the straight side of the mountain, running along it until it was swallowed by distance.

"No," Nessa said, shaking her head vehemently.

"It's either this way or backtracking," Hunter reasoned.

"I'll go with the second option."

"It will take us at least another five days to get to the city."

Nessa sighed, eyes darting between Hunter and the chasm. "I don't like either of those options."

"Well, think of it like this," Hunter said. "Five days of crossing harsh terrain verses forty-five minutes of utter terror."

Nessa frowned. "You're not selling either of them."

"Perhaps not." Hunter crossed his arms, waiting. "But those are the two options we have at present."

"Hmm." Nessa gave it a bit of thought. "I don't like this one bit."

"It will be over before you know it."

"If I fall to my death, I reserve the right to haunt you for all eternity."

"I fully respect that decision."

"Excellent." Nessa bundled Aoife into the messenger bag, wanting her hands to be free.

Shaking just a little bit, Nessa edged onto the ledge. It held steady, nothing coming loose. She let out a nervous breath and moved further along, angling herself so that none of her clothing would catch on the rocks.

Hunter waited for her, smiling in reassurance, and then started off again, albeit at an incredibly slow pace. Aoife squirmed in the bag, not quite fitting into it as well as she had upon first hatching, and Nessa put a calming hand on her. She could sense Nessa's unease, it seemed, for she settled down.

Nessa continued along the ledge at a snail's pace, hugging the stone wall and keeping as far away from the edge as possible. It was a long, winding journey, and Nessa's didn't enjoy it at all. The further they went, the worse the condition of the ledge became. In a couple of parts, it had weathered away to nearly nothing, and in one place, it was gone completely. There was no greater terror than having to jump from one narrow ledge to another over a black, bottomless chasm.

Although the ledge was in a terrible condition, Nessa could see that some poor soul had attempted to make some repairs to it. In one place, a huge crack had appeared in the mountainside, renting a gaping fissure that was too wide to jump. There, a couple of long wooden planks had been laid across it, forming a makeshift bridge. In those particularly hazardous spots, Nessa noticed, someone had also gone to the pains of carving small curled crosses into the rock face. Sometimes there was just the odd one or two, but occasionally there was a cluster of ten or more.

"What are these?" Nessa asked as a way to distract herself. "Do they mark the dangerous bits?"

"In a manner of speaking, I suppose."

"And generally speaking?"

"They are markers to show where some unfortunate person has fallen to their deaths."

"Oh."

"Think of them as little grave markers."

That was not what Nessa had wanted to hear, and she fell silent, focusing on putting one foot in front of the other.

Nessa's forty-five minutes of utter terror must soon be over, for there, in the near distance, was a wide plateau. The ledge ran right to it.

Not much further to go, Nessa told herself.

The ledge widened and the worst was over.

Nessa stepped onto the plateau and breathed a sigh of relief. She hurried away from the edge, not wanting to be anywhere near it. Hunter, though, lingered. He pointed to the side, at the small freshly carved cross there.

"Poor bugger must have got overexcited at being at the end," he said. "Fatal mistake."

"How unfortunate," Nessa murmured, half tempted to kiss the solid ground in jubilation.

Hunter went over to her and clapped her on the back. "See, I told you we'd make it safe and sound."

Nessa raised a brow. "A large part of me still thinks that backtracking wouldn't have been such a bad idea."

"Rubbish," Hunter scoffed. "It got your blood pumping with excitement."

"I think you're getting excitement and fear mixed up."

Hunter shrugged. "Same difference."

"No," Nessa said slowly, "I think they're quite the opposite of one another."

Hunter just looked at her. "We're going to have to agree to disagree."

"Fine," Nessa said, rolling her eyes. "Whatever." She surveyed the plateau. It was surrounded on three sides by tall rocky walls that allowed very little sunlight to reach the floor. It was swathed in thick shadows, which gave the air a ghostly chill. Despite a fair amount of fallen debris ringing the edges, the middle was empty, as if a path had been cleared.

Nessa stepped forward, leaving the chasm

behind her, and followed the pathway. She stepped around a boulder that was taller than her, and came face to face with an entrance to a deep, dark tunnel.

She stared at it, then at Hunter, who came up beside her.

"I'm beginning to think that you enjoy putting me in situations that you know I don't like."

"Nonsense." Hunter grinned from ear to ear. "It's all character building."

"My character is just fine the way it is, thank you very much."

"What's a dark tunnel compared to the ledge?"

"Moderately less unpleasant?"

"Exactly. It only gets better from here."

"That's a small comfort, I suppose."

Hunter snorted with mirth. "Come on," he said, "if we hurry, we'll get to the city in time for dinner."

"Dinner?" Nessa looked up, nearly cricking her neck in the process. Despite the blanket of shadows wrapped around them, she found that the sky was still bright blue, no indication of dusk being near. Hunter followed her gaze.

"Hungry?" he asked.

Nessa's stomach answered for her, growling loudly.

"Fear not." Hunter reached out, opening up her messenger bag. "Nature was kind enough to provide for us." Aoife raised her head, eyes expectant. "Out the way, medium sized reptile." He reached in and pulled out a handful of those strange husks he had picked earlier.

"You can actually eat those things?" Nessa eyed them, finding their appearance to be less than appetising. They were about the size of an apple, thick skinned and shrivelled, looking as tough as old boots.

"Not the whole thing." He crushed one in his hand, the dry skin crunching. He snapped off the broken pieces, casting them to the ground until he held a palm full of small pebble-like nuts. "But you can munch on these little beauties."

"Yum," Nessa mumbled.

"No need to be sarcastic," Hunter said, popping one in his mouth. "They're a lot yummier than they look."

"They'd have to be," she said, taking one and rolling it between her fingers, finding it to be surprisingly hard, "because they don't look yummy at all."

"Eat the damn nut."

Nessa placed it her mouth and bit down, expecting an unpleasant taste to be forthcoming. She blinked in shock. The nut, contrary to its withered appearance, actually tasted alright. Nothing to brag home about, but it was, at least, edible.

Hunter raised his brows. "Tasty?"

Nessa grudgingly said, "It's okay."

Hunter snorted and ate another one, then handed Nessa the rest. She held them in her cupped hand, slowly nibbling them.

Hunter nodded to Aoife, who, whilst still sat in the bag, had poked her head out, sniffing curiously at the air. "You'd best keep the dragon hidden," he said. "We'll soon be coming across people and it's best if no one sees it."

Nessa nodded.

Aoife was unimpressed at having to remain in the bag. For some inexplicable reason, Nessa felt the dragon's irritation as her own.

She shook the idea away, finding it ludicrous.

"Ready?" Hunter asked.

Nessa eyed the dark mouth of the tunnel.

"Let's get it over with," she said, popping another nut in her mouth.

༄✦༄

The darkness of the tunnel was absolute. There wasn't even the slightest hint of illumination, nothing to see their way by. Hunter held Nessa's hand in his own, guiding her. Using his cat-like senses once again, she supposed, swearing to herself that he must be able to see in the dark. Nothing else explained how he never tripped over or led them astray.

For a long time there was nothing but darkness and silence.

Then, when it felt as if hours had passed by, a pinprick of light shone up ahead.

It was far in the distance, but it was there nonetheless.

They hurried towards it, eager to be out of the dark.

As they drew closer, Nessa's ears picked up a faint sound, a low murmur. At first she thought it was the thunder of running water, but a few minutes later, when she stood at the end of the tunnel, she realised what it actually was: Voices, so many voices merging together in a large cavernous space, heard from afar.

"Wow," Nessa whispered, taking in the sight that was spread out before her.

"Welcome to The Hidden City," Hunter said, amber eyes aglow.

Chapter 25

Hunter had been right. After seeing The Hidden City, Nessa never wanted to leave.

The tunnel opened up onto a small balcony that was perched high up, offering a bird's eye view of the city.

What a city it was, stretching far and wide, hidden deep in the belly of the mountain.

Nessa was amazed. Never before had she seen such a thing.

The cave was immense, the sheer size of it almost unfeasible. Either end was out of sight, and the ceiling, hundreds of feet above the ground, was riddled with huge stalactites that reached down like grotesque claws, twisted and curved. Covering the ground was a sea of multicoloured tents of every size and shape. People filled the narrow walkways, the calls and shouts just reaching Nessa's ears. It was a hive of activity.

A city under a mountain was a curious thing in itself, but even more curious was how it was illuminated.

Growing on pale logs were ethereal glowing mushrooms.

They were everywhere. They lined the walls, the sides, and they were dotted throughout the sea of tents; amazingly enough, some were even suspended from the ceiling, the logs on which the mushrooms grew hanging down on thick ropes.

Nessa giggled at the absurdity of it. *Glowing mushrooms. Who would have thought?*

Their glow was radiant and distant, filling the gigantic space with soft light.

A narrow, winding staircase was to Nessa's left, leading to the city below. She went over to it, practically skipping down the first few steps. She ran a hand over the rope banister, feeling the coarse texture against her palm as it guided her downward. Her gaze roamed everywhere, drinking in the sight that was The Hidden City. Hunter was quiet as he followed behind her, just letting her take it all in.

Nessa paused when she came across a group of those ethereal mushrooms, taking the opportunity to look at them up close.

They were small and delicate, only a few inches

in height, a cluster of five that sat on a smooth white log. Their caps were bell shaped with a waved edge, and had a little frilled skirt that just peeked out from beneath. Diffused light came from somewhere within the mushrooms, making them appear to have a slight translucence to them.

"They come from far up north," Hunter said. "From the Whyte Woods."

Nessa gently ran a finger over one, the light making her fingertip glow red.

"How beautiful," Nessa said.

"There are other ones down in the city, all shapes and sizes. I'll show you my favourite ones if we come across them?"

Nessa nodded and, somewhat reluctantly, stepped away from the mushrooms, continuing down the stairs. The smell of food, delicious hot food, reached her nose and propelled her forward. Aoife, it seemed, scented something that caught her interest too, and squirmed, wanting to be free. Nessa rested her hand on the bag, sending the dragon a calming thought. Aoife quietened, although Nessa could tell that it wouldn't be for long.

As soon as Nessa stepped off the stairs, she was swallowed by the hustle and bustle of the city. The tents were pushed up against the side of the cave, creating a narrow walkway that teemed with people. Hunter grabbed her hand before she was caught up by the current, and nodded, indicating that they should cross the street, tugging her over to a small tent opposite.

The front section of the tent was pulled up, held in place by two wooden poles, creating a sheltered porch-like area. Large fire pits sat inside, spewing smoke and steam that was let out by a couple of small flaps, and nestled on top of them were a number of pots and pans, cooking sausages and a mixture of other delightful things.

Nessa's mouth watered and her stomach growled as they neared.

Dropping her hand, Hunter shot her a grin and rifled in his pocket as the chef came to stand behind the counter. He ordered and pulled out a couple of small copper coins. The chef pocketed them in his grease stained smock and barked at his assistant, who hurried around the cramped tent, pulling out a couple of plates and piling them high with food. Dinner was handed to them a few minutes later, and Hunter swiftly led them over to a quiet area by the side of the cave. They sat down, resting their backs against the stone, and dug in.

Nessa discovered that she was hungrier than she had first thought, and the scrambled eggs and bacon practically vanished. A single sausage remained when restraint kicked in, restraint, and a feeling that Nessa was sure came from the bag. She opened it carefully and peered in accusingly. Aoife looked up at her, blinking big eyes.

Nessa looked around, making sure that no one

saw, and slipped the sausage into the bag, much to Aoife's delight. Her angular head darted forward, snapping at it like a striking snake. Nessa flipped the bag closed, hoping that no one noticed that it was moving slightly.

As Hunter leisurely finished, Nessa gazed around, finding it all a little overwhelming. People were everywhere, shouting, laughing, talking as they went, walking down the streets, looking at the wares that were on offer. Like every city, there was the centre, filled with markets and shops, and it seemed that Nessa and Hunter were right next to it.

The people were fascinating, dressed in vibrant clothes of reds and purples and royal blues, in silks and velvets. They had the feel of nobility to them, or maybe they were wealthy merchants. They were something of that sort. Nessa eyed them as they passed, her imagination working in overdrive. She wondered what it must be like to wear such things, such bright and rich dresses and robes. It was a very girlish thought, Nessa knew, but she couldn't help but desire to be in their shoes, quite literally, even if only for a day.

Maybe you could, if only you stayed, a quiet voice whispered to her.

Nessa froze, wondering where that had came from. It hadn't been her own musing, that was for sure.

"I hope that dragon of yours is behaving?" Hunter asked, knocking Nessa out of her thoughts.

"She's a little hungry," Nessa said. "But I have her under control. I think."

"Good, good." Hunter stood. "No one can see or know about it."

Nessa got to her feet, holding the bag against her side so as not to jostle Aoife too much. "And what if someone was to see her?"

Hunter shifted and looked around, uneasy. "It'd depend on the person, but I reckon most people would hand you over to the authorities. Remember, there's a bounty on your head, a nice juicy bounty. And many people who have come here have fallen out of favour in the Kingdoms. This is a safe place for many, and most of them are content to be here. But not everyone wants to spend the rest of their lives living in a cave. If someone gave you to Margan, or even to the king, which you really don't want to happen, then they would be set for life, all past misdeeds forgotten."

Nessa swallowed nervously. "Best to keep the dragon secret then."

Hunter nodded and took her empty plate, stacking it on top of his own, and returned them to the food vendor. When he came back, he looked at her expectantly. "Do you want to have a look around, or are you eager to find Orm?"

Nessa deliberated quickly, desiring to explore the market but unsure whether Aoife would tolerate it. "Perhaps a quick peruse around?"

"Excellent."

They wandered around for a time with no particular direction, just going with the flow of people. There were the mundane stalls of fruit and vegetables, trinkets and cloth, and other such things, but mixed in with the everyday stalls were those that sold the extraordinary, the unusual and the strange.

One tent was filled with shelves covered in coloured bottles sealed with wax, potions and tonics. Jars of bones and other equally creepy things were also dotted throughout, little glass rings with tiny monster skulls inside, matching pendants too. The air had been thick with the scent of incense, making their eyes water. They hadn't lingered in there for very long. Another shop had an array of books that screamed when opened. The seller had informed them that they make particularly good diaries when Hunter had demanded to know what the point of them was, ears ringing.

Hunter had strode way, fuming at such an explanation.

"Stupid bloody idea if you ask me," he muttered.

"I dunno," Nessa said. "No one would ever want to open it to read your secrets."

"No, I don't suppose anyone would. I also doubt that anyone would be able to stand the noise long enough to write their secrets in the first bloody place."

"Mmm."

Onward they ventured, past tents of all colours,

sizes and shapes. Some were plain, others ornate with silver or gold trim. All of it was illuminated by those beautiful ghostly mushrooms that were everywhere.

Hunter suddenly pulled her over to the side. "Here," he said. "These are my favourites."

A large branch sat beside a dark entrance of a mysterious tent, its bottom dug into the hard ground and its spindly twigs splayed upward like reaching talons. From it sprouted a number of peculiar glowing fungi, possibly the most fanciful Nessa had seen so far.

"They're like witches' hats," laughed Nessa.

With a wide brim and a pointed tip that had a slight curl to it, the description suited them perfectly. They were small and dainty, with most of them being a plain translucent white. Others, though, had large knobbly spots that had a faint greenish tinge to them.

"Witches hats?" Hunter shook his head. "You must not have met many witches in your life. I've never seen one wear a hat that looks remotely like these."

Nessa chuckled, not able to find a suitable response.

Hunter nudged her with an elbow. "So, what do you think of them?"

"I can see why they're your favourites."

"I like the spotty ones more," he said. "They're more fun to look at."

"If you say so."

"I wonder if someone sells them. I want to buy some."

"I imagine that if someone sells screaming diaries, then someone's bound to sell glowing spotty mushrooms."

Hunter murmured in agreement, standing on tiptoes to see over the crowd as he searched the street. Nessa turned back to the mushrooms, gazing at them, trying to pinpoint exactly where the light came from, and not being met with much success. There was the beat of wings and the branch trembled, making the mushrooms quiver and sway. Nessa looked up, finding, of all things, a raven perched on the top.

A raven that stared down at her with familiar blue eyes.

"You," Nessa whispered in recognition.

It was the winged menace from the ruined town, the one who had incidentally led her to the mirror.

The raven *cawed* in confirmation, flapping its wings, buffeting the air.

Slowly, Nessa reached out to it. Why, she didn't know. To touch its feathers? To catch it?

A hand clamped onto Nessa's wrist, pulling her up short.

She looked over, finding that it was Hunter. His eyes were locked onto the bird's, and something passed between them, something that made Nessa's spine prickle with misgiving.

"It's best not to touch strange animals," he said quietly. He brought her arm down, pressing it to her side. "We should go find Orm."

Nessa found herself bewildered. "Right," she said, puzzled as to why he was staring at the bird with such intensity.

"Like, right now."

"If you say so." Nessa allowed him to pull her away, casting a confused glance over her shoulder as they were swallowed by the tide of shoppers.

The bird stared after them with keen eyes.

A shiver of warning crawled over her.

Hunter tugged her through the sea of tents and stalls, and the blue eyed raven soon vanished from sight, although her suspicions didn't leave her so quickly. That bird was the one that had led her to the mirror, Nessa was sure of it, but if that was so, how had it come to be there, of all places?

Was it just a coincidence?

Hunter directed her over to the other side of the cave. The wall was rugged and played host to several smaller caves and a couple of tunnels that branched from it like limbs. They went down one, a tunnel that was shadowed and cramped. The sides pressed in and there were few glowing mushrooms to light the way. The air was cold, and Nessa felt as if there were eyes on her, but when she looked around, she could see no one there.

The tunnel was empty for a short distance, then, when they went around a shallow bend, doors appeared, lining either side, all irregularly shaped, fitting badly into the door frames, and painted bright colours. Although there was a more residential feel to the place, Nessa did see a couple of signs hanging above wonky doors, so it wasn't completely devoid of shops altogether.

They stopped in front of a door that had peeling red paint. Pale light shone from around the edges where it didn't quite fit into the frame, and a quiet, melodic sound of reed pipes could be heard.

"Well," Hunter said. "This is Orm's place, and it sounds like someone's home."

Nessa looked at him, her doubt clear for him to see.

Without further ado, Hunter pulled open the door and Nessa prepared herself to meet the mysterious Orm.

The man who might know the answers to so many of Nessa's questions.

The man who she had travelled for a hundred miles to find.

Chapter 26

Nessa didn't know what she had been expecting, but it sure as hell wasn't the scene in front of her. The air held an overwhelming amount of scented smoke, thick and heavy, filling the round bubble-like room with an eye-watering haze. It was hard to see clearly, but there were things everywhere, bookshelves, piles of clothing, large statues. The list was extensive.

In the middle of the room was a circle of wooden chests, on which sat an array of smoking incense sticks. In the centre, on a bed of pillows, was a man. He was sitting cross-legged, his eyes closed and a small reed pipe resting on his lips, emitting a strange tune.

Nessa stood by the doorway, unable to step inside. Hunter too, seemed likewise inclined, and remained out in the street, using the door as a fan. The smoke billowed out in a cloud of sandalwood and champa flower. Nessa couldn't help but sneeze.

"Damn it, Orm," Hunter coughed. "How have you not suffocated?"

The music stopped as Orm slowly lowered the pipe. "Now," he said without opening his eyes, "who do I know that's rude and annoying enough to interrupt my musical playing-ness?"

The air now clearer, Hunter ushered Nessa through the door, closing it behind them. He sighed, "Boiled to the gills, aren't you Orm?"

Nessa took that meaning as drunk. Orm was drunk. Or something of the kind.

She stared at him, finding that he had a fine scattering of blond stubble on his chin and a shaved head. His nose was a little on the big side, adding a bit of character to his face, and even though he was sat down, Nessa could tell that he was tall. She could see the defined shapes of muscles under his baggy tunic.

He wasn't anything like she had envisioned.

Nessa turned to Hunter, wondering if he had been bullshitting her all along. Orm couldn't even open his eyes, let alone answer any questions.

Hunter, it seemed, was less than impressed with his friend's current state, and went over to him. At least, he tried to. The chests acted as barricades, and the pillows really didn't help matters, slipping underfoot as Hunter straddled a chest, trying to get over it without burning himself on one of the smouldering incense sticks.

Nessa watched his struggles, contemplating whether she should give him a hand or to just stand by and see how it played out.

She chose the latter.

She didn't feel bad about that at all.

Orm opened an eye. Not both, just the one. He looked at Hunter as he struggled, smiling faintly. "'Ello, Hunter," he murmured, not moving a muscle to help his friend. His eye landed on Nessa and his smile grew. "And hello Hunter's friend."

Nessa gave him a lazy grin and a small wave, fingers wiggling.

Orm blinked and gazed at Nessa and Hunter with both eyes open, his curiosity obvious. "Welcome to my humble abode," he said. "It is my pleasure to have you here this fine eve. How may I be of assistance?"

Hunter managed to get over the wooden chest without breaking himself, and promptly collapsed on the pile of pillows, sinking down into them.

"We need you to sober up," Hunter puffed, "and answer some questions."

"Sober?" Orm laughed. "Who says I'm not sober?"

"I do."

"And I second that," Nessa murmured.

Orm paused, considering their words. "Maybe I am, maybe I'm not. In any event, I didn't know that the two of you would be coming and found myself growing bored. You can't blame a man for simply passing the time."

"Just passing the time, is it?" Hunter managed to extract himself from the pillows and sat up, red faced and irritated.

Orm nodded solemnly.

"And what are you passing the time with?"

Orm chuckled, and from under the pillows, he pulled out a small wooden box. He opened it, revealing that it was filled with a number of cigars made from a dark flaking material. Nessa scrunched up her nose, having no idea what they were, although they couldn't be normal, judging by the way Hunter rolled his eyes.

"You've fallen back into bad habits, my friend," Hunter said, crawling forward, reaching out for the box. He went to grab it, but Orm squirrelled it away, hiding it. "You promised me you'd stop smoking this stuff."

"And you, Hunter, my lad," Orm pointed an accusatory finger at him, "promised to meet up with me three months ago for some fun at Silverman's. However, you never turned up. You abandoned me and our wonderful, wonderful plans."

Hunter shook his head and settled back against the wooden chest, giving up with wrestling the pillows. "Well," he began. Nessa, sensing that the conversation was going to continue for some time, decided to join them. She managed to hop over the chest with more ease than Hunter had, and settled down beside him on the pillows, which were less of a bed and more of a bottomless pool. "It was a little hard to meet up with you," Hunter continued, "since I was imprisoned in Ironguard."

Orm was amused. "Oh yes, I remember hearing all about that." He grinned from ear to ear. "Interesting and mildly entertaining it was, listening to the tales of your arrest."

"So you had heard?" Hunter looked displeased. "I had wondered. Thanks for the gallant rescue."

Orm shrugged. "I had intended to help, but then something happened and I got into trouble and blah blah blah, and so on and so on…"

"And so you left me there," Hunter finished. "For *three months*."

"I was in a lot of trouble," Orm argued. "Anyway, don't try and guilt trip me. Clearly you didn't need my help. You escaped that dreary place all by yourself. Bravo. And managed to end up in such fine company too. Double bravo."

Nessa couldn't stop her lips from twitching into a small smile. Orm, it turned out, amused her greatly, and had inadvertently given her a small glimpse into Hunter's past that got her thinking.

"You see," Orm said, "it was the Gods' way of getting the three of us here, together. A rather long and roundabout way of getting us here, I agree, but they got us here nonetheless. And for a reason, I'm sure. You can't be mad at me when I was merely a pawn in the Gods' divine game."

"And which divine game is that?" Hunter asked dryly.

Orm chuckled. "Who knows? The Gods work in mysterious ways, my friend, and they have yet to reveal their intentions."

"Huh." Hunter scowled.

"Come now, Hunter," Orm said, placating. "It all worked out for the best. Here we are, the three of us, happy and healthy, and in reasonably good spirits. It is a time to rejoice, and I can think of no better way of celebrating our gathering than with a good old smoke." Orm rifled around in the pillows, hunting for his box of strange looking cigars. He found it, setting it on his lap with a wide grin.

"Orm," Hunter said firmly. "No."

Orm pulled a face. "Come on. One smoke won't do us any harm."

Hunter looked at Nessa beseechingly. Seeing as it was unlikely she would be getting any decent answers anytime soon, Nessa resigned herself to wait until the morning and shrugged. Hopefully Orm would be lucid by then.

Hunter sighed as Orm opened the box and pulled out a flaking cigar, smiling like an imp as he did so. He popped it in his mouth, and with his other hand, clicked his fingers. A small flame flared between his thumb and forefinger, igniting the tip of the cigar.

Nessa jumped, startled. He had no matches, no

lighter. It was by no normal means that he had conjured that flame. It was magic. Orm had magic. It unnerved her to see such a blatant display of it. Then understanding dawned on her. Hunter believed Orm might know how she had been brought to the Twelve Kingdoms because Orm knew about magic, he could use it himself. Nessa looked at Orm with renewed interest.

Orm wiggled his eyebrows as he took a draw on his cigar. "Let's get this party started," he said around it.

Hunter, head in his hands, murmured, "This isn't going how I had planned it to."

"In all honesty," Nessa said, "I don't think anyone could plan this."

"Hmm."

Orm blew out a lungful of smoke and looked at them with drowsy eyes. "That's so much better."

"Yes," Hunter muttered, "it must have been so hard for you here, tucked safely away from your problems."

Orm shot him a halfhearted glare. "I'll have you know that the woman who lives opposite is incredibly annoying."

Hunter glanced at Nessa, who raised her brows, smirking.

"Irritating," Hunter said to her. "He finds his neighbour irritating."

"Must be a living hell," Nessa replied.

Orm pretended to look wounded. "Those words

are mean."

"So is leaving your friend to rot in prison," groused Hunter.

Orm took a long drag on his cigar. "Ugh, you're just going to keep bringing that up, aren't you?"

"Yes."

"Fine, fine." Orm waved a hand. "The next time you wind up in prison, because let's face it, it's more than likely to happen, I swear on my mother's grave to come and rescue you."

Hunter frowned. "Your mother's alive."

Orm paused in his smoking, actually having to give that a bit of thought. "Huh," he said after a little while. "So she is. I should probably write to her or something."

"Or something," Hunter muttered.

Orm began looking around, as if he was going to do such a task then and there.

"So… Um…" Nessa started, unsure of what to say, but wanting to keep Orm's attention on something relevant, at the very least. "Hunter says that you might be able to help me?"

"I will endeavour to help you in any way I can, pretty girl."

Nessa's eyes slid to Hunter.

"He'll be no good to us for at least another eight hours, I'd imagine," he told her.

Nessa believed that, and sank back against the chest, shrugging off her bags. Orm was quite happy in a world of his own, thanks to that strange cigar of his. He took another draw, making the cigar's end flare green. Smoke billowed from his nose in twin streams a moment later. Despite Hunter's attempt at airing the room out, it was quickly filling with smoke again, both from the cigar and from the incense sticks.

While Nessa acted like she was fine, she was, in fact, getting desperate to go somewhere else. The smog was growing ever thicker, making her eyes water and burn. Her lungs too, ached a little as she was forced to breathe in the fumes. She looked over at Hunter, wondering if it would be considered rude to ask if they could go elsewhere, just for some fresh air.

Then time seemed to lose all meaning, and Nessa's awareness to the world around her became warped and disjointed.

Hunter was speaking, his mouth moving and his eyes twinkling, but Nessa heard nothing but a quiet murmur, the words escaping her ears. Her gaze moved to Orm, seemingly in slow motion, finding him once again playing his reed pipe.

Nessa's mind turned foggy, filled with a strange haze. A purple filter settled over her eyes, giving everything a slight amethyst hue. Weirdly enough, she didn't care. It was as if all her worries had suddenly flown away, the weight on her shoulders gone. It was a wonderful feeling, to have one's fears fade away. Nessa smiled, relaxing further into the pillows. *Yes*, she thought faintly, *this will do quite nicely.* If the smoke still made her eyes water or burn, Nessa didn't notice as her eyelids grew heavy. *Yes,* Nessa decided, *this will do very well.*

Nessa's gaze was drawn down and she noticed something odd. The smoke from Orm's cigar and the incense sticks had condensed around her, shimmering gently, and her hand practically glowed. Her eyes went wide as she slowly realised that it wasn't actually her hand that shone, but the scar that was wrapped around it.

The light hovered on and around it, a thin and delicate web. Her eyes traced it, and found that the light wasn't just isolated to her scar, but also streamed way from it in a drifting thread, one that flowed to her messenger bag.

Nessa frowned, wondering why, of all the places, it went there.

With slow, clumsy movements, she opened the bag. Aoife's head popped out, large eyes blinking. Nessa didn't move as the little dragon slowly clambered out, stepping onto her lap. She was too busy watching as the thread of light shifted with the little dragon.

Nessa's fog-filled mind wasn't able to think straight, and it took her a long minute to realise that the thread wasn't connecting her to the bag, it was connecting her to the dragon, to Aoife. Nessa stared at the light that hovered around Aoife's chest, just as it did with her scar, tethering the two of them together.

Binding them together.

It struck a chord and a burst of fear stabbed into Nessa's chest. Her heart began to thunder and her breaths quickened. Something wasn't right.

This wasn't right, her mind screamed at her.

Aoife looked up at Nessa, and something profound clicked into place in her head, and she knew that nothing would ever be the same again. It was like a light bulb turning on in the darkest of places, illuminating secrets and hidden things. There was no going back for Nessa. She knew that right then, saw it with her own eyes. It was written on her skin and inside her. She could feel herself changing.

An unbreakable bond had formed between her and Aoife, binding dragon and girl together.

There was nothing Nessa could do about it.

The ground suddenly felt as if it had opened up and swallowed her whole.

Chapter 27

Nessa woke to the heinous sound of snoring. She held her eyes shut, trying to find the blissful darkness of sleep. It was not to be found, though, as the snoring was jarring and without much rhythm.

Snore... snort... sputter... silence... Then it started all over again.

Nessa groaned and rolled over, discovering that she was on a narrow bed with a blanket thrown over her. She frowned, the snoring momentarily forgotten as she gazed around the dim room, wondering where she was and how she had got to be there.

It was a small room, filled with soft shadows. The ceiling and walls were rounded and smooth, as if someone had blown a bubble into the rock, and the floor was made up of uneven planks of wood. The door was over to the side, small and hidden mostly by a heavy drape that allowed minimal light through. There was another small bed beside hers, and atop it was Hunter, stretched out on his back, feet overhanging the end, his arm thrown over his eyes. His mouth was wide open, emitting the dreadful noise that had awoken her.

Nessa scowled at him. It wasn't the first time he had sounded like a goddamn foghorn, but hell, it was giving her a headache. She sat up, hoping that the pain behind her eyes would go away. It didn't. However, she did find Aoife curled up at the bottom of her bed, fast asleep, which was a small relief.

Careful not to wake the hatchling, Nessa swung her legs over the side of the bed and sat on the edge. Someone, presumably not her, had been thoughtful enough to remove her boots before putting her to bed. The floor was cold against her bare feet, and she scrunched up her toes as she searched for her socks.

Then everything came rushing back to her.

Orm.

His shop.

Her light bulb moment.

Nessa gazed around, wondering if Orm was somewhere in the room, sleeping in a corner. Not that the room actually *had* a corner. In any event, he wasn't. It was then that Nessa realised she wasn't in his shop anymore.

"Huh," Nessa murmured, trying to put all the pieces of the puzzle together. The only problem? Nessa was missing a couple of them.

She stood and crossed over to Hunter, the floorboards shifting under her.

"Hunter?"

She gave him a shake. He snorted and tried to roll over. Nessa growled and gave him a quick whack.

He startled awake. "What! What's happening?"

Nessa frowned. "Nothing. I just wanted you conscious."

"Oh." Hunter relaxed, closing his eyes. "Well, I don't feel like being conscious at this precise time, thank you very much."

"I just wanted to know where we were? And how I came to be here? I don't remember going to bed."

"We're in the apartment above Orm's shop."

"Right." Okay, that made sense.

"And as for how you got up here," Hunter continued. "I believe that I carried you, and Orm carried me. Or something like that, I think."

That made less sense, but Nessa couldn't bring herself to comment.

Hunter rolled out of bed with a moan. "Since I'm awake now, I suppose we'll see if there's anything to eat. I'm famished. Is Orm around?"

Nessa shook her head. "I haven't seen him, nor have I heard anything. Although, in all honesty, I haven't been up for very long."

Hunter stretched, moving over to the drape that acted as a door. "Well then, I suppose we should find him and invite him to breakfast."

Nessa trailed behind Hunter as he disappeared through the drape, and having no desire to lug a squirming dragon hatchling around, she decided to leave Aoife where she was.

The door opened onto a rather small and cramped hallway. The sides were wonky and the ceiling was low, forcing Hunter to stoop a little. There were two other doorways, both hidden behind mismatching drapes, and a steep, compact staircase that wound downward. Instead of those ethereal glowing mushrooms, the hallway was illuminated by a candle that was tucked away in a nook.

Both of them couldn't fit in the hallway together, so Nessa hovered in the doorway as Hunter poked his head around the one opposite.

He quickly reappeared, sporting a peculiar half smile.

"Orm's not in there," Hunter said, cheeks pink. "Although someone else is."

"Oh?"

Hunter didn't elaborate and Nessa didn't ask as he started down the stairs, swiftly but also with a touch of caution. She noticed that they were uneven and had a tendency to move around a little. It was clear that someone without woodworking skills had put the floors and stairs in, and their lack of craftsmanship was showing. Nessa kept a hand on the wall, helping to steady herself as she descended.

At the bottom, thankfully, was a solid rock floor. It was bumpy and uneven, but it didn't shift when she took a step. Hunter moved forward and Nessa found herself in another small bubble-like room, one that acted as a hall. There was one rounded doorway just in front of them, and another to their right, both hidden behind curtains.

Hunter went straight ahead, dipping his head to fit under the doorway. Nessa paused, wondering what the other doorway led to, and she pulled back the edge of the curtain, finding herself greeted by the sight of Orm's shop. It was dark, and all she could make out were a few vague shapes and the front door, which had a seam of light around the edges where it didn't fit into the door frame properly. Nessa let the curtain drop and went after Hunter.

She found him in another rounded room that had been turned into a makeshift kitchen. A small fire pit sat in the centre, a pan perched in the middle of the flames. The smoke rose up to the ceiling, where it disappeared into a small hole that acted as a vent. A number of boxes and crates were placed around the side, acting as tables and worktops.

Hunter and Orm sat on pillows by the fire pit, watching whatever was cooking in the pan. They were chatting away, and Nessa suddenly felt a little unsure of herself. They were close friends, had known each other for years, and their ease with one another made her feel like an intruder. Neither of them noticed her hesitation, and Hunter gave her a grin as Orm leapt to his feet, striding over to her on long legs. He seemed to be in a fabulously fine mood, and offered her a gratuitous bow.

His manner calmed her nerves, and Nessa found herself smiling.

"Hello hello," Orm said in welcome. "Due to a lack of manners last eve, I would like to formally introduce myself." He took her hand, giving it a quick kiss. "Orm, at your beck and call."

"Pleased to meet you," she laughed. "I'm Nessa."

"Nessa," Orm grinned, "come, take a seat. Or more accurately, come and take a pillow. Breakfast is nearly ready." Orm took his own advice and Nessa followed suit, plonking herself down on a rather plush pillow.

"I do hope you like eggs," Orm continued. "It's all I have at the moment."

Hunter leaned over, whispering in her ear, "And all he's able to cook, and even then it's hit and miss."

Orm served up the eggs, which were scrambled and slightly burnt. Nessa didn't complain, all politeness, and wolfed them down. Hunter, on the other hand, turned up his nose. "Is this really the best you can do?"

Orm glared and raised his spoon threateningly.

"Are you going to take some of this delicious

food up to your lady friend?" Hunter asked with a sickening amount of fake sweetness.

Orm looked confused. "What lady friend?"

"The one naked in your bed."

Sudden realisation crossed Orm's face. "I was having a bit of fun shortly before the two of you came," he explained with a sly grin. "She's still there? She is alive, isn't she?"

Hunter shrugged. "She was breathing."

"Huh. I suppose I had better go and see her out."

"Yes," Hunter advised. "You don't want any more angry fathers turning up on your doorstep."

"Husbands," Orm corrected as he stood. "It's usually husbands."

Hunter rolled his eyes. "Of course." He looked up at Orm. "If you didn't know she was still up there, then where did you sleep?"

"I'm not completely sure," Orm confessed, "but I think it was in the gutter outside Marie's place."

"Still trying to win her over?"

Orm shook his head as he exited the kitchen. "No, but old habits die hard."

Hunter murmured his concurrence, and picked at his scrambled eggs.

"He's completely out of his mind," Nessa said when she heard the stairs rattle with Orm's ascent.

Hunter nodded, not disagreeing. "But he knows about all kinds of things, so he has some use."

"You honestly think that he might know how Margan brought me here?"

"He's one of the best options I could think of. The nearest, too."

"And if he doesn't know, what then?"

"Then we'll search for someone who does. Simple as that."

"Simple as that?" Nessa repeated, surprised.

Hunter grinned. "Simple as that. If Orm doesn't know himself, then he'll probably know of someone who does."

"Right," Nessa said with false brightness. On the inside, though, she was beginning to wonder if it really mattered anymore, especially after what she had come to realise last night. She shook herself, not wanting to dwell on such negative thoughts. "That sounds good to me."

"Excellent." Hunter stole the last of the eggs from the pan, practically inhaling them as soon as they hit his plate.

Feet pounded on the stairs, two pairs, and Nessa guessed that Orm had managed to rouse his lady friend. There was a murmured conversation and then the sound of the front door opening and closing. Orm reappeared a moment later, and beckoned them into the shop, which seemed to double as a living room. Nessa was beginning to have doubts that it was actually a shop, and that Orm was just a hoarder of unusual things, using a shop as a guise.

Orm moved around, lighting a number of candles that were dotted here and there by merely touching the tip of his finger to the wick. No matches needed. The flames first flared green before settling down to the usual yellow-orange. The room was filled with dancing light, which caught strangely on the rounded rock, illustrating the fact that there were no windows, a reminder that they were deep in a mountain's belly. Nessa was beginning to find the absence of natural light unnatural and claustrophobic.

Finished with lighting the candles, Orm jumped over the circle of wooden chests, settling himself down on the bed of pillows. "So what, my lovelies," he said, eyes twinkling, "can I do for you?"

Hunter heaved a long suffering sigh and crossed over to the front door, sliding the bolt home, keeping any unwanted ears away.

Orm's interest grew. "It's for my ears only. How fantastic."

Hunter gave his friend a withering glare. "Are you cockeyed?" Orm looked at him blankly. "Drunk?"

"Sadly no," Orm replied, sinking deeper into the pillows. "Although I really wish I were."

Nessa swallowed her laughter and joined Orm on the pillows. He smiled and gave her a wink as Hunter sat beside her, a unified front.

Orm gazed at them, the easy grin slipping from his face.

"Oh Gods," Orm murmured. "This is serious, isn't it?"

Nessa grimaced as Hunter merely nodded. This probably wasn't going to be a particularly pleasant conversation.

Orm groaned. "You know I'm not good with serious problems."

"Well," Hunter said dryly, "you're all we have right now, so you'll just have to suck it up."

Orm pulled a face. "Fine. What have you done now, Hunter?"

"Me?" Hunter was outraged. "What have I done, you ask?"

"It's always you," Orm argued. "It's either you or me. And I'm not the one that's spent three months in Ironguard."

Hunter sputtered. "You!"

Orm grinned from ear to ear.

"Actually," Nessa said, sensing that they were a few words away from a punch up, "it's to do with me. Or more accurately, what was done to me."

Orm's eyebrows shot up.

"Ha!" Hunter barked, triumphant.

Both Nessa and Orm ignored him.

"You?" Orm murmured thoughtfully, eyes keen and assessing. "You don't strike me as someone who searches for trouble."

"I don't," Nessa said, "but in this instance it found me."

"Is that so?"

Nessa nodded.

"Huh."

"Nessa," Hunter interjected, "why don't you go get problem number one?"

Nessa frowned, not understanding what he was talking about.

"The small purple one," he insisted.

Nessa was surprised. "Oh. You sure that's a good idea?"

Hunter nodded. "It will help speed this along."

"Right." She clambered out from the pillows, over the chests, and left the front room. She rushed upstairs, making them groan and squeak as she went. Before she had even got into the spare bedroom, Nessa knew that Aoife was no longer asleep. In fact, the little dragon was sat by the curtained door, waiting for her.

Nessa didn't dwell on that, and just scooped up the dragon, hurrying back downstairs.

Orm had his back to her, slouched as he was, and didn't notice her return. She hopped back into the circle of pillows and sat down beside Hunter. Aoife squirmed in her arms and without much of a fight, Nessa released the dragon hatchling. Aoife didn't wander far, staying near Nessa, sniffing at the pillows around her.

Nessa looked over at Orm, finding that his face was a perfect picture of horror and shock. He stared at Aoife, white as a sheet.

"D-d-dragon," he sputtered. "There's a bloody dragon in my home!"

"Only a little one," Hunter said helpfully.

Orm scowled. "A dragon is a dragon. I don't care how bloody big it is."

"Well, you'd care a lot more of it was the size of a cow instead of a cat."

Orm's scowl deepened. "True, but you're trying to distract me from the matter at hand."

"Maybe just a little."

"You're not doing a good job."

"Oh dear."

"This isn't your dragon, is it?"

Hunter shook his head.

"You didn't steal it either, did you?"

Another shake of Hunter's head.

Orm turned to Nessa, his whiskey coloured eyes uncharacteristically serious. She gulped nervously under the weight of them.

"Your hand," Orm said, holding out his own imploringly.

Nessa knew what he was asking for. She rolled up her sleeve, revealing the purple-hued scar, and placed her hand in his. He turned it this way and that, making it shimmer in the dancing candle light, seemingly coming alive. Orm swallowed and released Nessa's hand. She immediately shoved down her sleeve, hiding as much of the scar as possible. This didn't go unnoticed, though neither Hunter nor Orm made to comment.

"Well," Orm muttered, "this is something I never expected to happen."

"Join the club," Hunter said. Nessa gazed at him,

scowling.

"What House do you belong to?" Orm asked quietly.

"That's problem number two," Hunter interrupted before Nessa could answer. "She thinks it's unlikely that she's from one of the Twelve Houses."

"Nonsense," Orm scoffed, "she has to be." He looked at Nessa. "You have to be. You have to be from one of the Twelve Families, either by noble birth or by a bastard line. Otherwise the egg would never have hatched for you."

Hunter spoke up for Nessa again, and she was grateful. It was round two of the argument she had just a few days ago, only he was on her side this time round, fighting for her rather than against. It was an improvement. "Ah, this is where we run into problem number three," Hunter was saying. "Nessa is, shall we say, not exactly from around here."

"You mean she's from up north?"

"No, I mean that she's been brought here from another world."

"Literally from another world?"

"Very literally," Nessa confirmed.

Orm, bemused, pursed his lips. His eyes darted between Nessa and Hunter, weighing up the possibility of them actually telling the truth or if they were just making it up.

"How did this happen?" he eventually asked.

Nessa blinked. "How did what happen?"

"How did you come through the Veil? How were you brought to the Twelve Kingdoms?"

"Uh... I was pulled through a mirror, an old one that was corroded and had flickering green lights dancing all over its surface, like lightening. When I went near it, Margan reached out and grabbed me."

Orm's eyebrows shot up to his hairline, or they would have, if he actually had some hair. Nessa frowned, wondering, not for the first time, at how old Orm was. The shaven head threw her off a bit, making him seem older, but his eyes were bright and there were no wrinkles around them save for a few laughter lines. Nessa thought that he was perhaps in his late twenties.

"Margan," Orm mused, completely oblivious to Nessa's pondering. "That can't be good. You sure it was a mirror?"

"I'm sure."

"Like, a hundred percent sure?"

"Yes."

"Huh." Orm leaned back, crossing his arms, looking utterly perplexed.

"I take it Margan didn't use the standard magical abduction method?"

"No," Orm murmured. "In fact, he used a way that should be impossible."

"Impossible?" But it was possible, as Nessa had discovered.

Orm nodded. "It wasn't a normal mirror that you were pulled through, but a portalling one."

"That makes sense."

"Indeed it does, except that nearly eighteen years ago every portal was destroyed."

"Clearly not all of them," Hunter muttered.

"No, it seems that not all of them were destroyed," agreed Orm. "Margan must have found one that had escaped the destruction its brothers had met. He must have used it to bring Nessa here." His thoughtful whiskey eyes landed on her. "To bring you here," he amended. "But why?"

"I haven't got the faintest idea," Nessa told him honestly.

"No?"

"Nope."

Orm's eyes slid to Aoife, who was sat by Nessa's side, busy cleaning her scales. "It can't have been just to get a new Rider. There are more than enough bastards running around. Why go to all the difficulty of finding a portal, something everyone had thought were destroyed, just for another Dragon Rider when there are so many easier options available? Unless, of course, you are different and worth the trouble Margan must have gone through to get you?"

"There's nothing remotely special about me, if that's what you're getting at."

"I wouldn't be so sure if I were you."

"No?"

Orm shook his head. "I cannot even begin to fathom how he found a portal in the first place, let alone the spell that would open it. For nigh on eighteen years, countless magic users, and many mortals too, have searched all corners of the known world for even a whisper of such a thing. None have come close, not even remotely. It is curious then, that Margan, of all people, should happen upon it, and in secret, too. It is very curious indeed, for I can guarantee that not even King Kaenar knows about this. And he knows everything that happens in his kingdoms. Margan stands to lose everything if the king finds out what he's done. King Kaenar will see this as disobedience, as treason, so there must be a bloody good reason for Margan to choose you over countless others."

"There isn't," Nessa argued. "I'm normal, boring even. Maybe Margan made a mistake."

"Margan isn't one to make mistakes."

"There's always a first for everything."

"Not in this."

"What makes you so sure?"

"I just am."

"Oh?"

"The time… The research… The magic needed… What was at stake… Margan wouldn't dare make his move unless he was absolutely sure."

"Then it must have been a coincidence."

"No," Orm said slowly. "I think there is more to you than meets the eye."

Nessa stared down at her lap. "I don't think that's true."

Orm snorted softly, his disbelief evident. However, much to Nessa's immense relief, he changed the subject slightly.

"It is a puzzle," Orm murmured, "how he found an intact portal to begin with, and it's a complete mystery of how he managed to use it. I'm finding this all quite baffling."

"What's so baffling about that?" Hunter asked. "He managed to find a portal and the spell that made it work. Tricky, maybe, but clearly he managed it."

"Even with the spell, it shouldn't have worked."

Nessa frowned, confused. "Why is that?"

"Because the pathways between the portals were broken. Even with an intact portal and the spell, it shouldn't have worked because there was nothing for the portal to connect to."

"How did that happen?"

"No one knows," Orm sighed. "Portalling has always been a fickle and dangerous business, and very few people have ever done it. You're more likely to die than make it to the desired destination. A tiny number of people have ever succeeded. It's not a thing that many seek to try."

Nessa scowled. "Nice to know that Margan could have killed me in the process of bringing me here."

Orm gave her a smile. "But you didn't die, so it's all good."

Nessa was still unimpressed.

Orm stood and made his way over to a

bookshelf. It was a sad thing, tilting to one side, the shelves broken and seemingly held up by books. It was messy too, papers and scrolls tucked into every available nook and cranny, over flowing. Orm rummaged around, sending things falling to the floor.

"Ah-ha!" he cried triumphantly, picking up a thing that had once been a book. The cover was in tatters, the spine held together by just a few threads. A couple of pages fluttered loose, drifting down to the floor like falling autumn leaves. Orm paid them no mind, jumping back into the circle of pillows and laying the poor old book in the middle. He opened it, flicking through the pages until he came upon an elaborate illustration.

It was not unlike a medieval manuscript, hand drawn and illuminated with silver and gold. In the centre was a tree, thick trunked and with far reaching branches. Nestled within its clutches were nine flat worlds, their seas spilling over the sides, dripping onto the tree's roots. The border around it was an ornate pattern, filled with lines and sigils. At first, Nessa glossed over them, finding the illustration of the tree far more interesting, but then something about a couple of the sigils stood out to her. She recognised them. Sort of.

Hunter noticed. "Have you seen this before?"

Nessa began to shake her head, ready to deny it, but then stopped. "Not this exact picture, but yes, the tree does ring a bell. It's Yggdrasil, isn't it, from

Norse mythology?"

"Perhaps that's what it's called where you're from," Orm said. "But here we call it the Erith Tree."

"The Erith Tree?"

Orm nodded. "This is how the portals were destroyed." Orm tapped a branch that connected to one world. "The pathway that led to our world was severed, the branch cut. Without our connection to the heart of the tree," he ran his finger down the branch to the tree's trunk, "we are unable to portal to any of the other worlds." His finger ran up another branch and rested on a different world.

"Fascinating," Nessa murmured.

"That wasn't all you recognised," Orm said. "Something else sparked a memory."

"Indeed." Nessa pointed to a couple of the sigils. "I've seen something very similar to these in the town where the mirror, excuse me, *portal* was."

Orm frowned. "Similar, but not exactly like these?"

"The ones I saw were more angled, sharper."

"Huh." Orm rubbed his head. "What about the others, do they seem familiar?"

Nessa peered at them. "A few," she said after a minute. "But they still differ a little from the ones I remember seeing."

"You sure?" Orm pressed.

"Yes," Nessa said, slouching back against the wooden chest, "I am completely, one hundred percent sure."

Hunter gazed at Orm. "Does this mean something important?" he asked his friend, who was starting to look troubled. "What does it mean?"

"What does it mean?" Orm mused. "I haven't got the faintest idea. This is well beyond my realm of knowledge. That's all I know for certain."

Hunter scowled. "That's all you know?"

"Well, I also know that whatever Margan did to get the portals to work is old magic, very old magic. And that can't be good. Not good at all."

"How have you come to that assumption?"

Orm tapped the illustration. "This is a copy of the oldest manuscript about the Erith Tree. I know every sigil out there and none look remotely like these. What Nessa saw must predate them. That means that they are old, a relic of a forgotten language."

Nessa grew worried. "And that's bad?"

"It's not good," Orm said. "Magic is a volatile thing, difficult to control under the best of circumstances and with spells that have been painstakingly adapted over hundreds, if not thousands of years, for a specific purpose. These sigils," he pointed to the ones in the book, "are early spells, practically raw magic. Anything predating that," he shivered at the thought, "isn't something people like Margan should be using."

"Which is very, very bad," Hunter summarised, crossing his arms.

"Absolutely," Orm confirmed.

"But what does that mean for me?" asked Nessa. "Will I be able to get back home or not?"

Orm raised a brow. "Do you want to go back home?"

"Yes?"

His eyes darted to Aoife for a millisecond. "Are you so sure of that?"

"Yes."

Orm weighed the honesty in her words. "If that's what you really want…"

"It is," Nessa said stubbornly.

"Then I suppose we should find out what sigils Margan used, since they are the best bet of understanding how he brought you here in the first place. Perhaps then, we might be able to use them to send you back."

"Good."

"Right then," Orm stood and stretched, "I'll find you some paper to draw what sigils you saw. Then I'll start searching for someone who might know something about them."

"Okay," Nessa agreed.

"But in the meantime," Orm said, "I suggest you think very carefully on what you actually want, rather than what you think is right. It seems to me that you have come to a crossroad in your life, a very important one, and one that affects more lives than just your own. I wouldn't make any hasty decisions if I were you. But then again, I would also suggest that you make your decision before someone makes it for you."

Goose bumps broke out on Nessa's arms at his words. There was a note of finality about them.

But the decision has already been made, whispered a voice that echoed in the back of Nessa's mind. She looked at Orm and Hunter, startled, thinking that it must have been one of them who had said that. But they were busy talking to each other.

I'm going crazy, Nessa decided.

No, you're not, argued the whispered voice.

"Here," Orm said, surprising her. He handed her a charcoal stick and a scrap of ripped parchment. Nessa set them down on top of a chest, using it as a makeshift desk. The charcoal was delicate in her hand, light and easily broken if she was to apply too much pressure, and the parchment was soft under her palm as she held it still.

Conscious of the two pairs of very curious eyes on her, Nessa tried her best to recreate the sigils that she had seen in the town's ruins. She was hesitant to start with, her strokes slow and measured as she drew upon her memories of them, aware that she was far from the best artist in the world. Correction: *Worlds.* Plural, because as it turned out, there was more than one of them.

After the first one was eked out onto the pale parchment, the charcoal looking rather blunt and inelegant, Nessa found that she was able to sketch another five or so before she was unable to remember anymore.

"Right," Nessa said, setting down the charcoal stick. "That's the best I can do."

"That's enough to start with, I'm sure." With nimble fingers, Orm plucked up the scrap of parchment, careful not to smudge the charcoal. He gave it a quick once over, his eyes growing cautious, and then rolled the parchment into a tube, stowing it away in his tunic's pocket. Nessa told herself that it was just her imagination that made her think Orm was handling it like he expected it to spontaneously combust.

"Alrighty then." Orm cast them a cheery smile as he headed over to the front door. "You two sit pretty here while I go and ask some questions relating to these," he patted his pocket, "and I'll be back shortly. Hopefully in time for my lunchtime drink."

"And what do you expect us to do while we wait for you?" Hunter asked, offended at being left behind.

"You should clean yourselves up," Orm advised as he slipped out. "You're less than fresh."

Chapter 28

With instructions to bathe and help themselves to any clothing they came across in the shop, Orm was gone, leaving Nessa and Hunter behind. Hunter fumed for a couple of minutes, insulted at being called dirty. Nessa, though, could see where Orm was coming from. They had been travelling nonstop for a week, a week where showers and a good bath had been nonexistent. Being told that they were 'less than fresh' was considered polite.

Nessa gazed at Hunter, noticing that he did look rather dishevelled. His clothing was travel worn, covered in grime and badly wrinkled. His hair was a mess and he was in need of a good shave. In all fairness, he had tried to a few days ago, but his blade hadn't made the job easy, and the result was that Hunter looked a bit scruffy.

As if he could sense the direction of her thoughts, Hunter ran a hand over his jaw, feeling the patches of stubble. "I guess a bath wouldn't be so bad," he said. "I suppose we might smell a bit."

"Might smell?" Nessa laughed. "I'm pretty sure we do."

Hunter snorted. "You want to go first or shall I?"

"You," Nessa said. "I'm going to take up Orm's offer of some clean clothes." Her eyes swept over the disorganised chaos of the shop. "I just need to find them first."

"Good luck with that." Hunter smirked as he headed upstairs.

Nessa stood, wondering where the clothes might be. They weren't out in the open, so she went over to the circle of chests, hoping that there might be something of use in them. The first one she opened had nothing but old books, the second, peculiar little bottles. She pulled one out, lifting it up to the light. It was small, shaped like a pear but with a long thin neck. Black wax sealed the cork, running down the sides in rivulets, and inside was a bizarre globular red liquid. The label was old and faded, the lettering indecipherable. Nessa set it back in the chest with a grimace, and having no desire to find out what the other bottles contained, she shut the chest, locking away the strange and creepy collection.

The next chest, thankfully, was filled with neatly folded clothing. Nessa smiled, grateful that she hadn't discovered anything else unsettling, and began to rummage. There was an ongoing theme with the clothes, mostly consisting of tunics and leggings, similar to what she had been wearing since her arrival to The Twelve Kingdoms. She found a long sleeved top; whilst the temperature in the cave systems was constant, it was a bit on the cold side for her liking. Next she found a top to go over it: a half dress in earthy tones of rich browns with a touch of green and orangey-reds. It had dainty bell sleeves and a ribbon lacing up the front.

She tucked it under her arm, along with the long sleeved top and a pair of dark leggings, and waited for Hunter to finish.

Nessa spent a few minutes watching Aoife, perching a hip on a wooden chest, finding herself quickly spellbound. The little dragon had slipped between two pillows, becoming somewhat wedged. Not that she seemed to care, as she appeared to have fallen asleep. Her scales twinkled as she breathed, sparkling like amethyst stars. Nessa found it unbelievable that such a creature existed, let alone that one was in front of her, contently napping in a weird little shop, in a hidden city that was under a mountain.

It seemed too bizarre to be real.

But it was real, and there Nessa was, gazing at a dragon in a weird little shop, in a hidden city that was under a mountain.

"Hey." Hunter appeared at the curtained door,

knocking Nessa out of her daydreams. His hair was wet and he had shaved. He had also changed into some clean clothes. "The bath is all yours."

"Good." Nessa hopped off the chest and crossed over to the doorway. "There's nothing better than a good wash after a long journey."

"Having just had one, I couldn't agree more."

Nessa grinned and moved past him, heading upstairs.

"Ness?" Hunter called from the bottom of the rickety stairs. She turned around, surprised at his use of a nickname that few used.

"Yes?"

"Would you like me to feed the dragon for you?" he enquired.

Nessa began smiling, but he then ruined the sweet thought by adding, "Before it gets hungry and starts munching on innocent people."

"Maybe the dragon will do me a favour and munch on you," Nessa said dryly.

Hunter laughed and disappeared into the shop.

Nessa grumbled to herself as she stood on the landing. By process of deduction, she found the bathroom. The curtained room to the left was the spare bedroom, and the one to the right was Orm's, which left the doorway directly in front of her.

Wonky floorboards gave way to solid rock as she stepped over the threshold. It was a small room, and incredibly hot, the air filled with steam. Over in the far end, sunken into the floor, was a pool, vapour swirling over the water's surface. It was naturally formed, judging by the look of it, and water drizzled in from above, running down a couple of stalactites, not unlike a shower head. At the same rate that the pool filled, it emptied. A little whirlpool sat to its side, the water draining out by a little hole. A handful of candles and some bars of soap were dotted around in some nooks, near at hand.

Nessa quickly stripped off, eager to be out of her grimy clothes, and dipped a toe in the pool's water, testing it. It was hot, like a peel-your-skin-off type of hot. Nessa bit her lip, and since there were no taps to change the temperature, she slowly lowered herself down. Instantly her skin pinkened and she held herself rigid as she slowly acclimatised. Soon, though, Nessa was able to relax, and slipped down further into the pool. The water came up to her shoulders and steam gently brushed against her face. Her bath at Margret's had been nice, but this was something close to heaven.

The cave room, the natural hot water, the flickering candle light... Nessa could easily pretend that she was at a spa.

It was hard to tell how long she simply mulled in the pool, as the water never grew cold, but once the tips of her fingers began to prune, did she finally reach for a bar of soap. An added perk of the constantly replenishing pool was that the water remained clean, no matter how much dirt Nessa scrubbed off her skin. Only when she thought that

Hunter was probably wondering where she had got to, did she unwillingly leave the water.

Nessa swiftly dressed in her commandeered clothing, and discovered that there was a narrow full-length mirror tucked over by the door. She crossed over to it, wondering how she looked.

She ran her hands down her front, smoothing out a couple of creases and adjusted the ribbon so that it lay neatly. The top of the half dress was tight fitting until it hit her waist, thanks to the lacing, making the most of her modest curves and accentuating her small waist. It then flared out, skimming over her hips and ending just below mid thigh. The leggings were form hugging and dark, either black or deep brown. It was hard to tell in the soft candle light.

Nessa had never been a voluptuous girl. She was, and would forever be, a beanpole, albeit a petite one. But there, right then, she actually had some feminine shape to her. She twisted, trying to see herself from another angle. Her hair, still wet, was a dark spill that reached down to her waist, and while she didn't have a tan, despite all the time she had spent outside, her fair skin had a healthy glow to it.

Yes, Nessa thought to herself, *this will do nicely.*

She left the bathroom and went in search of Hunter. She found him down in the kitchen, along with Aoife. He was sat on one of the wooden crates, watching with avid eyes as the little dragon nibbled a large smoked sausage.

"She's eaten three of them so far," Hunter said as

Nessa joined him. "This is her fourth."

"Are you overfeeding my dragon?"

"I'm curious to see how much a small dragon can eat."

"Well then," Nessa said, "you can clean up after her when those four sausages reappear."

"Your dragon, your mess to clean up."

Nessa crossed her arms. "We'll see."

"I—" He turned and blinked, suddenly tongue tied. "You... Um... Look different."

Nessa decided to take that as a compliment. "As I said, there's nothing better than a good bath. I feel like a whole new person."

Hunter cleared his throat. "You kinda look like one."

"Thanks?"

Hunter was saved from having to respond by the clatter of the front door. "Sounds like Orm's back," he muttered, hopping off the crate.

"That was quick."

"Not really. You were in the bath for bloody ages."

Nessa followed him into the shop. "I wasn't in there for that long."

Hunter looked doubtful.

"I have a lead," Orm declared as soon as he spotted them.

"Oh really?" Hunter said brightly. "And would this be an actual lead, or just one that you think is, but turns out not to be?"

"I reckon there's a fifty-fifty chance of it going either way."

"Sounds more promising than usual."

"Will we be going far?" Nessa asked.

"Nah," Orm said. "I found someone here, in the City."

Nessa was pleasantly surprised. "That's good, I suppose. Are we meeting them now?"

"No time like the present."

Hunter gazed at the dragon coiled around his ankles, looking up at him with large hopeful eyes. "Are we bringing this little menace with us?"

Nessa had to wonder, was that a hint of growing fondness in Hunter's tone?

Orm nodded. "Yes, because I don't want it to mess up the place, or get its greedy little claws on my expensive imported sausages. I've been saving them for a special occasion."

Hunter blanched and Nessa was forced to hide her smirk behind a hand. Those sausages were long gone, and Aoife had received a helping hand at getting her claws on them.

"Well," Hunter coughed. "That's all sorted then. We're bringing the dragon."

"Aoife," Nessa corrected. "We really need to start calling her by her name."

"Fine then." Hunter clapped his hands, eager to be off. "Pack up *Aoife* and let's get going."

Nessa gave him a look that conveyed her ire at being ordered around, but nonetheless, did as she was bid. She collected her messenger bag and boots from the spare bedroom and then rejoined Hunter and Orm downstairs. Aoife was once again bundled into the messenger bag, much to her displeasure, and Nessa shouldered it, grimacing at the growing weight.

They left immediately, heading back to the main cave where the market was held. Despite what Nessa assumed was the early hour, it was surprisingly busy, making for slow progress. With Orm leading the way, they wormed through the crowds. At first Nessa thought that they were just going to the outer reaches of the city, but when the tents came to an abrupt end, Orm continued on, striding past them without hesitation.

With a touch of trepidation, Nessa trailed behind him. They entered onto a wasteland of barren stone that stretched as far as the eye could see. There were almost no glowing mushrooms to show the way, and the shadows were thick. There was hardly a soul around, and the few people they did see were sat off to the side, nestled around small campfires, watching them pass with feral hunger in their eyes. Nessa found their stares unnerving, and she sidled closer to Hunter.

Orm, thankfully, led them away from the darkened cave, taking them through a crack in the wall. It was narrow, making them go in a single file. Orm went first, then Nessa, and Hunter brought up the rear, keeping a watchful eye on those who gazed after them.

The fissure ran for about twenty feet or so, then opened onto another cave, one that was a good deal smaller than the main cave, but still big enough to house a small community. It was brighter there than it had been in the rocky wasteland, but not by much. There was an aura of darkness, of despair. The stone was a dreary grey, and the tents were subdued hues of blues and reds. It was not a cheery place to be. Not even the glowing mushrooms could do much to add any sort of ambiance or beauty.

Nessa shivered, wanting to immediately leave and never come back.

Orm seemed to be of a different mind, striding straight ahead without so much as a pause.

Hunter came up beside her. "You alright?"

"This place gives me the chills."

"It is pretty cold in here."

"That's not what I meant and you know it."

"I know," Hunter laughed, not at all fazed. "But it was funny, you have to admit that."

"I think 'funny' is a bit of a strong word for it. Perhaps amusing or mildly humorous are a better fit."

"Fine then," Hunter said. "It was mildly amusing, you have to admit that."

Nessa smiled, keeping a cursory eye on those they passed. The people, something about them put Nessa on edge. She couldn't put her finger on it; perhaps it was the way they stared at them with strangely deep eyes? Then she had to correct herself. They weren't staring at the three of them as they went through the camp, they were staring at *her*. Not outright, but from the corners of their eyes. It was subtle, and for some reason, Nessa found it more alarming because of that. She hugged her arms around her middle, telling herself that it was just her imagination.

It's the stress. Stress makes you paranoid.

But it wasn't paranoia that made a woman at a nearby booth selling necklaces halt mid-sentence to a potential buyer. Nor was it mere paranoia that made the woman's brows pull together in a frown. Nessa stared back, thinking that if the woman realised that she had noticed the unwanted attention, then the woman would turn away. She didn't. Her lips quirked up into a little smirk, and her hand came to rest on her peculiar necklace.

Nessa gazed at it. It was a large, drooping low on the woman's chest, composed of a bar of curled wire that a number of items hung from. There was a fine quartz wand and a collection of gems threaded into long strands, and in the middle was a long white bone and a dainty skull of a songbird. The woman's fingers stroked the bones as if they were a live pet.

Nessa's eyes darted up, instantly snared in the woman's gaze. Her eyes were a flinty grey, deep set and troubled. She was not youthful, and had threads of silver in her thick black hair and creases around her mouth and across her forehead. There was something about the woman, something that made Nessa commit her face to memory. The way that her gaze went straight through Nessa reminded her of Helen. Nessa shivered and forced herself to turn away. But even so, she could still feel the woman's stare on her back, and that feeling didn't leave until distance and tents severed the connection.

Nessa breathed a sigh of relief when Orm finally brought them to a stop. However, her relief was short lived when she saw their destination.

Tucked away by itself in a gloomy alcove was a tent. It was large and round, a rich cream colour edged in gold, the middle of the roof raised in a towering point. It looked out of place amongst the smaller and darker tents around it. But the truly unsettling thing about the tent was the aura of power emanating from it, deep and formidable.

"What is this place?" Nessa whispered. The people, their deep eyes and hidden stares, the waves of power that came from the tent...

"They said that it might be him," Orm muttered. "But I had hoped that they had been mistaken."

"I presume you know whoever resides in this delightful place?" Hunter asked.

Orm nodded. "I do." He didn't sound particularly happy about that either.

"And?"

"He doesn't like me much."

"Does anyone around here?"

Orm looked wounded. "Plenty of people like me, I'll have you know."

"Oh yeah, like who?"

"Uhh..."

"Guys," Nessa interrupted. "Stop dithering around."

Hunter smirked. "Dithering?"

"Dithering." Orm rolled the word on his tongue. "That's a good one. I like that word. Dithering."

"I'm so glad," Nessa remarked dryly. "Now, can we get on with things? I don't want to be here any longer than I have to be."

"I agree," Hunter said.

"Fine, fine," Orm grumbled. "But first things first, I must give you a warning, specifically you, Hunter, my boy."

Hunter's eyebrows went up and he grinned, amused. "Oh?"

"Don't speak unless spoken to," Orm continued. "That means no sarcastic comments, no stupid questions, and no damn jokes. I don't even want to hear one teenie tiny, minute quip out of you. Out of either of you."

"Fair enough," Nessa said, more than happy to let Orm do all the talking.

"And, if you value your eyeballs, do not stare."

"Huh." Hunter frowned. "That's delightfully concerning."

Orm turned, and with a trembling hand, pushed

aside the tent's flap, revealing a dark void beyond. He stepped inside, and was almost immediately swallowed by the lurking shadows. Nessa stared after him with a feeling that was akin to horror. A voice told her to run, to pull Orm back and get as far away from there as possible. But just as there was an impulse to flee, there was a stronger force that pulled her forward, and before she knew it, the tent's shadows closed in around her.

Chapter 29

At first there was nothing but darkness, and then ever so slowly, light began to bloom. With a whisper of breath, candles suddenly came to life, small flames jumping up and dancing merrily away. There were hundreds of them, ringing the edge of the tent, every size and shape imaginable. Despite the numbers, though, the tent was still bathed in muted shadow. It was as if something was holding the light at bay, some unseen entity half-smothering the flames, making them burn weakly.

Nessa swallowed nervously as the whisper came again, blowing softly across the ground. Mist appeared, drifting up out of the rocky floor, first in trailing fingers that soon turned into a thick blanket that floated around Nessa's ankles. Aoife squirmed in her bag, sensing Nessa's growing unease, and Hunter moved closer to her side.

"Well," Orm said with forced lightness, "it seems that no one is here. I propose we leave before they come back."

Orm was right. Save for the candles and mist, there was nothing else in the tent other than them. Nessa started turning, ready to leave, when a low, ominous chuckle filled the room. Nessa could feel it deep in her bones. Unease transformed into dread, and her hand somehow found its way into Hunter's, gripping it tight.

"It's far too late for that," said a deep, cold voice.

Shadows parted like curtains and a figure was revealed.

With a hunched back and bowed legs, an old man shuffled into the middle of the tent, the mist stirring in his wake. His hair was wiry and grey, falling around his shoulders and down his back, and his face was down-turned, partially hidden from Nessa's wide, staring eyes. His clothing was dark and tattered, hanging loosely from his emaciated frame, and clenched in one age-spotted hand was a twisted walking stick.

His appearance was less than intimidating, but he radiated power. It came off him in waves, almost palpable.

Whatever he was, Nessa was sure that he wasn't human.

Orm's warning came back to her, and she was

beginning to understand his worry. Her eyes darted to him, finding that he stood rigid, a pained smile fixed on his face.

The old man came to a stop, standing in the centre of the tent, and lifted his head.

Nessa barely stifled a gasp.

His face, deeply lined by age, was devoid of eyes. There were no empty sockets or withered flaps of skin, or even scars. In their place were two smooth, shallow hollows. The sight was, to say the least, startling.

He smiled, as if he delighted in her shock.

Orm took a step forward, a very small, very unwilling step. "We're he—"

The man snarled, his smile vanishing, and bared his teeth. "Yes, you and your companions, coming in unannounced. That's very rude, you know."

"Bu—"

"And speaking of your companions," the old man hissed. "Who are they? I find myself most curious."

"Well," Orm said slowly. "This is Hunter and N—"

"Nessa," the old man interrupted with a sigh.

"How do you know my name?" Nessa blurted, troubled.

The man's eyeless face turned towards her, as if he could actually see her. "Because, girl, I know many things. The Veil of this world fluttered and shifted when you came through. The wind whispers your name when it blows, and the ground remembers where you had stepped long after you have passed. Trees sing at your touch when you brush against them, and animals watch you with reverence. It has been a long time since this world has seen one such as you, and it remembers. Oh yes, it remembers. As do I."

The back of Nessa's neck prickled at his words, and a shiver ran down her spine.

"That doesn't sound alarming whatsoever," breathed Hunter.

"Come come," the old man cackled. "Let us sit and talk." It wasn't so much a request but an order. He waved his hand and the mist around him shifted and churned. It pulled together, rising and solidifying, and turned into a circle of four chairs.

Orm didn't budge as the old man settled himself down into one, and neither did Nessa or Hunter.

The old man growled.

"Sit," he barked. "Now. Before I lose my temper."

Orm shot Nessa and Hunter a cautionary glance, and then did as he was bid, sitting down to the old man's right. Nessa reluctantly let go of Hunter's hand and followed suit. She stepped around a chair, resting a hand on its back as she did so, feeling that, despite it forming from mist, it was as solid as a real one. She sat, half expecting the seat to vanish beneath her. When it didn't, she relaxed a little. Hunter grudgingly joined them, forced to take the remaining chair to the old man's left. He did so with distaste, and Nessa was glad that she was sat between him and Orm.

"There we go," the old man sighed happily. "This is so much better, so much more civilised. Now we can perhaps talk like sophisticated people."

"People?" Hunter muttered under his breath.

Nessa had to clamp her lips shut to stop a nervous bubble of laughter.

Orm shot them a glare of warning, and they quietened down like a pair of scolded school children.

The old man set his walking stick down and leaned back in his chair. "Yes," he murmured. "This will do nicely. Now, since I know your names, I shall be fair and tell you mine. You may call me Chaos."

Nessa blinked. "Chaos?"

"That's what I said."

"But that's not a name."

"It's my name," Chaos all but snarled at her.

Nessa gulped. "And what a lovely name it is."

Chaos instantly calmed, his demeanour suddenly turning to something you'd expect from a normal elderly man. "So what do I owe to such an unexpected visit?" he asked almost pleasantly. There was still a hiss to his voice, but Nessa was beginning to think that's just how he sounded.

Orm responded first, pulling out the rolled up piece of parchment with the sigils Nessa had drawn on it. "We were wondering if you could tell us anything about these, particularly about the language and their usage." He handed it to Chaos, who lazily took it between two fingers.

Nessa wasn't quite sure what she expected to happen, considering that Chaos had no eyes, but it wasn't what followed.

Chaos lifted the parchment to his nose and inhaled.

Nessa's eyebrows shot up.

He leisurely sniffed at each of the charcoal sketches. Nessa didn't know what to make of such an odd display. Chaos stilled, the parchment held in front of him. A muscle ticked in his cheek and his head turned to face her, giving Nessa the impression that if he could see, then he would have been staring.

"You bring these to me," he asked. "Why?"

"Because I want to know what they are," Nessa said slowly, sensing that she was treading on thin ice when it came to the being sat across from her.

"And why is that?"

"Because they have something to do with how I was brought here."

"And?"

"And they might be able to send me back home."

Chaos snorted. "But my dear, you are already home. Why ever would you want to leave?"

"Because this isn't my home," Nessa murmured. "I don't belong here."

"You belong here more than you think you do."

"You're wrong."

"Am I?" He shook his head. "No, I don't think so. I think you are exactly where you are meant to be."

Nessa denied it. "You're wrong."

Chaos batted her words away with a wave of his hand.

"You're wrong," Nessa argued, gripping the chair's arms. "You are wrong."

"No, I am not," Chaos said with a cruel twist of his lips. "And a part of you knows it."

Something in Nessa's chest constricted painfully, and tears welled in her eyes. She took a shuddering breath and stared Chaos down. He seemed to sense the torrent of emotions swirling inside her and shifted in his chair, uncomfortable under her gaze.

"I don't care if the wind whispers my name or if the trees sing at my touch," Nessa said through gritted teeth. "I need to go home. I have to."

"You have no idea, do you?" Chaos whispered, almost too quiet to hear. "She never told you."

Nessa dug her fingernails into the chair's arms, focusing on the discomfort so that she didn't snap and do something she might regret. "What do I have no idea about?" she demanded. "And who didn't tell me?"

"How extraordinary."

"What is?" Nessa cried.

Hunter reached over and pried her hand open, fitting it into his, holding it tight. His thumb ran over her knuckles, slow and methodical, trying to soothe her.

"How very extraordinary," Chaos repeated, thoughtful. "You really don't know, do you? You don't have the slightest inkling of how rare you are."

"We already know what she is," Hunter said. "We know that she's from one of the Twelve Houses. And trust me, there's more than enough of them around for anyone's liking."

"THE TWELVE HOUSES!" Chaos bellowed, making everyone flinch. "You think she has those curs blood running through her veins?"

Finally, Nessa thought, *he says something agreeable.*

Hunter blinked. "Uh..."

"Told you I wasn't," Nessa muttered.

"Indeed you're not," Chaos agreed, his tone making her pause. "What you belong to is a much more prestigious bloodline. Isn't that right, Orm?"

Nessa turned to Orm, who had been uncharacteristically quiet so far. His face had gone bone white, and he stared at Chaos with troubled eyes.

"Maybe," he said slowly, hesitant. "But there is one thing that strongly indicates that she does, in fact, belong to one of the Twelve Houses."

"If you are referring to the dragon hatchling that is in her bag, then you are misinformed. That means nothing."

Nessa frowned, not knowing what they were talking about, and rested a hand on her bag, which was sat on her lap. Aoife had been quiet and still since they had entered the tent, and Nessa wondered how Chaos knew that she was there. Nessa looked over at Hunter, hoping he might be able to shed some light onto what was happening, but he appeared to be as bewildered as she was.

Orm sounded like he was reciting something. "Only those with blood from the Twelve Families—"

"—Can hatch and bond with a dragon," Chaos cut him off. "Yes, I know what most have been taught. However, there's more to it than that."

"I am so confused," Nessa muttered.

Hunter's hand tightened on hers, a small comfort, but one she clung to like it was a lifeline.

Chaos sighed. "I can see this is going to be more difficult than I originally thought."

Nessa looked between Orm and Chaos, feeling that a panic attack was fast approaching. This wasn't going how she had thought it would. Something loomed on the horizon, something big and life altering. Something scary.

"Can someone please explain what you are talking about?" Nessa all but pleaded. She regretted entering the tent, and she regretted it more because she found it impossible to leave, despite the growing misgivings in her gut.

"Fine, fine," Chaos huffed. "But I want some tea before I start. I find tea is always a nice way to help unravel the truth of things."

Orm spoke up. "I don't think this is the best way of dealing with something like this."

"Quiet, half-breed," Chaos snapped. "The minute she entered your pathetic excuse of a shop, you knew what she was. You could have told her. You could have saved her from this."

Nessa gazed at him in question. "Orm?"

Orm shook his head mournfully, unable to look her in the eye.

"I presume, girl," Chaos said, "that you know why and how the bonding between human and dragon came about."

"Hunter explained some of it to me," Nessa murmured hesitantly.

"Good. Now for the tea." Chaos lazily clapped his hands together and, out of thin air, a steaming mug appeared. Nessa caught it before it had a chance to fall, more than a little startled. She peered into it, finding that it was some kind of herbal tea. Nessa grimaced. God, what she'd give for a brew of proper English tea right then.

Nessa looked at her companions, finding that they were holding identical beverages. Hunter, like her, was less than impressed.

"My kind has inhabited this land since the dawning of time," Chaos began, slurping his tea. "We were here long before the humans arrived and we will be here long after they leave. We are beings of magic, it is who and what we are. Dragons, too, are creatures of magic, and together we are tied to the weft and warp of the world. What harms us, harms the land. And what harms the land, harms us.

"When the humans first came to these lands, they brought a great number of things with them; knowledge of things that we had yet to discover, how to build mighty castles, how to kill one another over land and materialistic goods. But they also brought with them a terrible sickness.

"It decimated the dragons population.

"As a result, my kind and the land began to suffer. We came together, forming a spell that would save the dragons from the sickness. Since it was the humans who had caused it in the first place, we decided that they would be the ones bonded to the dragons, in case there were any side effects from the spell.

"We are not stupid creatures. We knew that the humans had a lust for power. They did back then, and they still do today. We knew that binding them to the dragons would give them an advantage, give them supremacy over lesser beings. So we wove in a loophole, a means that, should the Dragon Riders ever get out of control, we would have a way to rein them back in. You, Nessa, are our loophole."

Nessa sat quietly, absorbing his words.

"What kind of loophole are we talking about here?" Hunter asked.

"Well," Chaos smiled grimly, "we wouldn't give the humans all the power of the dragons without saving some for ourselves, now would we?"

Something clicked. "Your loophole is..."

Chaos cackled. "Yes. The loophole is an Old Blood."

Stunned silence.

"Impossible," Hunter breathed.

"Not as impossible as you think, little human," Chaos snapped.

"But it is," Hunter argued. "The Old Bloods have been hunted to extinction. There is nothing left of them but descendants, mixed bloods like Orm."

"You know nothing, boy," Chaos spat. "You are sat in a room with two of them."

"Two and a half," Orm muttered. "If you want to be precise."

Their argument finally sank in, and Nessa snorted. "You think that I'm one of these mysterious Old Bloods?" That was even more ludicrous than thinking that she belonged to one of the Twelve Houses.

"I don't think," Chaos growled. "I know."

"Impossible," Hunter murmured again, staring at her with wide, wondrous eyes.

Perturbed, Nessa swallowed her growing panic, feeling like it was about to choke her. "I agree with Hunter," she said. "It's impossible. I think I would have noticed if I belonged to a race of magic beings. Come to think of it, I'm pretty sure I would have noticed if my parents did as well."

"Not if they weren't your real parents," Chaos

said quietly.

Nessa was shocked into silence. Then, when it felt as if she could breathe again, she was caught in a bubble of nervous laughter, startling Hunter and Orm. Chaos sat looking rather impassive, waiting for her brief moment of hysteria to end.

"You think I'm..." Nessa raised a hand to her mouth, unable to finish, trying to force back a snicker.

"Adopted," Chaos bit out. "Yes. I am almost certain that you are adopted."

Hearing the word out loud was like having a bucket of freezing water tipped over her. Nessa slumped back in her chair, feeling like the very earth had been ripped open, swallowing her whole.

"How can you be so sure?"

"I am a Wraith," Chaos said as if that explained everything. "I know many things."

"A Wraith?" Nessa mumbled.

"Impossible," Hunter said, using his favourite word of the hour.

"Quite possible," Chaos hissed. "I assure you."

"But all the Old Bloods have been hunted to—"

"Extinction," Chaos cut him off. "Yes, I heard you the first time you said that. You're repeating yourself. Open your ears, boy, and try not to be so stupid. Yes, we have been hunted, near on five hundred years, and yes, we are close to extinction, but we're not there yet. A few of us are left, clinging to the edge of society, forgotten by most, fading to nothing more than stories told to scare children. I am the last of my kind, but I will be here long after your bones have turned to dust."

Hunter wisely swallowed any response.

A hand touched Nessa's arm, and she looked up, finding Orm gazing at her with compassion.

"Are you alright there?" he asked gently.

"Fine," Nessa said automatically. "I'm fine."

"She's lying, just so you know," Chaos sneered. "She's just realised that her whole life has been nothing but a lie."

"Don't think of it like that, Nessa," Orm said. "I'm sure your parents had a very good reason for not telling you."

The thing is, Nessa thought miserably, *it's very hard not to think like that.*

She didn't respond. There were no words that could express what she was feeling.

Orm patted her arm, then settled back in his chair, asking, "Do you have any idea of what kind she might be?"

Chaos shook his head. "I'm not completely sure. She could be several different things."

"A half-breed like me?" Orm sounded almost hopeful.

"No," Chaos snorted, "she is most certainly not a mongrel like you. The light I see around her is too strong for that. A pure breed, I am sure. Though what, I do not yet know."

"You don't know," Nessa muttered. "You tell me

this... this horrible thing, and you don't know what I am, only that I'm not human."

"I know many things," Chaos answered. "It is rare that something turns up that I cannot figure out immediately."

"Lucky me then," Nessa grumbled.

"I am a Wraith," Chaos said. "I always find the answers to the world's mysteries, sooner or later."

"A Wraith," Hunter snorted. "No, you're not."

Chaos snarled. "What would you know about it, boy?"

"I've heard the stories."

"Oh, the stories?" Chaos gave a sinister smile. "And what do those stories say?"

Hunter gulped, beginning to sense the aura of danger that permeated through the air. From the corner of her eye, Nessa saw Orm slump, head in his hand, eyes squeezed shut.

"I did tell him to keep his mouth closed," Orm moaned. "I swear."

It seemed that Nessa was the only one who heard him.

"Well," Hunter continued after a little pause, "I heard that you were a sight to be reckoned with, formidable and unearthly, with wings and eyes that could see into a man's soul." He shook his head. "And right now, you're not meeting my expectations."

That probably wasn't the best thing to say.

Nessa closed her eyes in acquiescence as Chaos

shot to his feet.

"YOU INSULT ME SO?" he bellowed. "I'VE KILLED PEOPLE FOR LESS!"

Hunter stammered an apology.

There was a heart stopping noise. The sound of crunching bone and popping joints. Nessa's eyes sprang open, fearing that Hunter was meeting an unfortunate end. He sat cowering in his chair, face bone-white, his gaze fixed with terrified fascination on Chaos.

Nessa stared.

Chaos' humped back twitched and shifted, moving like there were large snakes under his clothes. Sickening pops and cracks sounded, painfully loud, making Nessa flinch with each and every one of them. Then, erupting from his back, ripping through his tunic and overcoat, were two enormous wings. Scarred and tattered, riddled with holes and with razor sharp talons jutting from the top joint, they were a horrifying sight to behold.

Nessa recoiled in her chair as Chaos straightened.

Gone was the blind, withered old man, replaced by a creature that would best suit a nightmare than real life.

His grey hair was now dark, falling as straight as a pin to his waist, and the wrinkles had vanished, restored to smooth, youthful skin. But the most astonishing transformation, second to the wings, were his eyes, which were now deep set and a pale, piercing blue, almost indistinguishable from the whites. They seemed, as Hunter had mentioned, to possess the ability to stare into a man's soul. Around them was a thick ring of jagged scars, as if something or someone had tried to claw them out.

"I am a Wraith," Chaos snarled, his tone ominous. "A knower of life and death. I see many things, Hunter Greyson, and I see that death and grief linger around you. They reside deep in your heart. Do not cross me again, or your mother will have another body to bury."

Hunter, if it was at all possible, went even paler.

Chaos turned those eerie eyes to Nessa and Orm, who blanched.

"Now," Chaos growled. "Get out of my tent."

They couldn't leave fast enough.

Chapter 30

The journey back to Orm's home was slow and done in silence. Chaos seemed to have rendered Hunter mute, and Orm was absorbed in his own thoughts, his long legged strides taking him far into the lead. Nessa, well, she just wanted to be left alone, so the silence was oddly welcome. Her mind and emotions were in turmoil, and her shoulders were tense. A headache was quickly building behind her eyes and she wanted nothing more than a dark room where she could hide from everyone, and a blanket that she could bundle herself into while she cried her heart out.

Yes, she thought, *crying seems like a fine idea.*

Adopted.

The very word brought tears to her eyes. Out of all the things that Nessa had thought Chaos might reveal, that was not one of them. It felt as if her entire world had been thrown into doubt. Suddenly being told that your parents weren't your parents, there was no coming back from that. There was no forgetting.

Adopted.

Surely it can't be so?

Maybe Chaos was wrong.

But what if he was right?

Though Nessa hated to admit it, to even think it, what Chaos had told her rang true in a profound way. Memories besieged her, those of the hushed arguments that had always happened at night between her parents when she was younger. The arguments that, though subtle and indirect, had been about her.

Nessa sniffled and her arms tightened around her messenger bag, holding it and the little dragon inside closer to her chest. Aoife was still, perhaps sensing Nessa's growing distress and not wanting to add to it.

She recalled that when she was small, particularly during school, she had always felt as if she didn't quite belong, as if there was a glass wall between her and the rest of the world. She could see people, and they could see her, but there was an invisible barrier between them. Not to say that she had a terrible time of it all. There were a few friends over the years, someone to sit with at lunch and occasionally meet up with during the weekends. But those friendships had never ran deep. Sooner or later they would go their separate ways and that was the end of that. They would never talk or see each other again, and so the cycle would continue, repeating itself, never changing.

It seemed like nothing would ever be the same again.

At the time, Nessa had put it all down to childish insecurity, but now she had to wonder. Was it because she didn't belong there? Did everyone else sense her different-ness and that's why no one had ever got particularly close to her?

That idea was fuel for her troubled thoughts.

Orm had his front door open before Nessa got there, and she stepped into the happy mess that served as both the shop and the living room. No semblance of peace came over her, no tranquillity. In fact, the desire to run and hide grew to an overwhelming degree.

Hunter came in behind her, shutting the door after him.

"Well," he said finally, breaking the silence, "that was a very unpleasant experience."

"You're telling me," Nessa grumbled, shuffling over to the other side of the room.

Hunter watched her go with shadowed eyes. "Hey, I didn't mean it like that."

"I know you didn't." She began ascending the stairs, making them groan.

"Do you want some company?" Hunter called

from the bottom. "A shoulder to lean on?"

"I just need... I just need to be alone for a while."

Hunter sounded like he was going to protest, but then a murmured voice made him pause. Orm. He had a hand on Hunter's arm, capturing his attention and allowing Nessa to slip into the spare bedroom.

It was almost pitch black in there, the candle burnt down to little more than a puddle of molten wax with a sad little flame clinging to the last of the wick. The bed beckoned and after letting Aoife out of the bag, Nessa laid down and pulled the blanket over her head, as if it could shield her from her problems.

She could hear a conversation downstairs. Hunter's and Orm's voices floated up, muffled by the thick stone walls and the curtained doorways. Nessa didn't let them bother her. It didn't sound like they were coming upstairs at any rate, judging by the sound of things, which suited her just fine. She was pretty sure they were having a hushed argument. What about, Nessa couldn't even begin to guess.

Tears leaked from under closed eyelids, and Nessa rolled onto her side, burying her head under her pillow, hoping that it muffled her sobs. She cried until she could cry no longer. Her eyes became puffy and her nose blocked up. Nessa was a mess and felt no better for it.

Her bed jumped as something settled on it. Startled, Nessa pulled down the blanket and peered over her shoulder, finding Aoife standing over her, staring with wide cat-like eyes.

"Hey, little one," Nessa croaked. "It's alright. I'll be fine. I'm just a weepy old thing today, eh?"

Aoife stepped forward, clambering over her side and sat down, tucking herself against Nessa's stomach and curled into a neat ball.

Nessa sighed unhappily and rested a hand on the little dragon, taking a small amount of comfort from the silent companionship, and closed her aching eyes, finally managing to stem the flow of tears. She sniffled, wishing for a tissue but not having the energy or the inclination to go find one.

Time passed, although Nessa didn't know how much. Hunter and Orm's apparent argument wound down and there was a period of quietness. Faintly, she could hear sounds of movement from downstairs, but that was about it.

As it turned out, learning that your entire life had been built on a lie was tiring business, and before Nessa knew it, she was slipping into an unsettled doze.

༄◆༅

Just like the other times it happened, light slowly bloomed until the whole picture came into focus. At first it felt like she was having a dream, then she looked down and saw her translucence, and she realised. She was in one of her waking dreams again.

Nessa swore. "Oh, for the love of God. Why now? Can't I just have a break? Just one little one? Damn it."

Nothing. No magical response. No waking up in Orm's spare bedroom. It seemed that she was there for the foreseeable future. Or until she was sent back to the real world, since she had yet to figure out how to escape on her own.

Nessa looked around, finding herself standing in an old alleyway. A layer of dirt partially covered the cobbled ground, and the buildings crowded in on either side, towering three stories high, blocking out much of the night's sky. Their wooden shutters were closed and no light shone from around their edges. All was still and deathly quiet. A few tall iron lamp posts sat on one side of the street, casting small rings of soft illumination at intervals. They looked similar to antique Victorian ones.

A sound reached her ears, faint at first but growing steadily stronger. It took Nessa a second to place it, but then she realised that it was the click of hurried footsteps on the cobblestones. She turned around.

In the distance, a small cloaked figure was moving swiftly towards her.

She couldn't tell much about them, but as they neared, Nessa knew that they were female, even though a hood was pulled low over their face. In their arms, half hidden beneath the edges of their cloak, was a small bundle. Judging by the way it was carried, Nessa guessed that whatever it was, was precious and fragile.

The woman strode past Nessa without seeing her, and continued down the street. After a moment of deliberation, Nessa followed, feeling that maybe some universal force was showing her this for a reason. It was a long shot, but something useful might come out of these strange things. Maybe.

The woman turned a corner, quickly glancing behind her as she did so, and vanished from sight. Nessa looked, but saw no one there. Was the woman being followed? Her bearing certainly suggested that she thought so.

Nessa hastened around the corner, not wanting to lose sight of the woman, who was already a surprising distance away, moving at a pace that was almost a jog. Nessa chased after the woman as she went around another bend, and when she caught up with her, Nessa found herself in a small courtyard. A sense of déjà vu came over her.

There was little illumination, nothing save the full moon that hung low overhead.

The courtyard was perfectly round and surrounded by tall walls. In the centre was a pond-like feature that sank deep into the ground, with a narrow staircase that hugged the side and curled into the impenetrable darkness. The woman hesitated at the top of the stairs, and then descended down them, holding the little bundle tighter to her chest.

Nessa stepped forward, coming to a stop just as the woman had. She peered into the darkness below, barely able to discern the clocked figure, and swallowed her nerves. With slow, cautious steps, Nessa followed the woman, careful as to where she put her feet.

The déjà vu grew stronger once Nessa reached the bottom, for there, set in the opposite wall, was a mirror that gently flickered with light.

Nessa stared in disbelief.

"Not possible," she whispered.

The town and the courtyard were different, meaning it wasn't the one that she had come through, but the mirror itself was identical except for the lights that chased their way over its surface. These were a stark white, whereas the ones from before had been green, matching Margan's eyes.

Hope flared in Nessa's heart. There was another portal, one hidden away somewhere. She could find it, use it perhaps, and stand a chance of going home and discovering the truth about herself.

The lights were sporadic and not particularly bright. Little of the underground room was visible to Nessa, and it took her eyes a few minutes to adjust to the gloom. The woman stared at the mirror with the same kind of enrapture as Nessa did, although maybe with a touch of fear, judging by the way she stood.

A noise came from behind them, startling them both. The woman let out a little shriek as she turned, spotting a hunched figure shuffling out from under the stairs. Nessa frowned, mouth parting in confusion when she realised that it was Chaos. He was in his blind old man guise, his walking stick gently tapping against the flagstone floor. *What's he doing here?*

"Fear not, Melissa," he said. "It is only I."

Melissa visibly relaxed. "You gave me a fright."

"So I saw." The amusement quickly faded from his voice. "Have you been followed? Do they know?"

"They know," Melissa murmured, gazing down at the bundle in her arms. "They are close. We do not have much time."

Chaos moved over to Melissa, his gaze following hers. "Is this the one?"

Melissa nodded.

"Where is the mother?"

Melissa shook her head. "They knew. They were waiting for us. She...She didn't make it."

Chaos sighed, his shoulders sagging. "This is a terrible loss."

"I promised her that I would care for the child, that I will raise it as my own."

Curious, Nessa crossed over to them, peering over their shoulders.

Wrapped tightly in thick blankets, nothing visible but one tiny fist and the face, eyes closed tight in sleep, was a baby.

Though Nessa didn't have much experience with

babies, she could easily tell that it couldn't be much older than a few hours. Nessa understood Melissa's meaning that the mother was no longer alive.

Chaos' head snapped to the side, as if he heard something, although Nessa and Melissa hadn't.

"We must hurry," he said with urgency. "They are near."

"What do I do?"

"Stand by the mirror," Chaos instructed, waving her forward. "I have already started the spell. All it needs now is to be completed."

"By the mirror," Melissa muttered nervously as she went to stand before the flickering lights.

From his pocket, Chaos removed a rolled up piece of paper. It was too dark to read down there, but that didn't hinder him. Just as he had earlier, he lifted it to his nose and inhaled. Barely above a whisper, he began to chant, reciting the words on the paper, the spell. They were lost on Nessa, who only heard the occasional one, but even so, she could tell that the language of which he spoke was ancient and held great power.

The lights flared, suddenly blinding. Nessa knew what happens next.

"May the Gods be kind and protect you both," Chaos said as he finished the incantation.

And then, with a crackle and a flash, Melissa and the baby vanished through the mirror.

Chaos stood in silence, staring after them for a long moment, then he shook himself, standing as straight as his hunched back would allow.

"Now for the hard part," he grumbled. He dropped his walking stick to the ground, and it landed with a sharp clatter that seemed too loud in the quietness of the underground room. Chaos rubbed his hands together, clicked his fingers, and raised his arms, palms out, aimed at the mirror.

Something happened. A charge filled the room, heavy and static, making it feel alive. Then, with a mighty *crunch*, the mirror fractured and shattered into a million pieces. Silvered glass rained down, hitting the floor with delicate sounding *pings*. With the air still vibrating with power, Nessa somehow knew that the mirror wasn't the only one that had been broken.

She also knew that she wasn't in the present.

Nessa was in the past. Again. She was sure of it.

༄ ✦ ༄

Nessa awoke with a gasp. At first, the darkness was the same as that of the waking dream's, but then she became aware of the soft mattress beneath her hip and the dragon curled up beside her. She relaxed when she realised that she was back at Orm's, and not completely alone either.

The curtain over the doorway twitched as someone went to leave.

"Hunter?" she called, still groggy with sleep and a little disorientated by the lingering grip of the waking dream.

He turned around. "You're up," he said, surprised. "I didn't mean to wake you."

"You didn't," Nessa assured him, sitting.

"Oh." He appeared relieved. "I was just seeing if you were alright, and to bring you this." He held out a plate that was piled high with food. "Thought you might be a bit hungry. I didn't think that you would be asleep."

Nessa leaned back, settling against the wall. "I'm not asleep now."

"No," he said, going over to her. He held out the plate and she took it, setting it down on her lap. Nessa looked at it, but couldn't see what was on it. It was all just a dark shape.

Hunter noticed. "Here," he said, slipping out in to the hallway. He was back a second later, holding the hallway's candle. "It's not the best, but it will have to do."

"It's fine," Nessa murmured. She saw that dinner, at least she presumed that it was time for it to be considered dinner, consisted of a rustic sandwich. Ham and cheese in a homemade bun. "This is lovely." She began eating although she wasn't particularly hungry. She supposed that it just gave her something to do.

Hunter placed the candle on the floor and clambered onto the bed next to her. He picked up Aoife and placed her on his lap, much to the little dragon's irritation. Even so, she quickly settled down, curling up into a ball again.

"Orm was going to dish out his specially imported smoked sausages," Hunter said, "but then he discovered that I had fed them to your dragon."

"And how did he handle that revelation?"

"Well, that's kind of why I assumed you'd be awake. I thought the shouting would have even roused the dead. You must have been out for the count."

"I suppose I must have been."

"There were death threats and everything."

"Death threats," Nessa murmured thoughtfully. "I'm almost sorry I missed all of that."

"Mmm. He was so angry, he actually had me fearing for my life."

"Impressive."

"Yeah."

"Aoife liked them, though, if that's any consolation to him."

"It wasn't."

"Oh dear."

Sandwich finished, Nessa leaned across the bed and put the plate on the floor. When she sat back, she was closer to Hunter, her arm gently touching against his. Neither of them moved. Then, feeling rather forlorn, Nessa sighed and rested her head on his shoulder. Hunter held himself still, as if he feared that the slightest twitch might scare her away, as if she was a skittish animal. Then, ever so slowly, he relaxed, and Nessa loosely wrapped an arm around him, her hand finding its way into his, their fingers twining together.

The solitary candle did little to illuminate much of the room other than a small ring around it. The light barely reached them, giving them the sense of privacy, of secrecy.

"How you holding up?" Hunter asked, voice barely above a whisper.

"I don't know what to think anymore," Nessa confessed.

"That's understandable."

"Is it?"

"Sure. You've had a lot happen to you in the last couple of weeks. You know, since you came here."

"An awful lot," Nessa agreed.

"And it will take time for you to sift through all of it and see how you feel."

"Time," Nessa murmured. "That's the one thing I don't really have much of."

"Oh?"

Nessa sighed. "You see, this is where things get a little messy."

"Intriguing."

"My mum, at least the woman who I thought was my mum, is expecting a baby." She tried to keep the bitterness out of her voice, although she didn't quite succeed. "I want to be there for her when she has it, you know, to support her and stuff."

"That doesn't sound messy."

"No, when it's put like that, I suppose it doesn't.

But I have to admit that I wasn't kind to her when the pregnancy was announced. You see, it isn't papa's child. It's my half-sibling, as I was led to believe. Mum had an affair; fell in love with another man and... When papa found out that she was pregnant with another man's child, he lost it. He was so angry, furious. Mum and I were kicked out. He didn't want anything to do with either of us ever again. It broke my heart, hearing him say that. I blamed mum, and I... I suppose that I was horrible to her. Since papa didn't want anything to do with us, we were forced to move up north, in with mum's, for a lack of a better word, lover."

The words were spilling from Nessa of their own accord. "I hated it there. It was the complete opposite to what I was used to, to what I had grown up with. I'm a city girl, born and bred. The remote countryside was an alien world to me. And the man, mum's new love, the baby's father, I didn't like, not at all. I held him accountable, you see. I felt that he was just as responsible for what had happened as mum was. They were both to blame, I guess, but not in the way I originally thought."

Nessa cringed at the memory of how she had behaved. "I had a lot of time to myself in Ironguard. In that time I did a lot of thinking, and I came to see the truth of things between my parents, and I now understand something. What mum did wasn't as selfish as I had first thought. Her new man loves her, I see that now. He loves her with all his heart, and she loves him back. Love is an honest thing, I think, and I cannot blame either of them for it. Not now, though I wish I had seen it sooner. I've made it difficult for them, and I want to set things right between us, especially before the baby is born."

Hunter was meditative, absorbing her words. "I find it hard to imagine you being horrible to anyone."

"I was. It was hard on her, losing papa and dealing with the pregnancy. She was ever so ill the first few months. I could have helped her out more, but I didn't. I was spiteful and selfish."

"You were hurting," Hunter corrected her gently. "The man who raised you threw you and your mother away. No one would be thinking straight after that, not for a time at least. No matter how you act, a mother's love never fades, not completely. No matter how you behaved towards her, your love for her never lessened. She would have known that."

"You think?"

"I know."

"You can't."

"I do," Hunter argued. "And the fact that you now feel guilty about everything and wish to make it up to her tells me that you were just reacting to the situation. Your actions were not malicious. That speaks volumes."

"It does?"

"Yes. So I suggest that you relax a bit."

"Words of wisdom?"

"An order."

Nessa shifted, just a little, and looked up at Hunter, finding him gazing down at her. "I am a horrible person though."

Those amber eyes of his met hers. "What makes you say that?"

A week. That's how long they had known each other, and it was a week that had made everything start to change. The lines that had been so defined to her had now become blurred. Nessa wasn't sure where she stood anymore. Did she listen to her heart or her head?

"Because," she murmured, "for all the wanting of making things right between me and mum, a growing part of me wants to stay here a little longer."

"Is that so?"

"Yes."

And then it just happened.

Nessa wasn't quite sure how. One second they were staring into each other's eyes, and the next, Hunter's lips were pressed against hers, warm and soft. Was he the one to move first? Was it her? In any event, she found herself not wanting it to stop, and her heart began to jump in a skittering dance.

Quite suddenly, Hunter pulled back, looking just as surprised as Nessa felt.

"I didn't..." he whispered.

Someone cleared their throat and whatever Hunter was about to say was abruptly forgotten as they turned to the source. Nessa was mortified to discover that Orm had poked his head around the curtain doorway and was staring at them, smirking.

"Well well well," he said. "What do we have here?"

Nessa's cheeks burned red, and she realised that Hunter had an arm around her waist, tucking her up against him. How had that happened without her noticing? She scooted back, and Hunter's arm slid away.

"What?" Hunter demanded, glaring at his friend, flustered.

Orm gave them an owl-like blink, slow and knowing. "We're needed downstairs."

"Why?"

"There's trouble." Orm retreated, his footsteps sounding on the rickety stairs.

Hunter gave a long suffering sigh. "I di—"

Nessa hopped off the bed and began tugging on her boots. "We should go down and see what that's about."

"Right." Hunter coughed. "Of course." He rose and went over to the door. "I'll... umm... Just go down, then?"

Nessa nodded as she tied the laces. "Sure. Yeah. I'll be down in a sec." She couldn't bring herself to look at him just yet, not with her lips still tingling.

"Right," he said, leaving, slowly making his way downstairs.

With him gone, Nessa breathed a small sigh of

relief. *What the hell am I doing?* she wondered. *Did that actually happen?*

Yes, yes it had. Her heart fluttered in her chest as confirmation. She pressed her hands against her cheeks, feeling them burn against her cool palms. *Damn it, Nessa. What do you think you're playing at?*

It was a momentary lapse of judgement, surely?

Right.

That's what Nessa told herself. It was nothing more than a momentary lapse of judgement. Reciting that in her head, Nessa squared her shoulders, ordered her cheeks to stop being so damn pink, bundled Aoife in the messenger bag, and went to join the others.

In Orm's shop, she found him and Hunter there, and even more worryingly, Chaos as well.

Chaos was the younger, more monstrous version of himself. His glacial blue eyes landed on her as she moved over to them, the scars deepening and looking even more ghastly, if that was at all possible. His horrifying batwings were tucked neatly against his back, the talons peeking above his shoulders, and his face was grave.

"They are here," Chaos said. "They have come for you."

Chapter 31

A shock wave ran through the shop. None of them were able to fully digest the news. Instinctively, Nessa's hand went to her bag, resting on Aoife. Shadow's promise of returning for her echoed in her mind.

"Who has come?" she found herself asking, hoping, praying that she was wrong.

She wasn't. It was worse.

"Margan and Shadow,"

It was like being punched in the chest. "Both of them?"

Chaos inclined his head. "And their beasts."

"Beasts?"

"Their dragons," Hunter muttered, troubled.

"Dragons," Nessa repeated. "They have dragons. They're Dragon Riders?"

Nods all round.

"Both of them?" Nessa was horrified. "That's not possible, is it?"

"It is," Orm said. "They are both Riders, and have been for many years. They are the Riders for House Sliðen and House Íren. Their dragons are mature and powerful. You are no match for them. We are no match for them. At least not yet."

The revelation slowly filtered in, and Nessa recalled her first meeting with Margan, when he had pulled her through the mirror. His hand, which had since been bandaged, had born a mark. A scar, Nessa realised, which was not dissimilar to her own. Shadow; she had seen his, although it had been twisted and stretched. She hadn't yet put all the pieces together, but it began making some sense to her.

"What do we do?" Nessa asked, panicked, searching for an answer.

Orm sighed, running a hand over his head in thought. "We need to go."

"Go where?"

"Away from here," he said, coming to some kind of decision. "We need to get as far away as we can from Margan and Shadow. Then we'll decide what to do next."

"We're all going?" Nessa was surprised. "As in you and Chaos?" Both of them nodded, although Chaos looked less than pleased at the prospect.

"We can't very well have you and Hunter

gallivanting off by yourselves, now, can we?" Orm said. "You two clearly need chaperones."

Nessa's mouth fell open and she went bright red. Hunter shot his friend a warning glare, which was promptly ignored.

"We need to hurry," Chaos growled. "They are nearing the city."

"Which way are they coming from?" Hunter asked.

Chaos turned his head to the side, as if he was listening to something from a great distance. "The southern entrance."

"We'll leave through the northern tunnels," Orm said.

"That way is like a maze." Hunter frowned. "We can't risk getting lost."

"We won't get lost," Orm sighed. "I know that way like the back of my hand. And anyway, it will be nigh on impossible for them to follow us if we go that way. Their dragons won't fit through the tunnels. If they want to follow us, they'll have to do so on foot. In which case, they risk getting lost, giving us extra time to leg it."

Hunter nodded his head in approval. "Sounds like a good plan when you put it like that."

"I'm so glad," Orm said dryly.

Hunter scowled.

"Stop bickering," Chaos snapped. "They have arrived at the cave's entrance. They will be upon us soon."

"Oh no," Nessa whispered. Her worst nightmare was becoming real. Shadow without a dragon would have been bad enough, but Margan and two dragons coming to retrieve her as well? The thought of them getting their hands on her made Nessa's blood turn to ice.

"Come," Orm said as he strode over to the front door. He held it open and ushered them out, locking it behind him. "I bloody expect it to be in pristine condition when I return," he muttered as he pocketed the key. "I've paid next month's rent in advance."

"Pristine condition?" Hunter mocked as they set off. "Are you expecting someone to come and clean up while you're away?"

"I have no idea what you're talking about."

"The place is a mess."

"It's a shop," Orm argued. "It's meant to be filled with things."

"You're a hoarder and use the shop as a front for your bad habit."

"Lies. Malicious lies."

The banter came to an abrupt end when they entered the main cavern. It was bedlam, a city in alarm and confusion. Thousands of people rushed to-and-fro, arms filled with belongings, panic on their faces. The city was being evacuated with no clear order, and instantly Nessa and her companions were swept away with the wave of people. They didn't fight against it, and just went with the flow.

Orm, with his impressive height, towering above most people by at least a head, led the way, cutting through the crowds with ease. Chaos helped too, since people endeavoured to stay as far away from him as possible once they caught a glimpse of his scarred eyes and huge bat-like wings. Orm took them along the cave's wall, heading, Nessa presumed, northward.

They were quick in reaching the far end of the cave, and looming before them was a dark fissure that stood like a gaping mouth in the stone. A handful of people disappeared into it, but other than that, no one ventured near, preferring to leave via a couple of larger tunnels opposite in a mass flood.

They had just reached it when Chaos raised a hand, gesturing for them to stop. They skidded to a halt, hardly daring to breathe. Then they noticed it.

The earth beneath their feet trembled.

Gently at first, but with growing strength. Soon loose rocks began to rattle and the stalactites above shuddered.

Thud.

Thud.

Boom.

The rocks started to jump and bounce.

Boom.

Boom...

...Boom...

A hush fell over The Hidden City as thousands of

eyes turned to the southern end of the cave.

BOOM!

The ground shook with enough force to send more than a few people to their knees. Nessa reached out, grabbing the wall for support, feeling a level of fear and dread that was nearly as powerful as the shaking.

BOOM!

"What is that?" Nessa cried. "An earthquake?"

Hunter, eyes alarmingly wide, shook his head.

BOOM!

The southern end of the cave exploded.

Boulders the size of small houses were flung into the air as if they weighed nothing, and the cavern was instantly filled with dust and debris that smothered the glow of the ethereal mushrooms, plunging the cave into murky darkness.

From the gloom and the falling rubble, a monster emerged.

Then the screaming started.

The dragon released a torrent of green tinged flame and let loose a deafening roar. Even in the semidarkness, it sparkled like the finest jade. Its claws, teeth and the spikes that ran down its spine were as white as snow and shimmered like pearls. In the dragon's eyes, which were the colour of emeralds, there gleamed a terrible glee as it beheld the sight of people fleeing in terror. Fixed on its back, nestled between two spikes, was a saddle. In the saddle sat Margan. Even from afar, Nessa knew that it was him.

Nessa stood frozen, and before she knew what he was doing, Chaos ripped the messenger bag from her shoulder, handing it to Hunter, who looked incredibly shaken.

"What are you doing?" she snapped, reaching out to grab it back.

Chaos caught her wrist in an iron grip. "It will be bad enough if they capture one of you," he growled, glacial blue eyes sparking dangerously. "It will be the end of us if they get both you and the dragon. It is wise to take the precaution of separating you until we lose them. The boy is of no interest to them. They will not suspect that he has the dragon, not at first. It is better this way."

Nessa reluctantly saw the sense in his reasoning, although she didn't particularly like it much. Her feelings weren't improved when she felt a small amount of displeasure from Aoife when Hunter shouldered the bag. The dragon disliked being carried by someone other than Nessa.

The debris began to settle with a gentle patter that was painfully similar to raindrops, and Margan and his monster of a dragon stormed into the cave. People screamed and cried, running for their lives. A stampede was created.

Nessa and her companions were pushed up against the cave's wall, nearly crushed, saved only by Chaos spreading his mighty wings, channelling people around them.

"Quick!" Chaos barked. "Into the tunnel."

Orm dashed in first, swiftly followed by Hunter and Nessa. Chaos brought up the rear. The fissure, after the first couple of steps, was plunged into darkness. The light from the main cave didn't reach far, and there were no glowing mushrooms to show the way.

They were running blind until Orm clapped his hands and a flame appeared in them. It was small and Orm cupped it in his palms, sheltering it as best as he could from the wind that was funnelled down the tunnel. The light was weak, and caught on the craggy sides and the low ceiling, casting long, haunting shadows that seemed to come alive as the group ran past.

Through the haze of panic and urgency that had settled over Nessa like a cape, she noticed that the tunnel was part of a much larger network, with caverns and other passageways branching from it. Nessa understood Hunter's concerns over getting lost. It was a labyrinth down there. She couldn't even begin to imagine how Orm knew where he was going.

For miles they sprinted through the mountain, and all was silent save for their hurried breaths and the sound of their steps. Then, when they thought that they could relax and slow down a little, a dreadful resonating rumble shook the rock around them. A few stones clattered to the ground and the group ran with all their might, barrelling around corners and through chambers.

"Are they trying to bring down the mountain?" Hunter cried as the tunnel quaked with an ominous grumble.

"It seems like they're giving it a bloody good go," Nessa yelped, smashing onto the wall before righting herself and continuing on.

"There's a turning just ahead," Orm shouted. "Once we clear that we'll be able to see the exit. We'll be safe from whatever Margan and his beast are doing."

The turning in question appeared in the near distance, two passageways that forked away from one another. Orm took the one to the right, he and Hunter disappearing down it as Nessa slowed, a thought creeping into her mind.

"Margan and his beast..." Nessa murmured. "But where is Shadow and his?"

She turned to Chaos, intending to ask where Shadow was, and realised that he was nowhere in sight.

"Chaos?" Nessa called, voice echoing down the tunnel. There was nothing but still, impenetrable darkness staring back at her. "Chaos, are you there?"

No answer.

Hunter heard her and pulled Orm to a stop, beginning to turn back for her. The tunnel shook again, stronger and for longer. Stones on the ground bounced and danced, and dust rained down from above. Nessa's eyes flicked up as a mightily *crunch* filled the air. Fracture lines appeared in the ceiling, spreading out in a deceptively delicate pattern. Hunter's eyes widened in alarm and he made to run to her, but it was too late.

"The other path!" Orm bellowed. "Two rights then a left!"

With a thunderous roar, the ceiling came crashing down.

꽁◆ℭ

The dust was slow to settle, and the silence that followed was complete, the darkness absolute. Nessa waited, hoping that her eyes would adjust, but without Orm's light, she was left blind.

Slowly, she pushed herself up, realising that she had been thrown to the ground by the cave-in. Rocks had fallen everywhere, littering the floor with shards as sharp as broken glass. They bit into Nessa's hands, cutting them as she scrambled backwards, trying to find the tunnel's wall. At least then she would be able to place herself. It hit her back sooner than she expected, surprising her. Nessa leaned against it, trying to calm herself down so that she could formulate a plan to get out of there.

The darkness was disconcerting, so solid that Nessa couldn't tell if her eyes were open or closed. There wasn't the slightest hint of light in any direction. She knew that it was unlikely anyone would stumble across her any time soon. She was alone. Orm and Hunter were separated from her by several tons of rock. There was no chance that either of them would be able to dig through it. And Chaos? She had no idea where he was, didn't know when he had fallen behind... or had left... or had got lost. But whichever one it was, he wasn't there now, and if by some miracle he did turn up, she wasn't sure she could trust him completely. There was something about her waking dream, something that niggled at the back of her mind about him and Melissa.

"Right," Nessa said, reasoning with herself, "you can't see, so you're going to have to feel your way out." Probably easier said than done.

Nessa pulled herself up, standing with one hand on the wall. "Slow and steady wins the race," she murmured, taking her first hesitant step. Stones rolled and crunched underfoot, threatening to unbalance and trip her over. "Two rights then a left, that's what Orm said."

She took a minute to place herself, not wanting to go the wrong way and get lost, or worse, end up back at the main cavern where Margan surely waited. Once she was confident that she was facing the right way, she set off at a snail's pace, keeping a hand on the wall.

Progress was painfully slow, and Nessa lost her footing on more than one occasion, tumbling to the ground, receiving scraped hands and knees for the trouble.

Two rights then a left... Nessa kept repeating. *Two rights then a left...*

It was almost a prayer.

The route that Orm originally intended for them must have been a shortcut, for the way Nessa was now forced to take seemed never ending. It was nearly an hour before she stumbled across the first turning.

One right down, one to go...

The darkness was unrelenting and the silence ironically deafening. It played tricks on her mind. Nessa lost all perception of time and distance. Her steps, though, became surer and she tripped over less often, which was a welcome thing. Her hands and knees were raw and she could feel the blood seeping into her leggings and down her calves. The stinging was nearly unbearable and Nessa didn't think she could cope with another fall without bursting into tears. The pain, oddly enough, also served as another motivation for finding freedom. The sooner she got out of the tunnels, the sooner she could meet up with Hunter and Orm and dress her wounds. It was a nice thought, and one that kept her going even when she wanted nothing more than to stop for a rest.

Hunter and Orm, Aoife too, were often in her thoughts during her lonely and dark trek through the passageways. She hoped they were alright, that they were safe. Over and over she kept seeing the horror in Hunter's eyes as he tried to get to her as the ceiling collapsed. Worry became her new best friend. She worried that Hunter and Orm had been injured in the cave-in. She worried that they were trapped too. These were terrible thoughts to have, and no matter how hard she tried to ignore them, they were persistent and loud.

It was a small comfort to know that Aoife was unharmed, for she could sense the little dragon through whatever bond there was between them. Nessa told herself that surely meant Hunter was alive as he had possession of Aoife at the time of the cave-in.

Something else she worried about was another cave-in. Although there had been nothing but stillness, not even the faintest of tremors beneath her feet, Nessa still feared that the rock above her would come crashing down again.

It was then, whilst her mind was occupied, that Nessa didn't notice what was beneath her feet. The ground disappeared between one step and the next, and Nessa pitched forward, hitting the floor hard. Stones tore at her already raw skin, and the scabs that had only just formed were ripped off. She lay stunned for a heartbeat or two, body singing with pain, then she groaned and tried to pick herself up. She suddenly discovered that the strength which had carried her so far had fled.

Tears came to her eyes and Nessa, unable to stand, curled into a ball, sobbing. She was bone-numbingly tired and every inch of her body hurt, being either bruised or cut. She'd simply had enough, and didn't have it in her to do anything other than lie on the ground with her bleeding knees drawn up to her chest, her arms wrapped around them.

Nessa cried and cursed. She wasn't proud of that, but it did make her feel marginally better after a while. When she was finished, she was drained, but the determination to find her way out of the darkness had returned. Nessa told herself that Hunter and Aoife were waiting for her, that they were worried. She blindly swiped away the tears that clung to her cheeks, smearing blood from her palms as she did so, and stood.

And blinked.

And stared.

There, in the distance, a small light flickered and danced, barely bigger than a candle flame.

Hope flared, and Nessa thought that she had been found, before she realised that the light was stationary and no one else was in sight.

Nessa frowned, wondering what had caused the strange little flame to appear in the middle of the desolate tunnel, chasing away a small section of darkness. It was such a beautiful and simple thing, the ball of light, and Nessa wanted to yell with joy and run towards it. Something stopped her though, a sense of warning perhaps, or the knowledge that nothing good could possibly come from a magically appearing flame.

She thought about her options, which she was reluctant to admit were pretty limited. It was either forwards, towards the mystical light, or backwards, which only had the promise of either getting lost or facing Margan.

"Towards the magic flame it is," Nessa murmured.

Hesitantly, she approached it, and when it did nothing out of the ordinary, she took a second to examine it.

Hovering a couple of inches above the ground, there was no candle or wick, nothing to explain its existence. The little flame simply sat in the air, burning happily away. The light it produced was weak, barely reaching a few feet around it. Even so, Nessa wished that she could take it with her, not wanting to return to the darkness that surrounded her. She bent down, reaching out a hand, wondering if she could hold the flame in her palm just as Orm had with his.

The flame winked out.

Instantly the darkness came flooding back, a tsunami of despair. It didn't last for long, though. Twenty or so feet away, another little flame sparked to life, breathing a minuscule amount of light back into the tunnel. Swallowing her growing misgivings, Nessa approached it. Just like its predecessor, once she neared it, it blinked out, only for another to replace it further down the tunnel.

So, for awhile, Nessa continued in this fashion, chasing after a magical flame.

The second turn came, and Nessa ticked it off the directions she was following. *Nearly there... Nearly there...* Then, a great distance later, she came upon the left and final turning. She paused at its entrance, the sense of unease growing to an almost paralysing degree.

Danger lurked at the end of the tunnel, Nessa was sure of that.

I will be coming to fetch you when the time is right, Shadow had promised. It seemed that he was a man of his word.

With trepidation, Nessa entered the tunnel, feeling like she was about to run the gauntlet. As she did so, the air changed, becoming heavy and charged. *Puh...puh...puh...puh...* sounded out, and one after the other, little flames sprang up on either side of the tunnel, lining it.

Nessa paused, deciding that she really didn't want to go any further. *Maybe I'll just wait here until Hunter and Orm come,* she thought. *They know the route I've taken. They'll come looking soon enough.* Happy with that idea, she turned, intending to sit opposite the tunnel, wanting to be a safe distance away, yet close enough to see if anything was to come down it.

Nessa slammed into something and rebounded, taken by surprise. She stared, seeing nothing but empty air, and reached out a searching hand. It came across an invisible force that was as cold and as smooth as glass, and as hard as metal. She pushed against it, but it didn't move an inch. There was a barrier preventing her retreat.

"Well," Nessa said wryly. "This can't be good."

It got distinctly worse when the invisible barrier began moving, forcing Nessa down the tunnel. She tried to resist, to fight, pressing her back against it, digging in her heels, hoping that it would move no further. But for all her efforts, there was no give, and it continued to inch forward, ushering her unwillingly onward.

"Oh, fine," Nessa snapped, taking a few quick steps away from it, refusing to be corralled any further. "I'm going. I'm going. Not that I have a choice."

With the low sconces showing her path, Nessa walked slowly down the passageway, the barrier just a few short feet behind her, there as a reminder that she couldn't turn back, no matter how much she wished she could. She rounded a bend, and there, looming before her, was the exit.

Shadow stood just beyond it, framed by the tunnel's mouth, standing tall and imposing, a figure in black waiting for her. Sunlight danced in his dark hair, and his sapphire blue eyes gleamed when he caught sight of her. *I will be coming to fetch you when the time is right,* he had said to her. It appeared that time had come.

With her back straight and her head held high,

Nessa marched forward as if she was going into battle.

Maybe she was…

Chapter 32

Where it Starts and Ends

Darkness.

At first, disorientated and confused, Nessa thought that she was back in the tunnel. Had she been knocked out in the cave-in? Were the magic lights that Shadow had sent been nothing more than a dream? She shivered, cold and more than a little afraid, and went to sit up, only to find that she couldn't. It was then that she felt the harsh bite of metal against the skin of her wrists and ankles. Horrified, she realised that she was chained, hand and foot, to a slab of stone that acted as a table.

Nessa's heart began to race, and panic gripped her with its claws.

No no no no... This can't be real. This can't be happening...

But it was.

Terrible thoughts crept into her mind, and she imagined, with frightful creativity and vividness, all the things that Margan could have planned for her.

Oh, Hunter, where are you?

Far away, she hoped, safe from Margan's clutches. Him and Aoife both.

The air was icy and dank, and seeped into her bones, making her tremble uncontrollably. She listened, praying to hear the sound of rescue, but heard nothing save for the roar of blood in her ears.

How had it come to this? Nessa wondered.

Will I ever be free...?

Enjoyed HOUSE OF FEAR AND FREEDOM?
Then find out what happens next in
HOUSE OF GORE AND GOLD

Looking for something else to read while you eagerly await more from The Wyrd Sequence? Then why not try
THERE IS ONLY DARKNESS?

Death is meant to be the end. For Alfie, it was only the beginning.

Four years ago, eighteen-year-old Alfie's murder and resurrection forced her into a world invisible to humans: the Underworld, where grim things from folklore skulk in gloomy doorways and hidden corners, waiting for the perfect prey to stumble past. Demons. Warlocks. Little beasties.

For years, Alfie has been running from this world, hiding from those who hunt her, but the time for running is nearing an end.

As Alfie's past finally catches up to her, and she is pulled deeper into this sinister world, she discovers that its shadowy history is starting to repeat itself. A war is brewing; a war in which Alfie and the dark power of necromancy she unwillingly possesses may have an unfortunate role to play.

Where can Alfie run to when the man who killed her reappears, leaving a trail of bodies and chaos in his wake?

Who can Alfie trust in a world built from secrets and lies?

What can Alfie do when those she cares about most become entangled in a wicked web of deception and ruin?

ABOUT THE AUTHOR

Kimberley J. Ward, aka The Creator of Curiosities, is a dyslexic introvert who grew up in rural Dorset. She loves a good ale and a decent night's sleep. When she isn't looking after her ever-growing menagerie of animals and avoiding social interaction as much as politely possible, she is either writing or making something arty or jewellery related, or having a nap

You can find her curious creations at:

www.kimberleyjward.co.uk

Follow Kimberley J. Ward on:

Facebook @CreatorofCuriosities
Instagram @creator_of_curiosities
Pinterest @CreatorofCuriosities

Acknowledgements

This book has been in the making for longer than I care to admit, and during that time there has been a handful of people who've been vital in helping me get it out into the big wide world. So here's a big shout out you helpful souls.

A special thanks to Liz Nicholl, Nicola Young, Karen Nuttall and Samantha Presslee. All of whom have not only helped with this book throughout various stages of edits/reading, but who have also given me numerous words of encouragement over the years. It's all appreciated, ladies. Truly.

To Jessica Burgess, who has been a lifesaver when it comes to the edits, not only to this book, but also to the ones that I'm (still) working on. Seriously. You're a lifesaver. I swear that editing these things will be the death of me one day.

Most of all I would like to bring some attention to a few wonderful members of my family. Without you this book wouldn't have happened, the first page would never have seen the light of day. Your no shit attitudes towards me following my dreams kept me going during the rough times.

My annoying sister, you've read and reread this damn thing so many times you can quote it now. I'm sorry (not sorry). Granny-wanny, from getting me the beautiful antique desk on which I write to the nonstop words of support, I have so many things to be grateful for. You rock. To my fantastic uncle, Rob, there's far to many things for me to list that you've helped me with. You are invaluable. Finally, to my mummy-wummy. It's an impossible task to put down everything you've done for me, but just so you know, you are my best friend, and in general, the best. I wouldn't trade you for anything (well, almost anything).

Finally, my arsehole pets, you wake me up in the mornings with your demands for food, thus giving me an early start even if I hadn't planned on one. For some reason I cannot fathom, I love you little monsters.

Lastly, to my annoying sister, who really wanted to be acknowledged twice... here you go.

✠✠✠

www.ingramcontent.com/pod-product-compliance
Lightning Source LLC
LaVergne TN
LVHW091527060526
838200LV00036B/510